THE
SHAAR
PRESS

THE JUDAICA IMPRINT
FOR THOUGHTFUL PEOPLE

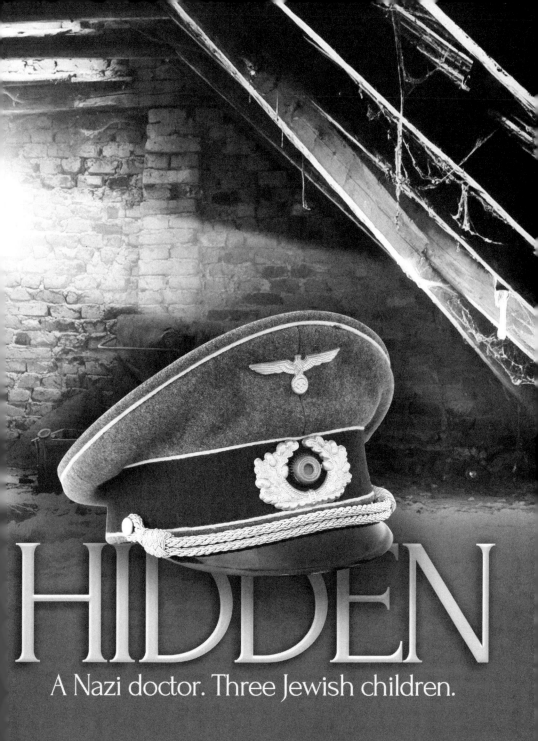

HIDDEN

A Nazi doctor. Three Jewish children.

A novel by Rochel Istrin

Published by **SHAAR PRESS**
Distributed by MESORAH PUBLICATIONS, LTD.
4401 Second Avenue / Brooklyn, N.Y 11232 / (718) 921-9000

Distributed in Israel by SIFRIATI / A. GITLER
Moshav Magshimim / Israel

Distributed in Europe by LEHMANNS
Unit E, Viking Business Park, Rolling Mill Road / Jarrow, Tyne and Wear, NE32 3DP/ England

Distributed in Australia and New Zealand by GOLDS WORLD OF JUDAICA
3-13 William Street / Balaclava, Melbourne 3183 / Victoria Australia

Distributed in South Africa by KOLLEL BOOKSHOP
Northfield Centre / 17 Northfield Avenue / Glenhazel 2192, Johannesburg, South Africa

ISBN 10: 1-4226-1564-2 / ISBN 13: 978-1-4226-1564-5

Printed in the United States of America
Custom bound by Sefercraft, Inc. / 4401 Second Avenue / Brooklyn N.Y. 11232

PART I

AN UNLIKELY REFUGE

1

NOVEMBER 1943. THE DAMP AUTUMN LEAVES SCATTERED across the windswept parking lot swallowed the sound of the approaching footsteps, which meant that the children were trapped before they had a chance to move to a more secure hiding place. Huddled as they were in the narrow space between the large black Mercedes-Benz and a retaining wall, the sight of the Nazi officer ended their slim hope of finding refuge from their pursuers. With no route for escape, the two eldest instinctively squeezed their eyes shut and whispered *"Shema Yisrael..."*.

Dr. Karl Emsbach was beyond weary after nearly 24 hours of surgery. His senses were so dulled by fatigue that the delicate beauty of the first rays of sunlight barely penetrated his awareness, though he did glance up at the foreboding clouds in expectation of more rain. Water dripped from the bare tree branches and his boots squished on the leaves. Only when the youngest turned in the girl's arms did he notice the three waifs huddled against the back wheel of his car.

When he reached for the door handle, the girl recoiled, turning to protect the small child clinging to her. For a timeless moment her dark eyes, stark against the cold whiteness of her face, met his blue ones. The surgeon was momentarily stunned by the intensity of her gaze — until it was torn from his face and directed to the street behind him, where a crescendo of hoarse voices could be heard. The doctor recognized the chilling sound of a pack hot on the scent of its prey. The children's predicament grew obvious as the shouts drew nearer.

Abruptly, the Nazi officer set his briefcase on the pavement. He unlocked the lid of the car's trunk and gestured at the nearly empty space inside. Two pairs of panicked eyes searched his incredulously.

"*Shnell!*" Dr. Emsbach commanded.

The boy was first to unfreeze. He scrambled over the bumper and scurried deep into the interior of the trunk. After a brief hesitation, the girl dropped the child inside and slipped after it into the unexpected hideaway. At precisely the moment that the bloodthirsty horde of Hitler *yugend* swarmed into the parking lot, the lid slammed shut. Without a pause, the Nazi officer whirled to confront them. Standing at attention, arm stiffly extended, he called out, "*Heil Hitler!*" in a commanding voice.

The gang of thugs halted in almost comic unison, presenting Dr. Emsbach with a forest of raised arms and clenched fists, accompanied by an enthusiastic chorus of "*Heil Hitler! Heil Hitler!*"

Their eyes, taking in his uniform and rank, shone with admiration. The boldest strutted forward. "Major, sir!" he bellowed, "We have sighted some stray Jewish dogs in this area! They must have passed by here in the last few minutes. Did you see which direction the animals ran, sir?"

The young man's drunken leer was meant to impress, though the acne-covered skin and buck teeth somewhat diminished the impact. Concealing his contempt, Dr. Emsbach bared his own teeth in a thin, forced smile. He pointed condescendingly toward a path leading down to the river, then turned his back and opened the Mercedes' front door.

"*Danke schön*, major! *Heil Hitler! Heil Hitler!*"

By the time the key turned in the ignition, the raucous shouts were already fading into the distance.

Swinging carefully onto the main street, Emsbach made a conscious effort to analyze what had just transpired. Impetuosity was so totally out of his character that the man was baffled by his own behavior. *It must be exhaustion,* he concluded. *What other reasonable explanation is there?*

In any case, it was imperative to consider the urgent practical consequences; mainly, what in the world was he going to do with his unplanned passengers?

One by one, he mentally crossed off the alternatives as they arose in his mind. Could he conceivably pass off the children as a servant's distant relatives and hide them with a good German family in a rural area? *No, not realistic,* he told himself. *The children are obviously Jews. Even the best forged identity papers would pose an unreasonable risk. They'll stand out against any background.*

Leave them in the forest to fend for themselves? He turned on the windshield wipers against the morning mist, pondering how long they would survive. Hide them in the cavernous basement of the hospital, near the boilers that guaranteed warmth as winter closed in? No, this was *not* getting *him* anywhere. He frowned.

I should just turn them over to the Gestapo.

The moment the obvious course of action formed, he knew with absolute certainty that he could not bring himself to do it. Though he deeply regretted allowing himself to fall into his present predicament, he was incapable of voluntarily identifying with the monsters that were defiling his Fatherland.

Perhaps it is because of the rumors? Dr. Emsbach wondered wearily. Too often in his work as a surgeon in the military hospital, patients under the influence of anesthesia babbled of blood-chilling atrocities. Adding these to his Uncle Heinrich's war stories, he could not escape the feeling that something inconceivably horrible was taking place in this war.

Absorbed in his thoughts, the military checkpoint loomed ahead before there was time to form a reasonable plan for dealing with it. The bored sentries waved the Mercedes through routinely, but once on the other side and around the corner, reality registered and Karl Emsbach began to tremble violently. It was necessary to pull over to the side of the road until he felt calm enough to continue.

Of course the guards recognize me, he reassured himself. He was in uniform, and his automatic response of *"Heil Hitler!"* was the same as it had been yesterday and every day before. *But what if they had opened the trunk?* The realization that his own life was in jeopardy jarred him back to reality. He made a concerted effort to concentrate as he continued driving along the familiar route out of the city, his palms damp with perspiration despite the chilly autumn weather.

The moment he turned into the alley leading to the car shed, the clouds burst and a stormy torrent of rain descended. Dr. Emsbach threw open the driver's door and quickly opened his umbrella before stepping out. The habitual movements involved in unlocking and opening the garage doors calmed him. He returned to the purring Mercedes and carefully parked it inside, then slammed the wide wooden doors shut with a satisfying thump. The single bulb, dimly illuminating the darkness, sent shadows scampering to the recesses of the musty shed.

He stood listening to the rain plummet down on the roof before methodically removing his carefully folded greatcoat from the front passenger seat. Karl noticed a paper packet of sweet rolls, and vaguely remembered requesting the scrub nurse to buy him something to eat from the hospital canteen. There had been no time to eat, and afterward he'd been so absorbed in this unexpected drama that he'd forgotten about them entirely.

He closed the car door and walked to the back of the Mercedes, his steps echoing dully on the sawdust-covered floor. With a quick release of the latch, the trunk lid popped open. Dr. Emsbach could see the children cowering inside, bunched into a corner as if making themselves smaller would somehow grant a greater degree of security.

He found it hard to meet their eyes. Unfolding the heavy wool coat, he spread it across the three of them and ordered, "Remain very quiet. I will return later. Do not try to move from here." As an afterthought, he dropped the paper bag with his rolls inside before securing the trunk and letting himself out of the garage through the creaky side door.

Karl Emsbach closed his eyes for a moment, letting the rain fall on his face. Overhead, tree branches swayed drunkenly in the wind. Otherwise, all was silence.

Walking up the stone path to the kitchen door at the rear of the house gave him the opportunity to gauge if there was any sign of life in the darkened building. The curtains were not drawn, and the windows stared back at him blankly.

Funny — he could not even remember the last time he'd been left entirely alone. Yesterday, before he left for work, his cook Beatrix and her husband Otto had requested permission to visit their daughter in town for the day. Of course, he had consented. He had driven his housekeeper Rhea to the train station on his way to the hospital, which meant that there should be no one at all left inside the house.

Dr. Emsbach's parents had died in an aviation accident when he was 10 years old. Since that time, Rhea had filled the role of his mother. The elderly servants, Bea and Otto, had been on the house staff when his own father was a child, and they were as much a part of his home as the towering walnut trees in the vast yard. Bea's nephew, Hans, was a loyal groundskeeper. The man's ferocious appearance belied his deep devotion to the orphaned boy now grown to manhood. Hans had been caretaker, gardener and Karl Emsbach's unofficial bodyguard ever since he could remember.

Reaching for the handle of the kitchen door, Emsbach was startled by the creak of a board on the porch behind him. He turned quickly, but it was only Hans.

"Will you be needing me for anything today?" Hans asked in his rough voice.

"*Nein, danke schön*, Hans. I'm going straight to sleep."

"You're not wearing your coat."

"I must have left it at the hospital."

The gruff giant grunted his disapproval. Emsbach smiled with affection.

"I will wear my old coat if I decide to go out again, Hans. Don't worry about me. I'm no longer a little boy."

"You would think a doctor would set a better example," Hans grumbled. "A man could catch his death walking about on such a cold morning without a warm coat."

"*Jawohl*, you're right. It was careless of me. I'm just tired, Hans. I wasn't thinking."

"There is a fair in town today. It is time to buy feed for the horses and some of the gardening equipment needs replacing."

"How long will that take?"

"Most of the day."

"Do you need help?"

Hans was offended. "Go to sleep, *Herr Doktor*! What kind of old man do you take me for? I can manage fine on my own."

After Hans left, the doctor held the screen door open with his shoulder and pushed hard against the heavy wooden kitchen door. As usual, it stuck for several seconds before abruptly yielding with a protesting groan. Stepping inside, he savored the warm familiar room and his tension relaxed. All was quiet in the empty house except for the faint background murmur of the dripping icebox.

Emsbach regarded it as propitious that the house and all the grounds in close proximity would be empty for the next few hours — enough time to put into action the plan beginning to take form in his mind.

He peered through the kitchen windows at the expanse of yard and garden between the house and the shed. The slow, steady drizzle would severely limit anyone's vision. It was not the kind of weather in which a person would choose to be out of doors. He carefully drew the blackout curtains closed and secured them.

His meal was set out on the kitchen table where Beatrix had left it, but he felt no hunger. He paced nervously until he was sure that enough time had elapsed for Hans to have left for the fair, and then pulled on two raincoats, one atop the other. He took his wet umbrella and one of Otto's homburgs from the peg beside the back door and retraced his steps to the car shed. Emsbach let himself in as quietly as possible. The only audible sound was the soft patter of rain on the shingled roof. He let out a sigh, reassured that nothing had changed since he'd left the hospital an hour earlier.

Opening the trunk of the Mercedes, he whispered, "*Arous!*"

The girl emerged first. The boy handed the little one to her and then climbed out to stand beside them. Their quiet seemed unnatural, but Emsbach was glad of it. He looked them over. The boy's head reached the girl's shoulder. *He must be about 8*, he thought. In the pale light they appeared very dirty, dressed in rags and skeletally thin. The smallest was 2 or 3 years old at the most. He clung to the girl, his face buried in the curve where her shoulder met her neck. She was older than he'd originally thought, though not old enough to be their mother. She appeared about 16. Her eyes looked much older.

He draped one raincoat around her shoulders, covering the child as well, and set the hat on her head where it sat ridiculously, covering her eyes, nose and ears. Automatically she tilted her head back to be able to see.

"No, don't!" he hissed. "Incline your head forward so that your face is hidden."

She nodded and complied while he draped the second raincoat over the boy. Satisfied that it was impossible to identify them from a distance, he pressed a warning finger to his lips and added a stern expression that brooked no disobedience. "Come after me!"

Emsbach led the children out of the garage and slowly up the path to the back porch. In the unlikely event that prying eyes observed anything at all, they would only see the doctor escorting two elderly gentlemen to his house — a most unremarkable sight.

When he finally had them all indoors, he relaxed slightly.

"In here," he said, leading the way to the kitchen.

Silent as wraiths, the children followed him.

2

INSIDE THE WARM KITCHEN, DR. EMSBACH METICULOUSLY hung up the wet coats and set Otto's hat on its peg beside the door. He indicated that the children should sit on the bench at the long wooden table that Bea used as a work counter. The boy's eyes widened as his benefactor loaded the table with whatever came to hand from the pantry and icebox.

"*Ess!*" Accustomed to command, his voice was curt. The children sat frozen, regarding the feast fearfully as if it might vanish at any second. The girl spoke, her soft voice breaking the silence.

"*Bitte schön,* may we wash our hands first?"

Although he agreed that it was necessary, Emsbach marveled at their restraint. "*Ja,*" he pointed at the sink and took out a dish towel from the cabinet.

The girl washed her hands with soap, rinsed them and then washed the boys' hands and faces. Before leaving the sink, she filled a cup with water and poured it first over one hand then the other, her lips murmuring something the German officer could not hear as she dried them with the towel. The older boy followed suit, though the small one just clung to the girl's skirt, waiting to be picked up.

The two oldest children each lifted a roll in both hands and whispered something unintelligible before biting into them. After that strange ceremony, all the food on the table was devoured indiscriminately, down to the last crumb. Karl Emsbach watched them, wondering how long the children had been without proper nutrition. He poured mugs of milk, which they drank thirstily. After a while, the little one curled up next to the girl and fell asleep, his small head resting on her lap and his mouth half open. On her other side the older boy leaned against her and was soon fast asleep as well. Her expression was loving as she gazed from one to the other, a look that was maternal despite her youth. Then her head dropped onto the table, and the steady rhythm of her breathing indicated that she, too, was sleeping.

They look as if they have been living liked hunted animals, Emsbach thought. *I have not seen a live Jew for nearly three years, but they couldn't have been on the streets that long.Someone must have hidden them, and either they were discovered or turned out.* A feeling of compassion swept over him, even as he berated himself for the weakness of allowing emotion to hamper his judgment.

These are the enemies of the Reich, he thought, tasting the bitter irony behind the words.

Leaving the children deep in slumber, Emsbach climbed the creaking, wooden back stairs to the second floor where the bedrooms were. His own chambers were at the front of the house, but there were plenty of guest rooms. Entering the one nearest the bathroom, he opened the closet door. For a moment he was flooded with childhood memories. As a very lonely only child, Karl Emsbach had repeatedly explored the nooks and crannies of the large old house. In this particular room he had made an exciting discovery: above the clothes closet was a hidden entrance that led up to the attic.

He easily scaled the makeshift ladder of parallel boards nailed discreetly along the back wall of the closet, each just wide enough for a toehold. The trap door overhead opened when he pushed it, showering him with accumulated dust. Hefting himself through the opening, Emsbach surveyed the large attic by the light of his flashlight. It had been undisturbed by any intruder for many years. Great shadowy shapes indicated where old draped furniture stood forlornly. His secret playroom from so long ago would now become a sanctuary for a few poor, hunted Jewish children.

With determination, Emsbach shoved away crates and boxes until a space about the size of a small room was created at the far end of the attic. Daylight penetrated faintly through the dirty glass of a single small window. He pulled the covering off a long-forgotten brass bed and dragged it over to the outside wall. Adding a small table and chair beside the bed, he regarded his labor with satisfaction.

It was cold here. He could see his breath when he exhaled, but there was no way to heat such a vast empty space. A couple of feather comforters would have to suffice. Not exactly hotel accommodations, but certainly an improvement over being drenched by the late-autumn rains and hiding from hostile eyes in dangerous urban alleys.

Repeated trips up and down, and linens, blankets, a water jug, basin and towel were neatly arranged. Returning to the kitchen, he found the group still motionless. Emsbach wondered what their names were, or if he'd known their parents before the war. Hoping to wake them gradually, he busied himself clearing off the table, replacing the food in the cupboards and icebox and sweeping away crumbs. *If Bea notices anything later, she will just assume that I helped myself to a generous snack,* he reasoned.

The children slept on. Beginning to feel the weight of his own fatigue, Karl Emsbach stood restlessly beside the table, debating how to wake them. Finally, he called out softly, *"Madchen! Yugend!* Girl, boy, wake up! You must come with me. Wake up, *shnell!"*

Their transformation from deep sleep to alertness took place with no discernible transition. The older children opened their eyes and jumped to their feet. Recognizing her benefactor, the girl's initial terrified expression resolved into apprehension as she waited tensely.

"Come after me," he instructed, turning and leading the way up the bare wooden steps from the kitchen to the upper story.

She swiftly picked up the still-sleeping toddler and followed soundlessly, the boy trailing behind. Only the soft creak of their weight on the stairs confirmed that the children were behind him. Their eyes darted from side to side as they climbed, taking in the faded rose garlands on the aging wallpaper and the loops of long twine threaded through little metal eyelets leading along the wall from the overhead light at the top of the stairs down to the ground floor. At the top, Emsbach pulled the string and extinguished the light. A few steps further stood the open door to the bathroom.

"Wash the children and take a bath yourself," he said, opening the door to the lit room. "I've put some clean garments on the shelf for afterward." Indicating items on a decorative toiletry table, he added, "You may use anything you need." A moment later he had disappeared into another part of the house and they were alone.

Fraydl looked from one of her nephews to the other. "Chaim, you go first," she whispered to the older boy. "Yanky and I will wait beside the door until you're finished."

Chaim stepped hesitantly into a chamber that looked almost like a palace. There were sparkling white tiles, large fluffy towels neatly folded over a softly hissing radiator, and a great white enamel bathtub on clawed legs. The boy closed the door. From the other side Fraydl heard the sounds of running water and then splashing. Ten minutes later, the door opened to reveal Chaim with a shy smile on his face, wet hair plastered against his head, wearing a pair of men's pajamas with the cuffs inexpertly rolled up. In spite of herself she smiled, and then began to cry.

"Wash Yanky now," Chaim whispered, "and then I'll watch him when it's your turn to wash."

She nodded and sniffed back her tears. The tub was filthy from Chaim'ke's bath. She scrubbed it thoroughly and filled it again. Tenderly she undressed her little nephew and then slid him into the bath water. Yanky clung to her in terror, his frightened eyes and grasping fingers seeming to scream in the silence as she washed the little boy clean from the accumulated filth of countless weeks. She dried him and wrapped the child in one of the pajama shirts like a nightgown. It would have been comical had the icy fingers of fear not been gripping her so tightly.

Now it was Fraydl's turn. Chaim took his little brother and sat on the floor beneath a window to wait. She scrubbed the tub and filled it with clean hot water. Gazing at the tiny wisps of steam rising from its smooth surface, she feared she must be hallucinating. It had been literally years since she had bathed properly. For so many months, their only access to water had been the rain. Was this really happening, or was it a cruel dream from which she would awaken to the real world of being a fugitive once again?

Fraydl put in one foot cautiously, then both feet and finally slipped into the indescribable bliss of the bath. Heedlessly submerging in the blessed warmth, she allowed herself to savor the embrace of the water and revel as her stiff taut muscles slowly relaxed. It was with great reluctance that she climbed out later, her tangled blond hair soaking the towel she wrapped around her head. The bath towel on the radiator was toast-warm and felt delicious against her skin. She quickly pulled on the warm woolen pajamas and rolled up the sleeves. Before she pulled the plug, she washed out the children's clothes and squeezed the wet articles as hard as she could. She didn't know how long it would take them to dry, hanging on the rack over the tub, but she hoped it would not be long. Before emerging from the bathroom she once again scrubbed the tub clean and checked to see that the room was as tidy as it had been when she first saw it.

Satisfied at last, she cautiously opened the door and found her two nephews waiting nearby. A moment later their rescuer stepped out of the shadows, his face expressionless like most German faces. Deep blue eyes regarded the children seriously, but the malevolence they were accustomed to seeing was not there. Karl Emsbach nodded, and gestured for them to follow him. He led the group through a utility room and turned into an adjacent guest room.

Before she could protest, the Nazi scooped up little Yanky and vanished up a nearly undetectable ladder through a trap door in the closet's ceiling. The child was as light as a feather. Emsbach bent down to give Chaim a hand, and the boy soon disappeared after them. Fraydl climbed slowly, feeling her way along the footholds until she, too, had entered the attic.

The air was stale and cold. She blinked as her eyes adjusted to the faint light and saw the small living quarters, so meticulously prepared while the children were asleep in the kitchen.

"You must maintain absolute silence." The intensity of his warning frightened them. "There must be no moving about unless I inform you that no one is in the house. Do you understand?"

They nodded. Moments later he was gone, the trap door securely closed behind him. Fraydl took Yanky into the bed with her, while Chaim snuggled into a feather comforter on a straw mattress beneath them. The three were asleep almost instantly. The girl's last thoughts before slumber claimed her were that perhaps the man was *Eliyahu haNavi* in disguise. But then, it couldn't be. The prophet Elijah would never appear in the uniform of a Nazi officer. So their rescuer must be a real live person after all.

And then she was asleep.

3

KARL EMSBACH DESCENDED THE LADDER SLOWLY AND painstakingly closed the trap door behind him. He checked every detail as he retraced his steps to the bathroom, and then down to the kitchen. There must be no indication of anything out of the ordinary that the servants might notice.

Satisfied that no sign remained, Emsbach exhaled slowly, only now aware that he had been holding his breath. The point of no return had been passed. Even without a rational explanation to justify the dramatic steps he'd just taken, there was no denying a tiny pinprick of satisfaction that made him stand just a little straighter. In a small, hidden way he was defying the German führer and the disgraceful regime of thugs that had hijacked his country and thrust his compatriots into a bloody war. The dissonance of wearing the uniform of a Nazi while being repelled by what it represented subsided last, and the exhausted doctor fell into a long-delayed sleep.

He awoke reluctantly several hours later to the familiar sounds of Bea preparing a hearty supper. He listened drowsily to Otto moving heavily about the rooms, checking that all was well. Suddenly,

Emsbach remembered the children. His drowsiness disappeared in a flash. Quickly he dressed and hurried down to the kitchen, his steps cracking like thunder on the bare back stairs.

"Our young master must be hungry!" Beatrix exclaimed.

"Our young master should remember his manners!" Otto added affectionately.

"*Guten Abend*," Emsbach greeted them.

"*Grüss G-tt*," the servants responded together.

Bea gestured at the table. "Come, Karl. The food is ready."

"I smelled it all the way upstairs," he complimented her.

"*Guten appetit!*" she smiled.

"*Danke.*"

"What would you like to drink?'

"Löwenbräu, *bitte.*"

She handed him a foaming mug. Everything appeared routine as he was served his supper with the servants' usual good-natured attentiveness. They inquired about his day and told him about theirs. Having worked for the doctor's grandparents when his father was a small child, Bea and Otto often treated their employer as if he were their grandson. Otto caught him up on the news from the 6 p.m. broadcast, mostly politics and war propaganda. While her plump and wrinkled hands deftly lifted and stretched the strudel dough, Beatrix complained about the price and poor quality of fresh produce.

After his meal, Emsbach took the evening newspapers and pretended to read while sending out silent feelers to monitor for tension in the air. Had they noticed anything? Was there any difference from yesterday or the day before? Just as he concluded that there was none, he realized that he was idly turning the pages of the *Neueste Nachrichten*, a daily he purchased for appearance's sake in order to avoid the suspiciously raised eyebrows of his Nazi colleagues when they saw him carrying only the *Post*. He hastily set it down beside its ideological twin, the *Vulkischer Beobachter*, and took up the *Post* to peruse the headlines, unhappily sensing Otto's puzzled frown at this minute deviation from routine.

Emsbach's thoughts returned to the children. How had they

passed the day? Judging by the degree of their exhaustion, it was probable that the three had slept the entire time, just as he had. The girl's name was Fraydl. There was something oddly familiar about the sound of it. A diminutive from the Teutonic word for joy, he decided. Later in the evening, when the house was empty, he would bring them down for a meal and there would be time to talk and learn further details. Meanwhile, several elective surgeries were programmed for tomorrow, and this was the time he usually planned them out. He must observe every habit of his normal schedule so as not to arouse suspicion.

Hans returned from the fair at around 8. He knocked respectfully and then gave his employer a succinct report of the day's purchases and his plans for the morrow. Afterward, Otto and Beatrix bade him good-night and left for their quarters in the carriage house.

Emsbach checked and double-checked that all the doors were bolted and the windows secured. Alone at last, the large old house was dark except for his study. He added a log to the fire burning in the stone hearth, and rearranged the wood until warmth permeated the room. He slid the etched-glass screen back into place and returned the poker to its stand.

The quiet evening was periodically interrupted by the tinkle of scattered raindrops blown against the windowpanes, and the tapping and scraping of branches in the wind. For the first time in years, Emsbach noticed the sound that the polished hardwood floorboards made as they settled. His own footsteps on the linoleum kitchen floor seemed overly loud. When a chunk of ice dropped into the pan under the icebox he jumped in alarm, and then smiled in self-deprecation. Yesterday none of these familiar background noises would have even registered on his mind.

The clock tolled nine mournful times. It was still early enough for a visitor to come by. Until 10 o'clock he was available for medical consultations, although it was rare for someone to brave the elements this late. Emsbach arranged food on a tray and left it on the side table beside the tapestry-upholstered sofa in his study.

Sitting at his desk, he tried to focus on the case studies in his files, but his concentration wandered as his mind rebelliously pulled him into ever-deeper reflection. Again and again he probed his thoughts and feelings, trying to make sense of them. There were no regrets. In fact, he was pleased. Since his service in Czechoslovakia, he had not felt so much at peace with himself as he did today.

Contrary to his adult image of self-control and authority, Karl Emsbach had once been a very sensitive child. His parents' disapproval notwithstanding, the little boy had often returned home with disabled wild creatures from the fields near their home. Otto and Hans had loyally helped him nurse them back to health, discreetly burying those that did not survive his best efforts to save them. Later, he'd turned his compassion and desire to heal into a medical career. Was it conceivable that his impulse to hide these children came from that same innocent period of his life, when he'd idealistically dreamed of bringing healing and life to the injured?

Karl Emsbach had been a model son: precocious, excelling in intellectual pursuits, neat, obedient and desiring to please. His industrialist grandfather's fortune was made because he'd had the prescience to invest his modest firm's profits in precious stones during and after the Great War. In the period between the world wars, rampant inflation had rendered the Deutsche mark virtually worthless. As banks folded and unemployment reached catastrophic levels, Wilhelm Emsbach's investments were transformed into unheard-of wealth. A mostly absentee parent, Karl's father, Mikhail, had been preoccupied with international business transactions and went abroad often on business.

Helga Emsbach was a socialite, entertaining the socially prominent aristocracy. Her prestigious salon was well known for its cosmopolitan company, including politicians, artists, entertainers, diplomats and military brass. Maternal contact with her only child was limited to the occasions when the boy was called upon to perform before her guests. Afterward he would quietly remain in the room and listen raptly to the adult conversation, until his mother noticed and sent him away. In general, Karl Emsbach was benignly neglected, spending hours in the company of his books, the doting servants and his vivid imagination.

Due to delicate health, his early education was in the hands of private tutors. All of this changed shortly before his 10th birthday. His parents were away on a trip to Italy and he'd been left in the capable charge of their housekeeper. He was reading when the doorbell rang that day. Minutes later, he heard Rhea call him to receive an unexpected and unpleasant visitor: his mother's only brother, Heinrich Mauer, a high-ranking career officer in the *Wehrmacht*.

Uncle Heinrich had always taken an unusual interest in the boy, but his presence unfailingly chilled Karl to the bone. His childhood nightmares often included being pursued by this man, who for some inexplicable reason seemed to his nephew to exude evil.

"*Guten tag, Onkel,*" the child stammered politely, clicking his heels together in a sharp snap as he'd been taught.

"A good day to you too, Karl," the older man said severely. "I bear unfortunate news for you. There was an aviation accident in Bavaria. Your parents were on their way home, and their plane went down in a remote forest. There are no survivors. Most tragic... I have come to make the necessary arrangements for your welfare."

The boy had stared at him blankly, not really comprehending. His uncle frowned in disapproval.

"Thank your uncle, Karl," Rhea prompted from the side, where she was waiting unobtrusively. Her voice was thick with shock at this unexpected tragedy.

"Thank you, sir," he responded mechanically.

The next weeks were a blur. The pampering of his childhood ended abruptly. After his parents' funeral, Heinrich enrolled the young boy in a military boarding school. At first, the experience was an unrelieved trauma for the youngster. Eventually, however, he learned to observe the strict rules and regulations of the academy and succeeded in stifling his own feelings.

Naturally shy, young Karl never really felt part of the social milieu. His academic success ensured him a certain status, but his reticence formed a wall between him and other boys. For years he blamed himself when his occasional efforts to fit in did not bear fruit, but with maturity he accepted the reality that he was simply different.

He dreaded his illustrious uncle's monthly visits during those years, when he was examined and cross-examined until the man was satisfied with his progress.

"What is this lackluster performance in sports?" Uncle Heinrich would demand in fury. "A soldier must conform and be an integral part of his company. For an army to succeed, each man must be a cog contributing to the whole! There is no place for an individualist in our society."

Mauer ignored his nephew's accomplishments in equestrian events and competitive racing, insisting that he make his mark in a team sport. Karl managed to mollify him by joining the rowing team. Unexpectedly, the boy discovered a real sense of fulfillment in this activity. The hours spent pulling the oars of the academy scull developed him physically. The previously weak boy metamorphosed into a handsome and powerful young athlete. His muscular appearance alone discouraged the bullies who had taunted him during his first years at the academy, and his uncle's scalding castigations gradually faded away.

Emsbach's physical strength made him a valuable member of the team, and he learned to love the pleasant high he experienced after his muscles burned with the effort required to win a race. Often he rose alone at dawn to take out a kayak on the misty ripple-free lake: the perfect time and place for thinking. These precious hours allowed him to connect with his inner thoughts, and gave him strength to endure the discipline and rigor of his military education.

Despite the antipathy he felt toward his uncle, there were advantages in being related to him. The academy's administrators were in awe of the high-ranking official, and some of their respect rubbed off onto his nephew. He was permitted certain benefits and privileges which made the years slightly less intolerable. As time passed, his naturally dreamy and gentle nature developed a surface layer of logic and self-control. At the age of 18, Karl Emsbach personified the image of German destiny: tall, handsome, blond, with a barely discernible trace of tragedy in his aloof blue eyes.

The year he graduated from the military academy, Adolph Hitler coerced President Paul von Hindenburg into signing a decree that appointed Hitler chancellor of Germany. The Reichstag's powers were then usurped by the Austrian upstart, who assumed full power and haughtily withdrew Germany from the foundering League of Nations.

Heinrich Mauer made his displeasure known when his nephew did not opt to pursue a military career. Instead, Karl Emsbach applied and was accepted to Heidelberg University. A talented and serious student, he completed his undergraduate studies in only two years and immediately enrolled in medical school.

Emsbach recalled those Heidelberg days with some nostalgia, for it was then that he first experienced comradeship with others his age. Rigorous internships divided the students into two main groups. The larger group escaped the pressures of learning in beer halls and cabarets, while the smaller, more select company sought intellectual fulfillment and stimulation through literature and discussion of ethical questions.

This was the first direct contact he'd ever had with Jews, and it was also the first time he had serious competitors for his scholarly standing. Even today, Emsbach was distressed by the combination of envy and attraction Jewish people aroused in his heart. He was also disturbed by their inexplicable disappearance from the university and the increase in blatant anti-Semitism that followed Adolph Hitler's rise to power.

At first, young Karl Emsbach had not taken the National Socialist German Worker's Party seriously. In his opinion, the brown shirts were a bunch of hooligans, best ignored. Who in his right mind expected the world to go insane? He attended exactly one rally — out of curiosity — and it was unforgettable. He remembered thousands of people pushing their way into the sports stadium well before the appointed hour, and the cacophony of their individual conversations blending into a hum that filled the air.

A staccato sound of drumbeats suddenly charged the atmosphere with electricity. Row after row of SS soldiers appeared at the entrance gate, marching in perfect time. Dressed in identical brown uniforms with jackets cinched at the waist, their knee-high black boots were polished to an ebony shine and brown military caps covered their heads. The leading marchers held long staffs aloft, bearing huge, nearly transparent cheesecloth flags. The spidery black swastikas, set against a white circle on a blood-red field, snapped in the wind. Emsbach was impressed in spite of himself.

When the first line of marchers reached the center of the field, the rows split seamlessly apart precisely down the middle and continued stepping in time. The führer strode into the gap between his men: posture erect, stiff legs strutting proudly to the beat of the drums. The response of the waiting crowd was deafening. When Hitler passed by, he clearly saw the trademark mustache on the leader's thin upper lip, the slicked-back black hair and the piercing blue eyes that stared straight ahead.

Frenzied cheering continued for many minutes. Tears of joy and pride glistened in the eyes of the fat Bavarian to Emsbach's right. A rhythmic stamping of feet pulsed through the stands. He did not recognize anyone in the procession of Nazi officials that followed Hitler into the stadium, but then, he had never taken much of an interest in politics. A group of bodyguards brought up the rear, forming a cordon between their leader and his admirers. Standing in a row with feet apart, the guards clasped their hands behind their backs and glared menacingly at the cheering spectators. After the last official had climbed onto the improvised stage, a company of Nazi soldiers smoothly closed ranks and marched to their designated places on either side.

Adolph Hitler took the podium. At first he stood motionless, looking out over his audience and apparently basking in their admiration. Then he lifted his arm in a salute, which was followed by a reverberating roar, *"Sieg Heil! Sieg Heil!"* Emsbach was shocked to see that the führer's face was flushed like a madman's. Jaw thrust forward with determination, Hitler waited patiently until the stadium was as quiet as a tomb before he began to address the crowd.

Although he spoke like someone possessed, his voice was mesmerizing. It was disconcerting to hear the way Adolph Hitler flitted back and forth between charm and insanity. The essence of his long drawn-out discourse was that Jews were leading the world into war. With an ominous frown, the führer warned the Jews of

Europe that they would only bring destruction upon their own heads. Since he was actually preaching to the converted, every few sentences were interrupted by applause and shouts of *Seig Heil!*

Within weeks, the coordinated actions of *Kristallnacht* convinced Karl Emsbach that the Nazis might not be just a passing phenomenon. Overnight, his Jewish professors, lab assistants and fellow students of Jewish extraction disappeared without a trace. Oddly, no one demanded an explanation. When he inquired about a particular study partner, he was informed that the young man had been repatriated to Poland — and good riddance. He graduated from medical school with honors in 1939, and was immediately inducted into the German Army.

Returning home briefly before leaving to serve with a medical team on the Czechoslovakian front, he'd hoped to find a relief from warmongering. Instead, he discovered that soldiers were now popular heroes. How proud they all were of him! Rhea, Bea, Otto and Hans. The women wiped tears from their eyes, and the men stood straighter as they saluted him. Emsbach had smiled and accepted their compliments, while inwardly wondering why his life felt like a burden that was almost too heavy to bear.

Now, at age 28, Emsbach was still the loner. The home front no longer regarded the war as such a glorious undertaking. Most able-bodied young men had been drafted for combat duty, leaving women, children, the elderly and the handicapped behind. Emsbach's connections and professional reputation got him reassigned to a military hospital near his home, where he honed his surgical skills.

Since his promotion to brigadier general, Uncle Heinrich was too busy to interfere excessively in his nephew's private life, which suited Emsbach very well. Two elderly uncles, his father's brothers, lived in nursing homes. Karl visited them as often as necessary, to fulfill his obligations and pay for their board and medical treatments, but he felt no emotional connection to them. In general, despite a certain *weltanschauung* that haunted the moments when he wasn't otherwise occupied, his life was agreeable. Perhaps, after the war was over, it would even be good.

In the hospital, young Dr. Emsbach was a respected figure on the surgical ward. His curious lack of arrogance and his ability to listen made him favored by the patients and the nurses. His best hours were spent in surgery, when all else faded from his awareness except the application of his adept mind and skilled hands. Sometimes he became so carried away with what he was doing that he sensed a mind other than his own guiding his hands and his decisions. No one else would have understood that feeling, but it was a sensation he craved and cherished. Those were the only times when he felt passionately alive.

4

T HE CHILDREN SLEPT FOR MANY HOURS. WHEN FRAYDL awakened, dusty light beams were filtering through the smudged window, offering enough light for a preliminary examination of her new surroundings. The attic was huge. Dim illumination shone from another window at the far end. A column of bricks from a rising chimney cut through the middle and cast a shadow through the dusky center of the room. Draped shapes — presumably out-of-use furniture — occupied most of the visible space, along with trunks of various sizes and numerous neatly stacked cartons.

Their host had piled some of the boxes in a low protective wall between the corner where the children slept and the rest of the room. A person coming up through the main staircase would not perceive anyone lying under the blankets, but when Fraydl sat up she could see all the way to the other side. Their wet laundry was hanging on a line tied from a nail on the wall to the end of the bed. The clothes were still very damp. A porcelain commode had been placed in the corner. Fraydl blushed, but she appreciated her host's consideration.

On the other side of the chimney it was possible to make out handrails, indicating a stairwell leading down to the house. Everywhere she looked beyond the partition of cartons, Fraydl saw a heavy layer of dust. There was a distinct possibility that, if she tried to explore further than her corner — which their rescuer had chivalrously mopped clean while the children were bathing — she would begin sneezing. Footprints on the dusty floor could also betray her presence if she was unwary.

Although the attic was cold, she was grateful to be sheltered from the biting wind outside. Two warm down comforters covered her, and the mattress was infinitely softer than the ground on which she was accustomed to sleeping. Fraydl snuggled deeper into the blankets and gazed up at the rafters under the roof until sleep claimed her tired body again. The children dozed off and on through the rest of the day, occasionally drinking from the pitcher of water the German had left on the table. Fraydl felt indebted to Hashem for granting them another day of life.

Whoever the Nazi officer was, he did not seem to mean them harm. His were the first eyes with human expression that she had seen in a very long time. Fraydl murmured the daily prayers with especial gratitude for Hashem's mercy in saving them so miraculously, and tearfully begged Him to protect them and to save all His tortured people. The concept of a normal life, even just sleeping in a bed, seemed unreal after years of hiding and fleeing.

Fraydl snuggled deeper into the warm bed. As she relaxed, memories from the past played through her head. Although it seemed so far away now, it had really been only a few years ago that she was a girl in her parents' home. A certain level of latent anti-Semitism was taken for granted in Vienna, although their gentile neighbors were usually decent and courteous. The Mertzbach family had felt safe in Austria, compared to the treatment Fraydl's grandparents had been subject to in Galicia before the Great War.

The reign of terror began in the spring of 1938, when Nazi Germany annexed Austria and Jew-hatred became official government policy. Fraydl had been on an errand to the corner pharmacy on the day German troops marched into their city. She watched with curiosity as crowds lined the streets and cheered, welcoming Hitler like a hero.

Within hours, Austrian Nazis began an orgy of persecution against all Jewish citizens. Jews were chased through the streets. Fraydl's brother-in-law, the oldest son of their holy Rebbe, was forced to scrub the sidewalks with a toothbrush while passersby joked and laughing Austrian women wearing high heels stomped on his fingers. Jewish stores and homes were pillaged, and many people were driven from their confiscated houses into the streets. Formerly friendly neighbors were suddenly ferocious anti-Semites.

Nazis appeared in the middle of the night and stripped their home of valuables, including the trousseau her mother had begun preparing for her youngest daughter. Fraydl's father and brothers were taken away. For weeks, the women of the family searched for them desperately, but none returned.

Officially, the Nazis encouraged emigration, while at the same time making it nearly impossible. Fraydl's remaining family stood in line all night to apply for passports, and then waited in an even longer line to obtain the coveted forms that would enable them to leave Austria. After submitting their visa requests to consular officials from other European countries, months passed but answers never came. To get a visa, Jews were required to present a certificate of financial solvency together with a recommendation from the local police that they were commendable citizens. In the end, it all came to nothing. They were trapped.

As the youngest child, the responsibility for comforting her elderly mother and helping her married sisters with their small children fell heavily on 11-year-old Fraydl. Civil liberties for Jews were revoked. Yellow badges made them frequent targets of public harassment. Jewish organizations and institutions were closed, even the *shtiebels*. Jewish property, schools, hospitals and cemeteries were vandalized. Every day more Jews were rounded up, interrogated and then interned in labor camps.

Within a year, most of Fraydl's extended family had disappeared or moved to less-conspicuous locations. Fraydl's sister Malka moved in with them after her husband and oldest daughter were killed trying to cross the border into Switzerland. Malka was also the first to go into hiding when the janitor of their building agreed to allow her and her two remaining children to hide in the boiler room. Fraydl's sister Yocheved and her husband Moshe stayed in the apartment, helping the rebbetzin and her youngest daughter as much as they could.

The stress took a terrible toll on Fraydl's mother. The gentle and noble rebbetzin faded to a shadow of her former self. Realizing that her time in this world was coming to an end, she summoned her remaining strength and arranged for a gentile neighbor to hide her *mizhinkele* in his cellar until the danger passed. He was given much of the family's jewelry and cash reserves for this service. Yocheved and Moshe moved into the attic over the stairs with their young son, Chaim. There the loyal janitor brought them food and news of the world.

Fraydl moved into Gerhardt's cellar in late 1940, after her mother's death. An elderly couple had also bribed the man to hide them from deportation, so she was not alone, but the weeks and months passed in fear and boredom, cold and hunger.

Days after settling into her hiding place, Fraydl heard the Nazis break into the house next door where Malka was hiding with her children. The heartrending cries of little Mendel and Yudel echoed in the emptiness long after they were gone, and, in her heart, forever.

By early spring in 1943 all their former Jewish neighbors were long gone. When Gerhardt had run through the money he had been given to conceal his former employer with his wife and the young Mertzbach girl, his motivation to continue hiding them waned considerably. No longer able to live with his conscience, Gerhardt confessed to his priest and was absolved of sin. Early the next morning, the Gestapo kicked down the cellar door and arrested the three mortal enemies of the German Reich. As she was led away, Fraydl glanced surreptitiously up at the attic window of her parents' house, and was comforted to note that her sister and Moshe had not been betrayed as she had.

The young girl and the elderly couple were taken to a shed behind the police station, where they were crammed inside together with other detainees. Fraydl was surprised to discover that she was no longer afraid. Perhaps circumstances had sapped her will to live, as it had her mother's. Fraydl waited dispassionately for the end, sitting cross-legged on the earthen floor and ignoring her surroundings. She even enjoyed the rays of sunlight that caressed her face through the barred window. After months in a dank dark cellar, it was heavenly to breathe fresh air.

In the darkness of night, Fraydl felt a finger poking her ribs.

"We can escape!" whispered a girl about her age who had been brought in a few hours after Fraydl. "There is a space under those boards big enough for us to slip through. Move in front of me so the guard can't see what I'm doing, and I'll dig out a larger passage."

"We won't get far," Fraydl argued in an even softer whisper. "They'll just catch us outside."

"If we stay, we're lost!"

The girl mouthed the words silently, but Fraydl understood. She looked around, and in the dim light from the guard's lantern she caught the eyes of the gentleman who had shared Gerhardt's cellar with her.

"Go!" his eyes seemed to plead. "Live, child. Live!"

Heart pounding, Fraydl inched her way between the girl and the door. She wondered what the girl's name was and where she was from, but was afraid to ask. The two teenagers took turns clawing at the dirt. Every hour the guard opened the door and briefly surveyed his prisoners. Somewhere near midnight, the unknown girl wormed her way under the boards and was gone. A few minutes later, Fraydl followed.

A full moon lit up the yard around the shack. Fraydl was wriggling herself out to freedom when she heard a commotion. The guard had spotted the escaped girl and was calling for reinforcements. Two policemen galloped off in hot pursuit, shooting their pistols as the nameless girl raced away from the shed.

It was too late for Fraydl to return. Torchlight was already illuminating the shack behind her and curses were flying as the guard realized that two of his prisoners were missing. Desperately, Fraydl buried herself underneath a heap of rubbish piled against the wall.

The rest of the imprisoned Jews were roughly dragged from the shed and pushed into a covered truck that soon peeled away with squealing tires.

Despite her thirst and hunger, Fraydl dared not move for the rest of the night and the following day. Only when darkness fell again and she could discern no activity in the vicinity did she finally stand up shakily and brush the refuse off her clothes as best she could. She did not know where her feet would lead her, but she knew that her life depended on getting as far away as possible.

That was the first of many nights of terror for Fraydl. Chained dogs howled when she passed, and each light that was turned on in the dark meant that she might have been discovered. Her own footsteps frightened her almost as much as the sudden hooting of owls or yowling of cats. The first light of dawn found her on the outskirts of the neighborhood where her elementary school had stood. With racing heart she ran on, unobtrusively hugging the shadows and pausing at intervals to be sure she was not being followed.

Finally, her steps reached the familiar neighborhood of her childhood. With the last of her strength, Fraydl let herself down the coal chute of her apartment building and into the cellar. Through the smudged window she followed the activities outside, and soon realized that not one of her Jewish neighbors remained. Where were Yocheved and Moshe? Were they still in the attic? From the sounds over her head it was clear that the house was presently occupied. It would only be a matter of time before she was detected. Covering herself as best she could with the remains of last winter's coal, Fraydl fell into an exhausted and fitful sleep.

When she woke the next morning, Fraydl's gaze was drawn to a heap of old clothes piled in the corner. She was debating whether to go through them in case there might be something she could use, when a little hand poked out from between the rags. Quickly she approached and pulled back some material to expose a small, thin face. Their eyes met and the toddler blinked uncertainly.

"Who are you, little one?" she whispered in astonishment. Who would hide such a small child under a pile of rags in this place?

5

AS SHE WAS PONDERING THE RIDDLE, A HEAVY OBJECT came barreling down the coal chute and thumped to a landing near her feet. Before she could react, it unfolded into a little boy. He opened wide eyes and stared at her.

Fraydl stared back at the apparition. He was so familiar; surely it had to be one of her nephews. "Chaim?" Her sister Yocheved's son would be the same age. "Is it you, Chaim'ke?"

A flash of recognition lit his face. "Tante Fraydl?"

She opened her arms and embraced the boy. "Where is your Mamme?" she asked, looking behind him as if Yochi might slide down the coal chute after the boy.

Chaim struggled not to cry. "They took Mamme," he whispered. His lower lip quivered. "The soldiers were on the ladder. They came up to the attic. Tatty shoved us under the bed and we didn't move. The soldiers took Mamme and Tatty away. I waited with Yanky for such a long time, but no one came except the old janitor. He told us we had to go away. I didn't know where to go, so I brought Yanky down here and waited until he fell asleep and then went to look for food. We've been here for a long time — days and days. We're so hungry, Tante Fraydl..."

The boy reached into his pocket and withdrew a few crusts of bread. He offered her one, but Fraydl shook her head. How long had it been since the policemen broke into the cellar and took her away from Gerhardt's house? Fraydl hadn't seen Chaim at all during the two years she'd been hidden, but he still looked the same. His baby brother, Yanky, was completely changed from the infant she remembered.

"Tante Fraydl," Chaim whispered, "Please take us to Mamme and Tatty now. I'm so afraid here!"

"I wish I could, Chaim'ke," she responded sadly. "But I don't know where they are."

"People go away and they never come back." His matter-of-fact voice made him sound far older than his 8 years. Chaim gave a crust to his little brother and Yanky sucked on it eagerly.

"I will try to find some more food," she promised. "When it gets dark I will go outside again."

Every night after that, Chaim stayed to take care of Yanky while Fraydl climbed back up the coal chute. Throughout the summer the children just managed to survive. Most of the time, Fraydl had no luxury to think or feel, only to run and hide and try to find food for the children. She grabbed fruit and nuts from beneath trees when she found them, and raw vegetables from gardens. Occasionally she discovered discarded bread or other edibles by rummaging through trash bins. She carefully balanced saucers of milk stolen from doorsteps, intended for cats by compassionate German *hausfraus*, and was happy to see the boys lick them clean. Fraydl was altogether too desperate with hunger to feel humiliated.

Things became worse when the weather turned colder as autumn approached. "What are we going to do now?" Chaim fretted. "Soon the neighbors will order fuel to heat the house. When the truck pours a load of coal down here, we will be buried alive!"

"Don't worry, Chaim. Hashem is taking care of us," his aunt promised, though she was nearly frantic with worry herself. A few nights later, as she prowled the neighborhood, the sound of a freight train gave her the idea of escaping the city and its dangers.

She woke the boys just as the sun was rising and led them to a spot near the central train station. Dodging between idle train cars, she spied one with half-opened doors and the children quickly scrambled in. Fraydl had no idea where its destination might be, but she innocently believed that anything was better than their present situation.

Some hours later, someone passed by and slammed the heavy door shut. Afterward the train jerked and screeched before rumbling away from the station.

"Where are we going?" Chaim asked.

"I don't know," she admitted. There was a small window overhead, so she stood on tiptoes and looked out. To Fraydl's horror, the tracks led north, toward Germany. Trapped in the moving freight car, there was nothing for the children to do but recite all the *Tehillim* that she could remember by heart as the train made its way deeper and deeper into Germany.

After her years in the cellar, the view from the little window was spectacular. Verdant fields and fat milk cows grazed in rolling pastures. Farmers waved and their red-cheeked wives looked up as the train rolled noisily by. At the approach to each town and city, the engineer applied his mournful horn. Then, after a brief stop, the journey would resume.

Late in the afternoon, the railroad car rolled to a stop outside a large station. There were shouts and noise as the cars were unloaded. The door of their empty car was unlocked and opened, but the worker did not spot the children cowering in the farthest corner. When darkness finally fell, Fraydl took Yanky in her arms and jumped down to the tracks, followed by Chaim.

"I'm hungry," the boy murmured, and the toddler moved petulantly in her arms.

"Be as quiet as you can and follow me," Fraydl instructed, picking her way along the railroad ties. "We will try to find something to eat."

They wandered nearly all night, but the search yielded very little. Starving and weak, Fraydl foolishly ventured out of the shadows and headed straight into a group of Hitler *yugend*, shouting obscenities and raucously singing off-key sentimental ballads extolling their love for the Fatherland. Still half-drunk from their night of carousing, the sight of a frightened Jewish face changed their focus instantly. The children were fortunate that the boys were tipsy, bumping into each other, reeling and staggering through the streets. Even so, in their weakened state it took enormous effort to put distance between them. At the end of her strength, Fraydl sought refuge behind a large automobile while she awaited the worst.

That had been yesterday. Today she was lying in a luxurious bed covered by warm blankets, clean and dry, with a tray of bread and jam on the table beside her and a Nazi officer to protect her from harm! It was so incredible that she could almost laugh — although, of course, she dared not make a sound. Only Hashem could orchestrate such events!

6

AFTER HER EXHAUSTED LIMBS HAD HAD THEIR FILL OF THE unaccustomed leisure, Fraydl nudged a sleeping Yanky aside and shuffled closer to the window to peer down at the world outside. It was late afternoon, and steady sheets of rain blurred her vision of the well-kept grounds three stories below. She could see a garden enclosed by a tall hedge, a cluster of bare trees and the car shed where they had arrived that morning. Further away was another long low building that appeared to be a stable.

She could see the stone path along which the soldier had led them to the house. A limp rope swing dangled from one of the trees, forlornly twisting in the rain. A very large man appeared suddenly, bald and hatless, with no apparent regard for the weather. Two German shepherd hounds strained at their leashes, pulling him toward the house. Fraydl quickly ducked away from the window.

By nightfall the children had finished their food and water and were waiting tensely, ears alert for the sound of approaching steps. The rain let up for a while and stars flickered between the clouds in the dark sky beyond the window. Hours passed in silence. Yanky played with a loose string on the quilt, twisting it and then letting it unwind. Fraydl whispered endearments in his ear and he wriggled bashfully.

Exactly at midnight, Emsbach cautiously pushed open the trap door and climbed into the attic. The children were momentarily blinded by his kerosene lamp, but he quickly put it behind his back when he saw their hands covering their eyes.

When the German stood erect, his hair seemed to brush the low ceiling. He looked around critically, but saw no sign that the trio had moved from their places. "I'll wait for you under the ladder," he said quietly, removing the tray. "Do you need help climbing down with the little one, or can you manage?"

"We can manage," Fraydl replied.

The children descended awkwardly and then followed the doctor as he led them through several rooms and down a broad, banistered staircase leading to the front entrance. The house was absolutely quiet and it was obvious that they were completely alone. This fact relieved Fraydl, but it also made her nervous. Who was this person, anyway? Why was he endangering his life by hiding fugitive Jewish children? What was his real motivation?

Emsbach opened the door to his study and gestured for them to enter. A fire blazed in the hearth and the room was warm. He indicated a tray of food waiting on the tea table, and busied himself pouring mugs of cocoa from a crystal pitcher. While young Chaim's eyes never left the tall, blond man, Fraydl's gaze wandered about the room. She took in the sage-green silk wallpaper, the heavy velvet drapes and upholstered chaise longue. The walls were high, with decorative carved molding along the edges of the ceiling. The space was dominated by a large desk, softly lit by an electric reading lamp. On it sat a calendar, a letter opener and an ornate inkwell holding a lone pen. This was a comfortable room, and an obviously masculine one.

"May we wash our hands first?" she asked hesitantly, fearing that he might be offended by her audacity.

"*Jawohl*, of course."

He showed them the way to the kitchen. Emsbach watched

quizzically as Fraydl and Chaim repeated their strange hand-washing ritual before partaking of the bread.

"We won't be disturbed," he reassured them. "My servants are quite elderly. They sleep in the carriage house, and no one is here at this time of night except me. The housekeeper is scheduled to return tomorrow, but the risk of detection is negligible right now."

Fraydl lifted her eyes from the food and looked at him. "Who are you?" she asked, taking in the non-threatening civilian clothes, the sweetish aroma of pipe tobacco and the undisguised sympathy in his blue eyes. "Why are you doing this for us?"

Chaim froze at her words. A tremor of fear passed through him. He, too, looked at their rescuer and waited.

"We will speak of this later," the German replied stiffly. "Now you must eat."

He leaned back in his chair and puffed reflectively on his pipe as the children turned their attention to the food. The only sound in the room came from little Yanky slurping his cocoa. The small boy licked his fingers, loath to miss even one sweet drop.

Chaim downed his cocoa in a few nervous gulps, barely tasting the thick, sweet liquid. His eyes caught Fraydl's but she turned away before he could discern her thoughts. He returned his attention to the plate of sauerkraut, wurst and boiled potatoes. "It's not kosher, is it?" Chaim whispered.

Fraydl shrugged. "How could it be?" she murmured under her breath.

"Is something the matter with the food?" Emsbach noticed the exchange between them. "You must be hungry. Why aren't you eating?"

Against the sound of the crackling of the fire on the hearth Fraydl nudged Chaim. "Eat!" she whispered. "I'm sure it's allowed. It's *pikuach nefesh*."

Her nephew pushed the wurst to the side of his plate. "I can't. I'm afraid I'll throw up. Even the smell makes me feel sick."

The German rose and walked over to where they were sitting. To his astonishment they averted their faces; their eyes appeared to be brimming with tears. "What is the matter?" he demanded. The children were obviously ravenous, but only little Yanky had made a dent in the food in his bowl.

The girl looked up at him helplessly. "We're not used to eating meat," she tried to avoid the real issue in order not to offend him.

"Well you must eat this meat, and you must eat it now." The command in his voice was unmistakable. "You are thin and weak and your bodies need the strength that only protein can provide." He stood there waiting.

Chaim cut a bite-sized piece of wurst and lifted it to his lips. "I can't!" he gagged and burst into tears. "It's not kosher! I've never eaten meat that wasn't kosher!"

"Please allow us to forgo the meat," Fraydl hastened to intervene. "It is so kind and generous of you to prepare this food. We appreciate your good intentions, but we are Jewish, and Jews are forbidden to eat meat that was not slaughtered and prepared according to the Torah Law." She paused anxiously to gauge his reaction.

Karl Emsbach did not know how to deal with this. He knew that Jews were peculiar, but he hadn't expected the hungry children to refuse his food. "Are you aware of how difficult it is to acquire meat these days? Our country is at war!" His words sounded ridiculous to his own ears.

Fraydl wrung her hands. She was only 16, an orphan herself and also responsible for her two nephews. She was fairly sure that it was permitted to eat the meat in order to sustain their lives, but what could she do if her body refused to cooperate? How could she explain such a dilemma to this gentile? They were completely in his power. If they offended him, who knew what fate would await the children?

"It smells delicious," she lied for the sake of peace. "I wish we could eat it, but we cannot. Neither of us has tasted meat in years, and now it makes us feel ill to even try. See? Even little Yanky ate only the potatoes and cabbage and left the rest."

The man turned to see the youngest child sprawled asleep on the carpet beside his nearly empty bowl. The doctor's face was expressionless and his remote blue eyes did not reveal the thoughts behind them. Fraydl looked up with pleading eyes, praying in her heart that Hashem would save them from the German's wrath.

Behind the mask he had learned to wear, Emsbach was impressed and also somewhat bemused by the children's stubbornness. It was unforeseen, but what would be gained by forcing them? The girl seemed truly distressed, while obviously taking care not to displease him. Tomorrow he would boil some eggs as a substitute for the protein they was missing by abstaining from meat. The wurst was delicious; he would eat it himself.

This is probably all for the best, he mused. *If I begin eating three times as much meat as usual, I can't imagine how I could hide it from Beatrix and Rhea for very long.*

"We are quite full," Fraydl offered with a shy smile. "The boiled potatoes and cabbage are very filling. If the *Herr* would be so kind as to show me where I can wash the dishes, I will be glad to clean up and put them away."

Emsbach regarded the girl thoughtfully. It was better that she learn to be independent, since every other day he worked straight through the night and she would have to manage competently by herself or the children would go hungry.

Frowning, he wondered how long this arrangement could continue.

7

FRAYDL WASHED THE DISHES AND PUT THEM AWAY, familiarizing herself with the cook's orderly kitchen and earning their rescuer's approval. Although it was very late, he did not want them to return immediately to their hiding place in the attic.

"Come back in here," he said, indicating the door to his study. "I know that it is late, but there will be all day tomorrow to sleep and I prefer not to put off our discussion any longer. There are important details that must be worked out to ensure a clear understanding of the issues involved."

Dread welled up and suffused her. With leaden legs, Fraydl reentered the warm study and perched cautiously on the edge of the sofa. This man had seemed so nice, so human, after all the mistreatment she and the boys had experienced at the hands of his fellow Germans. But who knew what might lurk behind those cold blue eyes? What unacceptable demands might he wish to exact in return for his protection?

The girl's obvious intimidation made Emsbach uncomfortable. His decision to help the children was taken, and he needed their trust and cooperation. Looking at the tense upturned faces, he was stirred by the same emotion that had repeatedly caused him to disobey his parents as a child, when he brought home wounded wild things from the forest in defiance of their express orders. Those small creatures had also been frightened of him at first, flailing desperately to escape when he bent to gently explore their broken wings or release them from a hunter's cruel trap. *When they know me, they won't be afraid*, he assured himself.

"Do you know who I am?"

Against the silence of the room his voice startled the children. Little Yanky began to cry in a most unsettling fashion, huge tears welling from his dark-brown eyes. His small mouth opened wide, but no sound emerged.

The older ones looked at each other in alarm. "No, sir!" they responded almost simultaneously, as the girl pulled the baby into her arms to soothe him. She brushed soft kisses against his forehead until he relaxed. The bigger boy put on a brave face, but he was trembling like a leaf.

"This won't do," Emsbach insisted with a frown. "Why are you so afraid?"

How could he know? Fraydl asked herself, glancing around the cozy study that seemed to be from a different planet from the one she and her nephews lived on. Then she thought again: *How could he* not *know?*

As these thoughts raced through her mind, the Nazi soldier seemed to read them. For a moment he froze, and then the man turned his gaze away from the children. "Forgive me," he murmured, unexpectedly overwhelmed with shame at his callous approach. Those two words did more to build their trust than all his previous kindness. When he addressed them directly a few moments later, the arrogance in his voice was no longer pronounced.

"My name is Emsbach. I am Dr. Karl Emsbach, a surgeon at the military hospital."

He continued speaking. The sentences were hesitant at first, but gradually began to flow as his confidence grew. The children sat before him, their serious eyes no longer reflecting the fear that had unnerved him before. After a while, their natural shyness and his introversion gave way to a mutual need for communication.

Fraydl tried to express her gratitude for his rescuing them, but the doctor shook his head in protest. "As an officer of my country, I am mortified at what has happened to Germany," he explained, real pain briefly visible on his otherwise expressionless face. "As a physician whose career is dedicated to saving lives, I am appalled." After a pause, he continued, "I've never understood anti-Semitism. When I was young it merely seemed illogical and gauche, something that characterized unrefined people. Now that it has become a way of life," he sighed, "it creates an onerous burden for anyone with a conscience.

"I have no logical explanation for how I responded when I saw your distress yesterday except, perhaps, that I am sick of this herd mentality and the shallowness that has taken over my once-beautiful Fatherland. I do not regret my decision to help you, and I give you my word as a gentleman that I will do my best to preserve your lives. When this war ends, as it must, I will be able to live with myself only because I have made this gesture."

One of the logs in the fireplace settled, sending a shower of sparks up the flue. Little Yanky was fast asleep, and Chaim rested his drowsy head against the back of the sofa. For the next hour, Fraydl answered Dr. Emsbach's questions. She told him of her home and family. Seeing that both the boys were sleeping, she allowed herself to express her incredulity that human beings could perpetrate the atrocities she had witnessed since the Reich annexed Austria, and her faith that right would eventually triumph.

Emsbach listened with absolute attention, realizing that his sympathy was the only medicine for her broken heart. After everything that could be said at this time had been said, they continued sitting in silence for a while, but it was a comfortable stillness. The trained physician in Emsbach appreciated that the children were weak and needed to sleep, but he found himself loath to bring their discussion to an end. He had not realized how much his heart ached until his feelings were put into words. Speaking with this young, intelligent Jewish girl left him with the kind of satisfaction he remembered nostalgically from his days as a medical student.

He stood up reluctantly from his place behind the great desk. "Are you and the youngsters comfortable?" he asked. "Is there anything else that you need?"

"You are very kind. We lack nothing," she replied. "This afternoon I looked out the window and saw a giant man walking outside in the rain with two dogs. When he glanced up, I moved back right away. I don't think he could have seen me, but you should know."

"That would have been my groundskeeper, Hans." Emsbach's tone was serious. "He is a very gentle giant, but despite his age his vision is still sharp. It would not do for him to suspect anything. You must not look out of the window when it is light out. Discovery would cost both your life and mine."

"I understand," she assured him. "I will be careful."

"Will you be able to control the little ones?" He looked at the boys with concern. "They must not move or make even the smallest sound during the day when my staff is in the house."

"We know how to be quiet during daylight hours," Fraydl assured him. "It has been a matter of survival for us. Even little Yanky seems to know, without actually understanding why."

Emsbach explained the routines of the house, and his work schedule. "Three nights a week I am at the hospital. I will leave food for you here in my private study, which is off limits for the servants when I am not present. After midnight you may leave the attic and come downstairs; only take care that your brothers do not move or touch anything outside this room. I cannot emphasize enough that if anything is moved from its usual place, it will arouse suspicion. There is a blackout order from the civil guard, so all windows are curtained at night and no one from outside can see in. Feel free to take any book from my library that interests you. If you need to communicate with me, you will find notepaper and writing utensils in this drawer. Write it down, then fold the paper and place it inside the appointment book in the top drawer of my desk.

"Once a week, on Sunday mornings, you will be able to move

freely about the house because everyone is at church from 8 in the morning until noon. I advise all of you to go up and down the stairs repeatedly in order to strengthen your muscles; otherwise, they will atrophy from the lack of exercise. Do you have any questions?"

Fraydl didn't, so he lifted the slumbering Chaim to his shoulder and together they carried the children back upstairs. He left a basket with an adequate supply of bread and jam, some apples and a bottle of water. Returning to his study, Emsbach gave his attention to his patients' files, easily completing the work he'd previously left unfinished. He could concentrate now. His mind was at ease.

8

A REGULAR ROUTINE EVOLVED FOR THE CHILDREN. THEY were soon familiar with the muted noises on weekday mornings, when Dr. Emsbach's housekeeper came to the house. Rhea worked until afternoon, a crew of village girls assisting her with the housecleaning, laundry and ironing. Limited by age and rheumatism, Beatrix and Otto never climbed the stairs to the second floor. Otto was extremely hard of hearing and the children could hear his wife's voice when she shouted at him. For many hours of the day, the quiet in the large old house was broken only by the occasional sighing of the wooden floors.

During the first weeks, the little family slept most of the time, their exhausted and malnourished bodies drinking in sleep as hungrily as the food they ate. But as their health was restored, the comfortable brass bed gradually became a prison. Unable to move about the attic lest the tread of their feet be audible downstairs, Fraydl's creativity was sorely in demand to keep the bored children quiet. With the resilience of youth, their memories of starvation and danger receded and it was torture for them to lie quietly for hours on end.

Chaim hated when he heard his younger brother plead, "Tante Fraydl, Yanky wanna go home now."

"Stop saying that!" he demanded. "We can't go home!" Chaim clenched his small hands into fists. "Home is gone, don't you understand? Mamme and Tatty are gone. Everything is gone."

"*Sha*, Chaim! He's too little to understand," Fraydl remonstrated, sorrowful at the 8-year-old's premature maturity.

Chaim hunched his shoulders and turned his face away. It hurt too much to remember his loving parents and the warm and happy home where he had spent his earliest years

Fraydl distracted Yanky with shadow games until he finally drifted off to sleep. "Chaim," she whispered to her older nephew. "I know it hurts, but don't forget where you came from. It's important to remember. One day this war will be over and we will go home again. I'm sure of it."

Chaim blinked away the tears and nodded. He didn't believe the war would ever end, but he didn't want to hurt Tante Fraydl's feelings and say so.

They must not forget, Fraydl thought to herself. *Our family was so special. Gedolei Yisrael were frequent guests in our home. I want Chaim and Yanky to remember their parents and grandparents, aunts and uncles and cousins, and what our lives were like. I was taught to cherish our family's heritage and I want them to grow up with that awareness, too. It's up to me to give them that connection, until our family is reunited after the war.*

On the nights Emsbach was home, he joined the family in his study, obviously enjoying their company. They always listened to the midnight news on the doctor's clandestine radio. News of the war on the BBC was not encouraging, but Emsbach liked hearing different perspectives. "I suspect it is closer to the truth than the Nazi propaganda in the local media," he mused, chewing pensively on his pipe and looking considerably more like a professor than a soldier. His captive audience listened politely as their benefactor expounded on whatever subjects interested him in current events or history.

There were times when he described his experiences at the university, amusing them with anecdotes from his life as a student.

Chaim noticed a chessboard on a shelf in the study and timidly asked Emsbach to play a game with him. Humoring the boy, the German agreed. Soon the two were bent over the desk, the thump of the chess pieces the only sound apart from the crackling logs in the fireplace. Predictably, the boy lost the first two games. But he was attentive, and by the third game he thought of a strategy that cost Emsbach his expected victory.

"How long have you been playing chess?" Emsbach complimented Chaim. "Don't ever reveal to my colleagues that I can be beaten by an 8-year-old!"

Chaim smiled shyly. "We used to play chess on *nittel nacht*," he started to explain, but stopped when he heard Fraydl gasp and saw her face pale.

"What is *nittel nacht*?" their host inquired absently, his attention riveted on the positions of the few pieces of ivory remaining in their fourth game.

Catching a glimpse of Fraydl's panicked expression, the boy stammered. "Umm. . ." He hesitated, but at that moment Emsbach swept his bishop from behind to trap Chaim's king, and the subject was forgotten as the doctor smiled in triumph.

Later, back in the attic, Fraydl warned her nephew to be more circumspect. "Never forget who he is, Chaim! Dr. Emsbach is not your uncle. He's not your friend. He's a Christian Nazi!"

Chastened, Chaim promised. "He was so nice," the boy muttered. "I forgot."

"I know, Chaim'ke, but we have no choice. We must be very, very careful."

"How much longer, Tante Fraydl?" His sad eyes made Chaim look very like his little brother.

"Only Hashem knows," she tried to comfort him and herself at the same time. "Maybe one day it will make sense. For now, we can only *daven* for Hashem's help. Look how He got a Nazi army officer to give us a home and protect us! There is a plan, whether we understand it or not."

The next night, Fraydl left a note for the doctor, explaining that boredom was making the boys fidgety and asking for something to occupy them. Emsbach dug through old trunks until he found a number of storybooks from his childhood, as well as a magnifying glass and an almost-complete set of dominoes. Together with paper and writing implements, Chaim now had the resources to quietly direct his energy during the daylight hours. Little Yanky posed a greater challenge.

"What do 3-year-old children play with?" Emsbach asked Fraydl.

"Balls and blocks, rocking horses and teddy bears," she recalled from her experiences babysitting nieces and nephews.

"I don't have anything like that in the house," Emsbach frowned. "I think my mother saved every toy and book I ever had, but I've never seen stuffed bears or building blocks here."

"Maybe he could string buttons on a piece of twine?" she suggested, and he nodded his agreement.

The next day, Dr. Emsbach gave them a tin full of every variety and color of buttons.

"Won't your housekeeper miss this?" Fraydl fretted as she inspected the contents.

"I don't think so. This belonged to my mother and no one has touched them in over 15 years," he replied.

Yanky poured the buttons out with a smile of delight. He dropped them back into the tin one at a time, fascinated by their diverse textures and patterns. Fraydl taught him to sort the buttons by shape or color, and began teaching him numbers by counting the buttons and arranging them in sets. The simple container of buttons became a source of endless activity for the child.

With the boys safely occupied, Fraydl read books from Dr. Emsbach's library or just lay in the brass bed and let her mind dream. It was icy cold in the attic, and all the children waited impatiently for nighttime when they could linger for awhile in the warmth of Emsbach's study.

The doctor kept his finger on the pulse of the household servants, gradually relaxing his guard as the plan appeared to be working successfully.

When he had time to think, he worried about Yanky. He felt he could trust Fraydl and Chaim, but the toddler represented a great danger. *I should find another place for the little one,* he thought to himself. *I should look for a family to take him in and raise him as their own.* It was not unknown for infertile couples to approach doctors about adoption. If he asked around, would it arouse suspicions? What about the fact that he just happened to have a 3-year-old who needed a home? Was there an innocent explanation for the child's Jewish face with its dark, intelligent eyes?

If there was, he had not yet managed to think of one.

9

E MSBACH PULLED OFF THE WHITE MEDICAL SMOCK THAT he wore over his scrub suit. Tired and hungry, this seemed like a good opportunity for a break in order to eat something before he was called to assist in another operation. At this hour of night the surgeries were all emergencies, the elective ones having been performed during the day.

"Going to the cafeteria?" The voice of his colleague, Konrad Winkelmann, followed him out the swinging door of the surgical ward.

"*Ja*," he responded, turning to wait for the young curly-haired surgeon to catch up with him. Winkelmann was the least offensive of his co-workers. The two men were frequently assigned duty together because they made a good team. In the cafeteria, the doctors filled their trays and made their way to an empty table near the exit in case they were paged.

"What do you think of the new orthopedic surgeon?" Winkelmann asked, generously sprinkling salt over his boiled potatoes.

"I haven't had a chance to get to know him yet," Emsbach replied noncommittally, crunching a juicy pickle and savoring the sour taste. He did not encourage Konrad because he did not like gossip in general, and also because his intuitive impression of Dr. Lothar Engelhardt was that the new man was a walking ego, a dangerous type to cross and an unpleasant one to work with.

"You know who he's related to, don't you?"

"Everyone here is related to someone in the upper echelons or we would be at the front," Emsbach responded cynically, taking another bite of his rye sandwich.

Winkelmann squirmed at the blunt truth in those words. "Yes, but do you know who Lothar's brother-in-law is?" he insisted.

"*Nein.*" Emsbach controlled his impatience. This conversation was even less agreeable than the bland hospital food.

"Just the Dr. Josef Grobke who is conducting all those medical experiments for the Gestapo we've been hearing about," Winkelmann chuckled conspiratorially, and was rewarded when his colleague nearly choked on the bite he was in the process of swallowing.

Pleased with himself for breaking this significant information to the senior resident, Konrad smugly waited for a response.

"I think my uncle mentioned him a few times." Emsbach affected boredom while parrying for time to absorb the unwelcome news.

"I wouldn't be surprised." Winkelmann took a big bite and continued speaking with his mouth full. "My father says he's one of the führer's favorites."

Emsbach toyed with his fork, sliding his food from side to side on the plate as his appetite deserted him. A slight commotion in the food line drew their attention to a new group entering the cafeteria. Lothar Engelhardt was leading a covey of deferential student nurses to an unoccupied table beside the window.

"Speak of the devil," Konrad muttered in admiration. "What do they see in him?"

Emsbach chewed thoughtfully. "Well, he's new. He's wealthy and well connected. And there are few enough available men for them to choose from." The young women, giggling and blushing, drew harsh glances from some of the older matrons.

Lothar looked around the room, soaking in the attention. Noticing his colleagues from the surgical department, he left his tray on the table and leisurely made his way over toward Karl Emsbach and Konrad Winkelmann.

What he lacks in intelligence he certainly makes up for in self-confidence, Emsbach thought with distaste as Engelhardt approached their table. Emsbach stood, politely offered his hand in greeting.

"Heil Hitler!"

"Heil Hitler!"

Lothar's hair was brushed back over his forehead in a conscious imitation of Adolph Hitler. Emsbach watched the man's eyes sweep the smoke-filled room with conceit. He was obviously convinced that all the diners were focused on him, following his every move and waiting to hear his every utterance.

Emsbach spoke first."I would ask you to join us, but I see you are not alone." It was an ostensibly neutral opening, but there was a hint of sarcasm that did not escape the newcomer's attention.

Engelhardt's pale-blue eyes flashed. He looked his colleague up and down for a long minute, frowning with displeasure. Major Emsbach was a head taller than himself, and considerably better looking. Lothar's competitive instincts warned him that this was a potential rival. He would have to be put in his place, to remove the threat to Engelhardt's still-fragile standing in the hospital hierarchy. Relying on past successes as a bully, the new man decided to employ a little humiliation on the veteran surgeon.

Speaking loudly enough to be heard over the low hum of conversation in the cafeteria, Lothar sniffed as though exposed to an offensive odor. "I smell a Jew in this vicinity," he said, pointedly staring at his adversary.

"I was not aware that a Jew could be detected by the olfactory senses. Is this something your brother-in-law is researching?" Blue fire danced in Emsbach's eyes, making it clear to the newcomer that he was not easily intimidated.

Engelhardt stiffened, his eyes darted from Emsbach to Winkelmann and back again. Winkelmann blinked uncomfortably, but Emsbach sat down nonchalantly and resumed eating. The tension was broken by the scratchy sound of the loudspeakers calling on all surgeons on duty to report for an emergency appendectomy. Emsbach deliberately wiped his mouth with a napkin, bowed ironically toward Lothar and exited the room with Konrad Winkelmann hurrying in his wake.

"Who is that man?" Engelhardt demanded in an angry whisper as he returned to his seat.

"Major Karl Emsbach? He's the nephew of General Heinrich Mauer," said an intern sitting at an adjacent table.

The murmur of low voices and the clink of cutlery resumed . The haughty doctor's face sported a mirthless smile as he belted out a hasty joke to deflect attention from the mortification that stung even after Emsbach's departure.

On the way home the next morning, Emsbach found himself remembering the episode. *Jews don't have a characteristic smell*, he assured himself sensibly. Still, he examined his hands, illogically wondering if there was something he wasn't aware of. Could it be that while shaking hands with Chaim, or touching something one of the children handed him, a smell clung to him? He shook his head in disgust. Those crazy Nazis were getting to him.

Approaching a crossroads, he made an impulsive decision. Instead of continuing home to sleep, he turned left and drove the car toward the bridge leading to the Austrian border. By midmorning he had reached the city where Fraydl and the boys used to live. Driving slowly, he was amazed that he could recognize landmarks just from the vivid descriptions the children had shared. His Mercedes seemed drawn by a magnet, and within an hour the doctor was on the very street where Jewish families had once filled the homes. Glancing at the house numbers, he soon found the exact address.

Embach sat in his car for quite some time, simply observing the neighborhood and trying to imagine what it had been like five years earlier. He never planned to and didn't know what made him open the door and get out, but somehow he found himself at the entrance to the house. There was no one in sight. He opened the door to the lobby and stepped in. Examining the tenants' mailboxes, he noticed the name "Gunther Gerhardt" inked over the previous resident's name: "Jacob Wolf Mertzbach, Rabbiner."

Emsbach climbed the wide stairs to the second floor and found the apartment the children had described. The upper right side of the door post was marred by a deep scratch of raw wood where the *mezuzah* had been torn off. Unexplained anger welled up inside the no-longer-weary doctor, propelling him to forge ahead. Gambling that his Nazi officer's uniform would arouse fear in the hearts of the inhabitants, Emsbach pounded on the door and loudly demanded entrance.

10

T HE DOOR OPENED AND AN ANGRY *HAUSFRAU* WITH A
dirty apron thrust a scowling face into the hall. At the sight
of the Nazi uniform, her manner turned obsequious. Two barefoot,
pink-cheeked little girls hung onto the woman's skirt, peering up
at him with round blue eyes. Behind the mother, an obviously
intimidated older boy raised his hand in the Nazi salute, croaking
"*Sieg Heil!*" Emsbach ignored him.

Looking down his nose at the anxious lady, he asked coldly,
"You are Frau Gerhardt?" He made it sound as if the name itself
was a crime.

"*Ja! Ja, mein Herr!*" she squeaked. Her eyes skittered from
Emsbach to the hallway behind him, in dread of more menacing
visitors.

"*Wu ist Herr Gerhardt?*" Arrogance dripped from his words.

The woman's hands fluttered momentarily, and then she stepped
aside and pointed at a heavyset man sunk in an intoxicated stupor,
his boots muddying the once-exquisite brocade sofa.

Emsbach pushed the *hausfrau* aside and took a step toward the
snoring drunk, roaring, "Criminal! Thief!"

The man stirred and mumbled in his sleep, but did not wake up. Hastily thrusting her offspring into the kitchen, the woman closed the door behind them and whined fretfully, "*Bitte schön,* do not wake him! He will beat us! Please, *mein Herr,* have mercy on the innocent children!"

From the discoloration around her eyes, it was obvious that she spoke from recent experience.

Emsbach shook his fist in her face, "Where is it? Where did he hide it?"

"Wh-what?? No one hid anything! I swear it! What are you looking for? Take anything you want." In her horror that Gunther would regain consciousness and discover this Nazi officer in the house, she was prepared to pay any price. Who knew how the good-for-nothing would react in his drunken state? He was likely to get himself arrested, and then she would be left with no one to provide for her and the children.

Emsbach brought his face near hers, and in a perfect imitation of his Uncle Heinrich's voice snarled, "You hid the Jewish treasure, you dirty thieves!"

"No! There was nothing. Only some old books, nothing else." The woman was verging on panic. "I know where they are. We'll get them for you. *Bitte schön, warten Sie ein minut!*" Hyperventilating, she cracked open the kitchen door and shrieked, "Dieter! Dieter!" She grabbed the boy's skinny arm and propelled him into the salon. "Quick!" she hissed. "Bring the box from under my bed! *Mach shnell! Du horst mir, dumkopf?*"

The boy, a Bavarian lad about Chaim's age, disappeared into the back of the house. Emsbach paced while the *hausfrau* wrung her hands, until the child reappeared lugging a heavy wooden chest.

"Oh, no! Not that one!" she moaned in dismay, cuffing her unfortunate son on the side of his head. "Put it back quickly or your father will kill you for sure! Bring the other one. *Der anderer!*"

She shoved him back, but it was too late. The Nazi intruder was already wrestling the chest from their hands, threatening, "You will be punished for the theft of Reich property!" Mother and son relinquished their hold as if scalded.

Emsbach seized the chest, glaring until they dropped their eyes and stepped back. Abruptly he left the house and carried it downstairs. After stowing the load in the trunk of his car, the officer sped away. The memory of the trespassers cowering against the wall left a bad taste in his mouth. *I should inform on that Gunther Gerhardt,* he thought, but he knew he wouldn't. His performance as a boorish Nazi disgusted him because it was so authentic. He was ashamed that he had pulled it off so successfully.

With the Mercedes secured in the car shed, Emsbach took a few minutes to pry open the lid of the chest and examine its contents. There were velvet pouches of varying sizes protecting tarnished objects of silver. *These are valuable,* he concluded with satisfaction. *They're worth a small fortune!* He was glad that he had succeeded in recovering them for the children. If Fraydl sold them she would be able to support herself and the boys for quite a long time after the war.

"Well, has the prodigal son returned?" Otto greeted his master gruffly, helping him off with his coat. "Bea, here is the young man at last."

"Karl! Where have you been all morning?" The old woman had obviously suffered distress on his account.

"*Es tut mir leid,*" he apologized. "I had some errands to take care of."

"Sit down now and eat. You should have phoned Rhea to tell us not to worry," Bea scolded with more affection than anger.

Emsbach sat at the table and ate mechanically, hardly tasting the food in his impatience to share his adventure with Fraydl and the boys. In the aftermath of his adrenaline-powered morning, exhaustion was setting in. His head nodded and his eyes felt far too heavy to hold open.

"Go to sleep, young master," Beatrix said sympathetically. "I'll warm up your food when you awaken."

"You're too heavy for me to pick up and carry to bed," Otto complained loudly, pulling at the doctor's arm. "Come on now, young man. To bed with you! The women have something important to discuss and you must be alert."

"What do they want to discuss with me?" he asked in alarm.

The two old servants laughed. "Don't worry, dear boy. We've been waiting to broach the subject for long enough. It can wait another few hours."

Do they suspect something? He frowned, shaking his head in an effort to free his mind from the blurry fog of fatigue. With Otto's hoary hand guiding him up the stairs, he soon found himself in bed, where sleep overcame him almost instantly.

Hours later, he woke up feeling unkempt and realized that he'd fallen asleep in his clothing. Always fastidious, Emsbach arose immediately to wash and change into clean garments. The morning's escapade seemed like a dream. From the head of the stairs he heard the clinking of dishes below and the aroma of dinner reminded him that he was starved. Hearing his steps on the creaky stairs, the servants greeted his appearance with inquiries about his health.

"I'm fine!" he declared. "And hungry."

"*Ach*, that's my boy," murmured Rhea as she adjusted her apron. "Sit down, Karl. Your food should be warm soon. Otto mentioned that Beatrix and I wish to speak with you about an important matter. . . Do you prefer to eat in peace, or to discuss the subject during your meal?"

Emsbach stared at his housekeeper, a lump of apprehension forming in the pit of his stomach.

11

DECIDING THAT PROCRASTINATION WAS THE BETTER PART of valor, Emsbach chose to eat before Rhea told him what was on her mind. He needed time to prepare for the eventuality that the servants had discovered some sign of the house's unconventional boarders. Conceivably Beatrix had noticed that her supply of food was diminishing at a more rapid rate than she was accustomed to. He sighed inwardly, recalling that just last week Rhea had asked for permission to dismiss one of the village girls after taking an inventory of the linen closet and discovering that a number of sheets and blankets were missing.

Unable to avoid it any longer, Emsbach summoned the servants to his study after he finished eating dinner.

Dear old Bea fixed him with a fond gaze and asked, "Why is the young master so tense? A body might think we were going to demand a raise in salary!"

"You're not, then?" he parried, looking from one to the other in a covert effort to divine their intentions.

"*Nein, nein.* This is much more important." Rhea brushed the levity aside. "Karl, you have been without a mother or a father to guide you for too many years. In this time of national emergency, we cannot expect your esteemed uncle to distract his mind from his duties protecting the Fatherland. Therefore," she paused to clear her throat, "we feel that it is our obligation to address this serious issue ourselves, as your beloved parents would surely have done if they were alive today."

Emsbach was nonplussed. He waited to hear what they would say, picking at nonexistent lint on his trouser leg and feeling about 5 years old.

"You are 28 now," his housekeeper informed him, "and with your excellent education and lucrative profession, it is time for you to marry. It is your responsibility to produce an heir to carry on the family name."

Having delivered this obviously rehearsed speech, Rhea dropped back into her chair with an audible exhalation of air. Beatrix patted her long-time colleague supportively, as the two women waited to see how the master would respond to their well-meant but irreverent interference in his personal life.

Almost speechless in his relief that the servants harbored no suspicion about the presence of Fraydl and the boys, Emsbach took several moments to compose his thoughts before he replied. "I appreciate your concern. Of course I intend to take a wife, but wartime seems hardly a propitious time for such an endeavor."

"It is the perfect time. There is no competition. The sight of you in uniform will win the heart of any girl you choose!" Old Beatrix waxed enthusiastic, her face wreathed in smiles.

"No, Bea. It's not that simple. In this time of great uncertainty, no one can be sure what the morrow will bring. I feel responsible for you servants and this house, as well as my work at the hospital. At this point, a wife would encumber me. Let us pray that this merciless war comes to an end soon, and then it will be a better time for building."

The two old women who had loved him ever since he could remember looked hurt and disappointed. In their eyes he saw reflected their hope that a woman in the house would bring back sunshine and life during these dreary times. Emsbach sensed how they longed for life to return to the way it had been when he was younger, when his mother's house was filled with parties and balls, laughter and noise. He hated to wake them from their happy though unrealistic dream, but he did not share their plans for his future. Privately, he doubted if the world would ever be the same after this war.

"Will you just agree to meet one young lady?" Rhea implored. Something in her voice warned him that a trap was being laid.

"You can't be so stubborn as to deny just one visit to give her a chance?" Beatrix added.

Their caring voices were more lethal than scolding or lectures. What harm would come of meeting the young lady they were so anxious to propose for his consideration? He wavered and they pleaded until finally, against his better judgment, he came close to agreeing. *Nohr einmal. Just once*, Emsbach thought to himself, hoping that such a gesture would persuade them to refrain from pressuring him further in the future.

"Her name is Liesa," Rhea said quickly. "Do you remember little Liesa Krieger, the daughter of your father's close friend Volker?"

Eemsbach nodded reluctantly, vaguely recalling the Kriegers from his parents' dinner parties. Volker Krieger had resembled a gnarled gnome beside his tall, willowy wife, Erika, and occasionally they'd been accompanied by a very young daughter whose name he'd forgotten. On several occasions his mother had instructed him to accompany the girl on his clarinet while she sang folk songs in a sweet, childish voice. He couldn't remember anything else.

"She's grown up now," Rhea continued. "A beautiful, talented and cultured young lady. I am sure your father and mother would approve of the match, and it just so happens that I met her not long ago and she expressed an interest in seeing you."

"Just like that?" he responded in disbelief. "Out of the blue, this young lady told you that she wants to see me?"

"Well, not exactly," the housekeeper admitted. "I was accompanying my daughter to the citizens' section of the Central Police Station to report her change of address, when I met Frau Krieger and her daughter. You must have heard that her father fell on the eastern front. They had come in to fill out the forms requesting his military pension."

Emsbach frowned, suddenly remembering Liesa's brother Ulrich. A loathsome bully, Ulrich had flattered his parents in their presence and tortured his younger sister in their absence.

Unaware of his thoughts, Rhea continued trying to interest the master in Liesa Krieger. "I hardly recognized the girl," she said. "She is as tall and slender as her mother, and very refined. I spoke with them and offered my condolences on their terrible loss. We continued talking as we waited, and the conversation came around to the days when your dear mother was alive and all the pleasant memories they have from that time. One thing led to another, until your name came up. Now you understand how I am able to assure you that the young lady in question is interested in meeting you."

Emsbach sighed. This was probably the last complication in the world he needed right now. "I'll think about it," he said, with little enthusiasm. "I appreciate your good intentions and I will seriously consider your suggestion."

The trio went into the kitchen, where Beatrix prepared a cup of hot cocoa for Emsbach while Rhea went through the house closing the blackout curtains on the windows. An hour later the servants had departed, and Emsbach was left alone at last.

They are correct in their assumption, he mused. *At my age, I should be considering marriage. The idea has some attraction. It is certainly a duty I must fulfill, but what shall I do? A wife would obviously need to become familiar with the entire house, including the attic. And the presence of anyone apart from myself would mean that the children could never leave their attic hideaway.*

There was no obvious solution. He faced the stark reality: from the moment he'd taken in the three orphaned children, life had ceased to be simple.

On the contrary, it grew more complicated by the day.

12

AT MIDNIGHT, THE CHILDREN DESCENDED THE STAIRS AND made their way to Emsbach's study, where a tray of salted fish and boiled potatoes awaited them.

"It's so good to eat something hot," Fraydl murmured in appreciation. The three made do with bread and jam during the day, which kept their hunger at bay but was not very nourishing. Their benefactor would have preferred giving them meat, but he'd resigned himself to devising other sources of protein rather than arguing about the subject.

He was home tonight. Emsbach sat at his desk and watched the children eat their supper, occasionally drawing on his pipe and causing the embers to glow. It gave off a pleasant scent. All was quiet and peaceful, and Emsbach observed with satisfaction that his "patients" were looking healthier.

"Shall I set up the chessboard?" Chaim offered cheerfully, while his aunt headed to the kitchen to wash the dishes.

"*Nein*, not tonight," Emsbach responded.

The child was disappointed, but he did not protest. He sat down on the rug beside Yanky and helped him line up the toy soldiers

Emsbach kept in a drawer for the boys to play with on the nights when he was not at home.

Fraydl returned, wiping her hands dry on her apron. She, too, was surprised at the deviation in their routine.

"Sit down," the doctor ordered. She complied obediently, confused by the formality but not unduly alarmed. It seemed to her that Dr. Emsbach used this official tone when he wanted to hide his feelings. Fraydl did not sense any hostility, though she noticed that the man seemed to be under some kind of stress.

A moment later the mystery deepened, when their host dragged a crate from behind his desk and set it on the floor before her.

"Do you recognize this?" he asked.

"*Nein, mein Herr.*" She shook her head.

"Perhaps you will recognize the contents?" He pried open the lid to reveal the velvet pouches.

Hesitantly, the girl took a bag and opened the drawstring. Her involuntary cry of distress brought Chaim to her side. Fraydl's fingers shook as the boy took the silver goblet from her hands and raised it to the light. "This is Zeide's *Kiddush becher!*" he whispered. Turning to Dr. Emsbach, he repeated the words in disbelief, "This is my grandfather's silver wine goblet. I remember him using it every Shabbos." The boy burst into tears.

Little Yanky looked from his brother to Fraydl and back, his lower lip quivering even though he did not understand what had happened. Chaim pulled out the rest of the pouches, one after the other. With streaming eyes and trembling hands, the girl gently handled the Chanukah menorah, the *besamim* holder, the filigreed *yad*, the *Megillah* and the challah knife. As each object was revealed, it was greeted by a fresh storm of tears from the older children.

Witnessing their broken hearts was unbearable. The German had anticipated that Fraydl would be pleased because of the monetary value of the objects. It had never occurred to him that the silver would trigger such a powerful emotional response. Clutching her mother's *leichter* against her lips, Fraydl whispered, "Tatte, Mamme," over and over again, her eyes shut tightly. Both boys were sobbing, their little hands stroking the tarnished silver and their tearful eyes on their aunt, who seemed transported to some faraway place.

Emsbach left the room for a moment, and returned with water. "Drink," he said, shoving one glass into Fraydl's line of vision and handing the other to Chaim. The girl took a few swallows. She looked around the room almost as if she didn't know where she was, until her eyes finally settled on him.

Since childhood, Karl Emsbach had been taught to repress sentiment. Strict self-control had been drilled into him during his years at the military academy. Fraydl's display of emotion was simply too raw. Overwhelmed by the intensity of the moment, he turned away from the children and stepped into a small, darkened chamber adjacent to his study, generally used as an examination room for his private patients.

Blindly, Emsbach approached the window and drew aside the heavy curtain. Staring out at the snow-covered world, he was bewildered by the wetness on his own cheeks. Inside his mind he could hear the plaintive echo of Fraydl's voice, crying, "Mamme, Mamme!"

It was a totally uncharacteristic reaction. His mother had always been Mutter, so why was he shaken to the core when he heard the word "Mamme"? It must be the natural empathy he felt at the depth of the children's feelings. Emsbach forced himself to focus on the immense black sky beyond the window, amazed that some part of him wanted to pound on the glass until it broke! "Mamme, Mamme," he whimpered, not even knowing who he was addressing. Perhaps G-d?

That thought angered him. Looking out into the darkness, he silently dared G-d to exist. Many years ago, barely out of childhood, when he had learned to stifle the unbidden feelings that arose in his heart, he had also learned to deny the existence of a supreme Deity. He continued attending services at the Lutheran church, where his parents had baptized him, because his membership furthered his career and ensured useful social contacts; otherwise, it was meaningless. Even as a child, enduring interminable sermons in the ornate chapel, he remembered pondering whether anyone really believed the words they preached or in the rites they performed.

By the time he reached adulthood, Germany was going insane. Emsbach was left with an impenetrable dilemma. On the one hand, Nature was perfectly ordered: something that his logical mind realized could never have come about by chance, especially when he was daily exposed to the complexity, intricacy and beauty of the human body in his work as a physician. On the other hand, if there was an omniscient Being, how could He allow men to commit unspeakable atrocities against each other? Emsbach's sensitive mind and intellectual integrity could not contain this contradiction.

Emsbach had been taught to believe only in objective truth that could be scientifically verified. *Still,* he asked himself, *where is the explanation of my life, and the series of events that have led me to where I am today?* The young doctor was too honest to believe that he deserved full credit for his surgical skills. He knew there were times when his hands seemed to move independently of his will: with lifesaving consequences. In his professional experience, he had seen cases that were considered lost go on to confound physicians when the patient recovered, while a person with a much more favorable prognosis inexplicably passed away.

And what about these Jewish children? Who could explain the extraordinary circumstances that had brought them into his life? In the few months they had been sheltering under his roof, he'd sensed a change in his outlook. After a lifetime of being emotionally frozen, he was beginning to feel warmth. Were not these children the trigger for this development?

Emsbach frowned. He saw himself as the embodiment of the Aryan ideal of complete control, where feelings existed in total submission to cold logic. After applying himself since childhood to systematically overcoming the weakness of his emotions, did he *want* to feel?He could not remember a time when he was not surrounded by walls that kept feelings at a safe distance.

Tonight, somehow, those painstakingly constructed walls had been breached, and he found himself as vulnerable as a little child.

13

FRUSTRATED WITH HIS LINE OF THOUGHT, EMSBACH carefully drew the curtains closed and returned to his study. The children were calmer now, murmuring together over the silver items displayed across his desk. When he re-entered the room, the older ones rose in respect.

"*Herr Doktor*, however did my parents' silver come into your possession?" Fraydl asked, her eyes searching his face.

Emsbach relit his pipe before telling them of the sequence of events that had taken place that morning on his way home from the hospital. Chaim was delighted to hear about the degradation visited upon the usurpers of his grandparents' home.

"You are a soldier, and you have a gun," he exclaimed innocently. "Why didn't you kill those bad people who took Baba's house?"

"It's not so simple, Chaim'ke." Fraydl nudged him.

"Someday they will be punished, I'm sure," Emsbach reassured the excited boy.

"Dr. Emsbach, I will never forget what you have done!" Fraydl said earnestly. "Words do not exist to express the gratitude I will carry in my heart for the rest of my life. G-d will surely repay you many times over for your kindness to poor orphaned children.

"This war is such a nightmare. I cannot bear to think of what has happened to my illustrious family. Perhaps only we three children are left." For a moment her voice choked, but she recovered. "With only memories to keep our past alive, I did not know how I would face the future. These precious heirlooms from my father's home are far more than just silver. In a way, you have returned our stolen identity to us as well."

The girl took each object in turn and explained its purpose and history to the German. Emsbach felt his heart churn with longing for the family warmth he had never known. He decided to steer the discussion in a more intellectual direction.

"I was taught that Judaism is a religion like Christianity or Islam," he commented, looking at the *klaf* of the *Megillas Esther* in her hand. "There were Jewish students at the university who looked and acted exactly like the German students. They ate meat with us in the school cafeteria. There was nothing different about them, except perhaps that they were more serious about their studies."

Fraydl frowned, wondering how to explain to this gentile the phenomenon of Jews who chose to leave religious observance behind but were still Jews nonetheless.

"How do you know that G-d exists? Where is He?"

There was a tremor of urgency in his voice, and the girl was taken aback. If her intuition did not fail her, a sincere longing for truth lurked behind his words. Fraydl looked at him silently, pained at her own inadequacy to explain what she felt so clearly in her heart.

Emsbach was surprised at himself. Although it seemed utterly absurd under the circumstances, the predominant emotion he felt was envy. It was not the monetary value of the silver objects that aroused this feeling, but the obvious attachment the children had to them. When Chaim held the goblet in his small hands, his face literally glowed with memories forever denied to his German protector. No matter how good his intentions, Karl Emsbach could only glimpse Chaim's world. He could never be a part of it.

The ache within the German officer was almost too much to bear, until he realized that his small act of courage in rescuing these children did give him a connection. Here, hidden in his house, a remnant was escaping the diabolical Nazi plan to utterly destroy such a rare and beautiful world. As he was contemplating this point, Fraydl began to answer his question.

"Before the war, I was only a child in my parents' home. I am afraid that I have forgotten many things due to the hardships we endured. After the war ends — may it be soon! — a Rabbi will be able to answer your questions much better than I…"

"Nevertheless," he urged, "try your best."

She inhaled deeply and tried to compose her thoughts into words. "I know that G-d exists, because my parents taught me this. They learned it from their parents, who learned it from their parents — all the way back to the Patriarchs of the Jewish people: Abraham, Isaac and Jacob. Throughout the generations, mothers and fathers did not have to tell their children to believe in G-d. By observing their parents, the children could see it was true."

"What are you saying?" Emsbach was intrigued by the notion that faith could actually be handed down from one generation to the next, but he was not convinced that character traits could be genetically programmed into chromosomes. "Scientifically," he told her, "it is known that an inclination to violence or bashfulness seems to run in some families, but belief in G-d obviously cannot be genetic if there are individuals who do not observe their religion's tenets."

"Closeness to G-d goes beyond just 'knowing,'" Fraydl tried again, wishing that her Tatte or one of her older brothers was present to better explain such abstract concepts. "This subject is very deep, *Herr Doktor*. I am not a scholar who can give you the answers you deserve. I am only a simple Jewish girl. I know that there are many learned works that discuss this matter from a philosophical viewpoint. My own faith in G-d comes from the closeness to Him that was a part of life in my family. I could feel it. It was always there."

Fraydl hesitated. *Hashem, help me! Please save me from error. Please give me the right words.* Forging ahead, she continued, "The Jewish religion is far more than attending weekly worship services.

There are rules and laws to be followed from the moment a Jew opens his eyes in the morning until he closes them in sleep at night, every day of his life."

"Why would anyone want to live such a constricted life!" Emsbach could not comprehend it.

"From the outside, these restrictions may look confining. But they are the practical means to free the soul from the physical world and attach it to the Divine. G-d is at the very center of a religious Jew's world, and everything the Jew does is with this perspective. In return, G-d gives us His love and protection."

"*Ach*, if this is love and protection I would think Jews should prefer *not* being His Chosen People!"

Fraydl blushed. With the best intentions in the world, she had made a mess of it. How could she correct the negative impression her words had caused?

"Despite all this violence, He is still with us. We are never alone. We are His people. Right now, His face is hidden and we are given over to the wicked rulers of the country, but we rely on His promise that He will never forsake us. Never!"

Karl Emsbach puffed on his pipe and decided that it was not necessary to force her to see reality. "Why would He hide His face, as you say? When you love someone, do you stand aside and let them be destroyed!"

"There is reward and punishment. When Jews keep G-d's laws, they are rewarded with success and prosperity. When they forsake His commandments, they are punished, just as a loving father punishes a beloved child who endangers his life with reckless behavior. As you pointed out, there are those who have chosen to abandon their Jewish roots and live like Germans. It seems that now He is using Hitler to forcefully remind the Jewish people that their mission in life is different than that of the gentile nations. Jews must live by the Torah."

"But how can you explain religious Jews being tortured along with their secular brothers? Did your parents and brothers and sisters deserve to be punished because Jewish students in Heidelberg ate food forbidden by your dietary laws?"

Fraydl was aware that her young nephew, Chaim, was listening to every word. She had to make it clear to the boy that the doctor's approach was in error.

"The Jewish people share one soul," she said quietly."Just as the entire body is affected by an injured limb, so the Jewish nation suffers for the failure of any individual part of them. This is the way it has always been, throughout our history."

The girl's bravado touched the German doctor. He remembered reading the Biblical portrayal of the Jews as a stiff-necked people, and it amused him to see how closely Fraydl exemplified the description.

If he could only get her to keep talking, she might unintentionally reveal something to still the storm that had arisen in his own heart.

14

M ORE THAN EMSBACH WANTED TO CONTINUE THE
discussion, Fraydl desperately needed some private time
with her own thoughts. Up until now, these weeks in the German's
attic had been totally disconnected from her life before the war, as
if the day would come when they would simply go back to the way
things were then. Some childish part of her wanted to believe that
when this terrible war ended, at least some of her family would
reunite and continue on from where they had been so cruelly
interrupted.

She'd been badly shaken by the doctor's description of the usurpers in her parents' home. Their former neighbors had taken possession of her family's house, were sleeping in their beds and using her
mother's fine china for their *tereifah* food! As Fraydl softly touched
the tarnished pieces, memories came to life. She could remember
her father polishing them every *Motza'ei Shabbos*. In her imagination, she could see the menorah displayed in refined grandeur
behind the glass in the breakfront, encircled by the smaller *bechers*
and the filigreed *besamim* holder with its turrets and tiny flags and

bells. Fraydl tried to control her tears, but it seemed beyond her strength to say another word.

Disappointed but realistic, Emsbach carried the chest up to the attic and left it there with the children. Perhaps he could pursue his desire for self-discovery another time, but further discourse was clearly inappropriate now. Preparing for sleep, his mind wandered to Liesa Krieger. *Perhaps my whole problem is just loneliness?* he asked himself. Rhea had said that little Liesa has grown up into a fine young lady.

I'll give it a chance, he thought, his eyes closing. *Tomorrow evening, I'll call her and arrange a meeting.*

The next morning dawned cold but clear. Yanky was the first one in the attic to awaken. Lying snuggled in the comforter, the little boy amused himself for a while by watching his breath make tiny white plumes in front of his face. If it weren't so cold, he would crawl out of the covers to look for something interesting to satisfy his insatiable curiosity, but it was freezing, and the bed was warm. Tante Fraydl had knitted a hat that covered his head and ears, but his nose felt like a chunk of ice. He tried pulling the comforter up over it, but that made it impossible to look around, so he tugged it back down again.

Slowly Yanky raised himself to a sitting position. Cold air rushed into places where the blanket was loose, and he shivered. Drawing his knees up close to his chest, the little boy tried to tuck in the edges all around.

Everything was quiet. Outside, he could hear the chirping of sparrows; they didn't seem to mind the cold. It was still early, and downstairs the housekeeper's cleaning crew had not yet arrived for work. He looked up at the small attic window, painted with bizarre and beautiful shapes by the frost. Sometimes late at night he was allowed to look outside, standing on tiptoes so just his eyes were over the sill. The moonlit, snowy landscape bordered by spidery trees and dotted with the tracks of animals mesmerized the child.

Born after the war was already in full swing, Yanky accepted the limits of his hunted existence without question. The rules of survival were instinctive. He knew that the most important skill was to be like a fawn in the forest, keeping absolutely still. Yanky could lie curled up under a blanket for hours at a time, half-asleep and half-alert, waiting for the signal that he could safely stretch his little limbs and still the pangs of hunger in his tummy.

Here in the doctor's house, it was much better than it had been in the coal cellar with his brother before Tante Fraydl found them. Now there was food to eat, at night they were allowed to move about and for a few hours it was warm and comfortable in the doctor's study. Yanky was trying to learn the *aleph-beis* and he already knew how to whisper his morning prayers.

Fraydl stirred, turned over and blinked sleepily. Yanky waited until her eyes met his, and then smiled. He toppled over sideways when she reached out to bring him closer.

"*Modeh ani,*" the girl whispered, and her nephew quickly finished the sentence, thanking Hashem for granting them another day of life. Fraydl helped him wash *negelvasser* after she'd finished doing it herself, and the sound of splashing water woke Chaim from his slumber under the bed. It was just another day, the same as the ones that had preceded it for the last three months.

But today felt different. Fraydl reached for the chest with its precious cargo. She gently opened the velvet pouches and set the cherished silver pieces in a row. At the bottom of the box she found something she had missed last night. A five-year Jewish calendar! What a treasure! "Look, Chaim!" she whispered, her cheeks aflame with excitement. "Now we can know the days of Yom Tov!"

Her older nephew took the pamphlet from her hand and examined it. "What year is it now?"

Her face fell. "I'm not sure," she admitted. The two of them studied the calendar and tried to reconstruct the passage of time.

"We can't use the calendar for the wrong year," Chaim pointed out skeptically.

"No, wait. We can figure it out. I was born in the month of Teves in the year 5687," Fraydl's brow wrinkled in concentration. "I was 8 when you were born, so that would be 5695. The *Anschluss* happened when I was 11 . Can you remember any of that?"

"Not really. But I remember when Baba Mertzbach was *nifteres* and my mamme cried."

"That was in 5700, the middle of 1940. You were 5 when your parents went into hiding just before she passed away."

"I remember when the soldiers took Tante Malka away and she never came back."

"That was the day before Rosh Hashanah, the year after Mamme died," Fraydl said sadly. She thought for a moment and then continued. "You were only 3 when the Nazis invaded Austria. Two years later your mother and father went into hiding. I moved into Gerhardt's cellar a year after that. I was 13 when Bubbe died, This is the third winter since then, so I must be 17 by now and the year is 5704."

They leafed through the pages until they found the year 5704 "Here it is!" Chaim proclaimed joyfully. Then he turned serious. "We found the year, but how do we know the month and day?"

"I assume it's Adar now. Let's ask Dr. Emsbach when Easter is on his calendar. The *talmid chacham* who lived next door to Zeide was an expert on the calendar. He claimed that non-Jews always set their holiday according to when Pesach comes out. He would say this so often that I remember clearly how he made his calculations."

Looking from one to the other, little Yanky tried unsuccessfully to understand why the two older children were so pleased. Finally, he snatched the pamphlet from his brother's grasp and examined it closely. As he held the calendar upside down a few inches from his nose, frowning in deep concentration, Fraydl and Chaim stuffed the corners of their blankets into their mouths to stifle their laughter. Sensing that their merriment came at his expense, the little boy pursed his lips and continued to study the pages with feigned dignity. Finally he gave up and put the corner of his blanket in his mouth in imitation of them, which caused the older children to laugh so hard that the brass bed beneath them shook.

It was just another day in hiding. But somehow, today was different.

15

D R. EMSBACH. DR. EMSBACH. YOU HAVE A TELEPHONE CALL at the nurse's station," came the announcement over the loudspeaker. Karl Emsbach closed the patient's chart he'd been reviewing, dismissed the interns who were assisting him this morning and walked purposefully down the hall to his private room on the surgical ward. He sat down at his desk and lifted the receiver.

"Dr. Emsbach speaking. Please transfer the call to my room," he requested from the operator.

"Karl!" It was Bea's voice, high pitched with hysteria. "Karl, it's Otto! He's fallen and can't get up! *Helf mir*! Tell me what to do!"

"Beatrix, tell me exactly what happened," Although he spoke calmly, his pulse quickened at the thought of his loyal old servant lying helpless and in pain.

Choking back tears, the old woman ranted, "The old fool! I *told* him not to do it."

"No one is blaming you, Bea. Just tell me what happened so I can try to help."

"For weeks now, he's been worrying that the weight of the snow on the roof will cause damage. That old ladder is far too heavy for

him to lift, so I never expected him to try it. This morning he got Hans
to mount the ladder in place, and then climbed up with a broom to
sweep the snow away. I didn't see anything, I was in the kitchen."

Her frightened sobs were deafening his right ear so he changed
sides for some momentary relief. "Go on," he urged. "What happened next?"

"I heard a loud yell and then a heavy thump. When I ran outside,
I found that stubborn old man lying on his back in the snow!"

"Is he conscious, Bea?"

"He was moaning at first, but when I got close to him he told me
to shut up and stop screaming."

Emsbach was relieved: it probably wasn't a head injury.
Apparently, the snow had absorbed at least part of the fall's impact.
"Cover him with blankets," he instructed her, "and give him something warm to drink until the ambulance crew comes. I'll send them
right away, but it might take a while before they arrive. Meanwhile,
keep him talking, but don't try to move him. Call me back if he
seems confused. Tell Rhea she'll have to lock up the house because
you will be coming in the ambulance with the medics. I'll be waiting for you here at the entrance to the emergency room. "

"Silly old man, I *told* him not to do it," she mumbled.

"Bea?"

"*Ja, Ja?*"

"Are you all right? Is everything O.K. with you?"

"*Jawohl*," she answered. "I'm going to tell Hans to put that ladder in the shed and to lock it to the wall with a chain."

"Beatrix, first go cover Otto up and give him some hot sweet tea.
The ambulance is on its way."

It was fortunate for Otto that the prisoner work gangs had managed to clear the roads. With the snow magnifying every sound, the
clanging siren of the emergency vehicle could be heard long before
it reached the house. Up in the attic, the sound sent the children
into a panic.

"Quick!" Fraydl stuffed Yanky into the drawer of a bureau that
formed part of the makeshift wall around their living space. "Don't
move until Dr. Emsbach or I tell you that you can!"

The girl's eyes skidded around the attic, searching desperately for a hiding place for Chaim. Without waiting for her, the boy wormed himself into a narrow space between the trunks and suitcases along the wall, completely disappearing from sight.

Listening to the rapidly approaching siren, Fraydl tried to calm her racing heart. She realized that there was no point in her hiding, because the arrangement in this section of the attic practically shouted that someone lived here. She could only hope that when the Gestapo burst into the attic, they would be satisfied to find one victim, and remain unaware of the presence of the boys.

The ambulance turned into the front drive and backed up to where Otto lay in the snow, surrounded by pillows and blankets. Armed with a steaming pitcher of tea, Beatrix alternated between offering him drinks and scolding him. Pale and embarrassed, Otto shrugged as the medical technicians took in the scene.

"I *told* him not to try to climb that ladder, but when does he ever listen to me? Deaf old man! I told him not to do it." Bea provided counterpoint as they strapped the elderly servant to a stretcher and loaded him into the ambulance bay.

Fraydl's whispered words of *Tehillim* were swallowed up by the shouting of voices down below. Like a nightmare, she kept replaying in her mind the sight of the old man's face when it had suddenly appeared in the attic window. Had he noticed them? If so, did he comprehend what his eyes were seeing? A split second after the man came into view, he'd vanished. Fraydl could not know that Otto had lost his footing and slid out of control back down the ladder. She only knew that he was there one moment and gone the next.

Some time later, the ambulance reversed back to the street and set off for the emergency room at the military hospital, the howl of its siren gradually growing fainter as the distance increased. The children remained subdued for the rest of the afternoon, huddling together as they anxiously awaited the relative freedom of the night, when Dr. Emsbach would be home to explain what had happened.

It took a long time to complete all the arrangements, including pulling strings to have Otto's surgery scheduled immediately instead of at the end of the week. Emsbach finally arrived home long after midnight, bone weary and out of sorts. He found the children in his study awaiting him. He looked from one to the other with concern, wondering why they were so pale and quiet.

"We heard a siren this morning," Chaim declared.

"Yes, that must have been the ambulance I sent," Emsbach nodded.

"Ambulance?" Fraydl's voice was incredulous.

"*Ja*," he affirmed, not grasping their misunderstanding. "My servant Otto climbed up the ladder to sweep snow off the roof. He lost his balance and fell."

"We thought it was the Gestapo," Chaim whispered.

It was the doctor's turn to grow pale.

"It was your servant, then! I saw him," Fraydl confessed.

"How could you possibly see what happened from the attic?"

"I looked up and saw his face framed in the window. He was wearing a red cap and there was a woolen scarf wrapped around his face. I was terribly startled... But before I could scream, he disappeared."

"It was only Otto." Emsbach spoke to them, but he was really reassuring himself. "He didn't see anything. If he had, he would have told me when I met him at the hospital. His hip is broken. The bones of elderly people tend to fracture easily."

Aware that he was babbling, he lapsed into silence, acutely aware of how precarious the children's position was. They might have avoided detection today, but who was to say they'd be as lucky the next time?

They were an unusually quiet foursome that night.

16

WITH BEATRIX STAYING WITH FRIENDS NEAR THE hospital in order to be close to her husband of nearly 60 years, Rhea took over the kitchen as well as her own duties. "I'm not as good a cook as Bea," the housekeeper apologized as she offered him a simple dinner of *wurst* and sauerkraut.

Emsbach reassured her, and dug into the food as if he were hungrier than he felt. Together with a loaf of rye bread, the meal was filling if not especially tasty. He missed the newspaper that Otto always put beside his place at the table, and he missed Bea fussing over him.

"How is Otto?" Rhea tried to fill the emptiness with conversation.

"Orthopedic surgery is very painful," Emsbach replied. "Dr. Engelhardt will be giving him morphine for another few days. We'll know if the bone is mending by the end of the week. I looked in on him several times during my last shift and he seems to be as comfortable as possible. Beatrix guards him like a lioness."

He'd been present during the surgery to realign the old man's hipbone into the pelvic socket, and he feared that Otto might never really recover. He suppressed a sigh. The uncontrollable changes in the outside world were hard enough to cope with when his private world was stable; now it seemed there were to be fundamental alterations at home as well. After a few days of Rhea's well-intentioned culinary efforts, it was obvious that he needed to hire a cook to replace Beatrix. Hans was an outdoorsman, so a new maintenance man to replace Otto was also inevitable. He rubbed his aching temples, wishing that life was less complicated.

"I have to go." Rhea put aside her mending and pulled on her woolen coat, knitted scarf and gloves. "Did you ever speak to Fraulein Krieger?"

Her apparent nonchalance did not fool Emsbach. The woman had obviously been waiting for a chance to broach this subject for days. He shook his head. "Not yet. I was going to, but I haven't gotten around to it yet."

"You are going to call her?"

"Yes, I already told you I would."

"Good. This house needs a mistress, Karl."

"I suppose it does," he agreed forlornly.

"Karl," Rhea delayed her departure for a moment. "This house is too big for me to handle in the few hours that I'm here during the day. I put up notices in the village and applicants should be arriving beginning tomorrow, but it may take some time to find replacements for dear Beatrix and Otto. Until the matter is resolved, I think I will stay here full time, so that someone will be available at all hours. "

Reluctantly, Dr. Emsbach nodded his assent.

With a friendly wave, Rhea hurried out the door to catch the tram home. The clock in the front hall struck five slow peals. He noticed that it was still twilight outside. In a few more weeks spring would arrive, and the rain would wash away the memory of snow. This winter of 1944 had been the hardest he could remember, and he was thoroughly tired of cold, overcast days.

He considered the possibility of a wife, someone who would deal with the domestic decisions he found so draining. Yes, he would call Liesa later tonight, after he finished the private appointments scheduled for this evening. And if she was not the right one for him, maybe it was time to be more receptive to other suggestions.

When Dr. Emsbach called, Liesa Krieger was out. He left a message that he would call again the next day. At midnight, the children came downstairs. While the boys played with their tin soldiers on the carpet, Emsbach warned Fraydl: "There may be some changes soon."

She raised her eyes with a questioning expression.

"I spoke with Rhea about interviewing applicants for the positions of cook and maintenance man. Because of his advanced age, Otto's injury is serious. I'm afraid it is possible that dear Beatrix and her husband may not be able to return to work at all. Of course, I will permit them to continue living in the carriage house, which has been their residence since before I was born. However, new servants will have to be assigned living quarters here in the big house. Obviously, this complicates our arrangement."

Fraydl waited silently. This was Dr. Emsbach's house and it had been a hospitable refuge for her and the boys, but she could understand that these unforeseen circumstances would necessitate a change. Involuntarily she glanced at the heavily curtained window. When she thought of the drifts of snow outside, icy fingers of panic closed around her heart. *Oh, no! This is a death sentence!* Then she caught herself and changed direction. *Hashem has taken care of us until now. I must believe that He will continue to do so.*

Reacting to the girl's slumped shoulders and changed expression, Emsbach asked, "What happened? What is the matter?"

When she didn't speak, he clarified, "Do you think I'm telling you that you must leave? Didn't I promise that I would do everything in my power to keep you safe until this war is over? You must trust me."

"Thank you, *Herr Doktor*." Fraydl's voice waxed soft with relief as she realized that they were not being turned away. "You have never given us reason to distrust you. I only wish there was some way to repay you for your kindness."

"I will feel amply rewarded if we all survive the war," he responded. After a moment's reflection, he returned to the former subject.

"The economic situation is very difficult right now. With their workers serving in the army, many nonessential businesses have closed their doors. The resulting high unemployment among the civilian population makes it likely that many applicants will be coming to the house tomorrow. I'm afraid we're very set in our ways here, which means that it may be an extended period before we find someone with the proper level of experience and training.

"I must caution you to keep absolutely silent throughout the day and the night, because Rhea will be sleeping here until replacements are found. I will be on duty in the hospital over the weekend. You children may not leave the attic again until I personally inform you that it is safe. Is this understood?"

She nodded. If they had to be quiet, they would do so as long as necessary. For her and the children, it was a matter of life and death. If only this war would end!

"I will give you medication to sedate the boys if necessary." He opened a drawer and withdrew a packet of powder. Glancing in Chaim and Yanky's direction, the doctor instructed her to add a few grains of the narcotic to a glass of milk, together with a tablespoon of sugar to disguise the bitter taste.

She accepted the medicine reluctantly, almost as worried about the idea of drugging her nephews as she feared their making noise.

"You know," Fraydl offered hesitantly, "if it proves to be difficult to find a good cook, I could prepare your meals. My mother taught us girls how to cook and bake, and I believe I could fill this role to your satisfaction. It would also save the *Herr Doktor* money, and give me a way to partially repay our debt."

Emsbach couldn't help smiling at the thought of this waif in Bea's kitchen. "It is kind of you to suggest that," he told her. "Let's wait and see how Rhea fares tomorrow."

17

BEING INCARCERATED IN THE ATTIC OVER THE NEXT FEW days was not as difficult as Fraydl had feared it might be. Among several volumes she had taken from Dr. Emsbach's library was a book about the life of Helen Keller. The last pages included illustrations of the alphabet used by many hearing-impaired people. For the children it would prove to be a treasure.

"What are you doing?" Chaim whispered, irresistibly curious about the strange contortions of his aunt's fingers.

"Look, this is a way to talk without making any noise." Fraydl mouthed the words, hardly making a sound. "Let's learn how to do it and then we can use it to talk to each other."

During their hours of forced solitude, the children managed to teach themselves sign language. They adapted the language to their own needs by inventing signs for concepts that little Yanky could understand without actually having to combine letters into words. It was a good way to keep active young minds occupied while their bodies were immobilized by necessity.

Beyond the attic window the sun appeared and began to melt the snow. In the mornings, Chaim called their attention to flocks of migrating birds sweeping across the sky, and for hours at night the honking of geese could be heard overhead. Snuggled under their warm blankets, it was almost possible to imagine an end to the cold.

Finally, on Sunday evening, they were reprieved. Dr. Emsbach called them downstairs and the three youngsters ate a hot meal for the first time in days.

"I have good news," he told the children. "Beatrix is coming back to work. Otto is progressing far better than expected, and he will be released from the orthopedic ward tomorrow. It will take more than a fall from a ladder to keep the old man down." His tone was affectionate, and it was obvious that their benefactor cared about the elderly couple.

"Otto will be staying in a convalescent home while he learns to walk independently again, but it is located relatively near here, so Bea is returning to the carriage house. She has asked to resume work during the day and will sit with him in the evenings."

"This is very good news for you," Fraydl responded. She had sensed that Dr. Emsbach was disturbed by the possibility of strangers coming to live in his home.

"There is a slight problem, though," he added with a grimace. "Beatrix is bringing her granddaughter to stay with her and help in the kitchen. I've met Monika before. She will undoubtedly provide support to her grandmother, but it is possible that she may become a complicating factor in other ways."

Emsbach's warning was an understatement. Monika arrived the next morning, and her presence was immediately felt by everyone.

Rhea found an early opportunity to complain about the girl, barely hiding her intense irritation, "Why did you agree to have her here? What does Monika do except get in the way?"

"Bea's granddaughter is supposed to be taking some of the burden off her grandmother's shoulders," he replied, stating the obvious.

"Well, she has a funny way of doing it," Rhea sniffed. "Whenever I see her she is usually stuffing her face with a pastry, or engaging my girls in conversation so they can't work, or just making herself at home as if she were the lady of the manor!"

Emsbach sighed. The plump and profoundly indolent teenager was decidedly a mixed blessing. But Bea was so proud of her plan to groom the girl to eventually replace her in the kitchen that he was loath to disillusion the doting grandmother.

Far from enthralled with the mundane tasks of peeling vegetables and scrubbing pots, Monika escaped her culinary lessons whenever she could invent an excuse to stay away. Other than eating, she did not seem to have any affinity for the kitchen, though she was respectful to her grandmother, who clung to the hope that the girl would improve with time.

Running into the crew of village girls as they aired out one of the bedrooms, Monika gaily informed them, "I love movies and I'm going to be a movie star. My mother says I inherited my talent for drama from her. She was an understudy for Marlene Dietrich before she married my father."

After Rhea's stern face appeared in the doorway to curtail that particular conversation, Monika was forced to dispel her youthful boredom by snooping around the big house. During the next weeks, she explored every nook and cranny, entering each room and opening every drawer and cabinet. Fraydl received a terrible fright when the girl opened the closet door beneath the trapdoor to the attic. The children could hear the scrape of hangers as Monika casually slid the clothes from side to side across the wooden rod, inspecting the contents of the rarely used closet. It was a miracle that the ladder nailed to the inside wall escaped her notice; or perhaps she did see it, and simply did not fathom its purpose.

The worst moment was yet to come. One morning Monika discovered the main entrance to the attic. Without hesitation, she climbed the stairs and opened the door to the loft. The shock of seeing a stranger step into the far side of the attic caused the children to freeze in a tableau of terror. Fortunately, Monika was immediately overcome by the dust and hastily retreated, to the accompaniment of percussive sneezes, without noticing the horrified occupants at the other end.

"Did you know that girl came up to the attic?" Fraydl asked Dr. Emsbach the next time he brought them supplies of food.

Alarmed at the close call, he exclaimed, "What?" After Fraydl described the episode, he added ruefully, "Perhaps I should have considered the possibility after Rhea complained to me about her. I'm sorry. I'll think of a solution."

At the first opportunity, he put a padlock on the door to the main entrance of the attic and locked it securely. *That will surely restrain Monika's natural inquisitiveness,* he thought to himself, hoping that he was not underestimating the girl's propensity to cause trouble.

That afternoon, Fraydl was dozing when she dreamed that the house was on fire. The children were locked in the attic with no route of escape, and she screamed for help in her sleep until her ashen-faced nephew shook her awake. "Tante Fraydl! Tante Fraydl! Wake up! "

Looking about in a daze, she realized it had only been a dream. "You were screaming," he told her.

"I'm sorry. It was a terrible dream, but it's over now. It was just a dream." Shaken, Fraydl was afraid to go back to sleep. None of them knew whether their secret had been revealed.

During their visit to Otto at the nursing home, Monika told her grandmother dramatically, "I heard frightful noises coming from the attic today. You should have warned me that the Emsbach house is haunted. There must have been a terrible murder there in years gone by. "

"Nonsense!" was Bea's curt answer. "I've never heard anything so ridiculous in my life!"

Otto was hard of hearing and paid no attention to their argument. Women's talk rarely interested him, and he usually tuned it out. Monika was deeply offended that her grandparents didn't take her seriously. She spent the rest of the visit sulking in teenage self-righteousness, refusing to take part in their conversation even as they made plans for Otto to come home again. The old man could walk reasonably well with a cane, and if Hans took over the heavy chores he would soon be able to supervise the house again.

"I am so happy," Beatrix told Rhea later. "Life is returning to normal at last. I hope that old fool has learned his lesson, and will stay clear of heights from now on."

18

"T ANTE FRAYDL, WHY IS THIS HAPPENING TO US?"
Chaim's innocent face was full of sorrow. There were many, many hours when the children had nothing to do but think, and the young boy had apparently been using his mind to try to make sense of his life. Sighing, she wondered whether he'd been disturbed by Dr. Emsbach's questions about Judaism, or if he was reaching his own conclusions.

"It is all part of Hashem's plan," she told him, remembering her father speaking the same words to her before he was arrested by the Nazis. "We may not understand it, but we believe with all our hearts that there is a purpose and that one day we will know what it is."

Almost from the beginning, their midnight excursions to the German's study had taken on a particular rhythm. While the children ate, their benefactor made conversation. Later, while Fraydl cleared up, he played chess with Chaim or turned on the BBC to listen to the news. Afterward he might speak of his own childhood and ask them questions regarding theirs, or relate anecdotes from his work in the hospital.

Fairly often, the doctor raised intellectual questions on topics that troubled him in politics, history or theology. These discussions with Fraydl often continued until the wee hours of the night, with the boys playing together on the carpet until they finally fell asleep waiting for the adults to finish talking.

At the beginning of the week, Fraydl had asked permission to use her mother's *leichter* to light Shabbos candles. "I promise to be very careful," she assured him fervently. "We will cover the window so that not even the faintest light can escape. It would mean so much to me, *bitte schön?*"

A shadow of exasperation crossed the German's face. "Why do you find such a ritual important?" he challenged. "What possible relevance can it have to your lives today?"

Fraydl looked down at her hands, resting in her lap. How could she explain to this man that just the memory of Shabbos at home strengthened her and made her feel connected and secure? Jewish religious observance did not make sense to the good doctor, as he repeatedly reminded her in their ongoing disagreement about her refusing nonkosher food. Did she dare add Shabbos to the equation?

"Like every human being, at times I have experienced a longing for something beyond everyday existence," Emsbach conceded, "but from there to embracing an illogical and incomprehensible ritual does not make sense. It is an irrational request!"

"I apologize for not being able to explain it better, *Herr Doktor*, but it is very important to me and the children to observe Jewish law as much as possible, especially our precious Shabbos. If you will give me permission to light my mother's candlesticks, I cannot describe what a kindness it would be."

Emsbach was not convinced, so Fraydl tried another tack. "Just as it is impossible to explain what a sunset looks like to a person who was born blind, or the taste of chocolate to someone who has never eaten it, I don't know how to show you how important this is to me. But I am absolutely sure that if you had seen my family on a Shabbos, you would understand. If you could step into a synagogue full of Jewish men praying or learning Torah, I am sure you would sense what I am so woefully inadequate at putting into words."

The physician's mind was trained to be precise, analytical and methodical. Even so, he was able to grasp this argument. A person's state of mind does affect his physical health. This metaphysical effect had been empirically observed. In the past he had sometimes grappled with the idea of a soul transcending the physical body. Now he looked at Fraydl thoughtfully and decided, *these children have suffered enough.*

"I will allow you to light your candles," he said. "I don't understand your need for it, but I accept the integrity of your request."

After she expressed her gratitude, he spoke again. "I really don't understand you, *Fraulein*. It simply does not make sense. How can you continue your loyalty to a G-d Who has forsaken you? Everything that is meaningful in your life has been stolen. Where is your anger? Your G-d does not deserve your faithfulness under these circumstances!"

As he spoke, the realization crystallized in Emsbach's mind that Hitler was actually waging a war against the Jewish G-d Himself. "When this war ends, do you think any Jews will be left?" he demanded. "When Germany is *Judenrein,* what will become of you? Will you still believe so strongly then?"

Fraydl sat motionless, her heart pounding as she pondered the best response. In spite of her host's friendly demeanor, she could never forget that the children were totally at his mercy. Emsbach treated them well, but he still wore the hated Nazi uniform and interacted with anti-Semites every day.

What would happen if she said something that caused him offense? She had seen the revolver in the top drawer of his desk. The man could shoot her on the spot and never have to answer for it. He could force the children back out into the inhospitable world outside, or turn them over to the Gestapo. She shivered involuntarily.

Emsbach's eyes were boring into her, but Fraydl was completely unaware of the reasons behind his interrogation. The very existence of the children in his life was turning his world inside out. Matters long repressed were struggling for expression and explanation. Wellsprings of longing, sealed shut by his cultural upbringing, teased and disturbed him simultaneously.

Aware that this moment in time was both an opportunity for *Kiddush Hashem* and fraught with peril, Fraydl whispered a prayer for wisdom. When she began to speak her pulse fluttered, but her voice was calm.

"As you point out, for all intents and purposes it does seem that G-d has forsaken us," she told him. "Jews are pursued without letup and persecuted beyond any other nation. We are completely downtrodden. Except for your miraculous intervention, *Herr Doktor*, my nephews and I would likely have been. . .torn to shreds. . .or worse. . ."

Fraydl shuddered at the memory, but her voice strengthened as she continued. "We Jews have a promise that G-d will never forsake us. It is a pact He made with our fathers for all generations."

This was said with such finality that Emsbach burst out, "Impossible! You cannot possibly believe your own words! Look at you — a fugitive! If you take the smallest step away from my protection, you will instantly find yourself in mortal danger. Where is your G-d in all this? Where was He when your parents, grandparents, Rabbi and friends were all torn away? Not forsake you? How can anyone be so blind as not to see that He has *already* abandoned you!"

"No," Fraydl repeated firmly, "not totally, and not forever."

19

EMSBACH STARED AT HER, IMPATIENCE VYING WITH incredulity. "Not totally? Not forever?"

Fraydl gripped the edge of her chair tightly and reiterated her firm belief in *hashgachah pratis*, "No, not totally. Didn't He send you to save us? Did He not put the thought in my mind to seek shelter exactly beside your car, at exactly the moment when you were leaving the hospital? Would you ever have opened the trunk for us of your own volition?"

The moment stretched between them. Fraydl dared not move while she waited to see how Dr. Emsbach would react to her words. Her self-confidence suddenly deserted her and she wondered what had made her think that this non-Jew could grasp the eternality of the covenant between G-d and the Jewish people.

Emotions flickered in rapid succession across her benefactor's face. Sensing the girl's scrutiny, Emsbach turned away, staring into the crackling flames of the fireplace as if searching for something terribly important that should have been there but wasn't. At last he straightened his back, tamped fresh tobacco into his pipe and lit it. His expression was blank, his gaze fixed on the ceiling.

Only when she resumed breathing did Fraydl realize that she'd been holding her breath. The quiet was broken by the ticking of the clock and the flickering fire. Chaim and Yanky had fallen asleep long ago, slumped against each other on the carpet, a tin soldier grasped in each small hand.

"Otto will be returning soon," Emsbach said casually, his voice neutral. Fraydl could draw no conclusions about the impression her passionate words had left on him. "Let's get the boys up to bed. Tomorrow is another day."

She lay awake for a very long time afterward, replaying their dialogue over and over. The doctor's intensity had nearly overwhelmed her. *I already have more than enough responsibility on my shoulders!* Fraydl thought to herself. *There is no one left but me to raise my two nephews as best I can, and to help them grow into erlicher Yidden. Why does it seem I have been chosen to educate a righteous gentile as well?*

Otto finally returned to the house, although his contribution now consisted more of offering unsolicited advice and complaining about the weather than anything else. It was difficult for the once-independent man to face the reality that his health had betrayed him in his old age. Otto spent more and more time napping in a sunny spot beside the window, a perpetual frown deepening the wrinkles on his face and an unread newspaper spread haphazardly over the woolen blanket on his lap.

"What are we going to do about him?" Beatrix asked rhetorically as she set the table in the kitchen for the servants' dinner. "He's just not himself anymore."

"We must ask the master," the housekeeper suggested. "He is very wise for all he's so young. He may have a solution."

"How are things going with our matchmaking efforts?" Bea winked conspiratorially. "How many times have they seen each other lately?"

"Three, by my count," Rhea laughed. "If we've done anything good in this life, it will be to get that young man safely married before we retire!"

"I pray that I will live to see the day when his children frolic in the backyard. *Ach*, wouldn't that do my old man good! Otto needs something like that to lift his spirits. How he used to love teaching Karl different skills. Do you remember when he showed the boy how to make a kite out of newspaper and sticks?"

"*Ja!Ja!*" The two servants sailed away on a wave of nostalgia as they recalled the master's childhood. "Do you remember the time he got a fishhook caught in his palm? What a brave little soldier he was while Otto worked it out."

"I remember how the mistress made him play his clarinet right afterward. I could see tears in his eyes from the pain, but he did it. He was such a good child. He never complained, not a single word."

"What's that noise?"

The women stopped their chatter and turned to see Hans standing at the foot of the backstairs, his brow furrowed in concentration.

Wondering what he was referring to, the two women stood still, listening, until they heard it as well. "It's coming from the front of the house!" Rhea exclaimed in alarm.

"No one is at home except us."

"Could it be Monika?"

"No, I sent her off to the market an hour ago. She couldn't be back yet."

The women turned their worried eyes to Hans. Otto stirred from his sleep and spluttered, "What? What's going on now?"

"Sh-h-h," Beatrix told him. "Listen!"

Hard of hearing, Otto heard nothing. He looked from one to the other and frowned. "Well, go see what it is! What are you waiting for?"

Hans squared his broad shoulders and headed for the hall that led to the front of the house. "Take this, boy," Otto called after him, raising his cane and offering it to his nephew. "You may need a weapon."

Hans hefted the heavy wooden walking stick in his hands and nodded with approval. He turned toward the front room and began to slowly advance, with the two women tiptoeing in single file behind him. When the strange scratching noise recurred, Rhea slipped her fingers around the scissors in her pocket and old Beatrix tightened her grasp on her rolling pin. Whoever was breaking into the house would soon have to deal with three very determined defenders.

Karl Emsbach looked up sheepishly when the train of servants appeared, one after the other, in the doorway. He was bending over an object on the floor, which they soon recognized as a cat. The creature mewed plaintively. Emsbach stroked her and whispered gently, his fingers methodically examining her soft body.

"She has a broken leg," he announced, standing up to face his staff, and feeling like a little boy caught doing something without permission. "I think that's the extent of her injuries. She was under the car in the shed. I decided to bring her in out of the cold."

"Why didn't you use the kitchen entrance?" Beatrice asked, slowly lowering the large wooden rolling pin she had fully intended to use in defense of Hans if he were overcome by an intruder.

"I supposed you were all in the middle of dinner and I didn't want to disturb anybody," he replied. "Look, Bea, she's hurt. See the angle of her poor leg. She must have been run over on the street and crawled into the garage to seek shelter."

"What are you going to do with her?"

"I'll splint her leg and she'll recover in a couple of weeks," he said with confidence, gently lifting the animal off the floor.

"And then what?"

He puckered his lips thoughtfully, stroking the yellow fur of the now-purring feline.

"We could keep her," he suggested.

"Whatever for?"

"She'll keep away the mice."

"There are no mice in this house!" Rhea insisted, mortally offended by the implied insinuation.

"No, of course not, Rhea. But recently Monika complained that she heard noises from inside one of the upstairs closets. It could have been a mouse."

"That girl is imagining ghosts, not mice. Mice squeak. They don't let out bloodcurdling screams, which is what she claims she heard." Rhea was not mollified, but the thought of Monika distracted her.

"Well, if there *is* a mouse, the kitty will soon find it and then we can tell Monika it was nothing to get upset about," Beatrix commented.

"Since she heard her 'ghosts,' Monika refuses to go upstairs anymore, which is a blessing in itself," Rhea pointed out.

Reassured that the situation was under control, Hans returned to the kitchen to eat his dinner while the women followed the doctor to his examining room and watched him carefully lay the animal on some newspapers before splinting its leg with tongue depressors secured by a few strips of bandage.

The cat bore the indignity with tolerance, sending the occasional haughty glance toward the servants observing the process. When Emsbach had completed his work, the yellow tabby licked her fur delicately, stretched and settled herself more comfortably on the papers.

"Well, she certainly seems to have made herself at home, hasn't she!" Bea exclaimed, still doubtful about the wisdom of adopting a stray cat.

"I don't want a cat in the house," Rhea protested. "It'll scratch all the table legs with its claws, and its long winter fur will shed all over the furniture."

"I'll put her up in the attic," Emsbch promised. "Is that a good compromise?"

"Well, it's better than leaving her down here." Though secretly relieved, Rhea pretended to grumble. The servants had learned long ago to put up with orphaned field mice and rabbits, fox cubs and squirrels, and ducks with broken wings. She supposed they would survive a cat.

DESPITE THE MASTER'S PROTESTS, RHEA INSISTED ON giving him a long list of instructions, from how to construct a scratching post out of a piece of old carpeting nailed to a wooden post, to filling an old carton with sand for use as a litter box. "You are a surgeon, not a veterinarian," she told him firmly. "I am giving you good advice and you should listen to the voice of experience."

While he set to work fulfilling the housekeeper's orders, Beatrix brought in a tin of sardines and placed it on the floor near the cat. The yellow tabby delicately ate the fish, licking the tin clean to the last drop.

"What will you call her?"

"What's wrong with Cat?"

"That's not very imaginative, is it?"

Regally the animal turned unblinking green eyes toward the women and stared.

"Cleopatra," Rhea decided.

"Yes, that fits. You can call her Cleo for short," Bea chimed in.

"Cleo it is," Emsbach agreed amiably, lifting the furry bundle and depositing it on an old pillow. "Dear ladies, please go and finish the meal that I inadvertently interrupted. I'll take Cleo upstairs later, after I finish my files. "

When the women had retired to the kitchen, Emsbach regarded his newest acquisition. "Cleopatra," he whispered, "You have a very important job to do here—and I don't mean catching non-existent mice."

The cat yawned in response. A moment later, Cleo pulled herself over to the fireplace and settled down on the warm hearth to sleep.

That night he introduced the children to their new roommate. The boys were delighted, but Fraydl regarded the feline with considerably less enthusiasm until the doctor explained, "Now you won't have to be so afraid if one of you accidentally makes some noise. Whatever Monika thinks she hears will be ascribed to the cat."

"I have never been this close to one before," Fraydl admitted. "And, truthfully, I am afraid of her. Don't cats bite and scratch?"

"For a stray cat, she seems extraordinarily gentle," Emsbach told the girl. "She let me apply antiseptic, stitch a wound and even splint her broken leg without any fuss. If you are gentle with her, I think she will respond in kind. You must make sure the boys don't tease or hurt her, though."

"Oh, they would never do that!" Fraydl defended her nephews.

"Most boys I have known do torment helpless animals," the doctor observed.

"Not Chaim or Yanky," she insisted. "It is forbidden. They would never do such a thing."

At his skeptical expression, Fraydl added, "There are many laws in the Torah regarding the treatment of animals. It is forbidden to cause them suffering. For example, a man must feed his domestic animals before he himself is permitted to eat."

Emsbach was impressed in spite of himself. "All right. Her name is Cleopatra," he informed the children. "You can call her Cleo for short. Her left back leg is broken so she won't be jumping around very much for a while. When you get to know each other better, I think you will appreciate her better qualities. Many fine ladies keep cats as companions, so regard it as a status symbol. Cats are fastidiously clean and require no human care except to provide meals."

Yanky stretched out a little hand and gingerly touched the cat's furry back. "*Ketzele* is soft!" he whispered to Chaim, stroking with increased confidence.

Not to be outdone, his older brother petted the cat's head.

"Look. . ." Emsbach demonstrated. "Scratch her behind the ears, like this. She likes that. Under her chin, too. "He turned to Fraydl. "I have a feeling she's in a family way and expecting to deliver fairly soon. You children won't be bored with a growing family of kittens to watch."

Fraydl did not want to offend their generous host, so she left her opinion of cats unspoken. Watching the animal give a pointy-toothed yawn, it was hard not to smile. She supposed it would be possible to tolerate the feline, as long as it kept its distance.

Cleo turned out to be a blessing. She kept the children in stitches with her antics as she explored her new home, clumping around the attic with her splinted leg and quivering whiskers. Naturally inquisitive, the creature roamed the loft freely while the children followed her progress from their corner. Once, her claws got caught in the furniture coverings and the cat fell over backward, pulling the whole sheet onto her. For a minute or two Cleo was a spinning, thumping ball of fur, until she was free again, limping away from the offending fabric with her head held high and long tail switching disdainfully.

By the time Emsbach removed the makeshift cast, Cleo was completely healed. She gave the injured leg a shake, obviously pleased with her new freedom from restraint, and then leaped gracefully onto her favorite perch at the top of a tower of trunks and cartons. Fraydl could not help being impressed by the beauty of the cat's effortless, almost fluid movements.

Cleopatra spent hours each day keeping her striated golden fur shiny and clean with her rough, pink tongue. The cat made friends with Chaim and frequently settled close to the boy, her throaty purr sounding as loud as a small airplane engine against the silence of the attic. When she wanted to play, Cleo approached Yanky, who gleefully threw wads of yarn for her to leap on and wrestle with. Even Fraydl eventually braved her natural antipathy and rubbed behind the animal's velvety ears, engendering a bliss so profound that it was impossible not to smile.

Cleopatra quietly became a mother early one morning while the children were still asleep. They awoke to discover that the cat had dragged their throw rug into a corner and was lying on it surrounded by a bevy of tiny, squirming kittens.

"*Mazel Tov,* Cleo!" little Yanky whispered. "Chaim, look! They're not asleep, but their eyes are closed. Why, Tante Fraydl?"

The boys sat cross-legged near the cat's corner and watched with interest. They counted and recounted, but it was hard to be sure exactly how many kittens had entered the world because the mother cat kept rearranging their places, tucking in this one and hauling that one to the other side. From time to time Cleopatra stood up, shook off her offspring and made the trip to the other end of the attic, but for the most part she was a devoted mother.

"There's one all-black kitten and two that are black with white spots," Chaim informed his aunt. "There are two yellow ones, like Cleo—no, three; and a gray one with black stripes. That's six!"

"Why is she licking them all the time?" Yanky puzzled.

Fraydl looked at the boys, wondering at the change she heard in their voices. She observed how eagerly they bent over the new kittens. Then she realized that it was the first time since they'd met in the coal cellar that the boys were relaxed and happy. Chaim and Yanky were acting like little boys and not like pint-sized grown-ups.

Her heart swelled with gratitude. *Let them just be children,* she prayed. *If only they could just be carefree children. . .*

21

SPRING SLIPPED INTO THE CITY WITH GENTLE SHOWERS AND budding trees. On its heels came an overwhelming desire to be outdoors and breathe the sweet fresh air. The attic felt stuffy and confining. The boys grew fidgety and kept picking fights with each other, complaining of boredom. At night, distant sirens warned of Allied bombers high overhead, and occasionally the sky lit up with flares and anti-aircraft shells.

"Is the war coming to an end, do you think?" Fraydl asked Dr. Emsbach, after one particularly loud explosion.

He glanced at the *Vulkischer Beobachter* on his desk and shrugged. Reports on his clandestine shortwave radio conflicted with the headlines in the Nazi newspapers, but the increasing numbers of seriously wounded officers being treated in the hospital did seem to lend some credence to the foreign broadcasts.

"There are always rumors," he told her thoughtfully. "Many people think that the war will end as soon as the Allies invade Europe, but that isn't realistic. Roosevelt is still lacking popular support to make the critical decision.

"Germany assumes that the American public doesn't have the stomach for a prolonged war, so even when the United States president eventually gives the green light, he will find our forces battle hardened and prepared to drag the war out for years. I'm afraid it is not nearly over yet."

"But it will end, won't it?" Chaim asked anxiously.

"Yes, of course it will. But not this year, and probably not the next, either."

The boy's expression was woebegone.

"Let's think of what it will be like after the war," Emsbach suggested. "You will able to go to school again and learn a trade. Maybe I can bring you some elementary textbooks and your aunt can use the time to tutor you."

"She's a girl!" Chaim declared. "She can't teach me Gemara. I want to go to *cheder*."

Emsbach looked at Fraydl questioningly.

"*Cheder* is a Jewish elementary school," she explained to their benefactor. "They learn the holy texts there."

"Well, you need to go to public school, Chaim, so that you can learn a profession. What would you like to be when you grow up? Perhaps a doctor, like me?"

"I want to learn Torah, like my father and grandfather did," Chaim answered.

"I don't know if that will be possible in Germany, even after the war," Dr. Emsbach said gently.

"Then I will leave Germany." Chaim stuck out his lower lip stubbornly. "I won't stay here if I can't learn Torah."

"Where will you go?"

"Palestine!" was the boy's unhesitant reply.

"Palestine?" Emsbach was incredulous. "What can you do there? It's all sand and Arabs."

"My father told me that Eretz Yisrael is the most beautiful land in the world. We used to get oranges and dates and *esrogim* from Palestine, so it is a fruitful land. After this horrible war is over, all the Jews in the world will go to live in Palestine and there won't be any more wars."

"If only. . ." Fraydl murmured sadly. "My oldest sister lives in Palestine," she mused. "She married and left Austria when I was about as old as Yanky is now. My mother always read her letters to us, and we often spoke about going to visit her one day."

"Tante. . .Rivka?" Chaim asked, wrinkling his brow as he tried to recall.

"Yes, her name is Rivka. Her children are just a little younger than I am. Imagine, Chaim, after the war we can go to Rivka and live with her in Palestine!"

The children perked up, their dejected mood brightened by visions of a sun-soaked land of sparkling seas, fruit orchards and tall eucalyptus trees.

Weeks passed, and the plum trees in Emsbach's yard bloomed with sweet-smelling blossoms. The flower gardens turned into kaleidoscopes of color. Using Dr. Emsbach's calendar, the children were able to calculate the days of Pesach and were careful not to eat *chametz* during that week. With Chaim's help, Fraydl improvised a rudimentary *Haggadah*; between the two of them they remembered much of it, especially the songs.

Little Yanky practiced every night, until he could belt out the *Ma Nishtanah* with confidence, more or less in tune. "Baba and Zeidy would *shep nachas!*" Fraydl praised the boys, her eyes moist with unshed tears. It was so sad to be making such a tiny *seder* in a non-Jews's house, but it was so wonderful to be alive.

Cleopatra continued to provide comic relief in the attic. The kittens opened their eyes when they were 10 days old, and shortly thereafter began exploring the world. The black one was the boldest. He crouched in ambush like a tiny panther, leaping on his unwary siblings, after which they rolled together in a furry tangle across the floor.

Chaim liked to hold a string of yarn just out of their reach, and watch the kittens dance on their hind legs and bat at it with their tiny forepaws until they lost their balance and fell over. During the first weeks, Cleo was the picture of a devoted mother, but when the babies grew big enough to eat food from her dish she seemed to lose interest in them. By midsummer, Emsbach decided that the kittens were old enough to find another home, and he took them away.

"Don't you miss your babies?" Yanky demanded of the cat. Cleo preened herself indifferently. It upset the little boy that his playmates were gone, and he couldn't understand why their own mother didn't seem to care. Fraydl distracted him with stories, but she wasn't sorry they were gone. As they grew bigger, the kittens had become too fond of jumping up on her bed and making themselves at home on her pillow. The lazy and regal Cleopatra didn't bother her anymore, but the boisterous kittens had made her nervous.

With the increasing heat of summer, the attic became stifling. The high temperatures sapped their strength and the children slept many hours during the day. It was a little cooler near the window, which Dr. Emsbach allowed them to open just a crack. From time to time they peeked down at the outside world and watched in wonder as people went about their normal routines as if there were not three children hidden high above them.

"Do you see that old man under the tree down there?" Chaim whispered to Fraydl.

"That's Otto, Dr. Emsbach's servant. I noticed that he's usually sitting on a chair in the shade by the garden."

"I feel sorry for him."

"Sorry for him? Why? *He's* not imprisoned in an attic."

"Do you remember the old men in the *shtiebel*? They were old like him, but they used to sit with their Gemaras and argue and get all excited. Every time I see Otto, he just sits there, doing nothing."

"I suppose that someone who never learned to use his mind when he was young and healthy would probably feel lost when old age takes away his strength," Fraydl agreed.

"Will that happen to me?"

"Why do you think it could happen to you?"

"Because I'm not using my mind for anything, either."

"Chaim, I think you *are* using your mind. You can't do anything else except use your mind as long as we have to be in hiding. And I'm sure the war will end long before you are old. When you are

Otto's age, you will sit in the *beis medrash* and learn just like your Zeidy did."

Day after day went by with almost no variation. Fraydl also felt like complaining about the boredom, but she had enough understanding to appreciate that the children were very fortunate to have the luxury of being bored. Dr. Emsbach considered her mature enough to hear information about the war, which he only shared with her when the boys were preoccupied with something else.

"My superiors at the hospital have been in a bad humor for several weeks, and we are all feeling the tension. According to the grapevine, the war effort is not going in Germany's favor."

"Is this good news?"

He grimaced. "Not for Germans."

22

EMSBACH PACED BACK AND FORTH IN HIS STUDY, LECTUR-
ing Fraydl on developments in the war. The girl was an ideal
listener. Beyond the fact that she was literally a captive audience,
her thoughtful comments and occasionally incisive questions
stimulated his intellect most agreeably. It crossed his mind that
speaking with this young girl was far more satisfying than his
conversations with Liesa Krieger. *Too bad she is Jewish*, he thought
to himself, and then smiled at the irony as he realized that otherwise
they would never have met in the first place.

Liesa was attractive and educated. She was a member of his family's social class. Their acquaintances had no doubt that Liesa would
be the next Frau Emsbach, and Beatrix and Rhea spared no pains
to reassure him that his own lack of certainty would pass after they
were married. No one, least of all Liesa, could understand why
Emsbach hesitated to finalize his courtship with a formal proposal.

"Your expectations are totally unrealistic," Konrad Winkelmann
said, shaking his head when Karl Emsbach confided in his colleague.
"Wives are not supposed to be your friends. For that, you have other
men. Wives are supposed to be beautiful, take care of your domestic

needs and give you heirs to inherit anything left from your fortune after she gets through with it." He laughed at his own joke. "A husband's role is to replenish the coffers and enjoy the envious looks on the faces of his associates, and that's all there is to it. To expect compatibility is a luxury, not a necessity! Be practical, Emsbach."

It wasn't that Emsbach hadn't tried. Despite his failure to become emotionally involved, he continued seeing Fraulein Krieger. They visited cabarets, attended concerts and plays, and even went horseback riding together. But no matter how attentively he listened to Liesa's lively chatter, Emsbach never felt the sense of connection he'd always assumed a couple should feel. He perceived her disappointment, and more than once decided to stop seeing her altogether, only to change his mind when her blue eyes filled with tears.

As he paced, Emsbach filled in the background of current events. "The Allies began bombing the industrial cities on the Rhine back in 1942. Now it is 1944, and Italy—Germany's main ally—has fallen. Everyone expects the Allies to launch their invasion. The only question is where and when it will take place."

"How do the officers you work with feel about that?" the girl asked.

"Oh, there is a lot of bravado about how the German forces will contain the invaders. 'Just wait, Churchill and Roosevelt will be sorry!' and 'Those Yanks will be running home to their mothers, licking their wounds.' There's a lot of laughter and backslapping."

"Do you agree?"

"Last month there was a massive bombardment on the Western front. Our troops rushed to respond. They're stationed away from the homeland. It doesn't look good."

A few nights later, June 6, 1944, Emsbach reported that the Allies had landed! "The BBC says that 135,000 American and English soldiers have established a beachhead at Normandy. The sheer number of Allied troops overwhelmed our fortifications before the armor could arrive to repulse them!" Because of the deception the Allies had practiced in the days and weeks preceding the surprise attack, only three German tank divisions were on hand to respond when the beaches were stormed.

Over the coming months, matters progressed even more quickly than Emsbach had predicted. First France was liberated, and then Belgium and Holland were invaded from the north. The children spent many days alone in the attic when Emsbach was called in for emergency duty at the hospital, but he always left them supplies of food to tide them over until he returned. Autumn was coming, and the temperature in the loft was finally bearable after the long hot summer.

In the hospital, no one was laughing or slapping backs about the cowardly Yanks anymore. A general being treated for gout stormed out of his room in a rage, colliding with Dr. Emsbach. Instead of apologizing, the infuriated patient sputtered, "I will have you posted to a combat zone, where you belong!"

Fearful that this was not an idle threat, Emsbach went out of his way to avoid that particular room for the remainder of the man's stay. He also realized that he had never considered what would happen to the children if he were transferred to a distant location. The most reasonable solution he could think of was to wed Liesa Krieger. She'd made it clear in numerous small ways that she was prepared to be his wife. Surely after they married she would take responsibility for the refugees under his roof?

He determined to broach the subject at the next opportunity. He would tell Liesa his true feelings about the Nazi regime, and gauge her response. If she was receptive, then he would reveal his secret to her and propose marriage. That way, the children would have another protector besides himself. If she did not support his political inclinations, it would mark the end of their relationship.

Caught in the throes of uncertainty about the future, Emsbach decided not to wait until he had time to contact Fraulein Krieger formally. After his shift, he showered and donned a fresh uniform at the hospital and drove immediately to her home. It was the first time he had ever come unannounced, but after so many months he felt that his lack of courtesy was forgivable, especially considering that he was planning on becoming a member of the family.

Emsbach rang the bell, straightening his military cap while he waited. Ulrich Krieger's valet answered the door. "I know the way," Emsbach said, brushing past the servant without waiting to be announced. Familiar with the layout of the house, he headed for the glass-enclosed atrium where they'd often conversed while she served him coffee and pastries. It was Liesa's favorite room and she spent most of her time there.

As he made his way to the atrium, he imagined her surprise and delight when she saw him. With a smile, he opened the door and stepped inside. The surprise was absolute for all concerned, because at the moment Liesa happened to be entertaining someone else.

"Karl Emsbach!" Lothar Engelhardt exclaimed, jumping to his feet from the sofa where he'd obviously been engaging his hostess in intimate conversation. "I didn't know you and Liesa knew each other." He turned to the young woman and asked, "Why didn't you tell me that you know Dr. Emsbach, darling?"

Liesa's face shifted rapidly from palest white to burning red. She opened her mouth to speak, but no sound came out. Her pretty blue eyes danced from one man to the other, incapable of deciding which response was called for in the situation.

Emsbach recovered first. "Forgive me," he said, bowing slightly. "I did not realize you had company. I know my way out." Turning abruptly, he walked back the way he had come, anger coursing through him like an electric current.

He heard the sound of footsteps as Liesa ran after him. "Please don't leave," she whispered. "I'll get rid of him, and then we can go somewhere together and talk. I will explain everything."

He glanced in her direction, but did not slow his steps. "No, Fraulein Krieger. We have nothing to discuss." He left the house.

As he backed the Mercedes out of the drive, his predominant feeling was one of relief. *I'm glad it happened like this*, he thought. *Imagine if I only discovered her duplicity after she was my wife!*

23

ONE MORNING IN LATE AUTUMN, UNCLE HEINRICH PAID a surprise visit to the Emsbach house. After welcoming him, Rhea watched with concern as the brigadier general's military driver entered the foyer, staggering under a mountain of uniform bags and valises. The driver was ordered to carry them up to the bedroom at the top of the main staircase.

"I will take tea in my nephew's study while you unpack," the General instructed the perspiring man, who pressed his lips tightly together in an effort to control the resentment engendered by his demotion to porter and valet. "Afterward, you will return the car to the base. Remember, if anyone discovers I am here, I will know that you were the one who revealed the information. Do not doubt that you will pay dearly for any lack of discretion!"

It was unfortunate that the young master was not present to tactfully persuade his uncle that he would be more comfortable in a different guest room. By the time Emsbach returned home, his uncle was firmly ensconced into the bedroom he had chosen and his uniforms were hanging neatly in the closet under the trapdoor leading to the attic.

Hearing unusual movement below, the children understood that it was critical to maintain total silence. There was nothing they could do except wait for Dr. Emsbach to rescue them as soon as he could. Within an hour, the servants' routine was completely altered to accommodate the brigadier general, who had no regard for his nephew's accustomed habits.

In the kitchen, Beatrix's face took on an uncharacteristic scowl as she prepared the menu ordered by Heinrich Mauer. "The young master was expecting shoulder roast stewed in beer and apples," she muttered. "He doesn't like pork loin, and he doesn't like pickled cabbage." The old woman's body language expressed her indignation more eloquently than words could have.

Monika bustled about, getting in the way more than she helped. The girl was thrilled at the opportunity to see the famous Heinrich Mauer in person. His name and rank were spoken of with a combination of fear and admiration by very important people. She could hardly wait to boast of how she'd served the brigadier general his dinner.

Rhea had known her mistress's older brother for over 30 years, since she first began working for the elder Emsbachs years before their son was born. She had a high regard for the man, in spite of his arrogance and reputation for cruelty. "He is one of our top-ranking soldiers," she explained to the village girls in a hushed voice. "Brigadier General Mauer has dedicated his entire life to service of the Fatherland. We may not question his demands!"

The housekeeper's patriotic admiration conflicted with her affection for the boy who had been left an orphan when her mistress was tragically killed. Rhea was aware that Mauer's demands had been extremely difficult for the child. In fact, there were times when, seeing the gentle boy overwhelmed by the strict regimen his uncle imposed on him, she'd slipped young Karl a treat late at night to comfort him. Her sense of guilt was eventually alleviated when the boy grew into a fine man and a source of pride to his country and his family.

After midnight, Emsbach carefully opened the padlock and let himself into the main entrance of the attic. "Well, it looks like we have a problem," he told Fraydl in a whisper as he set down a carton containing sandwiches and bottles of milk. "My uncle arrived without warning, and has taken up residence in the bedroom below you. There's nothing I can do until he makes the purpose of his visit clear. I will deal with it as soon as possible. Meanwhile, I rely on you children to keep absolutely quiet at all times. He doesn't usually stay long, but it may be a few days."

Fraydl nodded sadly. The three of them watched their benefactor exit the attic and then settled in for a difficult period. "Don't worry, Tante," little Yanky whispered in her ear. "I know how to be as still as a rock."

She gave the little boy a hug of encouragement, and then passed out the sandwiches. As they ate, the children were reassured to hear snoring from beneath their quarters. Presumably there was less danger as long as the man's snorts and grunts could be heard. Still, no one wanted to take a chance of moving about, and as soon as they finished eating they lay quietly in their beds until they finally fell asleep.

The next time Emsbach brought supplies, Chaim asked softly, "Will it be much longer?" It was increasingly difficult for the children to maintain silence, and their muscles ached to be stretched.

"I'm sorry, Chaim," the German replied quietly. "He is my mother's older brother. It would not be respectful to ask him to leave." Turning to Fraydl, he added, "My uncle has powerful connections in the army. It is vital for me to remain on good terms with him. I cannot refuse to allow him to stay for as long as he wishes."

Emsbach was not enjoying his uninvited guest. Brigadier General Mauer took over his study, sat in his chair, and rested his polished black boots on his nephew's desk. The vile stench of his cigars permeated all the downstairs rooms, causing Beatrix and Rhea to grumble with disapproval and open the windows despite the early winter chill. When the young master spent more time than was strictly necessary at the hospital, they nodded to each other with understanding.

In the beginning, Mauer rarely left the house. "I am not well," he admitted to his nephew. "I need a rest."

One week passed, and then another. Occasionally Uncle Heinrich ordered a driver to take him to important high-level meetings, but the majority of his time was spent at home. In desperation, Emsbach devised a ruse to at least dull the man's senses. Each time he returned from the hospital, he brought a few bottles of top-quality Scotch liquor for his uncle. Disregarding the rules forbidding black marketing, Mauer accepted the gifts and made quick use of them. "If this is the medicine you prescribe," he leered drunkenly, "you are a very good doctor!"

Uncle Heinrich prolonged his stay without further explanation. The nerves of all the members of the household grew taut. Over time, Emsbach observed that the man was becoming noticeably paler and thinner. Professionally, he might have diagnosed the symptoms of stress complicated by an excessive intake of alcohol, but as a victimized nephew he chose to ignore the signs and avoid any quarrel.

Unfortunately, the pressure Fraydl was experiencing was soon beyond her endurance. Night after night her dreams were broken by screams, her cries clearly audible in the bedroom below. Not even the whiskey could drown his uncle's senses sufficiently to make the man deaf. Chaim lay tensely on his mattress under the bed, helpless to prevent his aunt's nightmares. All he could do was wake her up whenever they occurred.

From his own bedroom, Emsbach woke up to the girl's screams and trembled with fear. Each time it happened, he expected his uncle to storm into the room and arrest him. After the first time, he tried giving Fraydl sleeping potions. The barbiturates helped for a few nights, but eventually her subconscious fears penetrated her dreams despite the medication, and the nightly cries resumed.

"O.K., I believe there is a G-d," Emsbach whispered to the sky outside his bedroom window. "There can be no other explanation for why Uncle Heinrich hasn't discovered the children in the attic directly over his head!"

24

T HE WINTER HOLIDAY SEASON ARRIVED, BUT BRIGADIER
General Mauer gave no indication that he planned to vacate
his nephew's home in the foreseeable future. Hans located a well-
formed blue spruce tree, which Rhea's crew of girls adorned with
the heirloom family decorations while the older women hung
up red-ribboned wreaths and sprigs of mistletoe. Afterward, the
servants gathered in the main entrance to admire their handiwork.

"Lovely," Beatrix breathed. And the housekeeper added,
"Perfect!"

Emsbach smiled, pleased by their obvious satisfaction, and then
turned his gaze absently toward the window.

"The young master is so distracted," Bea noticed.

"I think we were all expecting this holiday to be different," Rhea
murmured sadly. "We were hoping to see a new face here beside
him, a mistress for the house, and the renewal of old traditions."

"Well, we do have a new face," Otto said in an undertone, glancing at Uncle Heinrich.

The two women stared at him for a moment, and then continued
their discussion as if he hadn't spoken.

"This house is too big for just one person," the elderly cook concluded. "It should be filled with parties and children. It could have been so joyful if only things had worked out differently."

The devoted servants assumed that the master's melancholy stemmed from his broken romance with Liesa Krieger, but nothing could have been further from the truth. Emsbach was grateful that that miserable episode was behind him. The reason for his long face was his concern for the welfare of the children in the attic.

The doctor's thoughts were constantly directed toward finding a better solution. The war was going badly for Germany; it might be only a matter of a few more months until it would be over. Until then, however, every day that Uncle Heinrich was in the house was fraught with danger.

He considered moving the children—but where? During a break in his shift at the hospital, Emsbach slipped down to the basement and explored the general layout. An orderly, passing by on his way to fill an order in the underground pharmacy, took note of the surgeon and inquired as to the purpose of his unusual interest.

"Just considering the possibilities," Dr. Emsbach replied candidly.

"Possibilities, sir?"

"There are rumors that the Allied bombing raids are targeting hospitals. We may have to move our patients to a protected area, so I am examining the options available down here. You realize, of course, the importance of having a detailed plan in place before the crisis occurs."

"Oh, yes, doctor, *jawohl, jawohl*! Perhaps I can be of assistance?"

The man led Emsbach around the basement, pointing out which rooms were used for storage and could be vacated, and which it would be possible to alter in order to accommodate hospital beds. The orderly explained the variance in temperatures between the unheated corridors and storerooms and those areas nearer the enormous steam boilers, which were used to heat the hospital and provide an unlimited supply of boiling water.

Emsbach soon had enough information to conclude that the idea of hiding Fraydl and the boys here was not feasible. There were too many employees and too much activity both day and night. It would not be safe for the children in the hospital, even if he could overcome the challenge of how to transport them from the house and through the city without detection.

Inside his home, the cellar presented itself as a sensible solution. Careful neither to disturb his servants nor alert his uncle, Emsbach let himself through the door from the kitchen and descended the worn wooden steps in heavy darkness until his boots hit the packed dirt floor. He lit a kerosene lamp and, in its flickering orange glow, studied the chamber carefully. The stale odor from the fuel mingled with the musty smell of the earthen cellar, making it uncomfortable for him to breathe.

One wall of the cellar was lined with shelves where Beatrix stored jars of plum jam and the pickled vegetables that she put up every summer. Old trunks crowded the opposite wall, stacked one upon the other until they nearly touched the low ceiling. He knew that these contained tablecloths, dishes and cutlery that had been pressed into service when his mother entertained. On the third side were bins of potatoes, onions and apples that he frequently raided to prepare food for the children.

If air raids reached this secluded neighborhood, the members of the household would take refuge down here. The ancient cellar was approximately the size of the kitchen above, so there was very little space to move about. It would be no simple task to inconspicuously add three children and the paraphernalia necessary to make their lives bearable.

The doctor's eyes returned to the trunks. Could they serve as hiding places? Where would he hide their contents so that no one would notice? A trunk would be cramped for Fraydl, but the boys could both fit together in one. Emsbach extinguished the lantern and imagined spending days and nights into this dark and airless place. A wave of claustrophobia washed over him and he decided: *Only as a last resort.*

Exiting the cellar, he almost bumped into Monika. The girl's alarmed eyes widened as she glanced from the cellar door to the master of the house and back again.

"What's the matter, Monika?" he asked. "Do I look like an apparition?"

"*Nein! Ja!* I mean *nein, Herr Doktor,*" she stammered, nearly dropping the tray she carried.

When Emsbach realized that Uncle Heinrich was sprawled on the chair at the desk in his study, he beat a strategic retreat to the kitchen. From there, he listened to the brigadier general's voice arguing with someone on Emsbach's telephone, his spidery fingers beating a steady rat-a-tat-tat on the desktop.

Beatrix looked up with a smile when he entered. She was making strudel. As a child, he had loved to watch her pull the dough, stretching it until it was almost transparent. Her old hands were arthritic now, but her strudel was still the best he'd ever tasted. He took a seat at the kitchen table and she offered him a slice fresh from the oven, as he'd known she would.

"What's wrong, young master?" Bea scrutinized his worried expression.

"Why do you think something is wrong?" he evaded the question.

The cook stopped kneading her dough and gave him a sharp look. Emsbach shrugged uncomfortably, and quickly filled his mouth with hot strudel so she wouldn't ask more questions.

The delicate pastry burned his tongue, and he gratefully accepted her offer of a glass of milk. Hoping to sidetrack the direction of her questions, he changed the subject. "How is Otto doing lately?"

"*Ach,*" Beatrix sighed, "he's an old man. I know, I know. That means I'm an old woman. When did it happen? I don't know." She shook her head and began filling the dough.

"Where is Otto now?" Emsbach looked out the window at the gray clouds rolling across the sky and the tree branches whipping in the wind.

"Sitting by the fire in the carriage house," she grunted. "Just sits there all day, and then he complains at night when I tell him to get up and to go to bed."

Before Emsbach could say a word in response, there was a sudden shout from his study.

"*Karl!*" Heinrich Mauer's roars almost shook the walls. "*Karl!*"

25

Y ES, SIR! I'M COMING, SIR!" EMSBACH HASTENED FROM THE
kitchen to determine the cause of his uncle's agitation.

The brigadier general glared at him. Emsbach immediately realized that the older man was in physical distress.

"Let me help you to bed." He spoke calmly, in his professional
voice.

"Get your hands off of me!" Henreich Mauer grimaced. "It's
only my old injuries from the Great War. You're a doctor. Give me
something to take away the pain!"

Emsbach rummaged in his medical bag until he found an envelope of barbiturates. "I'll bring you a glass of water," he began, but
the old soldier interrupted him.

"*Nein!*" he panted. "I don't want your powders. Where is the
whiskey? Give me the bottle!"

"*Onkel* Heinrich, that is inadvisable. In a state like yours, drinking hard liquor could be very detrimental to your health," Emsbach
tried to reason with him. "It might even be lethal!"

Mauer lifted his arm so swiftly that Emsbach's reflexes had no
time to react. The brigadier general seized his nephew's collar and

twisted it so that his windpipe was blocked. With surprising agility, the old man pulled Emsbach's face down to his level and hissed, "If you disobey me, it will be the last thing you do in your life. *Verstehen sie?* I order you to bring me whiskey — now!"

"Yes, sir!" Emsbach gasped for air. Hands shaking, he poured half a tumbler of whiskey and set it on the desk in front of his uncle.

The dark amber liquid vanished into the brigadier general's mouth. Heinrich wiped his lips on the back of his shirt, closed his eyes and collapsed backward in the chair. Just when Emsbach concluded that his uncle had lost consciousness, Mauer bolted upright and snatched the bottle from his hands. Emsbach backed out of the room, followed by the sound of shattering glass when Heinrich hurled the now-empty bottle at the doorway where his nephew had just been standing.

Minutes later, Brigadier General Mauer stood up clumsily and staggered from the study, broken glass crunching under his boots. No one dared interfere as he lurched drunkenly up the stairs to his room.

Late the next morning, Uncle Heinrich again called for his nephew, but this time in a voice barely rising above a whisper. A hangover was giving him a splitting headache, and he wanted more whiskey.

"*Onkel* Heinrich." Emsbach spoke softly and soothingly. "You are very sick. I want you to come into the hospital for a few tests. It's possible we can alleviate your pain under controlled conditions. What do you say?"

"I say shut up and give me the bottle."

"No, *Onkel*. Not until you agree to come to the hospital with me."

Mauer's expression was homicidal, but when he tried to rise from his bed the pain overcame him and he fell back with a scream. "Give me a drink and then I'll go wherever you want. Bring the whiskey *now!*"

Emsbach hid his triumph. The idea of hospitalizing his uncle had come to him out of desperation, but it offered at least a few days' respite from the tyrant. Shaking a little sleeping powder into the glass before pouring in the whiskey, he ensured that the brigadier general would sleep for the next few hours—long enough for him to put his plan into action.

While the nurses settled Uncle Heinrich into his hospital bed, Dr. Emsbach went to discuss the case privately with Dr. Reinholdt Frank. The chief internist was well aware that he owed Karl Emsbach more than one favor. If it weren't for Emsbach's recommendation, he would be serving on the front instead of in a military hospital.

"You know, of course, that the brigadier general is a member of the *Oberkommando,* and we rely on your discretion," Emsbach informed him. "My uncle did not request medical leave. I practically had to kidnap him to bring him here."

Dr. Frank squinted over his spectacles, puzzled by this unusual development.

"Reinholdt, my uncle is as strong as a bull. I don't believe he is suffering from anything except possibly stress from the military situation, aggravated by alcohol consumption and sheer meanness. There is some discomfort from old war wounds, but I think that's just an excuse."

"So why did you bring him here? Surely you are aware that we are at war. This is a hospital, it's not a convalescent home!"

Emsbach cleared his throat. "I'll be forthright, Reinholdt. I need a break. My uncle moved into my house a few months ago and, at this point, if I don't have a few days without his constant interference in my private life, my sanity is at risk. *Onkel* Heinrich has made my life miserable since I was a child, and I can't take the pressure. He's never stayed this long on previous visits. Go examine him. If you talk to him for 10 minutes, you'll understand why I need this personal favor. Keep my uncle hospitalized for at least a few days. Order tests; rule out every possible disease and then get a second opinion. Try different pain-relief regimens. Just don't release him before he's detoxified. *Bitte*?"

Dr. Frank frowned. "Do you understand what you are asking?" Emsbach noticed a vein throbbing in the internist's neck. "If he becomes sober enough to realize that this is only an exercise. . .you and I will both find ourselves cannon fodder on the eastern front!

This is not just a cranky uncle we're talking about; this is Brigadier General Heinrich Mauer!"

Emsbach waited tensely while the internist paced back and forth, hands clasped behind his back and brow furrowed with tension. "I've got it!" he exclaimed at last. "I will give your uncle a medical referral for a certain treatment available only in Switzerland: some combination of hot mineral baths and mud packs. I'll recommend a month of recuperation before returning to active duty. How's that?"

"Brilliant, Reinholdt!" The two men shook hands, and then went to Heinrich Mauer's room. After exchanging Nazi salutes and the requisite *"Heil Hitler,"* Emsbach introduced his colleague. *"Onkel* Heinrich, this is Dr. Reinholdt Frank. He is one of the best internists in Europe. After he examines you, we will select the finest course of treatment medical science has to offer."

Mauer glowered at the two young doctors, but the humiliation of wearing an open-backed hospital gown had left him speechless. Reinholdt completed a very thorough physical examination in a most respectful manner, recording all the information in a leather binder and maintaining the most serious demeanor throughout.

"Brigadier General," he addressed the reluctant patient after the examination was concluded, "it is a miracle that you arrived here in time. Another day without treatment would undoubtedly have been fatal. Your nephew showed consummate wisdom by insisting on immediate hospitalization. Sir, Dr. Emsbach has saved your life!"

Heinrich Mauer's mind was still groggy from the barbiturate in his whiskey, and he shook his head to clear it. His legendary self-confidence seemed to be in temporary remission.

"I promise that you will receive the best treatment available for your rare and grave malady," Dr. Frank continued. "You are a V.I.P. patient of the highest order, and we shall do everything in our power to restore your health as quickly as possible. The Reich needs you, brigadier general! The German people need you. The war effort depends on you!

"Still, I must warn you that there is a great danger of relapse if the treatment is discontinued before it has run its full course. Can I depend on your cooperation, brigadier general?"

26

D URING THE FEW DAYS THAT BRIGADIER GENERAL MAUER
was undergoing tests in the hospital, Emsbach occupied
himself with finding a new refuge for the children. Not far from
the military hospital was an orphanage run by a Catholic order.
As a Lutheran, Emsbach's only connection with this institute was
noticing its proximity to his place of work. He decided to pay them
a visit.

"Major, sir!" The nun who answered the bell bent her head
slightly in acknowledgment of his rank. "How may I help you, sir?"

The woman was in her 40's, her stout figure covered by a starched
white apron over her black habit. The wimple on her head cut rather
cruelly into her plump forehead. She had a ring with many keys in
her hand and her breath smelled unpleasantly of garlic.

"I would like to speak to the priest in charge," Emsbach requested
formally.

The nun nodded slowly. Though she did not speak further, she
seemed singularly disinclined to relinquish her position block-
ing the door. His ears detected furtive movements in the chamber
behind her back, which aroused his suspicion. Taking advantage of

his uniform, Emsbach drew himself erect and ordered her to grant him immediate entrance. "You dare obstruct a soldier of the German Reich?" he frowned. His menacing tone had the desired effect and she stepped back. "Call your superior. I do not take kindly to waiting. *Shnell!*"

The woman responded grudgingly, obviously torn between fear of the stranger and loyalty to her order. Finally she turned and disappeared down a long dark hallway. Emsbach pushed the door open and entered the vestibule after her. It was empty, but on the other side of one of the doors sounds of motion could faintly be perceived.

Abruptly he opened the door and looked inside, but the room was empty. A second door on the far side of the room clicked shut. Before he could advance into the room, Emsbach was interrupted by the appearance of the priest.

"*A guten tag,*" the man's voice was pleasant and serene. "I am Father Matthew Hofmann. How may I assist you, sir?"

"I would like to speak with you privately," Emsbach said. The priest led him down the hall to a modest room. There was a warm blaze in the fireplace, and the men sat on chairs before it.

"May I offer you some refreshments?" Father Matthew inquired.

"No, thank you. I am not staying long."

"May I ask the nature of your business then? Please forgive Sister Angelina if she did not welcome you with the proper respect. We do not often have unannounced visits, and when we do they are invariably unpleasant. If you would care to examine our ledgers, I have them right here." He opened a cabinet and withdrew several thin leather-bound volumes. "The children are playing in the courtyard and will not disturb us. I thought it best, since they are war orphans and the sight of a soldier in uniform is distressing for them."

"I understand. How many children reside in this institution?"

The priest frowned slightly. It was obvious to Emsbach that he was debating whether or not to be forthright. After a slight hesitation, Father Matthew pointed to the ledgers in his lap and said, "We have approximately 100 boys at this time. Their ages vary from infancy up to about 12 years. As you probably know, older boys live in the monastery on the mountain and the girls all live with the nuns in the convent."

Two little boys could be hidden among a hundred without difficulty, Emsbach thought. "Where do the children come from?" he asked.

"As I stated previously, they are war orphans. Some of the children were brought by their widowed mothers or older siblings who could not care for them in these difficult times, and others were referred by village pastors or city authorities."

The priest was uncomfortable, and Emsbach sensed it. *I wonder why?* He asked himself, continuing, "What is your financial situation?"

Father Matthew sighed and raised his hands, palms up. "These are terrible times," he admitted. "We are partially supported by the tithes of our community, but the people have little to spare. The older boys keep a vegetable garden. We have a cow for milk and a few chickens for eggs. We manage, but there is nothing left over." He looked at Emsbach hopefully, wondering if this officer might have connections that could ease the orphans' plight.

"Do you have Jewish children here?"

The question struck the priest like a bolt of lightning. His complexion paled and his jaw muscles knotted visibly. "No! No! Of course not!"

"Perhaps you do," Emsbach continued, his tone sinister.

"No, I'm sure that all the boys here are good Christian lads. You can come to chapel and see how beautifully and fervently they pray. Please, have no doubts on this subject. I am well aware that such a thing is forbidden. I would never endanger my life's work by taking in a Jew."

"I think that you would. I think there are Jewish children in this orphanage!" Emsbach noted the beads of cold sweat that had sprung up on Father Matthew's forehead.

"No, sir! Such a thing would be out of the question."

"Well, perhaps a Jewish child might be brought here without your being aware that he is a Jew."

The priest swallowed and licked his dry lips. "It is not totally impossible," he admitted, "but I can't imagine it. No, I don't think so. No, no."

"I will inspect the children myself. Please call them in immediately. I am confident that if there is even one Jewish child here, I will identify him."

The priest appeared to age suddenly. "I will go and tell Sister Angelina to summon the children," he agreed with marked reluctance.

"No. I will accompany you to the courtyard and you will line them up for my scrutiny."

Why now, when the war is so close to being over? Father Matthew asked himself. *Just another few months. . .* But the officer towering over him left no alternative. Unconsciously wringing his hands, the priest studied the arrogant Nazi's face but found no sign of a softer human emotion. He led the way to the garden with a heavy heart.

When the two men appeared unannounced in the noisy courtyard, the children froze in their places. Complete silence reigned as several of the boys edged backward with pale frightened faces.

"The children are to stand in line for inspection," the priest instructed the nun in charge.

Boys were quickly pulled into formation, their shirts tucked in and hair smoothed back from their faces. "Shall I bring the infants as well?" she asked submissively.

"No, that will not be necessary." The officer spoke with authority, "This will take only a short time. Tell the children to approach me one at a time. After I have spoken with each one, they may resume their activities."

Emsbach sat down on a stone bench. His briefcase was stuffed with sweets wrapped in paper. As each child approached in turn, he asked the boy his name and age and gave him a bonbon. The children's tense faces soon shone with smiles, as they accepted the unexpected treat and willingly answered the visitor's questions.

The names given by the boys were all good German ones: Heinz, Franz, Hans, Georg, Dieter, Peter, Axel, Johann, Stefan, Martin, Erich, Joachim. Emsbach nodded and rewarded each with a candy.

When he had seen all the children, he invited Father Matthew to dismiss the boys and sit on the bench beside him.

"The boys Rudolph, Oskar and Friedrich are Jews," he said drily. "I assume you know this."

Emsbach had observed these three furtively mumbling something just before popping the bonbons into their mouths. Chaim and Yanky always whispered this way before eating and he knew it had something to do with being Jewish.

"They are not the only ones," he conjectured. "A more thorough examination will easily reveal the others."

Matthew Hofmann did not reply. Afraid to confirm or deny knowledge, he trembled uncontrollably at the danger hovering over his head. The soldier's eyes bore into him, demanding a response, but the priest sat helplessly as his own eyes slowly filled with tears.

"I am prepared to keep your secret," Emsbach's quiet words were barely perceptible.

Father Matthew held his breath. Had he heard correctly? The priest turned slowly toward the unwelcome guest, his mouth working futilely.

"For a price, of course," Emsbach added.

"We have nothing. I have no money to pay you." There was desperation in the priest's hoarse voice.

"I do not want your money."

Father Matthew wrung his hands, unable to fathom what price this Nazi might exact in exchange for not throwing him and his little flock to the hungry wolves of the Gestapo.

"I have a secret of my own." He waited a moment to allow his words to sink into the priest's consciousness.

Father Matthew looked at him sharply, his mind spinning as he tried to grasp the meaning behind the Nazi's statement. Sudden happiness flooded his heart. "You want to bring me a Jewish child?" he asked. "You have a Jewish child that needs a home and protection?"

Emsbach nodded.

In his relief, the priest felt like grabbing the man and crushing him in a hug. "Yes, yes, of course. Bring him!" he said, the tears finally spilling over onto his cheeks. He took out a handkerchief and blew his nose.

"Two boys," Emsbach said. "The older is about 10, and the younger is 3 or 4. I gave my word to care for them, but circumstances have changed and it has become impossible to continue sheltering them. They are clever children. You must prepare German papers for them. I suggest using the identities of orphans who died in the first years of the war. Do you understand?"

"*Jawohl, mein Herr!*" Father Matthew agreed emotionally. He felt like a man who has faced the angel of death and somehow survived. "Bring them tonight, after midnight. I will be prepared."

27

THE CHILDREN BURST INTO TEARS WHEN EMSBACH informed them that they must separate. It was difficult for him to witness their shock as they clung to each other and trembled.

"It's the best thing to do, under the circumstances." Emsbach averted his eyes from their faces. "The war is going very badly. They need fresh soldiers and I could be re-deployed to the front any day. *Fraulein* Fraydl, you are nearly an adult. Alone, there is a chance you will survive. Together with the children on the street, you don't stand a chance."

Choking back her tears, Fraydl nodded her acceptance of his logic. She whispered into Chaim's ear, "He's right. You must go. It's our only chance."

The thought of leaving was so terrifying that their little corner of the attic suddenly seemed familiar and inviting.

"We'll be so good. We won't move! We won't make a sound!" Yanky pleaded, but the decision remained unchanged. Within hours the boys would leave their aunt, and no one knew if the three would ever meet again.

Chaim drew himself up as tall as he could, and squared his

shoulders. "I will take care of Yanky, Tante Fraydl. You don't have to worry about us."

Yanky turned to Dr. Emsbach. "Are you sending the Tante away too?"

Karl Emsbach ruffled the little boy's hair. "If I can find a safer place for her, then your aunt will also go." He suddenly felt bereft. His charges were leaving.

Fraydl neatly folded her nephew's clothing and packed them into a carton. Emsbach pulled Yanky onto his lap and put his other arm around Chaim's waist. "I will visit you at the convent," he assured them. "Sunday afternoons are visiting days. If I come every week, people would get suspicious, but from time to time I will stop by."

"Will they put us in the attic?" Yanky asked.

"No, you will be with other children. You'll be able to run and play." Emsbach smiled. "You will have friends, and lessons to learn."

"But we have to keep everything secret," Chaim reminded his little brother.

Yanky blinked. "Everything?"

"Yes," Chaim told him seriously. "No one must ever know the truth. We have to be somebody else from now on. We aren't Chaim and Yanky anymore."

"But you won't forget who you *really* are!" Fraydl exclaimed. "You'll remember in your hearts always. When this war is over, you will go to Tante Rivka in Palestine, and then you will be Yanky and Chaim again. *B'ezras Hashem*, I will meet you there, too, and then we will always be together."

"When, Tante Fraydl?"

"I don't know, Yanky. But one day it will happen." She blinked back sudden moisture in her eyes. "You won't forget me?"

"No! Never!"

"Children, we must leave now." Emsbach took Yanky's small hand in his, and Chaim carried the box with the few belongings they had accrued since they'd come to the attic. Emsbach turned to Fraydl for a last word, "Pray that they will be safe," he said. "And that, no matter what, they will not reveal who they really are."

She nodded, holding back her tears. "They understand," she reassured him. "They will never give away their secret."

When they had left, Fraydl let herself cry. She wept for the two innocent children forced to play a dangerous masquerade in a Christian orphanage, and she cried for her parents and for *their* parents. Finally she *davened* with all her heart that when the war ended, her nephews would find their way safely back to *Yiddishkeit*.

The next morning, Emsbach found his uncle sitting in a chair beside his hospital window, looking pale and bilious. Having undergone countless tests and examinations since he arrived, the brigadier general was gradually becoming convinced that he was, in fact, seriously ill. After a token effort at polite conversation, Emsbach withdrew to seek out Dr. Frank.

"*Heil Hitler!*"

"*Heil Hitler!*"

The two men shook hands.

"Well, how'm I doing?" Reinholdt asked with a wink and a raised eyebrow.

"I'm eternally in your debt!" Emsbach responded.

"Glad that you know it," the internist said with a smirk. "You really owe me one, Emsbach! In less than two days, the brigadier general has managed to offend or terrify every person on the floor."

"So now you can understand my position. . ."

"Absolutely. On the other hand, if another solution isn't found soon, I'll be a candidate for the funny farm."

Emsbach nodded in resignation.

"I put in for a transfer for your uncle to the sanatorium in Switzerland," Reinholdt added. "The committee has granted approval. If only your uncle agrees to go, you'll be spared a few weeks of his noxious presence."

"Why shouldn't he?"

"The problem is that cooperation is not one of the traits with which Heinrich Mauer was endowed. We'll act as if he's already agreed, and proceeding accordingly."

"When can they receive him?"

"Tomorrow, or the following day. I'll order an ambulance to transport him."

The next day, Brigadier General Heinrich Mauer peremptorily refused to travel to Switzerland.

His temporary withdrawal from alcohol was causing a pronounced tremor in the man's hands. Flushed and dizzy as his blood pressure rose, Heinrich Mauer did not feel like a healthy man — but he was a stubborn one. "We are fighting a war!" he raged. "I must return to my duties immediately."

Dr. Frank and his colleagues gathered around the old soldier's bed and entreated him to reconsider. "You will come back 15 years younger!" Reinholdt appealed to the brigadier general. "You owe it to Germany. A few weeks of this treatment will give you the strength to win the war practically single-handedly!"

Heinrich glowered at the doctors surrounding him. Then his face relaxed and a smile appeared. "On one condition," he stipulated, his voice cold and vengeful. The physicians nodded like puppets, prepared to grant him any wish so that he would leave their ward. "My nephew, Major Emsbach, must accompany me!"

Reinholdt let his breath out in a sigh of relief. "That will be arranged, brigadier general." The doctors swiftly vacated the room before the old soldier could change his mind.

Emsbach took the news stoically. An army ambulance with a driver was assigned to take the brigadier general back to his nephew's house for the night, and the trio would leave for the Swiss spa before daybreak the next morning.

After Uncle Heinrich was safely settled on the sofa in the living room downstairs, together with the bottle of Scotch whiskey that he insisted on for company, the driver asked for a few words in private with Emsbach.

Kurt Liggett had sized up the surgeon and decided it was possible to rely on his discretion. "Major," he said confidently, "I have a mutually profitable business offer to suggest."

"*Ja?* What kind of business, private?"

"I'd like to do a favor for a friend of mine. He heard that I am driving to Zurich, and he asked me to bring something back to

Germany from Switzerland, something of considerable value for which he is prepared to pay handsomely." Liggett's grin was more a leer than a smile.

"You are speaking of contraband?"

Emsbach's severe tone caused the private some misgivings. Had he misjudged the surgeon? "Some might call it that," was his cautious response.

Major Emsbach frowned. It went against his nature to do anything illegal. With the children on his conscience, he certainly didn't need more trouble. On the other hand, the driver was indisputably correct in the assumption that an army ambulance with a high-ranking officer inside would not be closely inspected at the border.

His mind went into high gear. If it was possible to smuggle something into Germany from Switzerland, why couldn't they smuggle something *out* of Germany and into Switzerland? He looked at the driver. Was he trustworthy? If he discovered that there was a stowaway on the ambulance, would he inform the Gestapo?

On the other hand, Emsbach now had compromising information on the private; to wit, that he was a smuggler of contraband. This might give him enough power over Liggett to protect himself if Fraydl were detected.

Did he dare take the chance?

28

PRIVATE LIGGETT WATCHED EMSBACH'S FACE CLOSELY, trying to read his thoughts. It seemed to him that the major was coming around.

"There's a hefty profit in it for both of us," he promised, counting on the temptation of money to overcome the man's scruples, as it had his own. "I have some experience in this business. I've done this particular friend such favors in the past and it's as simple as pie."

"I'll want payment in advance," Emsbach told him.

"*Jawohl, jawohl*" Liggett was delighted. "*Nicht ein probieren!*"

"Where will you store the contraband in the ambulance?" Emsbach wanted to know.

"Come, I will show you!" the driver said enthusiastically. He was more than glad of an opportunity to boast of his clever advance planning.

The two men left the house through the back door and went down the stone path to the car shed where the ambulance was parked. Private Liggett opened the double doors in the back of the vehicle. Emsbach examined the interior of the ambulance closely, but saw nothing unusual. One side was lined with small drawers labeled with the medical supplies they contained, and the other side held a bench for passengers accompanying the patient on the stretcher, which took up all the space in the middle. There was a seat for another passenger in the forward section beside the driver.

Emsbach shrugged. "Diamonds, maybe?" he asked. There was not enough room for anything bigger.

Liggett grinned. "Look at this," he almost giggled. With a twist of his wrist he pulled up the seat of the bench, revealing a strap on the floor. "Pull the cord," he instructed, and a moment later a spacious compartment was revealed, hidden beneath the floor.

Emsbach's eyes lit up. He bent over and examined the underside of the ambulance to determine how the hiding place had been constructed.

"Ingenious!" he complimented Private Liggett. The secret space was completely invisible from the outside, but secure and able to bear weight. "Who built this? You?"

"*Ja!*" the driver said proudly.

"What time do you want to leave in the morning?"

"I'll be here at 5 o'clock, and we can leave as soon as the patient is ready."

"Excellent. It's already late. Where are you sleeping?"

"I'll drive back to the barracks."

"Would you like to take my car?"

Liggett's eyes bulged. He had never driven an automobile like the elegant Mercedes-Benz. His mouth opened in a wide grin. "Sure thing!"

Emsbach handed him the keys without hesitation. "Take care, private. If that car comes home with so much as a scratch, I'll have you hung for destroying Reich property."

Emsbach watched impatiently as the eager young soldier slowly backed the Mercedes out of the car shed. Kurt Liggett loved automobiles. He had earned his position as a military driver because he was an excellent mechanic, having tinkered with motors since he was old enough to handle a wrench. He knew how to take them apart and put them back together again, blindfolded. Private

Liggett knew how to appreciate the luxury of an expensive modern automobile. He would not be in a hurry to return before morning, as long as he could drive the luxurious Mercedes.

Emsbach locked the doors to the shed and opened the secret compartment under the ambulance. He sized it up approvingly and then returned to the house. Uncle Heinrich was snoring loudly on the sofa in the living room downstairs as Dr. Emsbach made his way quietly to the attic.

"Get ready!" he told Fraydl. "You are going to Switzerland!"

She was thrilled beyond words at the news that this time tomorrow she would be out of the reach of the talons of the Third Reich. "I can hardly believe this is really happening!" she whispered.

"You'll have to leave the chest with your family heirlooms," Emsbach pointed out. "There's barely enough room in the compartment for you and the quilts you must have for warmth, plus a supply of water and some food. After the war, send word to me where to find you and I will return them."

After the war, she thought. *Such magical words!*

Emsbach instructed Fraydl to put on all of her clothes in layers, one over the other. "This winter is the coldest and longest that I can remember," he told her. "It's still snowing, even though it's nearly April already. I'm afraid it will be a cold ride."

When she came downstairs, he had to smile at the shapeless result. "We must be quick," he warned. Indicating a basket with a bottle of water, a thermos of hot coffee and some sandwiches, he asked, "Is this too heavy for you to carry?"

"No, I can manage," she assured him.

Emsbach gathered up a feather comforter and a few pillows to cushion the long and bumpy ride, and then led the way out the front door into the dark night. "It's half-past 4 now," he whispered. "The driver will be here at 5. It won't be much longer."

The sidewalk was icy. They moved slowly, step by deliberate step. Emsbach realized that he was sweating in spite of the cold, and was relieved when they reached the car shed without mishap. He bundled the girl into the hidden compartment and hastily closed the trapdoor.

"Are you all right?"

There was a barely audible *"Baruch Hashem."*

"If you are in any trouble, knock on the floor above you. From my place on the bench, I should feel the vibration through my boots."

"I understand," came the muffled reply.

"Good. I wish you success. *Auf Wiedersehen.*"

Emsbach returned to the kitchen and waited until he heard the purr of the Mercedes' motor in the alley. His watch showed that it was exactly 5 o'clock. The trip was expected to take six hours. Fraydl would suffer from the cold, but there was no alternative. He inhaled slowly, anxious for the ordeal to be behind him.

Together, Dr. Emsbach and Private Liggett carried the stretcher back to the house, where they loaded a very drunk brigadier general onto it and strapped him in place. Emsbach kicked the empty bottles on the floor with disgust, grateful that the man had not smashed them into the wall as was often the case.

"If you have any more of that," Kurt Liggett advised, "bring it. If the old man gets difficult you may need something to calm him down."

"Right," Emsbach agreed reluctantly, securing two full bottles in his uncle's suitcase.

By the time the two had maneuvered the stretcher down to the car shed, it was beginning to grow light outside. Emsbach climbed in after his uncle and took his place on the bench while Liggett slipped into the driver's seat. The motor turned over and the engine was soon humming. It was obvious that the vehicle was kept in excellent condition.

Too late, Emsbach considered the possible effect of carbon monoxide in the hidden compartment. A wave of panic swept over him. Would they arrive in Switzerland, only to discover that Fraydl had suffocated from the poisonous fumes of the exhaust?

He felt so helpless. There was nothing to do except pray—if he could only remember how. Everything about these Jewish children seemed to bring him back to the question of G-d.

29

CURLED UP IN HER HIDING PLACE BENEATH THEIR FEET, Fraydl could hear the men's voices against the steady drone of the motor. As the kilometers passed, the conversation between Emsbach and Kurt Liggett gradually faded into companionable silence, occasionally pierced by the snorts and whistles of the snoring patient.

After working shifts that deprived him of sleep for long periods, Emsbach's inner biological clock was no longer attuned to day or night. If he was motionless for any significant period of time, exhaustion simply set in. The rocking of the car, together with his immobility, caused his head to nod and he soon slept where he sat on the bench.

The hours stretched as the ambulance sped along the icy highways on its way to the Swiss Alps. In the early-morning hours, the streets were mostly empty and whatever traffic there was gave way to the military ambulance. Later in the journey, the bustling streets in populated cities presented a difficulty. Private Liggett had his hands full threading a path between heavily clad pedestrians — their attention distracted as they attempted to hold onto their hats in the wind—motor cars, horse-drawn vehicles and swaying bicycle riders. School children in brown-and-green uniforms tended to dash into the road without warning, causing the ambulance driver to swear and slam on the brakes.

Emsbach woke with a start when the ambulance hit an ice patch and lurched into a skid. Kurt Liggett was a skillful driver. He quickly regained control of the vehicle, but Uncle Heinrich was shaken awake. Surprisingly, he did not seem to be upset at finding himself in the ambulance.

"Give me a drink," he growled at his nephew. "And you know I don't mean water."

Emsbach, resigned, handed him the whiskey, which his uncle guzzled straight from the bottle. Fortified with liquor, the brigadier general fumbled with his restraints and sat up, looking around with a scowl.

"Where are we?"

"A few more hours and we will be in Switzerland, brigadier general," Liggett answered. The patient lay back down and appeared to fall asleep. Emsbach was just dozing off again when he heard a strange sound. Looking at his uncle, he saw that the older man was sobbing drunkenly. With a slurred, whiskey-loosened tongue, Heinrich Mauer began to speak.

"It's those accursed Jews!" he snarled. "Even when they're dead they pursue me! I can't take it anymore!"

Emsbach's handsome Aryan features were distorted by distaste. He glanced at the rearview mirror and saw that Liggett was listening with amusement.

"It's all right, *Onkel* Heinrich." Emsbach tried to calm the old man, but Mauer would not be quiet.

"I hear them all the time!" he complained drunkenly. "Their screams follow me wherever I go. They even followed me to your house. They wake me every night."

Now I know why he didn't react to the girl's nightmares, Emsbach thought. *It serves him right.*

The brigadier general continued to rant, cursing the Jews and swearing revenge on the spirits that haunted him. Once he began,

Mauer was unstoppable. First he boasted of killing many Jews, and then he wept with self-pity because their spirits dared disturb his peace of mind.

As they crossed the border into the Austrian Alps, Mauer whispered dramatically, "The worst is *her* voice." He shuddered. "It echoes in my head without mercy. The damned Jewish dog!"

There was a pause. Emsbach dared hope the performance was over, but the Nazi general stirred again. "It was just an ordinary deportation train from the ghetto. A thankless job, getting all those unruly people on board in a disciplined manner, but there must be order. Someone had to do it, and Heydrich knew that if he wanted it done right, Heinrich Mauer was his man."

Again there was silence for several minutes before he continued. "In every *aktzia*, there are always troublemakers. Names are posted clearly. They know the hour they must be in the *mittelplatz*. 'Resettlement,' we tell them. Ha! Ha! Resettlement! A good joke… But there are always big shots with connections that get their names taken off the lists. Of course, that leaves us with no choice but to hunt for replacements. Such a waste of time. No sense of organization."

Emsbach held his breath, willing the whiskey to put the man back to sleep. He did not want to listen to any more of his uncle's confession, but he was trapped: a captive audience. "The quickest, most efficient solution is to grab kids from the streets," the bigadier general mumbled. "In less than an hour it's possible to fill up a truck and get them to the plaza. But, *ach*, such wailing and screaming!

"I stationed men to keep their parents from interfering, but a few mothers always broke through and tried to climb into the truck to join their children. It's such a bother throwing them out, but there are quotas to fill and adults take up too much space.

"There was one mother I'll never forget because she was so stunning — a real Semitic beauty with blazing black eyes. My men had scooped up three of her children and they were making the devil of a fuss calling to her. She ran from one side of the truck to the other, trying to reach them through the bars. She could see her brats and hear them, but there was no way for her to get to them.

"What a laugh we had, I can tell you, seeing that beautiful Jewess running around and around the truck, frantically calling out, 'Yanky! Moishy! Suri!'" Heinrich said the names in an artificially high voice, laughing until tears ran down his ruddy cheeks.

Emsbach clenched his fists helplessly. He wanted to shout, "Shut up!" Glancing at Liggett, he saw the driver shaking with mirth. Tears of frustration stung the doctor's eyes as the brigadier general continued relentlessly.

"Well, that beautiful dog caught sight of me, and somehow she understood I was the highest-ranking officer around." Heinrich paused for a coughing fit, spitting bloody phlegm into a stained handkerchief, before continuing hoarsely.

"She must have lost her mind. If it wasn't such a pleasure to look at her, I would have just shot her on the spot. The dog ran up to me and threw herself on the ground at my boots. My men were laughing so hard, I thought they'd split their sides. '*Bitte*, save my children,' she begs me. '*Ratava die kinder! Gevalt!*'"

If he keeps talking, I will kill him, Karl Emsbach thought. The knuckles of his fists grew snow-white from the effort to keep from smashing his uncle's face. The only thing that held him back was the knowledge that it would cost his life, and probably Fraydl's as well.

Heinrich turned to his nephew with a smile, clearly aware of his reaction. The brigadier general didn't look drunk anymore; in fact, he looked completely sober. Chills ran down Emsbach's spine. What did this evil man want from him? Was this whole journey a trap? He turned his head away and licked his parched lips with the tip of his tongue.

Heinrich smiled broadly. "Don't you like my story, Karl?" he asked, in a voice that froze his nephew.

The driver's voice broke through the tense exchange. "Don't stop now, brigadier general. Tell us what happened next!"

30

T HAT BOY IS MORE OF A MAN THAN YOU," HEINRICH MAUER sneered, jerking a thumb at Kurt Liggett and narrowing his eyes.

In a show of apathy, Emsbach turned away. To distract himself from the taunt, he concentrated on the small window in the rear door, instinctively understanding that his uncle was leading him somewhere he did not want to go. Anger would rob him of the ability to think clearly. In spite of the tremendous effort required to check his temper and remain calm, he must retain control of his thoughts.

The brigadier general lay back on the pillow, closing his eyes. "I let her beg, of course," he continued, addressing the driver. "I was curious to see what she would do. When I did not respond, the dog pulled herself up and looked me straight in the eyes. 'Have you no children?' she demanded, 'No wife? No feelings?'

"My wife died years ago," Mauer said, his anger escalating. "We were married over 30 years, but we were childless. It infuriated me to hear that Jewess refer to her. I unlocked the gate at the back of the truck and watched her striking black eyes light up with hope.

'Which child do you want?' I asked her. She showed me three little ones, all less than 8 years old. 'Only one!' I told her, 'You may have one child. If you do not choose immediately, we will take them all!'

"*Ach*, Liggett, I will never forget the look on her face. It was pure art. It was tragedy incarnate. Three little brats, shouting, 'Mamme, take me!' Six little hands reaching out, trying to catch her attention—and all she could do was stare at them, unable to move. Priceless. A scene from a pageant."

Heinrich sank into his memories, an appreciative expression on his face.

"What happened next?" the driver urged, clearly caught up in the narrative.

"*Ach*, nothing," the brigadier general said, flicking a speck of lint from the sleeve of his uniform. "It was only a few more minutes before the truck was full. There was no further reason for delay, and I gave the order to move on. There was a schedule to keep, you understand? Still, I'll never forget how that Jewess remained standing there like a statue in the middle of the road after they drove away, arms still extended for the children that would never return..." Uncle Heinrich's voice tapered off to silence as he drifted into sleep.

Emsbach blinked back angry tears. Who was that unfortunate woman? Where were her children now? On the stretcher, his uncle snored peacefully. Brigadier General Heinrich Mauer, proud officer of the Deutschland Army, believed himself to be a cultured man, the embodiment of a gentleman soldier. Emsbach felt nauseated at the man's lack of conscience or basic human warmth.

The vehicle stopped to refuel. Emsbach assisted his uncle to the restroom and then left Liggett with the unenviable task of waiting for the brigadier general to come out again. Returning to the ambulance, he looked around cautiously. After verifying that no one was watching, he leaned against the back doors and pretended to smoke his pipe. At the same time he lifted the lid to the secret compartment with his other hand to allow fresh air to reach the captive girl.

"Are you all right?" His eyes swept the area methodically, insuring that he was unobserved.

"*Baruch Hashem*, yes," was her soft reply. His heart skipped a beat with relief. His worries about carbon monoxide had been unfounded.

He fingered his woolen scarf. "Are you warm enough?"

"I'm fine."

"Do you need anything?"

"No, nothing," Fraydl reassured him. "It's just cramped. It'll be good to get out and move around when that will be possible. How much longer do you think it will take to get there?"

"We should cross into Switzerland in another hour, but it will take a while to settle my uncle in the sanatorium and I will need time to locate a safe place to leave you. I expected the trip to be over by now, but the weather slowed us down. We must drive slowly because of the fog and sleet... Get down, they're coming back!" He let the lid fall from his fingers, and used both hands to tamp down the tobacco in his pipe.

Liggett approached the ambulance, supporting a weak and cranky brigadier general. "Hello, major. How about a smoke?"

"I'll be glad to give you tobacco if you have a pipe."

"No, I prefer cigarettes."

"Sorry, I don't have any."

"I want a drink." Heinrich blinked peevishly.

"Just a minute, sir. Let us secure your stretcher inside the ambulance first."

Emsbach dug into the suitcase until he found the second bottle of whiskey. The men watched in amazement as Uncle Heinrich tilted it up and drained the entire thing in seconds.

"*Ach, sehr gut*," Mauer declared in a slurred voice, smacking his lips with satisfaction and wiping his wet mouth against his sleeve. "Bring another bottle, Karl. Give some to Liggett here, too."

"Thank you, brigadier general," Liggett responded. "I will be glad to drink with you in Zurich, but in this weather it is too dangerous. Besides, I am on duty and it is not allowed."

Mauer gave him a wink. "One sip? Just a taste?" he cajoled.

Emsbach's frown of disapproval was too clear to ignore, so Liggett shrugged in reluctant refusal and climbed into the driver's seat. He turned on the ignition and pulled out of the gasoline station, back wheels sending up a shower of slush behind them.

A few miles further along the road, Heinrich's face clouded, his mood passing from mellow to maudlin. Drunken tears flowed down his red face and he sniffed loudly between great shuddering sobs. "It is time for my dear nephew to know the truth," he blubbered, barely coherent. "He has been a good boy and he deserves to know. Karl, you owe your life to me. I made you into who you are. You are mine, boy. If it wasn't for me, you would be dead long ago."

Emsbach glanced at his uncle with a mixture of disgust and fear. The man was crazy. Abruptly, Heinrich fell into a deep, snoring sleep. Emsbach bent over and retied his shoe, unobtrusively tapping softly on the floor. Fraydl's answering knock assured him that she was all right. He wondered how much of his uncle's gruesome story the girl had heard. He hoped that the noise from the motor had spared her from his uncle's mad ranting.

Emsbach's eyes returned to the old man on the stretcher, and a daring idea came to him. There were ampoules of medication in his medical bag which were known to simulate a heart attack if given in excessive dosages. He felt dizzy, realizing that it was in his power to rid the world of this monster and no one would suspect!

Light beads of sweat formed on his forehead as he contemplated the deed. Would it be wrong to end the life of such a debased human being? He unlatched his doctor's kit and fingered the small glass bottles of drugs, easily identifying the exact one he would need.

Private Liggett's eyes remained focused on the slick road. Obviously, the driver needed all of his concentration to maneuver the unwieldy ambulance along the twisting mountain road. If the man occasionally glanced in the mirror, it was merely to check the traffic behind them. He would never notice what his passengers were doing.

Emsbach turned sideways to conceal his hands from the driver's view. Just one minute and the deed would be done. He had begun assembling the syringe when Liggett suddenly hit the brakes. The doctor was thrown forward against the partition behind the driver.

Emsbach's eyes flew to the rearview mirror in alarm. Had the driver witnessed anything? His mind raced to concoct an explanation if Liggett should ask him what he was doing. Surely the man's mechanical training had not included the study of pharmaceuticals?

Emsbach decided that he had nothing to fear. No ambulance driver would ever question the administration of an injection to a patient by a physician.

"Karl, where are we?" his uncle demanded petulantly, roused by the sudden swerve. The vehicle skidded to a stop.

31

THE REASON FOR THE SUDDEN STOP WAS MUNDANE: AN unmapped military checkpoint had appeared in front of them, immediately after a sharp curve in the road. Emsbach waited impatiently while a red-nosed soldier saluted *"Heil Hitler!"* and opened the ambulance's rear doors to inspect the passengers.

The recruit gave a cursory glance inside, saluted the brigadier general and waved them on without even inspecting their papers. Kurt Liggett grinned from ear to ear, his unspoken "I told you that's how it'd be" hanging in the air between them.

As they passed the last barrier, two soldiers ran over to the ambulance and banged on the roof.

"Hey, quit that!" the driver yelled.

"No harm intended! The officer on duty told us that you're headed for Zurich, and since we have urgent business in Geneva, we'd be indebted if you could give us a ride to the train station at the border."

Liggett shrugged. "I'm on duty," he said. "Ask the major."

When the taller soldier turned to request Emsbach's permission to join them, he broke into a smile of recognition. "Well, if it isn't little Karlikens!" he exclaimed, poking his comrade in the ribs with his elbow. "You haven't forgotten Karl Emsbach, have you, Bruno?"

His short, heavy companion stuck his head through the open window of the ambulance and peered at the occupants. "*Ja*, It's Emsbach," he confirmed. "It's been over 15 years, but I'd recognize that face anywhere!"

To say that Emsbach was dismayed would be an understatement. Fritz Heckmann and Bruno Johanningmeier were living reminders of the unhappiest years of his childhood. When he first came to the military academy after his parents' death, these two older boys had tormented him ruthlessly. He did not relish renewing his acquaintanceship with them.

"*Heil Hitler! Heil Hitler!*" They greeted Karl Emsbach jovially. Noticing Heinrich Mauer on the stretcher, Fritz assumed a concerned attitude and called out, "What is this? The brigadier general needs specialized treatment in Switzerland? *Ach*, it must be very bad if our German doctors cannot cure him!"

Uncle Heinrich squinted, scrutinizing the two soldiers. "Get in and close the door before you give us pneumonia!" he barked, adding in a hoarse whisper to his nephew, "Karl, move over and make place for these brave German fighters."

Much to Emsbach's discomfort, he had to put up with their coarse stories and vulgar laughter for the rest of the trip. His uncle soon sank back into his drunken stupor while Fritz and Bruno carried on a raucous conversation, oblivious to the aggravation they were causing their former schoolmate. With the two newcomers crowded onto the narrow bench beside him, he had no choice but to forget about his plan to inject his uncle with an overdose of medication. *Perhaps it is for the best*, he consoled himself, rubbing his aching temples and wishing the ride was over. *If it is meant to be, there will be another opportunity.*

Steadily falling snow slowed their progress as the road led to higher and higher altitudes. Uncle Heinrich was seized with a coughing fit. Emsbach helped him into a sitting position until he could breathe more easily. "Who are these men?" the brigadier general demanded, glowering at Fritz and Bruno. "What are they doing here?"

"They're getting out at the border," his nephew explained. "You permitted them to come as far as the train station."

Mauer shook his head. "Get them out of here!" he roared.

"We're at the border," Kurt Liggett called back to his passengers. Fritz and Bruno made haste to scramble out. The guard signaled to the ambulance driver that he could continue on into Switzerland.

"Halt!" The brigadier general roused himself. "Halt, I tell you!"

Emsbach bit his lip in vexation. What would his unpredictable uncle do next? Heinrich Mauer groped his way to the rear doors and opened them. He jumped unsteadily off the bumper and made his way into the station.

Private Liggett gave Emsbach a quizzical look. "What now?"

"I wish I knew," Emsbach sighed. "Pull the ambulance over. We'll just have to wait until he comes back."

Half an hour later, Emsbach sent the private into the station to learn the cause of their continued delay. Liggett returned with a grimace. "The brigadier general is having a few drinks with the captain," he informed the major.

"Would you like to wait inside, where it's warm?" Emsbach asked.

"Ja, I would."

"Go in, then. I'll stay out here in the meantime."

"You'll freeze," Liggett warned.

"It doesn't matter. I need some peace and quiet to calm my nerves."

Liggett nodded his understanding.

The moment he was alone, Emsbach lifted up the door of the secret compartment and passed Fraydl a cup of still-warm coffee from his thermos. She drank it gratefully.

"This is not Switzerland, is it?" It was less a question that a statement.

"We're on the border," he said encouragingly. "We just have to cover a few more feet and we'll be out of Germany."

She noticed that her benefactor's jaw was tight with tension and his blue-gray eyes were clouded like the stormy weather. "This trip is very difficult, isn't it?" she commented, trying to convey both sympathy and thankfulness. "Very few people would go to so much trouble for a total stranger. Dr. Emsbach, you are an extraordinary person—a hero. It has been a rare privilege to meet you. After the war, I will make sure that your kindness is recognized."

"After more than a year in the same house, I don't think we can be classified as total strangers anymore," he said lightly, deflecting the praise. "My reward, if I deserve one, will come from knowing that the world is a little bit of a better place than it would otherwise have been."

She sipped the coffee gratefully, allowing its rich warmth to course through her stiff, chilled limbs. Emsbach was relieved to see that she was in good condition in spite of the cold cramped quarters. Fraydl returned the cup to him with a smile, then fluffed her pillows a little and changed to a slightly more comfortable position before the lid closed again.

Private Liggett arrived a few minutes later. Noticing that the windows had frosted over, he tipped his cap at Emsbach and began scraping the ice from the windshield. "The brigadier general will be out shortly. He seems to be in a vile mood. I hope the liquor calms him so we can finish this trip before dark." His breath formed clouds of steam as he toiled to clean the glass. Emsbach stepped out to help him by cleaning the side mirrors.

Heinrich Mauer staggered out of the station. "Get into the car!" he commanded. "We're going back to Germany. I'm a soldier, and it is time for me return to my duties."

The private's eyes met the major's, brows raised in disbelief. Had the whole drive been for naught? Liggett took his place behind the steering wheel. If he was disappointed about the lost profit from the contraband, he concealed it effectively. Emsbach was too stunned to react. He just stood in the snow and gazed toward the Swiss border, so near and yet so far.

The brigadier general's fierce visage dared anyone to object. "Let's go. Now!" He got into the front seat beside the driver and glared at his nephew until Dr. Emsbach wordlessly moved around to the rear and climbed into the ambulance.

The tense quiet of the next hour was broken only by the hypnotic swish of the windshield wipers. From time to time, Heinrich Mauer turned and narrowed his eagle eyes, focusing intently on his nephew's face. *This is one of his tests!* Emsbach realized with a sinking heart. He vividly recalled the tests contrived by his uncle during his youth, supposedly to build his character.

Heaven help me! Will I never be free of this man's malice?

32

AN INVOLUNTARY SHUDDER WENT THROUGH HIM AS Emsbach remembered the most difficult test his uncle had put him through. It had occurred at the end of his senior year at the academy. Emsbach remembered the ceremony marking the completion of his officer's training course as if it were happening right now. Heinrich Mauer was the main speaker at the graduation. Emsbach had been nominated for an award of distinction, and he was confident that his uncle would be pleased.

Before entering the auditorium and taking their seats, the cadets paraded in complicated clockwork formation, goose-stepping in perfect synchronization. At each boy's side sat a young German shepherd, personally raised and trained as attack dogs from puppyhood.

Emsbach had let his hand fall to the side, where he could stroke Isar's silky ears while his eyes took in the impressive sight of the entire student body in uniform. *Why do I feel out of place?* he wondered. The feeling was familiar. Introspective by nature, he chastised himself for not sharing his fellow cadets' passionate adoration of the high-ranking officers on the stage. Far from idolizing those exalted figures, the most he could summon was admiration for their patriotism and loyalty to the Fatherland.

When Colonel Mauer rose to speak, he was greeted with thunderous applause. Emsbach sensed the envious glances of his comrades and thought, *If they only knew what he is really like...* Heinrich was a charismatic speaker, and the audience was soon on its feet shouting, *"Heil Hitler! Heil Hitler!"* The man waited until complete silence reigned again, and then summoned his nephew to join the officers up on the stage.

Apprehension caused young Karl's heart to beat erratically as he complied. His German shepherd, bounded along beside him, tail wagging with excitement. Cadet Emsbach shook hands with his uncle and the other officials, and then stood at attention.

"Put your dog through its paces!" Uncle Heinrich ordered him.

This was an instruction that his nephew was delighted to obey. Isar was an unusually intelligent and devoted animal, and it carried out each command with alacrity: leaping, crawling, fetching, turning over, locating hidden arms, attacking a mock enemy and defending his master. When the demonstration was over, the panting animal resumed its position at his master's side.

Emsbach stood on the stage, enjoying the admiration of the audience—until he heard Uncle Heinrich's voice over the loudspeaker: "Soldier, put down your animal!"

There was no time to think. He had been trained to obey, and he was being commanded to kill his dog. The cadets watched with bated breath as Emsbach knelt beside the beautiful animal, put his left arm around Isar's furry neck and nuzzled him for the last time. Knowing that any hesitancy on his part would have consequences that could ruin his own life, he unsheathed his razor-sharp hunting knife with his other hand. As the devoted animal licked its master's cheek, he swiftly slit the dog's throat.

Isar was dead instantly. Cadet Emsbach's face betrayed none of the emotions that were raging inside of him. He was standing at attention before the dog had even slumped to the stage floor in a pool of blood. The crowd went wild with approval, their cheers echoing from every side. But at that moment, Emsbach was so consumed with hatred for his uncle that he heard and saw nothing.

Dismissed from the dais, the young man made his way out of the auditorium and ran blindly into the woods, where he vomited until he feared he would faint. He had passed his uncle's test, but at the price of his innocence. The cadet who returned to receive a medal in recognition for his valor was not the same boy who had mounted the stage with his dog an hour before.

More than a decade later, Emsbach sat on the narrow ambulance bench and desperately tried to divine the purpose of this latest ordeal. Had Heinrich known about Fraydl all along? Was this just a game, like a cat with a mouse?

It was many kilometers before his uncle spoke again. The sick and drunken caricature had vanished. In its place, the general radiated something malignant, made infinitely worse by his cruel smile.

"One day I will kill you. Do you know that, Karl?" Uncle Heinrich's voice was low and gentle, his penetrating eyes glued to his nephew's face.

Minutes ticked by. Feeling like an actor who has forgotten his lines, Emsbach returned his uncle's gaze impassively, grateful for the years of training that allowed him to conceal his emotions.

The tension broke when the brigadier general laughed aloud. Mauer reached backward and slapped his nephew's shoulder. "I could almost love you, Karl," he said. "One has to admire your Aryan control."

Emsbach remained motionless, waiting for whatever would happen next—but nothing did. His uncle turned his face back to the windshield, and they did not speak again until the ambulance arrived back at his home.

"Come inside the house for a drink," Emsbach invited the driver, taking his uncle's suitcase and leaving Kurt Liggett to support the brigadier general. "You deserve one."

In the kitchen he handed each of them a full tumbler of whiskey, downing his own in two gulps. After a reasonable amount of time had passed, he excused himself. "I left my medical bag in the ambulance," he said. "Make yourselves at home. I'll be right back."

Back in the car shed, he released Fraydl from the hidden compartment and temporarily transferred her and her possessions to the trunk of his Mercedes. They were both exhausted and he avoided eye contact. There would be time to talk later, assuming that he'd be able to get her safely back to the attic.

After he returned to the house and bade farewell to Private Liggett, he methodically refilled his willing uncle's glass until the man lapsed into blissful insensibility. Helping his uncle to his study, he left the drunken man snoring on the sofa and let himself out of the back door to retrieve Fraydl.

The back stairs creaked like thunder to his ears, but Uncle Heinrich did not stir. As the girl wearily climbed the makeshift ladder back up into the attic, she reassured her benefactor, "Everything is from Hashem. I have known many disappointments, but there is always hope for tomorrow."

"You still have your faith?" His voice held a bitter note. "It was a good plan. We were so close! If your G-d is controlling things, as you claim, then He chose not to save you. He sent us both back into the greatest danger."

"There is a Divine plan, whether we understand it or not." She spoke the familiar words with conviction. "We can only try to do our best. When things don't turn out the way we expect, we must accept that it is for the best and go on."

Emsbach did not answer. "I'll bring you up something to eat as soon as I can," he promised, and she closed the trapdoor behind him.

Cleopatra had taken advantage of her mistress's absence to make herself comfortable on the duvet. The girl's reappearance reminded the animal that this was not permitted. The tabby stretched lazily, squeezing her eyes shut for a few moments before gracefully bounding to the floor and rubbing against Fraydl's ankles with a purr like a Mack truck.

Fraydl stroked her feline roommate's soft fur, thinking how lonely it would be without the boys. "When there's no fish, a herring is also a fish," she whispered to Cleo, who regarded her quizzically.

Emsbach brought up a tray of food through the main door and left it on the table. Cleopatra followed him back down to the study and settled herself possessively on his lap while he filled his pipe and sat back to smoke. Turning her emerald-green eyes toward Uncle Heinrich on the damask sofa, the tabby sheathed and unsheathed her claws irritably.

"You don't like him either, do you?" Emsbach whispered with a tired smile. He stroked the soft, burnished-gold fur idly, and tried to think of a new plan to cope with the unhappy state of affairs.

33

E MSBACH KNEW HE SHOULD SLEEP, BUT THE SIGHT AND
sound of his uncle snoring on the sofa reignited a smoldering
rage that he had been suppressing for years. The brigadier general
snorted, and rolled off the couch with a thud. Grudgingly, Emsbach
dropped the kitty gently onto a cushion and went to help his uncle
up off the floor.

Uncle Heinrich did not resist as he was led upstairs to his bed.
He only gestured for another drink, which his nephew supplied.
Let him drink himself to death, he thought angrily. His own bedroom was across the hall, facing the front of the house. For a long
time he lay awake, pondering the day's events and wondering
what he could do to save the life of the young Jewish girl in his care.

Some time after midnight, he heard the screams. Fraydl's nightmares had returned. This time, Heinrich Mauer awoke with a roar.
"NO-O-O! No more! I will kill you! I killed you once, and I will kill
you a thousand times if I have to, until you leave me alone!"

Emsbach went immediately to his uncle's room, but the door
was locked. He raced through the rooms to get to the other side,
where Heinrich's bedroom connected to the utility room beside

the bathroom, but that door was barred as well. From the sound of furniture being smashed inside, he understood that the man was searching for the source of the screams that haunted him.

Emsbach hesitated. Should he run for the key to the padlock on the main attic entrance, in the hope that he could somehow block the trap door from above—or was it already too late?

Fraydl woke from her dream to a furious pounding. Someone was trying to open the trapdoor! There was a small bar of wood nailed onto the floor that she always swiveled over the edge of the door to hold it in place. Dr. Emsbach had designed this simple device to discourage Monika's curiosity, but it was now cracking loose from the violent blows rained on the door from below.

Heinrich Mauer's voice echoed in the closet underneath the entrance, stridently cursing and swearing to execute her again! Cold fingers of panic closed around Fraydl's throat. The attic was dark, but she was accustomed to the dim light from the scimitar-shaped sliver of moon peeking through the window. Her eyes searched desperately for a place to hide, even as she realized that there was not enough time. The warm blankets on the brass bed would give her away. No matter where she hid, the madman coming up the ladder was sure to find her in the end. Fraydl huddled in a corner and whispered *viduy*.

Cleopatra had returned to the attic when Dr. Emsbach locked the main entrance. The cat's response to the brigadier general's pounding was to creep along the floor and crouch beside the trapdoor, the tip of her tail flicking in a slow, ominous cadence and her cold eyes staring in predatory anticipation.

The trapdoor burst open. Cleo's small furry body tensed like a coiled spring. When the top of the arrogant Nazi's head appeared, the little cat gave a bloodcurdling yowl and launched herself at the intruder. Heinrich Mauer found himself on the receiving end of a furious feline assault as Cleopatra landed on his face with unsheathed claws, all four legs scratching simultaneously.

The attack was so fierce, and so unexpected, that Mauer lost his grip on the narrow ladder and crashed down to the floor of the closet together with the biting, scratching cat. Recovering rapidly, he ran to the chair where his holster hung. He removed the gun and aimed it at Cleopatra. For several minutes he fired at her repeatedly, but Cleo raced around the room, leaping from the dresser to the curtains, running under the bed, knocking over the commode, and even jumping on and off the brigadier general's shoulders in a dizzying trajectory of yellow fur that he could not get a bead on.

The sound of the pistol being fired was too much for Emsbach. He threw his shoulder against the locked bedroom door until it splintered open. At the sight of his uncle in pajamas, his gun aimed at some indeterminate spot on the floor, the doctor froze. The instant the door opened, Cleopatra streaked past her master and disappeared.

"What happened?" Emsbach shouted in alarm. His uncle's face was covered with bloody scratches and the bedroom was reduced to a shambles, but Uncle Heinrich offered no explanation. Instead, he shoved his nephew aside and charged into the darkened house after the cat, determined to avenge his wounded pride.

It was almost daybreak before Emsbach managed to appease his uncle with a bottle of whiskey. For all intents and purposes, the cat had vanished.

Mauer endured the application of antiseptic to his cuts with poor grace. "That damned animal must be put down," he threatened, shaking his fist. "It attacked me! You can't keep such a dangerous creature in your house!"

"*Onkel*, why didn't you go up to the attic through the main door? The cat was startled when you opened the trapdoor from the closet, and she responded according to her natural instinct. She's a good mouser. When she shows up I'll lock her in the attic again. She isn't vicious, she's just a cat."

"No, she must die. After what she did to me, she does not deserve to live."

"I'll take care of it. Here." Emsbach refilled his uncle's glass. He had no intention of harming Cleopatra. At least now there was a good excuse to move his uncle to a bedroom farther away from the closet leading to Fraydl's hiding place.

Early the next morning, Heinrich Mauer came into the kitchen for breakfast. He found his nephew trying to explain to the servants why it was necessary to perform a thorough cleaning of the upstairs bedroom.

"What happened?" Rhea asked in disbelief.

"My *onkel* had a bad dream." Emsbach tried to downplay the incident. "He was under the impression that he was being attacked."

"That's what comes from too much to drink," Beatrix sniffed — and then caught sight of the brigadier general entering the room. "*A guten morgen, Herr Kommandant!*" She curtsied. The old cook quickly set a steaming plate of sausage and eggs on the table, and he sat down to eat. She wisely refrained from asking what had happened to his face.

"You!" he addressed Otto, who was staring at his scratched features, "Move my things out of the east bedroom into the front corner room. Do it without delay. And you," he turned to Rhea, "If you or any of your housemaids sees a yellow cat in the house, I am to be informed immediately. Is that clear?"

"Yes, sir," she responded, sensing a connection between the cuts on the brigadier general's face and his bizarre request.

"Yes, sir!" echoed Monika, when his eyes moved to her. She curtsied and ran out of the room to look for Cleopatra.

From the attic, Fraydl heard the village girls chattering below as they changed the linens, mopped the floor and opened the windows to air out the room. Their lilting voices were almost like music; it had been so long since she had heard such light conversation. From the window she could see that the sun was finally out again, but it was still so cold that she shivered under the blankets.

Before noon, the sound of approaching sirens pierced the air. Fraydl's heart did a somersault. *How much more must I endure?* she wondered.

The clanging of the vehicles came closer and closer, until the faint roar of motorbikes escorting an official cavalcade could be discerned. Abruptly, the sirens stopped. In the silence that followed she heard car doors slamming, footsteps running and male voices barking orders.

34

F RAYDL STRAINED TO HEAR WHAT WAS HAPPENING IN THE room below. The village girls were discussing the unexpected visitors.

"Do you know who just came?" a rather high-pitched, girlish voice asked in a tone of awe.

"How would *you* even know?" a second voice queried.

"I was bending out the window to clean the sill, and you can see the driveway from here. I saw limousines with flags on each fender. Men in uniform got out. They looked very important!" She lowered her voice to a pitch that Fraydl could scarcely catch: "Do you think *Herr Hitler* himself has come to visit the young master?"

"Why would the führer come here?" Fraydl heard that question clearly. Just thinking about it made her light headed.

"Don't you know anything?" The first voice was offended. "You're such a simpleton that you don't even know the master's *onkel*, Brigadier General Mauer, is a member of the High Command."

"Of course I know that!" the other girl defended herself.

"Well, let's sneak downstairs and have a peek!"

When the sound of their voices grew fainter, Fraydl understood that the speakers had left the bedroom. Silence followed.

In the attic, Fraydl waited anxiously but did not hear anything unusual. Time had never seemed to pass so slowly. A few hours later, there was a commotion outside the house as the official automobiles collected their passengers. Evening came and Rhea called farewell to Bea and Otto, locking the empty house before heading down to the tram station.

The silence was eerie. Dr. Emsbach was probably at the hospital, but where was his Uncle Heinrich? Sitting alone in the attic, Fraydl thought of Chaim and Yanky. She was grateful that they had not been here to witness the brigadier general's aggression. This was probably bedtime in the orphanage. She imagined a dormitory full of little boys, and prayed that her nephews would remember to recite their prayers before going to sleep for the night.

Cleopatra patrolled the attic, unhindered by the darkness. Satisfied that all was in order, she returned to her mistress and rubbed her furry side against the girl's ankles before curling up to sleep. Fraydl pulled the duvet up to her chin and passed the time watching the patterns splashed across the ceiling by the occasional headlights that passed through the alley. The cloud cover was breaking up in a restless sky, giving the impression that the moon was playing hide-and-seek.

After midnight, she heard a knock on the closet door below. This was Dr. Emsbach's way of summoning her. "Come to my study," he called softly. "You are surely starving. Your dinner is warm."

Fraydl climbed carefully down the ladder, wondering where Uncle Heinrich was. She knew that Dr. Emsbach would not risk bringing her out of the attic unless the brigadier general was out of the house. It was a relief to be able to move about normally.

"I have news," Emsbach told her after she'd washed her hands. While she ate, he revealed the sequence of events that had taken place earlier in the day. "My *onkel* had visitors: very important, high-ranking people. You were in the same house with Reichsmarschall Goering, Deputy Führer Hess and SS-Obersturmbannführer Eichmann."

Fraydl's stomach lurched. Her appetite fled and she toyed with the food as he continued speaking

"Those are my *onkel's* colleagues. Something secretive has been going on at the military base near the hospital, and *Onkel* Heinrich was summoned here to deal with it. Because of the urgency of the matter, when his health began to fail and he was hospitalized the mission was given to another officer.

"The whole High Command came today to discuss the results of their investigation. It has been discovered that a cadre of senior officers wish to sue for peace immediately. They believe that the war is lost, and they want to promote a transition to an orderly civilian government in order to enhance recovery after an armistice.

"My *onkel* and his supporters have embraced the opposite position. They demand that every soldier fight to the death, no matter how many lives are lost or how much damage is caused. They want Germany to go down in a blaze of glory as an everlasting lesson to our enemies. The Nazi bigwigs came here today with the intention of convincing my uncle to return to duty in spite of his medical condition.

"Obviously, the war situation is deteriorating. The German Army has its back against the wall on every front, and their ability to function is compromised by the irrational demands being placed on them by Hitler. The leadership of the hawk faction is counting on *Onkel* Heinrich to infuse morale and turn things around. The peace camp fears the brigadier general greatly — and rightly so."

"Now that he has returned to duty, what can he do?"

"Even if his hands are tied by the reality on the ground, he will never admit defeat. Anyone he imagines is a traitor, he will destroy. The remainder of the High Command will be bullied into making a last stand for the honor and dignity of the Fatherland. This desperate course means that the conclusion is foregone. Do you understand? It means that the war is ending!"

"How much longer?" Fraydl's voice choked with emotion. It had been so long. Could it really be almost over?

"A few weeks or a few months; it's impossible to predict. Much depends on whether the Allies see through the smokescreens that will be set up to protect areas of special interest."

"If it is inevitable, what is the point of dragging things out?" Fraydl didn't understand the contradiction.

"Adolph Hitler is not a soldier. He wears a *Wehrmacht* uniform and puts on airs, but he does not have a military mind. Even though I was present, the generals discussed quite frankly how the führer's political goals have been allowed to override the needs of the army. Yesterday, Hitler incredibly ordered the army to open an all-out offensive on the Western front against the Allied troops. The Chief of Staff, General Alfred Jodl, put up a fierce fight, but the führer refuses logic if it contradicts his wishes. You don't have to be a military genius to understand that moving soldiers to the west leaves our Eastern front vulnerable to the Russians."

Fraydl ate mechanically, hardly tasting the food on her plate. She listened politely to Dr. Emsbach's lectures on military strategies and battle plans, but his words did not seem real. Perhaps, after she was reunited with her family and they had picked up the pieces of their lives, she would have the patience to indulge in questions about the cause of the war and the significance of how it had ended. Right now, the only thing that mattered to Fraydl was survival. How much longer would she have to hide and live in fear?

Unaware of her lack of interest, the doctor continued pacing the room and analyzing recent events for her benefit. "You remember that our ally, Mussolini, was captured and hung by Italian partisans when he tried to flee Italy for Switzerland? Since then, the upper echelons in the military have been in total disarray. The generals told my uncle that Hitler is holed up somewhere in Berlin. There is no agreement about the next step. This has to be the end, *Fraulein*! It's impossible that it will continue much longer."

"I'm glad your uncle is gone, but I don't understand what the generals hope to accomplish. How could the brigadier general return to his duties if he knows the situation is hopeless—especially since he is not in good health?"

Emsbach stopped midstride to stare at her. "You don't understand the German mentality," he said, slightly exasperated. "When the people give their hearts and souls to a leader, they will follow him to the death. There is no alternative for a true German."

"So your uncle left with them?"

"*Ja.*" The doctor sat down and filled his pipe. "*Onkel* Heinrich put on his dress uniform, flaunting all his medals and ribbons as if he were going on parade. His orderly came and packed the rest of my uncle's belongings and took them away. I can hardly believe he is gone." He glanced toward the door as if expecting the truculent old soldier to reappear.

"I hope he doesn't return," Fraydl murmured.

"We share that wish," Emsbach said flatly, "but I expect that he will."

"Why do you think so?"

He sighed. "His last words to me as he went out the door were. 'We have some unfinished business, you and I…'"

35

F RAYDL STOOD UP AND COLLECTED HER EMPTY DISHES. Before she went to the kitchen to wash them and put them away, she paused to ask, "What did he mean? What unfinished business?"

"Who knows? I am convinced that my *onkel* is insane. Maybe the whole world has gone mad. I have decided that after the war ends I will sell this property and liquidate my assets. I want to leave Germany and put as much distance as possible between myself and my uncle and a lot of painful memories."

"Where will you go?"

"I would like to discuss that with you."

Fraydl regarded Dr. Emsbach quizzically. What difference did it make to him what she thought? As fine a man as the doctor was, they would be parting ways after the war was over.

Fraydl finished cleaning up in no time. Without Chaim and Yanky, there wasn't very much work involved. She returned to the study to say good night.

Emsbach was waiting for her expectantly. "Please sit down," he requested.

She wanted to refuse, but thought better of it. Fraydl felt uncomfortable alone in the house with him. She missed her nephews very much. "Will you visit the boys in the orphanage soon?" she asked.

"Perhaps."

Fraydl didn't understand why Dr. Emsbach had asked her to stay. He appeared preoccupied with his own thoughts as he sat at his desk and drew on his pipe.

"Were Goering and Hess and Eichmann really in the house?" The question was meant to remind him that she was still there. She wanted to hear what he had to say and then go back to her attic.

"They've been here before."

"While we were here?" Her eyes widened apprehensively.

"No. Long ago, when I was still a boy. My mother entertained a wide circle of guests. Rhea says that Mutter's parties were considered a status symbol and the most important people vied for invitations. She mingled with diplomats, society matrons, royalty, foreigners, politicians, *Wehrmacht* and *Luftwaft* officers, actors and movie producers, cabaret stars — you name it."

"Do you remember?"

"Of course," he smiled. "From the age of 6, I had to bring my clarinet and play so that everyone would know what a talented son my mother had. Usually, Mutter accompanied me on the piano, which she played very well. She preferred German composers like Bach and Brahms, and her guests were always enthusiastic."

He put his hand to his cheek. "Her guests used to pinch my cheeks until I cried out. I hated when they did that, and my face hurt long afterward, but there were often very interesting conversations if I didn't get caught eavesdropping."

"Do you still play the clarinet?"

"Sometimes. It soothes me. My taste has changed, though. I like modern jazz better than classical music. You know, like *Rhapsody in Blue*?"

She shook her head. "I only know Jewish music," she explained.

"The composer of *Rhapsody in Blue* is Jewish," he told her. "Maybe that makes it Jewish music?"

"I don't think so," she smiled.

Cleopatra sauntered nonchalantly into the room. Emsbach reached down and stroked her back as the cat rubbed lazily against his ankle, purring loudly.

"The tabby that took on the Third Reich," he laughed.

"It was a miracle," Fraydl said seriously. "I can't bear to think of what might have happened. Who would have thought she'd do what she did? She saved my life!"

"And mine," Emsbach added gravely.

"Yes, her actions saved your life as well," Fraydl agreed. Over the course of her young life, she had seen other miracles in which Hashem used ordinary means to bring about extraordinary results. But Cleopatra was decidedly among the most amazing of them all.

Accepting their admiration as her due, the cat settled down on the carpet, tucked both paws under her breast and stared into the distance, looking for all the world like the Egyptian Sphinx.

Fraydl yawned.

"Forgive me. You are still tired from the trip. I am selfish to keep you up."

She looked at him gratefully. "Yes, I suppose I am. Good night, then. Thank you for everything."

She returned to the attic alone. Emsbach remained sitting at his desk, brooding. *Why weren't you forthright?* He challenged himself. *What are you waiting for?*

Having no answer, he promised himself, *Tomorrow. I will speak to her then.*

As a distraction, he uncovered the radio that was locked in a hidden compartment in his desk. At first there was only static, but he manipulated the knobs patiently until the radio tuned in to the frequency of the BBC.

The main news story was the sudden death of the president of the United States, Franklin Delano Roosevelt. Emsbach listened to the commentator's elegy with concern. *How will this affect the war?* He wondered.

There was a detailed report on Roosevelt's successor, now President Harry Truman, and then an update of Allied movements in the war. "The Western Allies have crossed the Rhine River in the strategically important Ruhr region," the announcer intoned. "A large number of German troops are reported to be surrounded in Western Germany. Meanwhile, Soviet troops reached the outskirts of Vienna tonight. After initial losses, the Allies have recovered and are advancing in Italy. They are expected to cross into Western Germany within days."

Emsbach turned off the radio and replaced it in its hiding place. *The war is nearly over. So much destruction and death...for what? How many widows and orphans and cripples will spend the rest of their lives in wretchedness?* He felt very sad. *Life as I have known it is gone forever.*

Occasionally drawing deeply on his pipe, he remained sunk in his thoughts for some time. *What will rise from the ashes of this war?* If only mankind would learn a lesson from the devastation, perhaps a better world could be built. It was a solemn thought.

Feeling chilled, he noticed that the fire in the grate was burned down to embers. He stirred the ashes to extinguish it completely, then turned off the desk lamp and went to bed.

36

IN THE HOSPITAL CAFETERIA, THE DINERS WERE SUBDUED.

"Have you heard the rumors?" Konrad Winkelmann's appetite was clearly affected by the atmosphere. He stared at his pickled cabbage stew without interest.

"About Commander Judl?" Emsbach asked, mopping up the last of his gravy with a piece of bread.

Winkelmann nodded glumly.

"Do you have any idea what's happening on the Eastern front?" Emsbach knew that his fellow surgeon's brother was stationed on the border.

Winkelmann rubbed his aching temples with his fingertips. "*Ja.* It's not good, Emsbach. It's not good."

Having listened to the BBC before leaving the house that afternoon, Emsbach knew that Red Army troops were pouring into East Prussia. Soon they would close in on Berlin. As anxious as he was for the war to end, the speed with which events were unfolding was alarming. He was disconcerted to realize that he feared a post-war world.

The room fell silent as the intercom crackled to life. "All medical personnel, report to the main auditorium immediately. I repeat: all medical personnel, report to the main auditorium immediately."

"What's this about?" Winkelmann muttered anxiously.

"We'll know soon enough." Emsbach hastened to join the other doctors exiting the cafeteria.

General Erwin Schaefer briefly addressed the men assembled in the lecture theater. "It is my duty to inform you of assignment changes, effective from this moment." The man's monotone voice contrasted with the powerful message he was conveying. "The rosters are posted on the main bulletin board. Buses transporting officers east will be boarded at 21:00 hours. Units heading west are to depart from the train station at 23:00 hours. Medical personnel assigned to continue their work in the hospital are to make arrangements to remain at their posts until further notice. Dismissed!"

The sound of chairs scraping the floor was deafening. Emsbach joined the line of officers walking briskly toward the notice board. Three single-spaced typed lists were posted. Each man searched for his name with an unspoken prayer that he would not be traveling tonight.

Konrad Winkelmann gasped in dismay. He turned to his colleagues with a wan smile. "I always wanted to see Budapest," he said bravely. "It's supposed to be one of the most beautiful cities in the world."

Emsbach gave his friend's shoulder a supportive squeeze, simultaneously searching for his own orders. He felt a measure of relief when he saw that he was not on the same list as Winkelmann. Their eyes met momentarily, and then they parted as his fellow surgeon hurried away to collect his belongings.

Lothar Engelhardt smiled broadly. "Too bad Winkelmann is leaving," he told Dr. Emsbach. "At least you're staying to keep me company."

Emsbach concealed his revulsion for the orthopedic surgeon. Relieved that he was assigned to remain in his surgery, he saw that more than half the men were transferred out.

General Schaefer stood stiffly behind the doctors at the bulletin board. His face was expressionless, but Emsbach knew the man as an excellent physician who cared about his staff.

He saluted. "May I have a word with you, sir?"

"Of course, Major Emsbach. Do you have a question about your assignment?"

"No, sir. I have a request, sir. I need time to close my house and make arrangements for my dependents."

"Dependents, Emsbach? Exactly whom are you referring to?" The general's pale-blue eyes bored into the surgeon.

"My servants, sir. They are quite elderly and I would like to move them out of the city to a safer location."

General Schaefer nodded brusquely. "Very well. Return to your post by noon tomorrow."

"Thank you, sir." Emsbach saluted and left the hospital grounds. A friend of the senior Emsbachs, the general had been a frequent guest at his mother's parties and was personally acquainted with the household. The commanding officer understood that the surgeon would be better able to perform his duties if his mind was at rest about his longtime servants.

Emsbach stopped by the orphanage on his way home. The nun who answered the door bowed respectfully and led him to Father Matthew. When they were alone, the doctor inquired, "How are the children?"

The priest smiled. "Do you miss them?"

Accustomed to hiding his feelings, Emsbach shrugged. "I feel responsible for them."

"They are fitting in well. There are no particular problems."

"What do you do about the air raids?"

"The children sleep in the shelter." The priest sighed. "Will it get worse, major?"

"I'm afraid so, father. It would be better if the orphanage relocated to a more rural district."

"I have considered that possibility," Father Matthew agreed, his expression somber. "I am in contact with my superiors about it."

"Good." Emsbach shook hands with the priest and left. An hour later, he was at the house.

While Fraydl took her dinner in his study, Emsbach packed the belongings he would need over the next few weeks. By the time he returned downstairs she had finished.

"Tonight is my last night home for a while," he told her gravely. "I've been ordered to stay at the hospital until further notice."

"Did something happen?"

"It's a matter of reorganization. Some of the doctors have been transferred, and we are critically short of staff."

"How long?"

"Conceivably until the end of the war."

"Is it close?"

"Let us hope so. Meanwhile, I shall have Beatrix and Otto moved to the country. Monika will accompany them and be responsible for their welfare. Rhea informed me that her daughter's husband has been reported missing in action. It will be convenient for her to be released from her duties here in order to be with her daughter and help her at this time."

"Everyone is leaving, then?"

"Hans will be in the carriage house. I need him to care for the grounds and guard the property... but you will be alone in the house. As long as the blackout curtains are drawn, you may move about freely. For your safety, I ask that you go down to the cellar during the air raids. There is enough food in the pantry for a few weeks.

"When the war ends, it is likely that there will be anarchy in the streets for a prolonged period. Under no circumstances are you to leave the house before I return. Have you any questions?"

Fraydl returned to the attic in a state of repressed excitement. She looked out the small window at the moonlit, snow-covered lawn and clasped her hands together tightly. "Thank You, Hashem," she breathed the words into the cold night. "Please bring the *yeshuah* soon!"

Emsbach stayed up another hour, packing his files and arranging his papers. *I must speak with her,* he thought. *But now is not the time. Now I must serve the Fatherland until the bitter end of this terrible war.*

37

THE NEXT WEEKS PASSED IN A BLUR. BUDAPEST FELL. INSIDE Germany, troops were carrying out an impetuous scorched-earth policy, destroying crops and desperately needed resources. There were air raids every night, with the vibrations of hundreds of enemy propellers heralding earth-shaking explosions. Although many planes were shot down by Nazi anti-aircraft, eventually the defenders were overwhelmed by the sheer number of bombers overhead.

The first signs of spring appeared, although Emsbach had little occasion to notice. He was functioning with nearly no sleep, snatching short naps on a cot between surgeries when he could. Groggy with exhaustion, he thought of the Children's Home and hoped that Father Matthew had managed to spirit away the orphans before the situation deteriorated. It gave him a measure of tranquility to recall the three Jewish children he had rescued. Soon they would all begin new lives.

Back in the empty house, each time the sirens wailed Fraydl descended into the cellar accompanied by Cleopatra. In the depths of the underground storeroom she prayed that Germany would soon suffer total defeat. She did not mind the solitude, but she missed her nephews. As the attacks occurred more frequently, it became expedient to spend the entire night in the shelter rather than race up and down the stairs.

Waiting for the all-clear one night, Fraydl was shocked to hear the creak of the cellar door above her. Someone was coming down the stairs! Silhouetted against the weak light of the single lightbulb, she made out a Nazi uniform. But before she could react, he called out, "Don't be alarmed. It's only me!" She recognized the voice of Dr. Emsbach.

A moment later, the electricity shorted as the earth shook under the impact of repeated explosions. Emsbach lit a kerosene lantern to dispel the gloom and they waited together. Sooner than expected, the relentless bombing was replaced by silence and then the all-clear. Carrying the lamp, he led the way back up to the main portion of the house.

Shock waves had shattered some windowpanes, and shards of glass were sprayed across the kitchen floor. "They've attacked the refineries," Emsbach commented, taking a broom and dustpan to clean up the mess.

The curtains billowed like wraiths in the cold wind until Fraydl stuffed rags into the gaping holes. She peered out into the darkness, listening to the eerie wail of distant fire engines. To the west, the sky glowed crimson from burning buildings. Fraydl's nose crinkled at the faint, acrid scent of smoke. It stung her eyes and nostrils. An unexpected late snowfall descended steadily, as if it wished to cover the charred signs of destruction on the earth as quickly as possible.

"The planes stopped bombing because of the weather," Emsbach reasoned. "The navigators can't see through the cloud cover. It's really late in the season for such a heavy snowstorm. The trees have budded already, but now they will freeze." He sat at the table and rested his head in his hands.

"Would you like something to eat?" she asked.

He looked up with a questioning expression. "I baked bread this morning," she told him. "There are a few more jars of Beatrix's plum jam, and I can put up some potatoes if you're hungry."

Emsbach shook his head. "I just need sleep, that's all."

"When do you have to return to the hospital?" She filled the kettle and put it on the gas stove to boil water for tea.

He smiled at the irony. "The hospital has been evacuated. The mayhem there is indescribable. Ambulatory patients were released last week when the main building suffered a direct hit. Bedridden patients are still being transferred to other locations. Early this morning, General Schaefer and some of the other high-ranking officers abandoned the city. Discipline broke down to the point where we were essentially left to fend for ourselves. So I came home."

The teapot whistled. Fraydl placed tea leaves into two mugs and steeped them in boiling water. "There's no more sugar," she said regretfully, "but drinking something hot will make you feel warmer."

Emsbach sipped the hot tea appreciatively. "*Danke schön*," he told her. "I had to walk home from the hospital. There's no more petrol for the Mercedes. I left hours ago, but the streets are blocked by mountains of debris and I had to make countless detours." He shook his head. "This was once such a beautiful city. It's impossible to believe what has happened to it."

Fraydl remained silent. *What has happened to my beautiful people?* she thought to herself in anguish.

Emsbach seemed to read her mind. "Fraydl," he began, "I must speak with you about your future. The end of the war is here."

She lifted her eyes, surprised that he had used her given name instead of using "*Fraulein*" as he usually did. "Soon I will return home and wait for my family," she said, a tiny ray of hope shimmering in her eyes. "I'll take my nephews to my parents' house first; because that is the place where everyone will come. Then we'll all go to Palestine."

He shook his head. "It isn't that simple," he told her gently. "*Fraulein*, Europe is *Judenrein*. There are no more Jews left alive. They have all been murdered by the Nazis... Every last one."

Her dark-brown eyes stared at him without comprehending. "Of course not," she said in a flat voice. "How can you say that?" But even as she said the words, she intuitively knew that he was speaking the truth. No one could have survived the past seven years.

Emsbach's expression confirmed that his words were accurate, but her heart refused to accept them. "No!" she cried, standing up so abruptly that the tea in her cup sloshed over into the saucer. "No!" Her eyes scanned the kitchen blindly, and her hands shook. "No!" she whispered. "No, no, no." She sat back down on the bench, bowed her head and buried her face in her hands.

"I'm sorry. So very, very sorry." The grief in his voice was real. "*Fraulein*, listen to me. I knew all along what was happening, but I did not want to overwhelm you. I wanted to protect you and the boys from this knowledge, so I kept it from you. The world you know is gone forever. We must speak about the future."

Fraydl needed time to grieve, but Emsbach couldn't wait any longer to pour out his thoughts. At first she did not really listen to what he was saying, until she suddenly realized that she must pay strict attention.

"I have thought the situation over since the new year," he was saying, "and I came to the conclusion that we must not separate after the war. You and the boys will accompany me to the United States as soon as I can arrange papers for the three of you and apply for passports."

He scrutinized her pale face. "To avoid complications, we must formally adopt your nephews," he continued. "The whole procedure may take a few months; therefore I believe it is important that we be married as soon as possible. Even in these chaotic days, it is possible to find a judge willing to perform this service. We shall continue living here until our visa applications are accepted."

Fraydl tried to grasp what she was hearing. "Marry you?" she murmured in confusion. "*Herr Doktor*, I cannot marry you."

"I realize that it must be a civil ceremony," he replied, "but we cannot live together otherwise and you have no place else to go. It will not be possible to get United States visas as individuals, but as a family I believe it can be accomplished fairly quickly."

Fraydl stared at her benefactor in horror.

38

I T HAD NEVER OCCURRED TO EMSBACH THAT THE GIRL MIGHT question his plans. His awareness of the fate of the Jewish people in the lands under German occupation had convinced him that there was no future for a Jew in Europe. The Hebrew nation was ultimately following the same law of nature that relegated their contemporary nations, the Egyptians, Persians, Greeks and Romans, to history books. Even if a few individuals survived, no nation could recover from such total devastation.

Emsbach had corresponded with assimilated Jewish medical professionals living in the United States, and his impression was that religious and racial origins meant nothing in the new world. The best course for Fraydl and her nephews would be to relocate to an entirely different culture where their Jewish ancestry could be hidden. As citizens of a free country with endless opportunities, they and their descendants would lead satisfactory and fulfilling lives.

When the girl did not respond, he expounded further on his ideas. "I will buy a few acres in a rural state, perhaps South Carolina or Georgia," he mused. "People there have few preconceptions; for them the last war ended 100 years ago. Life is graceful and decent in the American South. *Fraulein,* you and the children can put the past with all its cruelties behind you forever. Chaim and Yanky will have a normal childhood like every other boy, attending school and playing with their friends. They will grow up to be proud and fearless men, doctors or lawyers, able to forget the terror that has shadowed their lives since birth."

Tears shimmered in Fraydl's eyes and her lower lip quivered in spite of her efforts to control it. Emsbach sighed. All things considered, she would need time to let go of the past. Until now, he had carefully avoided discussing the Nazi extermination plan and its repercussions. It had obviously come as a great shock to her.

The girl was so innocent, so sure that she would return home and be reunited with those members of her family who had been taken away to work camps. He frowned. It was regrettable that he had to be the one to destroy her illusions, but as long as she clung to them they would prevent her from seeing reality. Emsbach had grown very fond of her and the children, and felt confident that continuing their lives together was in the best interests of each of them.

He stood up and carried their mugs to the sink, leaving the girl by herself at the table. "We shall continue this discussion in the morning," he said, raising his voice over the sound of running water as he rinsed the cups and saucers. "It is understandable that you need time to absorb the facts before we make our plans more definite. I wish you a good night."

The wooden steps creaked as the doctor went up the back stairs. Left alone in the dark kitchen, Fraydl replayed their discussion in her mind. Her head spun with thoughts that made no sense. The war was essentially over—but so was the world she had grown up in. Contrary to Dr. Emsbach's assumption, she had found a cruel, new grip on reality. She realized that her family was gone forever. To stay in Germany was out of the question. The land was bathed in the blood of her martyred people. But at only 18 years old and alone in the world, how could she rebuild her life and raise her young nephews?

Fraydl tossed her head as if she could erase Dr. Emsbach's

startling proposal of marriage. Why did he have to introduce such a complication into a relationship that had always been proper and reserved? As kind, intelligent and responsible as the German was, they were from different and unbridgeable worlds. Fraydl leaned her face on her hands, wracking her mind to think of how to phrase her refusal in such a way that her benefactor would accept it without offense. Unfortunately, the more she thought about it, the more inadequate her efforts.

"Of course you will understand," she could try to express herself tactfully, "that marriage is the furthest thing from my mind because of the upheavals in my life at this particular time." *No, he will easily counter it with common sense.*

"You have given us so much already. We can never repay you for your kindness. I do not deserve such an honor as you suggest." *No, that sounds hypocritical. He will see right through it.*

"I am only beginning to put myself back together. It is impossible to make such a crucial commitment before I have achieved stability in my personal life." That didn't sound logical; Dr. Emsbach was offering her security, and her rejection could only come across as ingratitude after all he had done for them.

Fraydl was exhausted. *I will think about this tomorrow*, she thought wearily.

Tomorrow may be too late, an inner voice warned. *Dr. Emsbach is a man of action. Once he makes a decision, he follows through. You must not delay. Be honest, and make it clear that you can never be his wife!*

For just a moment, Fraydl allowed herself to envisage the safe and comfortable future her benefactor had described. She imagined a home of her own, far from this land of terror. Karl Emsbach would be a considerate and supportive husband. They would live in a beautiful house with respectful servants, cultivate friendships with refined and cultured people, and live a contented life with their attractive and obedient children. What would it be like to walk down a city street in the middle of the day without fear? To have a caring and intelligent husband to turn to whenever she had questions or felt overwhelmed by events…

She woke with a start. The kitchen was dark and the icebox dripped. She stood, rubbed her aching neck and straightened her shoulders before quietly feeling her way to the back stairs and up to the second floor, step-by-step.

A sense of dread accompanied her. Fraydl feared Dr. Emsbach's reaction when she told him that she would not be his wife. If he turned her out of the house, where would she go? She had no idea how she would ever find Chaim and Yanky again, and she had counted on having her benefactor's advice and support to regain possession of the family property in Austria.

It was cold. Pausing beside a window, she opened the curtain a hairsbreadth in order to look out into the yard. Snow was falling steadily, blown almost sideways by the capricious wind. She shivered and let the curtain fall back in place.

She noticed a light shining from beneath Dr. Emsbach's door. The fact that he was still awake disturbed her. Now that he had spoken of marriage, was she still permitted to remain in his house until the war ended and it was safe to leave?

She climbed the ladder up to the attic and sat down, feeling restless and wide awake despite her tiredness. For a few moments there was a break in the clouds, and Fraydl stared down at her quilt as the moonlight slid slowly across like the tide.

An hour later, her decision was made. With hands clumsy in the frigid air, she dressed herself in layers, sweater upon sweater, skirt over skirt, and several pairs of long stockings. Finally, Fraydl covered her head with a woolen scarf and stuffed herself into a coat, forcing as many of the buttons into their buttonholes as she could.

Her final act before leaving the attic was to pull the chest with her family's silver out from under the brass bed where it was kept. One by one, she lifted the objects to her lips and kissed their cold smooth surfaces. "I'll come back for you one day," she promised. Then the box was firmly closed and replaced unobtrusively in its corner under the bed.

Fraydl climbed awkwardly up on a chair and tugged at the window sash. Nothing happened. She strained with all her might, pushing and pulling until she nearly tumbled from her perch, before the wooden frame burst open with a mighty creak. Panting, she allowed the cold wind to caress her fevered face for a minute. The windblown snowflakes felt like cold tears on her cheeks. Not daring to look down, she turned her head to study the silhouette of the old walnut tree that towered higher than the roof, its branches spreading close to the house.

With one last look at the room that had sheltered her for so long, she turned and clambered gracelessly up onto the sill.

39

CLEOPATRA HISSED IN ALARM.

"Shh!" Fraydl whispered. "Go back to sleep, Cleo."

Not heeding her, the cat leaped up onto the windowsill beside her and pressed against the girl's cheek.

"Get down, Cleo!" Fraydl whispered fiercely, but the tabby only pressed closer and mewed. The soft fur tickled her nose and hindered her breathing. "Stop it, Cleo!" She shook her head sharply to dislodge the feline, and then edged further out the window, feet first, until the tips of her toes made contact with a narrow shelf.

Slowly and gingerly, Fraydl lowered herself down onto a ledge. Leaving the agitated cat on the windowsill, she began sliding, inch by inch, toward the nearest tree branch, clinging to the overhead eave for balance. At the end of the ledge, she cautiously extended one leg toward the tree—but felt only air.

Breathless from the effort, she shuffled another step and stretched her foot out until it rested firmly on the closest bough. Grateful for the pale moonlight to guide her, she leaned forward and grabbed hold of the last roof shingle, swinging out her other leg.

When planning her escape, Fraydl had not taken into consideration that the tree's limbs would be covered with a thin film of ice. Immediately upon transferring her whole weight from the ledge to the tree, both feet slipped out from under her and she lost control. There was nothing to break her fall but the frozen limbs of the tree beneath her perch. Grabbing desperately at the brittle branches, she managed to slow her freefall but not to halt it. Ricocheting from limb to limb, she plummeted helplessly down from a great height.

Pacing restlessly in his room at the other end of the house, Emsbach thought he heard a drawn-out scream in the night. Immediately he headed for the attic, assuming that Fraydl's nightmares were the source of the sound. In the back of his mind he noticed that the dogs guarding the grounds were barking hysterically, and wondered if there was a trespasser outside. Throwing the padlock aside, he shoved open the door and made his way between the draped furniture and stacks of cartons toward the other end of the attic.

The sight of the empty bed and an open window greeted him. Initially, he failed to grasp their significance. Poor Cleopatra was cowering on the windowsill, meowing and scratching at the wooden frame. It was only when he reached over to pull the cat back inside that Emsbach realized with horror what must have taken place. He dropped Cleo to the floor and thrust his head out the window. In the faint moonlight, it was just possible to make out a dark motionless shape lying in the snow beneath the tree, encircled by howling hounds.

The doctor flew down the stairs, his feet hardly touching them as he raced out of the door and around to the backyard. "Get back!" he yelled fiercely at the barking dogs, shoving them away from the prostrate form. The animals made way for him reluctantly, standing at attention a little distance away.

He yanked the scarf away from Fraydl's neck and searched for her jugular vein. The rhythmic pulsing of life left him dizzy with relief. "*G-tt zu danken*, she is alive," he murmured, rocking back on his heels.

The girl's eyes fluttered briefly open and then closed again. To determine her degree of alertness, he pinched her shoulder painfully. Fraydl groaned and resisted weakly. "*Madchen*, wake up! You must tell me where it hurts." His doctor's voice was calm and professional, far calmer than his racing heart. "I dare not move you before your injuries are evaluated."

It took a few seconds for Fraydl to regain full consciousness. She looked up at her rescuer and whispered brokenly, "Forgive me, *Herr Doktor*, but I had to do it."

That obviously didn't make sense. Perhaps she had a concussion. Ignoring the possibility for the time being, he ordered, "Tell me where it hurts. Does this hurt? Can you move?"

Fraydl obediently twisted her head from right to left, and flexed each aching arm. But when she tried to move her legs, red-hot pain surged up from her feet and she gasped, "I can't! They hurt so much… I can't move them."

Fortunately, her thick layers of clothing, as well as the snowdrifts on the ground beneath the tree, had cushioned her fall and protected the girl from a more serious injury. Emsbach straightened up and turned to the hounds. He grabbed their collars and led them to the shed where they would be confined until Fraydl was safely inside. Returning to the house, he found a blanket and some rope and brought them back outside. It took only a few minutes to fashion something between a hammock and a stretcher. Fraydl managed to wriggle onto it without using her injured feet, and he dragged it over the snow like a sled.

Inside his examination room, the doctor lit a lamp and cut away her wet and torn woolen socks as gently as he could, exposing grotesquely swollen and discolored ankles. It would unquestionably have been better to rule out fractures with an X-ray, but since this was unfeasible he could only treat her severely sprained ankles and follow her vital signs to be sure there was no internal injury. With her feet securely wrapped in long bandages and resting on a basin of snow, Fraydl was instructed to keep them elevated to alleviate swelling.

After seeing that she was as comfortable as possible, Emsbach put on a warm coat and went outside with a broom to erase as much evidence of the fall as he could. The unseasonable storm had not abated, and the wind had already half-filled the signs left behind. Hopefully Hans would not notice anything suspicious when he made his rounds tomorrow.

Emsbach released the dogs from their captivity, rewarding them with biscuits for their alertness. Back in the kitchen, he mopped up the wet floor where melted snow had become puddles and hung up the rag to dry. Only when order had been completely restored did the doctor allow himself to demand an explanation.

A world of hurt and anger was concentrated in one word: "Why?"

Fraydl met his stern gaze briefly, and then turned her eyes away. "I was afraid," she admitted softly.

"Afraid? Of what? Of whom?"

"Of you."

His expression was baffled. "Afraid of *me*? Have I ever given you reason to feel threatened? Have I ever harmed you in any way?"

She shook her head, feeling ashamed and guilty about her misguided adventure. "I was afraid that you would not accept my refusal to marry you."

Her words were met with silence. Finally he responded in a flat voice, "It seems to me that you really have no choice."

His matter-of-fact response stunned her. "But I do," she replied. "With all due respect and also gratitude for all you have done, I can never be your wife, *Herr Doktor*. It is out of the question for a Jew to marry a gentile."

"You will reconsider," he repeated calmly. "It is in your best interest."

She closed her eyes, wishing it was possible to escape the throbbing pain in her ankles. "Never," she whispered. "I cannot betray my parents or my people. It is impossible."

"I see." His face was expressionless despite the growing anger seething inside. "This is your final decision?"

"Yes," she whispered weakly, praying that he would accept it— and her all-pervasive, all-important identity as a Jew.

"You should know by now that I would respect your personal wishes, even though I do not agree with you."

Fraydl looked at him, searching for some outward sign that he understood her position. This time, however, the doctor looked away, avoiding her scrutiny.

"I never wanted to hurt you," she said gently.

He stiffened, but said nothing.

"Forgive me. I was afraid you would not understand."

When he turned to her, his eyes were like blue fire. "I would never force my will on another person," he stated. "It is not my nature to do so."

"I should have known," she admitted.

The tension between them was palpable. Fraydl felt that the German was holding something back, and an intensifying sensation of dread competed with the agony of her cuts and bruises.

"I am sorry that you do not grasp the danger you are putting yourself into, but it is your future," he continued. "I will arrange for you to be cared for until your health returns. As for Chaim and Yanky, you need have no worry. They are orphans and must have a guardian. I shall adopt them and take them with me to America. It is unlikely that the woman I eventually marry will care for them as dearly as their own aunt, but I promise to look out for their welfare and raise them, to the best of my ability, as my own sons."

40

Fraydl's eyes widened and tendrils of panic fluttered in her chest. "I could never agree to that," she declared. "Chaim and Yanky must stay with me!"

"The choice is yours."

She took a deep breath, gathering what remained of her strength to argue for the boys' lives. "For the same reason that I cannot marry you, my nephews cannot be your sons. I have already explained this to the best of my ability, and I am in too much physical discomfort at the moment to repeat it.

"*Herr Doktor*, you are an exceptional human being. I truly admire you and wish you all the good in the world. But a Jewish child has a soul that requires spiritual guidance even more than physical sustenance. It would be irrational to substitute a comfortable life in this world for the eternal rewards that a Jew can earn by learning Torah and observing the commandments."

"Your nation has been rewarded with Adolph Hitler." Emsbach's voice was bitter. "I cannot undo the war, but I *can* give Yanky and Chaim — and myself — a better life. I envisioned your place together with us, but you are mature enough to refuse my offer, if you so desire. The boys are still young children. As an informed adult, I accept responsibility for judging what is best for them. My decision is final and there is no further room for discussion."

Emsbach walked briskly over to the medicine cabinet and chose a narcotic analgesic. Ignoring her protests, he insisted that Fraydl swallow the medication and watched until it took effect. When her head nodded, he moved her to the couch in his study and covered her with an afghan for warmth. She stirred drowsily, but did not awaken.

Despite his exhaustion, his thoughts raced without pause. What earthly difference did it make if they were from different backgrounds? In his opinion, their similar outlook on essential matters was sufficient foundation to build a successful marriage. Absently, he rubbed his temples to ease the tension. Fraydl was an intelligent young woman, but incredibly stubborn. Tomorrow he would try to convince her, while avoiding confrontation. If he could be more patient, she would come around to his point of view. Setting a tray with food and water within her reach, he left the study and went up to his room for a few hours of sleep before daylight.

Under the influence of the drug he had prescribed for her, Fraydl was still sleeping deeply when he checked on her the next morning. Her breathing was regular and her temperature was not elevated. He pulled back the curtains and studied the weather outside. Yesterday's storm had passed and the sun was shining in a dazzling turquoise sky. He decided to go out for a walk to clear his mind.

The melting snow created rivulets of mud, and his boots squelched as he crossed the backyard. There was a slight indentation under the walnut tree where Fraydl had fallen, but it was hardly noticeable. Emsbach walked over to the stables. His two horses had been requisitioned by the army months before. He missed riding, the sensation of power the great animal gave him as he controlled it with a touch of the reins or a light pressure from his heel.

He whistled, and three dogs came bounding through the mud, tongues lolling. They leaped and danced joyfully about as he opened the kennel gate and dished out their food. It should be impossible to think of war and death on such a beautiful day, but the destruction he saw everywhere was an unavoidable reminder. His gait slowed as the weight of reality settled on his young shoulders.

Fraydl woke to a ray of warmth from a sunbeam that had settled on her face. Her ankles throbbed intensely, a harsh reminder of the previous night's adventure. She needed to get up, but the slightest movement caused her pain. Where was Dr. Emsbach? The profound silence inside the house led her to believe she was alone. She had to get away from here — but how?

Forcing herself to stand, Fraydl grabbed the back of Emsbach's chair for support and hobbled to the kitchen, step after painful step. The tight bandages on her feet helped. She washed *negelvasser* and splashed water onto her face. She couldn't get far and she couldn't move fast, but she was able to move.

The squeak of the screen door on the porch alerted her to someone's arrival. With a familiar rasping sound, the kitchen door scraped open and Dr. Emsbach entered. He looked in her direction, but said nothing. If he was surprised to see her up, it didn't show. He walked past her and went down into the cellar. Returning with a pail of potatoes, the doctor proceeded to peel them and drop the pieces into a pan of salted water to boil.

"There are some eggs left in the icebox," Fraydl spoke up.

He looked up as if noticing her for the first time. "How are you feeling?" he asked, taking out a smaller pan for the eggs and filling it from the faucet.

It was an ordinary question, but the air in the kitchen fairly crackled with tension.

"Better, thank you," she replied, wincing as she took a small step toward a chair.

"You must rest with your feet raised," he reproached. "Go back to the couch immediately."

Fraydl complied without argument, painfully shuffling from the kitchen to Emsbach's study. After eating breakfast, she accepted another dose of analgesic and sank into a dreamless sleep. She woke to the familiar wailing of the air-raid siren, but did not have enough strength to make her way down to the cellar.

She whispered *Tehillim* instead, until the all clear came.

Lying prone on the sofa, and still groggy from the narcotic, Fraydl watched tiny drops of light shimmer on the walls, tossed there by the prisms hanging from the doctor's desk lamp. Embach was obviously not home, or he would have helped her down to the cellar during the air raid. She was hungry and her mouth felt full of cotton wool.

With a moan, she rolled sideways and sat up, setting her feet carefully down on the floor. To her relief, it hurt less than before. She hobbled into the kitchen and washed up, then prepared herself a supper of bread and jam. While she was eating, Cleopatra sauntered in and regarded her mistress's bandaged feet with curiosity.

"Here." Fraydl set a saucer with milk and bread on the floor. "Eat, Cleo. It's not sardines, but you won't be hungry."

The cat apparently agreed, because she accepted the offering, daintily licking up all the milk before swallowing the hunks of bread without chewing. Tired from her exertions, Fraydl returned to the sofa and arranged the pillows so that her aching ankles were elevated. She fell into an uneasy sleep, filled with strange and disconnected dreams.

41

DAY FOLLOWED DAY IN THE EMPTY, ECHOING HOUSE. Recovering from her injuries, Fraydl spent most of her time reading or sleeping and waiting for something to happen. She lived on apples, boiled potatoes and the bread she baked for as long as the flour lasted. After one week there was no more milk or eggs, and not long after the canned goods were all used up.

Cleopatra became a nuisance, constantly rubbing against Fraydl's legs and meowing for food. Finally she summoned the courage to send the cat out to scavenge. A balmy breeze greeted her when she opened the kitchen door. Fraydl inhaled the spring air with longing before quickly shutting it again.

Where was Dr. Emsbach? He had not informed her that he would be away, and she knew the hospital was closed. The nights were quiet without the wail of air-raid sirens. *Wouldn't it be ironic if I am hiding here while the war is over already?* Fraydl's eyes fell on Otto's AM radio cabinet. She brushed away the dust and tried the power knob. Loud static was interrupted by the somber voice of an announcer reading instructions to the public.

Fraydl stared at the machine. The announcer was informing the public of a curfew that the Allied victors were enforcing in German cities. The war was over! She was free! Feeling suddenly faint, Fraydl collapsed on the nearest chair and wrung her hands. It had finally happened. The war was over.

What should she do first? She stood up, and then immediately sat down again. Nothing in her environment had changed, but suddenly, everything was different.

I must find the children, was her first coherent thought. *Where did Dr. Emsbach leave Yanky and Chaim?* She should wait for their benefactor to return in order to learn the answer to that question, but he had been gone for so many weeks that she'd lost track of time. Perhaps something had happened to the doctor? Her imagination conjured up an accident. She was certain that he would not abandon her, so the only explanation was that he was wounded, or worse.

Fraydl couldn't stay in this house forever, but she had nowhere else to go. A march playing on the radio galvanized her into action. She went upstairs to the bathroom and drew a bath. After she was dressed, she gathered her small wardrobe into a bundle and slipped out the front door.

It had been nearly two years since she had seen a normal street with motorcars and horses and pedestrians. People all seemed to be walking with their heads down. No one paid attention to the lone girl in a gray sweater who stepped out of the Emsbach house. Overwhelmed with the light and color and movement all around her, Fraydl was dazed. This city was totally unfamiliar to her. With a prayer in her heart, she allowed her feet to carry her forward in the hope that she would eventually recognize someone or something.

As Fraydl was making her way through the city streets, Dr. Emsbach unlocked the back door and entered his home for the first time in almost two months. The fastidious German was almost unrecognizable; his uniform was torn and unkempt, and his face was hidden by a blond beard.

"Fraulein?" he called. His hoarse voice echoed in the empty house. Alarmed, the doctor went from room to room, but his search did not turn up any sign of Fraydl. He sank into the chair in his study and ran his fingers through his hair. *Where could she be?*

What has happened to her? He looked around the tidy room. There was no sign of a struggle; it appeared that the girl must have left of her own free will.

"Oh, Fraydl," he whispered. "How could you be so foolish?" It was anarchy on the streets outside, and a lone Jewish girl would be an inviting target for the disappointed remnants of Hitler's supporters. Emsbach's shoulder slumped in defeat. Having risked his life to save the children during the war, he could not believe that fate had placed the girl in deadly peril at the last moment before the danger passed away.

There's nothing I can do, he told himself. *I can only hope that she will return before anything terrible happens.* He caught a glimpse of himself in a mirror on the wall and shook his head. It seemed like years since he had left for the black market with the intention of buying a supply of food to last them until the end of the war.

Emsbach leaned back in his chair, remembering the weeks he had been away after encountering the American soldiers at a roadblock on his way home. By the time he realized they were speaking English and not German, their menacing rifles were pointed directly at his chest. His identity papers were examined and translated, and a short time later he'd found himself under guard as a prisoner of war. Together with a number of other Nazi officers, he was transferred to a detention camp and forced to submit to repeated cross-examinations. Like all the other detainees, he claimed status as a noncombatant in a civilian position.

In the holding cell, he'd paced back and forth like a sentry on duty. Emsbach was worried about the children, and anxious to get out of internment as soon as possible.

"Don't worry so much," one of the other prisoners had advised him. "Sit down and relax. You're making me nervous."

Emsbach regarded the man who had spoken. "Do you have any idea what they are going to do with us?" he asked. "How long will we be here?"

Some of the other prisoners laughed at his naïveté, while others regarded him with suspicion. Emsbach thought he recognized an older officer. "Captain Horst von Trappen?" he inquired respectfully.

The man frowned and corrected him, "You are mistaken, young man. My name is Rolf Muller!"

Emsbach realized the man was using an alias, and apologized.

Radiating hostility, Von Trappen and the other Nazis in the group stared at Emsbach, sizing him up. "State your name and rank, officer!"

Automatically he saluted and replied, "Major *Doktor* Karl Emsbach, senior surgeon at the military hospital."

"Emsbach? Your uncle is Brigadier General Heinrich Mauer?"

He nodded warily.

Recognizing him at last, the captain relaxed and smiled. "This is the man who put me back together after I was wounded in France," he declared to the others, giving Emsbach a sharp slap on the back. "You can't be too careful," he explained. "The greatest danger for us now is an informer. We'll wear down those Yankee interrogators and their stoolie interpreters. It's just a question of time until they'll be forced to release us."

Emsbach's family connection was sufficient to gain the trust of his fellow prisoners, and the officers spoke openly in his presence. Most of their deliberations centered on alternative plans for escaping Germany in order to regroup in a foreign country. "They may have defeated us in the war, but the Reich will rise again!" was the common theme. Escape routes to Syria, Egypt, Paraguay, Brazil, Bolivia or Australia were frequently mentioned. They discussed rumors that the Vatican was assisting former officers, and that the American intelligence agency was willing to look the other way in exchange for information that would help them deal with the Soviet Union.

Emsbach sat on the side, withdrawn. He had too much time to think, and he cared nothing for his former comrades or their grandiose political plans. Finally, after weeks of hardship, he was brought before the military tribunal. After his name, rank, occupation and serial number were verified, his identity documents were returned to him stamped and signed by the interim military governor.

Grimy and rumpled, Dr. Emsbach was released from the detention camp and allowed to return home.

42

AFTER WEEKS OF INTERNMENT, IT WAS A DIVINE PLEASURE to shave and shower. Emsbach was not surprised to find that the icebox and pantry were bare. He knew there were terrible shortages in the city, and many people were suffering from hunger. At least he had been fed in the internment camp. There were still some potatoes in the cellar, which meant that Fraydl had not starved while he was gone.

A nap did a great deal to restore Emsbach's natural vigor. Wandering through the empty rooms of his house, the German half-expected to find the girl, but she was truly gone. With the arrival of darkness, he knew she was not likely to return. Drawn to the attic, he sat glumly on the chair beside the brass bed. The lantern sent eerie shadows around the corner of the room where the children had stayed. Noticing the crate with the silver still under the brass bed, his spirits rose. *The girl surely intends to come back if she left this here,* he reassured himself.

Emsbach went down to his study and tried to read, but it was impossible to concentrate. He kept seeing Chaim and Yanky in his imagination, playing with his old toy soldiers on the carpet. The orphanage had been vacated around the same time that the hospital was closed. Tomorrow he would return and begin making inquiries, trying to learn where Father Matthew had moved the children.

The sudden sound of someone hammering on his front door startled him. Who could it be at this late hour? Perhaps someone needed medical assistance. It took him only a few seconds to walk to the entrance and unbolt the door. At the sight of Brigadier General Heinrich Mauer, his heart sank.

"Aren't you going to invite me in?"

The saccharine tone and sardonic smile set Emsbach's teeth on edge. He stepped back so that his uncle could enter. The man was in civilian dress, but the bulge beneath his suit jacket indicated that his Luger was in its holster on his hip.

"Where is your luggage?" Emsbach asked, eyes scanning the porch behind his unwelcome guest in expectation of seeing an attendant swaying under the burden of a trunk or suitcases.

"The war is over, Karl, or didn't you know?" Mauer's sneer was more pronounced than ever. "I am on my way to Argentina, but you and I have some unfinished business. So I delayed my departure in order to come here first."

Emsbach didn't know whether to feel relieved or threatened. His instincts forebode ill and he hesitated, but the brigadier general did not wait for a formal invitation. He pushed past his nephew and strode briskly toward the kitchen.

"There's nothing to eat but boiled potatoes," Emsbach informed his uncle without regret.

"I didn't come for dinner. Bring me a bottle of whiskey and let's get this unpleasantness over with."

Emsbach fetched the liquor and a tumbler. "You're not joining me?" Heinrich asked facetiously, making himself comfortable in Karl's cushioned chair. He settled his shiny black boots on the desk and uncorked the whiskey. Mauer ignored the proffered glass and lifted the bottle to his lips, guzzling the brown liquid while his nephew stared at him with loathing.

"You have good taste," the brigadier general complimented, regarding the bottle with approval. He set the whiskey on the desktop and leaned back in the chair with a sigh of content. "I have been anticipating this day for many years."

Emsbach waited apprehensively.

"Close the door, Karl," Uncle Heinrich purred. His nephew complied.

"Stand in front of me so I can see you better."

Emsbach obeyed silently.

An enigmatic smile played about the brigadier general's lips. "I am proud to have the privilege of destroying the last Jew in Germany," he proclaimed, lifting the Luger and pointing it at his nephew's heart.

The girl! Emsbach's thoughts raced. *He knows about Fraydl! Thank G-d she is not here. The monster must have known about her all along.*

"I saved you for the very end," the old man continued with a modest shrug. "I will go down in history."

The man is totally mad, Emsbach thought with a frown. *Absolutely crazy.*

There was a menacing click as his uncle removed the safety catch and cocked the hammer of his weapon. Emsbach's heart began to race.

"Uncle Heinrich." Emsbach forced himself to speak as calmly and deliberately as if they were at a social event. "I am Karl, your sister's son. I am not a Jew. *Bitte schön*, put away the gun before someone gets hurt."

The Nazi officer's response was to laugh uproariously. After taking another swig of whiskey, he laid the Luger casually but watchfully on his lap. "Sit down, my dear nephew," he commanded, indicating the couch, "and listen well. You deserve to know the truth before you leave this world."

Emsbach's knees felt suddenly weak. He sat down slowly, never taking his eyes off of his uncle.

Mauer was enjoying himself immensely. "Your mother was never my sister!" he hissed. "My sister Helga was barren; she was physically unable to bear a child. You, my boy, were born in a Polish village near the Czechoslovakian border."

Karl Emsbach was thunderstruck. Were these words the meandering fantasy of a madman — or could there be some truth to his uncle's claim?

"Would you like me to tell you about it, before you die?" Uncle Heinrich's pale-blue eyes twinkled. He seemed to be holding back a great joke.

Emsbach nodded, his throat too tight to form words.

Mauer's expression grew unfocused as he waxed nostalgic. "My career was just beginning then, and I rose through the ranks like a meteor. The world was mine for the asking." The brigadier general paused for a moment, remembering. "My comrades and I were off duty and itching for action one Saturday morning, when one of the fellows suggested that we cross the border and have some sport with the Jews who lived in the village of Birnhack. It was a form of amusement we had engaged in before. And so, after a few rounds of beer, we swam our horses across the river and jumped the border fence. We were young and looking for fun, you understand?"

Without waiting for an answer, he continued.

"It must have been a Jewish holiday, because the men were inside the synagogue and there was a crowd of women and children milling around the courtyard. They all scattered when we approached, except for one little tyke who stood at the top of the stairs as if daring us to come closer. The boy couldn't have been more than 3 years old, with golden curls framing his face, and eyes as blue as the sea.

"We halted our horses right in front of the synagogue and sat there watching him, mesmerized. He looked like a little soldier, hands clenched into fists, ready to do battle if we came any closer. One of my companions declared, 'That can't be a Jewish child!' And we all agreed.

"Someone from inside the synagogue called to him, but before he could turn around I rode my horse up the stairs and snatched him by the back of his britches. Oh, how that little boy fought! Like a wolf cub! Twisting, kicking, biting! I was drunk, so it only amused me at the time, but the next day I had black-and-blue marks to show for it.

"I held him up in the air, and we laughed at his antics. Then I thought of my sister Helga, alone in this huge empty house with her husband away on business most of the time, and I decided it would be heroic to bring her a child to fill the void in her life. You were such a beautiful, golden *kind*. Later, when I sobered up, I realized it wasn't so, but at that moment it seemed to me that the Jews had stolen a Christian child. Your hair was so blond and your eyes are so Aryan blue. . .

"So my dear nephew, I was the one who brought you here to my sister. The rest is — how do they say? History. A little financial incentive to the right civil servant, and one small Jewish boy was officially registered as the son and heir of my brother-in-law, Mikhail Emsbach.

"And now you know why I have come to kill you today," he concluded, picking up his Luger.

43

THE ONLY WORDS EMSBACH COULD ARTICULATE WERE, "How *could* you?" Great waves of emotion rolled over him. It felt as if the air had been sucked from the room. The whole story was impossible! But the Luger was pointed directly at his heart, and he knew that the man behind the trigger was a deadly opponent.

"If this is true, then what is my name? Who am I?"

Mauer regarded the younger man with amusement, waving the gun slightly from side to side for emphasis. His pale eyes narrowed cruelly as he calmly lined up his target.

"Your real parents searched for you, of course. They traced you as far as Berlin, but my connections in the government were sufficient to stop them there. I will never know how they got the names of some of my men, but at one point they even sent messengers to me, offering to pay a fortune for information as to your whereabouts. You had a big family, plenty of brothers and sisters. It surprised me that they even noticed you were gone." Uncle Heinrich laughed at his own joke.

"My name," Emsbach said through closed teeth, struggling to control himself. "What are my parents' names?"

There was a moment of silence as the older man toyed with the decision of whether or not to reveal the information. "What difference does it make?" he asked at last. "They are all dead long ago. There are no Jews left in Birnhack. It will be my pleasure to help you join them, wherever they are."

Emsbach's hands were sweating. He wiped them on his trousers. "You're making this all up. I don't believe it ever happened."

Heinrich Mauer's face reddened. He downed a few more swallows of whiskey before responding to the taunt. "Stern, Karl. The family was Stern. Are you satisfied?"

Stern, Emsbach whispered to himself. The name triggered no memories.

"Their messengers followed me to Berlin." The brigadier general's voice was beginning to slur from the liquor. "I had to get rid of them, those smelly Jews in long coats with sidelocks and beards. My comrades were laughing at me; it became a matter of honor. I threatened to have Rabbiner Stern imprisoned for kidnapping a Christian child if they didn't stop harassing me. After that, I never saw them again."

Emsbach's attention was riveted on the barrel of his uncle's Luger. *I have to escape,* he thought. *I must find out if this fantastic account has any basis in reality.*

"Are you afraid, Karl?" Mauer tilted his head and smiled sadistically. "Why don't you beg for your life, boy? I would like to see that. You are always so cold and controlled. You act as if you think you're better than anyone else—but you're just a Jew. The last living Jew in Germany! And you are about to meet the fate I have been planning since you defied me and chose to be a doctor instead of a soldier. You could have been like a son to me and followed in my footsteps. All doors would have been open to you! But you chose the medical profession in spite of my direct wishes.

"Do you realize how I laughed when my colleagues praised you for being a model Aryan? They envied me, because you were so successful in the military academy. You could have been a poster boy for the National Socialist party. Ha! Ha! It's just too bad that no one but you knows the truth, and no one will be left to appreciate the irony."

Beads of sweat were gathering on Emsbach's forehead. He had to distract his uncle. Perhaps he could wrest the revolver out of his hands, but how? If he even moved, Uncle Heinrich would shoot.

The circumstances were clearly hopeless, yet even as he waited helplessly for the denouement of his life, an incongruous memory arose in his mind. Fraydl had once described the splitting of the Red Sea to him. That situation had appeared hopeless, as well, until G-d suddenly split the sea and the Children of Israel miraculously escaped their Egyptian pursuers. Fraydl argued that a Jew must always have hope, even when the blade of the sword is touching his throat, because a Jew has a personal relationship with the Master of the World.

If I am a Jew, then I also have a personal relationship with G-d, he thought. *Help me, please! Only G-d can save me from this depraved man!*

His thoughts were interrupted by a choking sound. As he stared, Uncle Heinrich's complexion began changing color: from bright red to ghastly white, and then a sickly hue of gray. The brigadier general's eyes opened wide before rolling up into his skull. He fell sideways, the revolver clattering harmlessly to the floor.

Mechanically, Emsbach checked for pulse and respiration, but he knew instinctively that the nemesis that had tormented him for so long was dead. Only a moment ago, this man had wielded such power, and now he was gone. Was it a coincidence ... or a miracle?

Shuddering at the thought of what had nearly transpired, he bent over the body, removed the holster belt and put it into a desk drawer together with the deadly pistol. Now what? The death was natural, but it must be reported. Emsbach had no desire to stay another minute under the same roof with his uncle's body, so he put on his jacket and headed for the police station to notify them and to summon a wagon from the morgue to take the brigadier general away.

His head spun. Everything felt unreal. Germany was defeated, and Uncle Heinrich was dead. Where were Bea and Otto and Hans? What had happened to Fraydl and the boys? Stars glimmered in the sky like randomly scattered diamonds. Against this background, Emsbach began to feel the confusion melt away. In its place came an incredible sense of peace.

"I would like to report the demise of my elderly uncle and request transfer of the body to the morgue," he explained to the guard at the precinct headquarters.

"Cause of death?"

"Stroke."

"When did the death occur?"

Emsbach looked at his pocket watch. "Fifty minutes ago."

"Has this been verified by a medical doctor?"

"I am a physician, and I am willing to sign the necessary forms."

Less than an hour later, everything was arranged. The officer on duty expressed sympathy for Emsbach and admiration for his legendary late uncle. "What a terrible time to pass away," the policemen shook his head. "The brigadier general deserves a state funeral, but the occupiers will never permit it."

"No," Emsbach agreed. "Few of his comrades would be able to attend anyway. I imagine the funeral will be a modest one."

The officer on duty authorized an ambulance to take Dr. Emsbach home and collect the corpse of the deceased. Altogether, things went far more smoothly that he had anticipated, and by midnight he was finally left alone with his thoughts. He went to bed, but sleep evaded him as the events of the day ran through his mind over and over again. He tried to grasp their significance in order to plan his steps for the future.

Fraydl was gone, Uncle Heinrich was dead and he was not the person he'd believed he was. In a single day, his entire life had turned upside down. Was it any wonder that sleep eluded him?

PART II
DIVERGING PATHS

44

AFTER A SLEEPLESS NIGHT, EMSBACH WASHED UP AND GOT dressed. It was time to take action to resolve his uncle's riddle.

The rain drumming on the window reminded him to don his hat and an overcoat. The need to think slowed his steps uncharacteristically. He was oblivious to the raindrops dimpling the puddles in the street. The scenes in his imagination felt far more real to him than his actual surroundings.

He pictured a father and mother whose little son was stolen in broad daylight, and tried to imagine how they must have felt during the years he'd been gone. What had happened to them? Could they ever forget their lost child? *If it were my son*, he thought, *I would never stop looking for him or thinking about him. Not as long as I lived.*

It was bitter for Emsbach to realize that his family would never know how things had turned out for him. Knowing the wartime professionalism of the Gestapo, it was unlikely that any Jews in the village of Birnhack had survived.

He wondered if his parents had been people like his Jewish

acquaintances at the university. There had been a fellow student in pre-med named Stern. He could have been his brother! Emsbach strained his memory to recall the fellow's features, but found no resemblance at all. Frank Stern had a swarthy complexion. He wore thick glasses, and had wide lips and a decidedly prominent nose — much like *Der Sturmer* caricatures.

Perhaps the brigadier general had invented the whole incredible story just to torment him? How plausible was it, really? Not plausible at all. No, not at all... The old man was unhinged. Emsbach's boot caught on a cobblestone and he looked up to get his bearings. He was on a pedestrian bridge above the river, and the rain was letting up a little. He stood there for a long time, gazing down at the swirling gray water.

The constantly changing surface was puckered with rain, and the restless river seemed full of secrets. "Tell me the truth!" he whispered. But the only response was the muted rush of its waves against the piles of the bridge.

"Do you need some help?"

He turned to see an elderly man with a cane standing quite close to him.

"No, thank you. I'm fine," he replied.

"You shouldn't stay here in the wet and cold," the concerned citizen protested. "You're a young man. You have your whole life ahead of you."

"I'm just leaving," Emsbach reassured the anonymous fellow, and crossed to the far side of the bridge in a few brisk strides. *I could never kill myself,* he thought in reaction to the old man's suspicions. *I wouldn't give Uncle Heinrich the satisfaction!*

The rain was beginning to soak through his coat. He shivered. It was time to be sensible and look for a tram heading in the right direction. While he waited at the nearest stop, Emsbach listened to the mournful whistles of the trains arriving and departing from the adjacent Central Train Station. For some reason, they reminded him of Fraydl and the boys. Where were the children now?

A tiny flame of anger flickered in his heart. *Why did the girl have to leave? I was there for them when they were in trouble, but now that I am drowning in doubts she has disappeared from my life.* The arrival of the tram brought an end to these irrational thoughts, and he directed his attention to the immediate task at hand.

Several stops later, Emsbach reached the neighborhood he was seeking. Alighting from the tram, he followed the narrow streets until he came to a sparsely populated and secluded lane. He followed the familiar stone path up to the porch of her cottage, and then hesitated. Closing his eyes, he let the rain fall on his face, listening to the steady ticking sounds made by the slow drizzle on the leaves of the rose-bushes. Finally he gathered his wits and knocked on the door. It was still early in the morning, but Rhea wouldn't mind.

As he expected, the housekeeper's face lit up with delight when she recognized her visitor. "Karl! Please come in!" she gestured toward the dim recesses of the small house. "What a pleasure to see you! It has been too long. Is everything all right?"

"*Onkel* Heinrich had a stroke last night." He wiped his muddy boots on the welcome mat and stepped inside. "He passed away shortly afterward."

"Oh! I'm so sorry," she responded in genuine sorrow.

Their eyes met briefly, and both knew that he was not mourning the loss of his formidable uncle. "It is a loss for Germany," Rhea added with a frown, closing the front door and leading the way to her tiny, neat kitchen. "Your uncle was a loyal patriot, and he dedicated his life to the Fatherland."

Emsbach followed, watching Rhea prepare him a glass of tea. It felt so natural to be taken care of. For the first time in many weeks, he relaxed.

"What else happened?" Her sharp eyes did not miss very much.

He stirred the brown liquid, watching the mint leaves dance in the wake of his spoon. "I must ask you something." The slight quaver in his voice alerted her to the seriousness of his visit. "And I beg you to answer me truthfully," he added for emphasis

Her brow furrowed with anxiety. "What do you want to know, Karl?"

Emsbach hesitated. Was the whole thing just a delusion of his uncle's sick mind? She was standing at the sink, peeling potatoes for a casserole for his lunch. "I want to know about when I was born," he told her. "You were with my mother then. Tell me about it."

Rhea's hands ceased working and the peeler dropped onto the pile of peels in the sink. "What exactly do you want to know?" she asked. The tremor in her voice revealed, better than any words, that the bizarre story was not a fiction.

"*Onkel* Heinrich, just before he died..."

"He shouldn't have told you," the old woman sighed. "You never needed to know."

"Tell me everything you know." It was a command. "I must know the truth!"

Rhea sank down on the wooden chair facing him, her fingers toying nervously with the ruffles on her apron. "I remember the day you arrived," she began. "Your uncle came unannounced in an army vehicle. You were so small and frightened, wedged between two soldiers with rifles on their knees. Heinrich Mauer demanded that I summon his sister right away. When she appeared, he scooped you up from the wagon and passed you directly to the mistress. Then he bowed ceremoniously, and declared, 'This orphan is now your son.'

"Your parents had been married for more than 10 years by then, and Helga no longer expected to ever bear her own child. We all understood that she was very concerned about her marriage. The master wanted an heir and had already threatened to divorce her a number of times.

"The mistress set you on the ground and looked you over. 'Why don't *you* and Andrea want him?' she asked her brother.

"I'm sure Heinrich expected her to respond with admiration for his gesture, but when she reminded him of his wife he became very angry. You remember that your Aunt Andrea was subject to periodic emotional breakdowns. 'It is out of the question,' he yelled. 'You don't want him? Just give him back!'"

"Helga wasn't impressed by your golden curls and blue eyes, but she saw that you were intelligent and that appealed to her. 'Leave him,' she instructed her brother. 'Don't be angry. It was an excellent idea.'

"Your mother asked no further questions, and I never heard any more information about your background. The mistress put your little hand in mine and told me to arrange for a governess. When the master returned from abroad, he and your uncle took care of the legal aspects of the adoption. The servants were told that the topic should not be discussed any further."

45

EMSBACH CLENCHED AND UNCLENCHED HIS FISTS IN
frustration. "I don't remember anything," he admitted aloud.
"Anything at all."

"It's best that way," Rhea soothed him. "There is no point in dig-
ging all this up. It makes no difference to anyone. *Herr* Emsbach
and *Frau* Emsbach were very proud of you. You were a better son
to them than if you were their own flesh and blood."

"You don't understand," Emsbach's voice was hoarse. "What
about my real parents? You can't just take a child away from one
family and give him to another!"

"Your uncle said your parents were dead, Karl. I'm sure that the
mother who gave birth to you would be grateful that the Emsbachs
took you in and raised you as their own. Your real parents would
certainly be glad that their son grew up in wealth and comfort
instead of in an orphanage. They would be proud of the fine person
you have become."

He stared at her for a moment, and then asked, "Did I cry for my
mother?"

"What?" Rhea dropped her eyes. She stared at her hands in her lap and sighed. In a low voice, she said, "For a little while you did. But then you got used to us."

"How did I call for her? Did I cry '*Mütti*'?"

Uncomfortably, Rhea shook her head.

"What name did I use? Tell me, Rhea!"

"You cried 'Mamme,'" the old woman answered softly, and for a moment her eyes filled with tears as she remembered the helpless child this man had once been. "You spoke a dialect that was different from ours. It was awhile before you were able to express yourself in proper German."

Emsbach turned his face away from her, his jaw set. "Tell me the truth, Rhea. Do you have any idea where I really came from, or who my real parents were?"

Rhea pressed her lips together so tightly that the skin turned white around her mouth. "*Genug*, Karl! Forget you ever heard about this. Just put it behind you and get on with your life, my dear boy."

"Rhea, please! I must know. I need to know."

"What did your uncle tell you?"

"He said I am a Jew."

She nodded sadly. "We suspected as much."

"Why?"

"For the obvious reason that you were circumcised. And that at first you would not touch any food we cooked for you."

"So do you think my real mother, my Jewish mother, would be proud that her son was a Nazi officer?"

Rhea recoiled as if she had been slapped. "Stop it! Don't think about it! If you don't put the past behind you, it will destroy your future. What's done is done. Be happy that you are alive, Karl Emsbach!" She rose from her place, shaking with suppressed anger.

The doctor stood up as well. His head throbbed. "Good-bye, Rhea," he said quietly, and left her standing in the kitchen. The rain had stopped, although leaden clouds drifted overhead with the promise of more. He walked aimlessly for a time, his mind in a fog. Eventually, his feet carried him to a tram station. *I will go home*, he decided. *It will be possible to think more clearly after I have slept.*

Hours later, Emsbach woke up and went down to his study. Withdrawing a sheet of paper from his desk, he began listing his priorities. He must contact Father Matthew about Chaim and Yanky. In his present state of mind it would not be a good idea to bring them back home, but he would renew contact and see that the boys had everything they needed. Fraydl? His heart ached with worry for her, but there was nothing he could do. She was gone.

The house. After knowing that she was complicit in hiding the truth from him for so many years, did he want Rhea to come back as his housekeeper? No, he decided. Whatever he might do with his life, he could not forgive her deception. He wrote on the list: *Settle a pension for Rhea*. Out of regard for her many years of service to his family, he would be generous, but her role in his life was over.

As much as he wanted to leave the cursed soil of Germany and immigrate to the United States, it was not a logical time to liquidate his assets. In addition, there was a slim possibility that he could still discover something about his past. Perhaps someone from the village of Birnhack had survived the war and could fill some of the yawning emptiness inside him? If he did not make the attempt now, he might never have another opportunity.

The next morning, Emsbach hitchhiked to where he had left the Mercedes. Now that the war was over, petrol was available again. He filled the tank and cleaned the dust-grimed windows. Driving gave him a sense of control, even if it was only an illusion. Several hours later he reached the border, where his passport and papers were stamped by the guards. Emsbach slowly passed from Germany into Poland.

His military bearing had an effect on civilians, even without the uniform. Emsbach stopped farmers on the road and followed their directions until he arrived at the outskirts of Birnhack. It was a drab village, hardly distinguishable from any other. "Where is the synagogue?" he called to a young man herding a cow with a long stick.

The bare-headed boy appeared struck dumb by the question, but an elderly man who overheard the exchange stepped up to the driver's window. "If you let me ride beside you, I can show you where to go," he offered, his eyes traveling over the Mercedes' plush leather interior with undisguised envy.

"Get in."

The Pole grinned, showing gaps where several teeth were missing. "My name is Viktor," he introduced himself. "You wouldn't have a drop of something to drink for a thirsty fellow?" His tone was wheedling, but Emsbach sent him a withering look that caused the old man to shut his mouth with an audible snap.

Except for Viktor's terse instructions, they drove in silence until the long-vacant shul came into view. "We use it for the cows in the winter now," his passenger volunteered. Emsbach removed the key from the ignition and waited impatiently for the fellow to vacate the automobile.

Viktor climbed out reluctantly, his bones creaking with age. He did not go about his business, but stayed beside the Mercedes watching the German climb the stairs and look about, apparently searching for something.

The heavy, ornate synagogue door was not locked. Emsbach pushed it open and peered into the dark interior. The smell of cattle was unmistakable. It pained him acutely that he did not recognize anything, nor could he dredge up a single memory. Perhaps the trauma had been so profound that it wiped the scene from his mind. Or maybe he had just been too young to remember.

The Pole was still standing beside the Mercedes when Emsbach returned to the car. Viktor tipped his cap and asked if he could be of any further service.

"How old are you?"

The old man blinked.

"I asked, how old are you?"

"My children have grandchildren," Viktor offered by way of an answer.

"Have you always lived in Birnhack?"

The Pole nodded. "Born and raised here."

"Show me the house where the Stern family lived," Karl ordered.

"The *Rabbiner*?" The man's previous indifference was replaced with surprise. This blond, blue-eyed stranger from Germany was obviously a soldier. What connection could there be between him and the forgotten Jews of his village?

Emsbach dropped a few coins into the old man's palm, earning another gap-toothed grin.

"Follow me," the Pole said affably. Quelling his own curiosity, old Viktor led the German through narrow alleys until they reached a simple, thatch-roofed cottage. A *Volksdeutscher* family was living in the house now, and the door was opened by a peasant woman clad in a dirndl. Disregarding her, Emsbach entered the dwelling and studiously gazed about the dwelling.

It was possible to recognize where *mezuzahs* had once adorned the doors, just as he had seen in Fraydl's family's apartment in Austria. "Who lived here before you?"

The nervous housewife clutched the hands of her two small children. Like the boy on the road herding his cow, she was too intimidated to speak. Emsbach wondered if there might be any treasure hidden here, something left from his parents like the ritual objects from Fraydl's home. But now that the war was over he could no longer pretend to have authority.

He searched the speechless woman's simple, round face. "Where are the silver objects that the Jews left behind?" he demanded.

"The Gestapo took everything," she whispered fearfully.

"Who lived here before you?"

"The Rosenheim family."

Emsbach looked at his guide. "Rosenheim?" he asked sharply. "I told you to show me the home of the Stern family."

"The Sterns left Birnhack years before the war," Viktor explained hastily. "This is where they lived. The Rosenheim family moved in after the *Rabbiner* left."

"Why did they leave?"

The Pole did not respond to his question, but Emsbach had the distinct feeling that the old man knew something. He reached ostentatiously into his pocket and fingered the coins there.

Viktor grinned with satisfaction. Convinced that the German's search involved locating valuables, he was not averse to amusing the stranger with the story that had long ago become a legend in the village. "The *Rabbiner* had a child who was stolen by a German officer on horseback about 30 years ago. The whole town witnessed it. There were many rumors about the child being sighted here or there (for which the Rabbi was always willing to pay a few *groschen*), but he was never found. The *Rabbiner's* wife was broken by what happened, and the family moved away to seek medical treatment for her."

46

KARL EMSBACH SLAPPED SOME MONEY INTO THE BEMUSED Pole's hand and returned to his automobile. The gaping door of the synagogue drew him once again. Stepping cautiously over the threshold, he made his way from the lobby to the main sanctuary, following the dim light that shone through once-beautiful stained glass windows.

The floor was covered with trash and dung. The wooden benches had been overturned and converted into food troughs. On the eastern wall the Holy Ark stood alone, bereft of its Torah scrolls and velvet curtains. Overhead, broken stems of crystal chandeliers still caught rays of light, turning them into rainbows that splashed incongruously on the ceiling.

He stood motionless in the silence, listening intently. It was probably only the wind, but he almost felt as if faint voices were calling to him. How he wished it were possible to turn back the clock and experience the last time he had been in this place!

The sun was setting. Soon darkness would reign in the old, abandoned synagogue. Emsbach picked his way back to the door, bitterly disappointed at the dead end he had reached.

At the border crossing, he engaged one of the guards in conversation. "Have any Jews returned?" he asked.

The guard took a drag on his cigarette and shook his head. "Not from Germany."

"I'm trying to locate a particular family," Emsbach said offhandedly.

"Why don't you try the Jewish Joint Distribution Committee in one of the big cities? I hear they are running DP camps and registering survivors."

"Thanks. It feels like searching for a needle in a haystack, but at least that's a direction to follow."

He drove home, emotionally drained by the reality of simultaneously occupying two diametrically opposed worlds. Despite his outward German appearance, his inner self was undergoing a revolution. *If it wasn't for Fraydl and the children, I would have simply ignored my uncle's revelation that I am the child of Jewish parents,* he reflected. *I would probably have filed the information away in my brain and then continued the same life that I was living before the war.*

A week passed before Emsbach was able to take further action. His days were occupied with finding a new housekeeper and cook, overseeing necessary repairs to the house and grounds and making financial arrangements to transfer his local assets to a central account. In postwar Germany, life was gradually beginning to return to normal. Commerce resumed as citizens tried to forget their humiliating defeat by setting their sights on a better future.

On a national level, the refugee problem was strangling the bureaucracy. Emsbach read in the newspaper that the Red Cross was gathering data from Nazi records. He traveled to their headquarters in Arolsen to begin his search in the archives that listed prisoners of the forced-labor camps and the death camps. There was a faint hope that Fraydl's name might appear in the DP section. At this point, she was the only person in the world with whom he would feel safe sharing the discovery about his past.

Hours of searching through wartime documents, deportation records and lists of prisoners left him overwhelmed and depressed.

On the way home after a fruitless day in Arolsen, he passed a former military base. Abandoned by the disbanded German Army, it was currently serving as a temporary camp for refugees and displaced persons. Emsbach parked his Mercedes in front and approached the entrance gate, which was guarded by indifferent British soldiers. No one attempted to stop or identify him as he passed through.

Once inside, he felt his body turn to lead. The grounds were crowded and unsanitary. The sullen inmates looked as though the severe shortages of food and clothing at the end of the war were still in force. When a group of people loitering near the gate edged closer to beg for a handout, Emsbach regarded them sharply. The former prisoners flinched involuntarily at his military bearing.

"He's a German!" he heard someone whisper.

"It's a German *soldier*!" a woman cried out in alarm.

More and more people congregated to see what was causing the disturbance, until a small crowd had formed. On the edge of the gathering a man, mentally imbalanced as a result of all he had experienced, picked up a stone and hurled it at Emsbach before fleeing into the interior of the camp. The rock glanced off his cheek. Instinctively, he touched his face, staring uncomprehendingly at the blood on his fingers.

Quick to discern that trouble was brewing, the guards went into action. Two armed soldiers took their places on either side of the tall, blond German, extricating him from the mob while other officers brutally and efficiently dispersed the crowd.

The British soldier who courteously escorted Emsbach out of the camp was apologetic. "They want revenge," he explained. "If we didn't keep them within the gates, they would attack innocent civilians and no one would be safe." The entire incident had lasted less than five minutes.

Emsbach returned to his car. He was in shock, lacking the emotional resources to deal with what had just happened. For a long time he sat in the driver's seat without moving, dizzy and confused. He didn't really know what he had wanted to accomplish by entering the camp in the first place. The humiliation stung. Wouldn't it be much more sensible to retain his familiar German identity: to go home and simply continue on with life as he knew it?

He touched his cheek gingerly. It was only a superficial cut, but the wound in his heart was deep. When he finally regained some measure of control, he turned the key in the ignition and drove home. Tomorrow he would try the border guard's suggestion. If that didn't bring concrete results, he would just have to accept his fate.

The following morning, Emsbach entered a large brick building in the city's industrial district. A handmade sign identified it as the Joint headquarters, and a secretary directed him to the third floor, where he faced yet another bureaucratic nightmare. Anxious people milled about the main room, waiting for access to the files containing population lists. Harried clerks strode back and forth between ceiling-to-floor shelves stacked with piles upon piles of records. The atmosphere was electric with urgency and desperation.

When Emsbach stepped into the hall, he immediately felt dozens of pairs of eyes on him. Was the scene at the DP camp going to repeat itself here? He stood impassively, eyes straight ahead, waiting his turn in the long line as the babble that had filled the room when he entered was replaced by a tense silence. Emsbach had no doubt that he was the cause of the transformation.

47

ONE OF THE CLERKS LEFT HIS PLACE AT THE HEAD DESK and wended his way through the crowded room to approach Emsbach. "May I help you?" His expression was wary.

Emsbach surmised that the clerk was more exhausted than hostile. "I wish to see the archives from a village in Poland named Birnhack. It's across the border from Gerlitz. I am looking for information about a *Rabbiner* named Stern."

"Follow me, please." The clerk led him to a seat near the windows. Fifteen minutes later, an assistant brought several heavy tomes to the table, set them down with a grunt and returned to the racks for more. To the doctor's consternation, he saw that the records were written in an unfamiliar script.

Biting his lip in dismay, he stole a glance at the other men seated near his table. Most were busy copying information from the record books, although some were still leafing through the pages with expressions of disappointment or distress. Emsbach noticed a tall, excruciatingly thin man, his reddish-brown beard streaked with gray, who seemed to be watching him out of the corner of his eye.

When their eyes met, the stranger cleared his throat and edged closer. "Perhaps you need a translator?" he suggested. "I am available for a reasonable compensation."

Emsbach nodded. "That's exactly what I need," he said. "Come, let us begin immediately. I am Dr. Karl Emsbach from Ravensdorf. It is imperative that I trace any survivors of the Stern family who resided in the village of Birnhack about 30 years ago."

"My name is Leizer Levine," the fellow said, taking a seat beside Emsbach. The two men spent hours delving into the endless lists of names. Eventually, as one day followed the next, Emsbach figured out how to read both the Hebrew and Cyrillic alphabets, but the information he sought about his family remained elusive.

Days later, he announced, "I give up." He was totally frustrated after so many hours of futile searching. Names of people and dates of birth swam before his eyes and haunted his dreams at night. Pushing the most recent volume away, he leaned back in his chair and stared glumly at the ceiling.

Leizer regarded him thoughtfully. The doctor had never offered an explanation for his unusual interest in the Stern family, but Levine was perceptive enough to know that Emsbach's search was far from academic. Also, the small sum he was earning for his efforts was very welcome. Without any other source of income, he would be sorry to lose this one.

"There might be more information in a different city," he suggested. "There are several organizations that keep records, and they don't always share their information."

"Are you prepared to accompany me?"

Leizer nodded.

"Won't your family worry if you are gone for a long time?"

Levine patted the book on the table. "My extended family is listed somewhere in these volumes," he said quietly. "I have not seen my wife since the war began, and I was separated from my children over a year ago. I pray that they are alive, and constantly search for their names at the same time that I help you."

This information made Emsbach look at the man who was assisting him, and really see him for the first time. "What did you do before the war?" he asked.

"I was a Talmud scholar."

Fraydl's brothers were Talmud scholars, too, Emsbach thought. Remembering the girl reminded him of Chaim and Yanky. *I have to get the children,* he decided. "No, Rabbi Levine, I have neither the patience nor the strength for any more research. Thank you for your offer."

The two men shook hands and parted. It was still early afternoon, so Emsbach had time to drive into the city and visit the orphanage. Perhaps someone was there who could tell him where to find the children.

The same nun redolent with the same potent smell of garlic answered the bell. She recognized the major and welcomed him politely, curtsying and stepping back so that he could enter the foyer.

"Is Father Matthew in?" Emsbach inquired.

"Father Matthew is dead."

"Dead?" Emsbach was aghast. "What happened? When?"

"Someone informed the Gestapo that he was sheltering Jews," she informed him impassively.

Emsbach reeled. The nun put out an arm to support him. "Sit down, major," she said. "I'll bring you a glass of water."

Emsbach had no idea how he made it to the chair, but he was sitting when the nun returned a few minutes later bearing a cup of water on a tray. He drank it down without the slightest awareness of what he was doing.

"I didn't know," he unthinkingly murmured.

"Of course not."

"When did it happen?"

"In the last days before the end of the war." The woman sighed.

"Were you with him?"

"No. I was transferred to the girls' wing, and Father Matthew took the boys to the village where he had relatives. We only found out later."

"Where are the children? What happened to the boys from the orphanage?"

"The archbishop divided them up and sent them to monasteries in the country."

Emsbach gazed at the empty glass in his hands. He wanted to hurl it on the floor and smash it to smithereens, like the lives of so many people shattered by the war.

"Would you like to speak with Father Gustav?" the nun asked. "He is the new vicar."

"Not today." Emsbach stood and walked heavily to the door. "The news of Father Matthew's death is a shock and I need time to come to terms with it. I will return another time. Good day, Sister."

It seemed incongruous that the sky was still blue and the sun was shining.

For all his lofty intentions, Emsbach realized that, in the end, he had failed to save the children. There was no one to confide in or seek counsel from. He got into the Mercedes and rested his forehead against the steering wheel for a moment, utterly spent.

Only a short while earlier, Emsbach had been absolutely sure of himself, in control of his life and his future. Now, the shards of his carefully conceived plans mocked him. His vision of a new life in America with the children he had rescued had vanished like smoke into thin air. The war was over and he had survived, but he was now a stranger to himself.

He felt a burning desire to pray, and it embarrassed him. Closing his eyes, he called out silently, *Dear G-d in Heaven, help me! If my real parents are still living, bring me back to them! If the children are still alive, bring them back to me!*

Feeling inexplicably calmer, he started the car and pulled out into the road.

48

INTOXICATED BY THE IDEA THAT THE WAR WAS OVER, FRAYDL continued walking for hours. Oblivious to the weight of the bundle she carried, she inhaled the fresh air and tried to absorb the concept of freedom after years of oppression. At one major intersection, her way was blocked by a crowd. She stood patiently among the others, watching as truck after truck of American soldiers rumbled by.

Seeing a pretty girl, some of the soldiers on the vehicles whistled, the American way of expressing appreciation. Fortunately for Fraydl, she did not realize that their attention was directed at her or she would have been mortified. A few called out to her in English, causing her to turn her head and smile pleasantly. One soldier plucked a branch of pink cherry blossoms from a tree and presented it to Fraydl in an overture of friendship as the convoy flowed by like an endless brown river.

Delighted, she held the flowers, her deprived senses enchanted by the soft, feathery petals. The procession of trucks disappeared into the distance and the knot of people moved forward. Fraydl vainly searched the crowd for a Jewish face because she wanted to ask directions to the train station, but she met only hostile expressions. *Of course they're bitter,* she shrugged. *They've just lost a war.*

Shivering despite the warm day, Fraydl quickened her pace. *Soon I will be in my own home again,* she comforted herself. Visions of her extended family reignited her excitement. Although she would never forget the day the soldiers took her father and older brothers away to the labor camp, it was possible that they had returned by this time. *Perhaps they are waiting for me right now? It will be so wonderful to be together again at last!*

She imagined telling her family about the ordeals she'd undergone since they'd been separated. *I won't tell Tatte everything,* she decided. *I don't want him to know how hard it was. It's bad enough that he will discover the Mamme is no long with us.*

Fraydl imagined returning to the Emsbach home, accompanied by her father. *Tatte will want to express his appreciation for all the Doktor's kindness, and we need to find out where Chaim and Yanky are now. We must also retrieve our silver.*

The war was over. Life could begin again. Fraydl regretted that her mother had not lived to see the triumph of good over evil. The sound of a locomotive's whistle reached her ears. What *siyata d'Shmaya!* While she'd been lost in her thoughts, the surging crowd had carried her to the very destination she needed!

It was pandemonium in the cavernous hall of the Central Train Station. The ticket booths were closed. Swarms of passengers elbowed their way toward teeming platforms, jostling onto cars whenever a passing train paused long enough to be boarded.

Fraydl heard a scream, and turned to see a young woman clutching a baby and pointing at a burly man who was rapidly pushing his way through the crowd with her suitcase in hand. "Thief! Thief!" the unfortunate mother cried helplessly. But in this time of anarchy, there was no one to help her.

Fraydl clutched her bundle tightly and slowly worked her way toward the southbound platform. It was hot, and she was so thirsty that her tongue seemed stuck to the roof of her mouth. For a moment, she wavered. Had it had been a mistake to leave Dr. Emsbach's house unprepared? She was spared further indecision when a train pulled into the station and she was swept along with the mob of refugees, all of them intent on boarding before the locomotive pulled out again.

Minutes later, Fraydl found herself pressed into a corner seat on the last bench. The scenery flashing by the open window elated her, and the wind tousled her hair. The sound of the wheels on the track seemed to repeat: *The war is over and I'm going home. I'm going home. I'm going home...*

Although there were stops at every single station to allow passengers to alight or board, the train made steady progress. It was still daylight when she saw the sign welcoming visitors to Austria. *Soon, soon,* she promised herself, although she wasn't at all sure where she would go once she stepped off the train.

At the first Austrian station, a group of rowdy young men shoved their way into the car, much the worse for having recently imbibed a generous quantity of good German *bier*. One of the newcomers pushed aside the travelers standing in the aisle and staggered over to Fraydl's relatively secluded corner. Noticing the girl, he leered drunkenly. She shrank back and the youth seemed to sober. Suddenly he yelled, "There's a Jew in here!"

His cry was met with raucous laughter. "Peter's had too much beer," one young man chortled to his companions. "Peter, there aren't any more Jews. Put your head down and sleep it off. You'll feel better when you wake up."

Peter stared at Fraydl. "Here's one that got away," he insisted, his coarse voice cracking.

Some of the other hoodlums edged closer and stared at her drunkenly. Fraydl turned her face to the window. She tried to ignore them but the thudding of her heart was almost audible. On all sides, passengers with stern expressions craned their necks to get a glimpse of her. Sensing that a confrontation was brewing, two British soldiers left their places and made their way down the aisle toward the rear of the car.

The drunken youth backed away from Fraydl in a display of disgust, wiping his hands as if he had touched something unclean. Before he could incite his friends to take appropriate action, the train rounded a steep mountain curve and the inebriated boys tumbled over themselves onto the floor.

"Get off me!" came a yell came from the bottom of the pile, followed by a mayhem of flying fists and elbows as a fight broke out between the ruffians. The British soldiers stepped in, adding their fists to the fray.

"Hey, Fritz!" The taller Brit addressed the belligerent boys with the collective generic name used by Allied enlisted men for all German males. "You fellows are getting off this train right now!" Moments later, as the train slowed, the two soldiers pushed the boys out of the car even before it came to a full stop.

"Sorry, *fraulein*," the soldier apologized to Fraydl with an exaggerated bow. "I don't think those barbarians will be bothering you anymore."

She looked at him in astonishment, grateful to be rid of the drunken teenagers but unsure how to respond to her rescuer. "*Danke schön*," she whispered.

The soldier acknowledged her words with a nod and returned to his seat. Despite the civilized attitude of the British soldiers, the atmosphere in the car remained openly antagonistic toward her. Fraydl could hardly wait for the unpleasant trip to end.

Night fell. The bright lights at the next station dazed her. It was Munichau, the last stop before her own. Most of the passengers disembarked before the overhead lights finally dimmed and the locomotive continued chugging along the track. To Fraydl's dismay, the train did not follow the familiar route that would lead her home. In fact, it seemed to be traveling in a completely different direction.

Afraid of drawing attention, she unsuccessfully strained her eyes to make out the road signs in the dark. The car was much less crowded than it had been before. Underneath one of the empty benches she spotted an abandoned basket containing a few apples. No one noticed as she helped herself to the first food she'd tasted all day. The apples satisfied both her hunger and her thirst, and the repetitive click-clack of the wheels lulled her into an exhausted sleep.

"Wake up, girl! Get off the train!"

It was a conductor, inspecting the cars. Fraydl jumped up, instinctively clutching her bundle of clothes, and quickly alighted. The surroundings were totally unfamiliar and she had no idea where she was. After so many hours sitting on a rocking bench, her ankles nearly buckled before she adjusted to the reality that the ground was no longer swaying beneath her.

The well-lit station appeared to be empty. "Go on home, girl," the conductor called after her, not unkindly. "It's too late for a young lady to be out on her own."

Fraydl wandered along the platform until she saw a gentleman in a uniform. "Can you help me, sir?" she asked.

He regarded her suspiciously.

"I'm lost," she admitted. "I was on my way to Vienna, but the train took a different direction."

"What business do you have in Vienna?" he frowned.

"My family used to live there."

"There are no more Jews in Vienna." His voice was flat, unmoved by her pained expression. "You'll have to go to the police station," he barked. "Go back to the terminal, and wait in the office until you can be processed properly."

She didn't know if she was more frightened of leaving the train station or of staying there, but in the end Fraydl found herself waiting her turn in a line of refugees as a sullen desk sergeant took down information and filled out forms.

Forced to deal with approximately eight million people who had been uprooted from their homes by the war, the Allied powers in Germany had appointed local officials to try to create organization out of chaos. These bureaucrats lumped all homeless civilians together as Displaced Persons. The small group of refugees from the train station was duly transported to a nearby DP camp, until recently the SS living quarters of a Nazi concentration camp.

49

AFTER A FITFUL NIGHT'S SLEEP ON A COT IN THE WOMEN'S dormitory, Fraydl woke to discover that she was now living under armed guard in the Austrian section of a Displaced Persons camp. Immediately after the war ended, homeless refugees were categorized by the occupying authorities according to their national origin. The inevitable consequence of this approach was that the tiny number of Jewish refugees who survived the Holocaust were imprisoned in intimate proximity to their worst enemies.

Fraydl's experiences in the war had made her sensitive to danger, and almost before she opened her eyes she sensed peril. As unobtrusively as possible, she left the barracks and searched for a way to escape — only to discover that the camp was surrounded by barbed-wire fences and locked gates guarded by armed sentries with ominous expressions.

Her mood plummeted, from the euphoria of the previous day to a black despondency. *Why was I so impatient to leave the safety of the Emsbach house?* Fraydl rebuked herself. *If only I had waited, surely Herr Doktor would have returned. What will become of me now?*

"*A guten morgen.* Come, I'll show you where to get something to eat."

Fraydl was startled to hear a voice just behind her. When she turned to face the speaker, her heart flooded with relief. She knew intuitively that this gray-eyed girl was a fellow Jew! "*A guten morgen,*" she replied, a genuine smile lighting her face.

The young woman had dark blond hair and looked about her age. "My name is Helene Lieber," she said quietly. "We used to live in Hallstatt."

"I'm Fraydl Mertzbach. I'm originally from Vienna."

"You look very well." Helene examined her critically. "With your face, how did you succeed in posing as a gentile for so long?"

Fraydl shook her head. "I've been in hiding most of the time. Since I was 14."

Helene's gray eyes bored into her face. "You're lucky." Helene did not conceal her bitterness. "My father's business partner agreed to tell people that I was his orphaned niece, but I had to act the part. Every day that passed was torture."

"It must have been difficult." Fraydl tried to imagine.

Helene shook her head. "You can't begin to understand. I had to work hard all the time and never complain. Every morning, when I woke up, I didn't know if I would still be alive that night. Anyone might betray me. I was afraid to open my mouth because the wrong word or phrase would accidentally give away my secret. I pretended to be stupid, smiling like an idiot no matter how offended I was by the things they said and did." The flow of words stopped abruptly.

"Have you been here long?" Fraydl asked, hoping that changing the subject would distract her new friend from the pain of her memories.

"About a month." Helene relaxed her tense shoulders and offered a half- smile.

"Why are there guards at the gates? Are we prisoners?"

"Yes and no. It's not a prison, and we're not criminals, but no one can leave without permission — and they don't give permission easily."

The two girls reached the front of the line and accepted trays with bread and butter, boiled eggs and orange juice — politely refusing the bacon and cheese. Helene was ravenous. During the time it took Fraydl to wash for bread, she finished her breakfast down to the last crumb.

"There are over a thousand people in this camp," Helene explained while Fraydl ate, "but less than a hundred are Jews. Some of the inmates are not even refugees, but former Nazis pretending to be displaced persons in order to escape arrest for their crimes in the war. Be careful. It is not wise to draw their attention."

"When did the war end?" Fraydl asked.

Helene gave her a funny look. "Where were you hiding?"

"Over the border, in Germany. My benefactor disappeared many weeks ago and I didn't dare go outside without knowing what was happening. When the supply of food was almost finished, I thought of turning on the radio. That's how I discovered that the war was over."

"Germany capitulated about two months ago."

Fraydl could hardly believe that she had left the Emsbach house only the previous morning. Remembering Dr. Emsbach's reports, she asked, "Are the stories about the annihilation of all the Jews true?" Her voice faded to a whisper.

Helene's expression grew hard. "Yes," she replied. "May G-d avenge their deaths! Everyone I know is gone. There is no one left."

The two young women sat together in oppressive silence. Fraydl's eyes filled with tears and she blinked them away. "I don't believe it," she insisted. "It *can't* be true! Surely the civilized world would not stand by and allow such a thing to happen."

It was Helene's turn to divert Fraydl's attention. Looking around to be sure they were not overheard, she whispered, "We must leave this accursed land!"

"Palestine." The word leaped out of Fraydl's mouth of its own accord.

"Yes!" Helene agreed. "Whoever is still alive must go to Palestine. There is no other solution."

"When can we leave?" Fraydl asked, the smallest flicker of hope momentarily kindled in her grief-stricken heart.

"A little more patience," Helene cautioned. "Technically, Germany has been defeated, but there are still pockets of Nazi resistance out there. Even surrounded by people who hate us for surviving, we are safer inside the camp right now. Soon, though, we will be in Eretz Yisrael."

It can't be soon enough, Fraydl thought. *If I can just find Chaim and Yanky, then we will be on the first boat to Palestine.*

Each passing day brought more refugees to the DP camp. The few Jewish survivors drifted together for mutual support, and occasionally Fraydl met someone who had known one of her brothers or sisters. As death after death was confirmed, she began to lose her own desire to continue living. *Why did I remain alive?* She questioned. Each time, she sat *shivah* for one hour, mourning another sibling who would never return. Fraydl began avoiding her fellow inmates, and spent hours lying motionless on her cot.

Helene, meanwhile, found herself drawn to a group of young adults whose conversation centered on their lust for vengeance. When former guards from the concentration camps were recognized, their lifeless bodies mysteriously showed up the next day near the perimeter of the barbed-wire fence. For the downtrodden survivors, the violent death of their tormentors was empowering. The Nazis masquerading as refugees feared and hated the vigilantes, while the DP camp guards pursued them relentlessly.

"Why doesn't your friend join us?" they asked Helene.

She shrugged. "Fraydl was in hiding during the war, so she had no idea of what was going on. Now she's been forced to face reality. She needs time to mourn."

"We need her support. Try and convince her that our activities are the best revenge for her losses. Bring her to our meeting tonight."

Fraydl listened listlessly as Helene employed her powers of persuasion to interest her in participating.

"I can't," she murmured. "Leave me alone. I'll think about it later. Not now."

That night, Helene was arrested along with her new friends. Left alone with her melancholy, Fraydl turned to Hashem with a desperate plea for His salvation.

50

TIME PASSED MONOTONOUSLY FOR THE RESIDENTS OF THE Displaced Persons camp. As Fraydl adjusted to her new reality, she often chose to escape the inhospitable dormitory and join the other Jewish refugees sitting idly outside the dining hall. She would usually take a seat on the side and listen quietly, rarely offering her own ideas or opinions.

"We have to demand an improvement in our living conditions!" Raya complained, swatting at a housefly. "This place is filthy."

Fraydl certainly agreed with that sentiment. Naturally fastidious, the dismal hygiene in the camp was a constant source of discomfort to her.

"Who cares whether you are satisfied or not?" Katya's voice shrilled unpleasantly. The daughter of an Austrian banker before the war, the poor girl had only learned that her maternal grandmother was Jewish when she was taken to Theresienstadt. Orphaned of her mother and disowned by her wealthy father, the once pretty and vivacious girl was now hollow eyed and bitter.

Masha had spent the war years posing as a Christian and working as a seamstress in a Bavarian textile factory. Practical by nature, she saw no point in complaining about things that could not be changed. "Be grateful for what there is," she reprimanded. "Outside these gates, people are starving. At least in here there is food to eat."

"We have to get on with our lives," Raya grumbled. "Day after day we sit here doing nothing. Do you want to be an old lady when they finally release us? We must do something to make things better!"

"What exactly do you suggest?" Katya's lips curled in contempt.

Silence followed. They all knew that they were powerless to change anything. A wave of chagrin swept over Fraydl as she recalled what had happened when she'd gone to the office to request a few sheets of paper and a pencil. She'd wanted to write a letter to Dr. Emsbach, to let him know where she was and to request his assistance.

"What do you need it for?" the clerk had responded.

"I need to find my two young nephews. I must write a letter to the person who was responsible for them," Fraydl explained.

"I'm sorry. Residents are not allowed to send or receive mail." He didn't sound sorry.

Intimidated by the man's hostile demeanor, she'd tried asking politely for a pass to leave the camp, "Just for a few hours, to take care of some private matters."

"Permission denied. No one is allowed to leave the DP camp."

Fraydl flushed in humiliation. *What is my crime? Why am I being imprisoned here?* she wanted to demand — but she didn't.

Unmoved by the disappointment on her face, the clerk continued, "Our priority must be to protect innocent Austrian civilians from harassment. If you are dissatisfied, you may forward your request to my superiors."

Fraydl stared at him for a moment before turning on her heels and exiting the room. Back in the dormitory, she comforted herself with *Tehillim* and the knowledge that, even though they acted as if they were in charge, the occupying authorities were not the ones running the world.

A few days later, the monotony was broken when a delegation from Palestine visited the camp. The Jewish Brigade Group was

interested in establishing contact with survivors. Their representatives enthusiastically encouraged the Jewish refugees to support
the Zionist cause. Many were seduced by their glowing promises
— but not all. Fraydl remembered her father's warnings about the
dangers of secular Zionism, and she resisted the visitors' persua-
sive arguments despite her own longing to be in Eretz Yisrael.

Over the next weeks, emissaries from various Jewish youth
movements and Palestinian agricultural settlement organizations
continued to visit the DP camp.

"Don't listen to them," Solly Bergman warned in a somber voice.
At 30, he was the oldest among the Austrian Jewish refugees, and
his opinion carried weight. "They know we all want to leave the
bloody soil of Europe, but the reality is not as rosy as they describe."

"How can you tell us not to go up to Eretz Yisrael?" young
Mordche Fisher asked in astonishment. He was very tempted to
sign up and join the underground.

"It's too dangerous," Solly reasoned. "We've only just survived
Gehinnom. Do you want to go and fight a war with the Arabs now?
The British have no intention of allowing more Jews into Palestine.
It would upset the delicate balance with the Arabs. Immigration is
illegal, and if they catch you — which they probably will — you
will find yourself in a worse camp than this one, maybe for years."

Fraydl approached each visitor with the request that they contact Dr. Emsbach for her, but as soon as the speakers realized that
she did not support their particular agenda, her personal dilemma
held no interest for them. "Have patience," one official from the
Jewish Agency reassured her, before excusing himself to go address
another group in a different section of the camp. "There are going
to be changes soon."

"What do you mean?"

"The maltreatment of Jewish survivors has come to the attention of the news organizations in America. President Truman will
need the Jewish vote when he comes up for re-election, so he's
appointed a mission to investigate the rumors. The situation
should improve soon."

Fraydl watched the Palestinian Jew hurry away to the Hungarian section of the camp. Without regular news from the outside, it felt as if the world had forgotten all about the refugees.

Weeks passed with no apparent change. She began to wonder if they would ever get out of this wretched place.

"Listen to them!" Raya shook her head cynically. "Politics! Isn't it just like men to sit around discussing political developments in the world, as if it makes any difference to us?"

Fraydl didn't tell her, but she thought it was a good sign. In a small symbolic way, life was becoming ordinary again. No longer were their thoughts limited to merely surviving for one more day. Now the men had both the leisure and the normal wish to know what was happening in the outside world. From her place in the corner, she felt comforted when she heard their raised voices and saw their gesticulations as they argued.

"The American delegation was shocked by the conditions in the DP camps," declared Kalman. "I glimpsed the headlines while the guard was reading his newspaper."

"I picked up the paper after the guard left," young Tuvia boasted with a mischievous grin. "I have it right here!" He pulled the crumpled pages from his shirt and carefully smoothed the creases. "Here, you can read the whole report."

Getzel scrutinized the date: 30 June 1945. "It's recent," he commented.

"So what does it say? Read it aloud!"

Kalman took the newspaper and held it up to the light. "Professor Earl G. Harrison wrote a scathing report in June 1945, notifying President Harry Truman that American policy gives the impression that the United States condones Nazi policy regarding the Jews," he read in a clear voice.

His audience leaned forward, nodding their agreement. This was encouraging news.

". . .and strongly recommending immigration to Palestine as the only feasible solution to the untenable situation," he continued.

Kalman's voice was drowned out by shouts and banging on the tables. Fraydl looked from one to the other, hardly daring to hope the words were true.

"Did you hear?" Getzel the Zionist sympathizer exulted. "We will be in Eretz Yisrael by Pesach!"

"Your optimism kept you alive in the camps, but it won't get you into Palestine," Solly Bergman commented sourly.

"Not with the Arab-loving British in charge," Yaakov Meyer agreed.

"Keep reading, Kalman," Geztel urged. "What else does it say?"

"British Prime Minister Clement Atlee made haste to spell out London's apprehensions to the United States, reminding President Truman that the Arab nations are likely to respond to mass Jewish immigration by disrupting vital oil supplies. In addition, he warned of the growing influence of the newly nuclear USSR in the Arab world. 'Opening the gates of Palestine to more Jews would be a disaster for the free world!' the chancellor told the American president."

51

SEVERAL AMERICAN SOLDIERS STOOD ON THE CORNER, trying to flag down a ride back to their base. Since this was in his direction, Emsbach decided that picking up a couple of hitchhikers might distract his mind from the dead end he had reached.

"Do you live nearby?" the shorter soldier asked in fractured German, opening the front door and sliding in beside the driver.

"No," Emsbach replied in English, gesturing to the second soldier to sit in the back seat. "Where are you from?"

"Memphis, Tennessee," the soldier in front drawled, followed by his partner's drawn-out, "Bahston, Mass."

"And where are you stationed now?" The doctor adjusted the rearview mirror so he could see his passenger as well as the traffic behind him.

"Not far from the former concentration camp of Mauthausen, near Ebensee."

Between the drawl of the one soldier and the twang of the other, Emsbach's college-English comprehension was receiving a good workout. Understanding them demanded his full concentration.

They will never get jobs as announcers for the BBC, he thought wryly, *but it is a good mental exercise for me.* "What is your assignment there?" he asked.

"The camp was requisitioned for homeless refugees. Our job is mainly to prevent disorder."

Recollecting his own experience at the Displaced Persons camp, Emsbach had no difficulty relating to the American soldier's words. Sunk in his memories for a few moments, he lost track of their discussion until the southerner mentioned that many visitors came to the camp, searching for relatives.

"Do they find the people they are looking for?" Emsbach was vaguely curious about this route of obtaining information.

"Most don't. It's real sad to see them coming with hope in their eyes and then leaving with the weight of the world on their shoulders."

There was silence in the Mercedes. "War is a tough business," the soldier from Boston added, and the others nodded their agreement.

"A couple of days ago, a committee of American rabbis came to our camp looking for Jews. One of them was asking everyone he met if there were any survivors from the village where he used to live — some place called Birnhack that no one ever heard of. I'm not even sure if it's on a map."

"Birnhack!" Emsbach involuntarily slammed the brakes, throwing himself into the steering wheel and his passenger against the dashboard. "Birnhack? Are you certain?"

"Yes," the fellow answered, rubbing his forehead where it had bumped the windshield. He regarded the German doubtfully, clearly questioning his sanity.

"Sorry. I also happen to be looking for someone from Birnhack." Emsbach spoke calmly and resumed driving, but his heart was pounding painfully in his chest. "Do you remember what the man's name was?"

"It was a German name. I thought at the time it was funny to call someone 'Star' so his name must have been Stern or something like that."

Emsbach caught his breath. He pulled the car over to the side of the road. It was impossible to focus on driving with stormy waves of emotion sweeping over him. "Do you know how I can find this American who was asking about someone from Birnhack?" he interrogated the soldier.

"The delegation has been at the camp every day this week. It's possible he's still there. If you'll take us to Ebensee, we'll get you inside the camp."

Emsbach's imagination was on fire. It would not do to raise his hopes only to be disappointed again. He pulled the Mercedes back onto the road and the men continued their journey, but Emsbach no longer had enough patience to try to understand their strangely accented English.

It took an hour to drive to the Displaced Persons camp where the hitchhikers were stationed. He parked the car and surveyed the camp. It appeared marginally better than the British one he'd visited previously. Accompanied by the American soldiers, he was received civilly despite the hostility that his Germanic manner triggered. Emsbach looked around for an officer to approach.

"Hello! How are you?"

Karl Emsbach smiled at the familiar voice, and shook hands with Leizer Levine. "Rabbi, what are you doing here?" he asked his former assistant.

"The same thing I was doing in the archives where we met," the tall thin man answered. "I am trying to trace anyone from my extended family who might have survived the war."

"Did you happen to meet a delegation of American rabbis?"

"I know they are in the camp, but I haven't spoken with any of them. How do you know about the rabbis?"

"I gave a ride to some soldiers who are stationed here, and they mentioned it."

Levine's expression was puzzled. "Of what interest are they to you, *Herr Doktor*?" he asked.

"I heard that one of the rabbis is inquiring about survivors from Birnhack. I thought he might know what happened to the family I'm trying to locate."

Leizer nodded. "They're meeting with the commanding officer

of the camp right now," he told Emsbach. "I'll take you to head-quarters, and when they leave the meeting you can talk with them."

"What are American rabbis doing here in the first place?"

"They're encouraging Jews to return to life, *Herr Doktor*," Levine said quietly. "Some of the Jewish refugees have been asking for a kitchen where they can eat kosher food, and they want a room set aside for study and prayer. Up until now, the authorities were not forthcoming, but the residents are hoping that the delegation of visiting American rabbis will have enough influence to get the officials in charge to agree."

The meeting was taking place in a barracks room, and it had reached an impasse. Several of the participants noticed Emsbach and Leizer through the open door. Relieved to divert his attention from the deadlocked discussion, the presiding officer turned to the newcomers and was favorably impressed with Emsbach's military bearing. "Are you looking for me?" he inquired.

"I would like to speak with the rabbis," Emsbach said.

"Yes?" The rabbi who was wearing a United States Army uniform did not look pleased at the interruption.

Emsbach looked at the men sitting around the table, and then addressed the rabbi who had spoken. "I understand that a member of your delegation is looking for survivors from the village of Birnhack."

There was a barely audible gasp. A gray-bearded man in his late 60's stood up, hands gripping the edge of the table. He fixed Emsbach with piercing blue eyes. "I am the one you are referring to," he informed the German intruder. "Do you have any information?"

"I am looking for information about the Stern family from Birnhack, Poland," Emsbach replied. The sensation of being stared at by every eye in the room was extremely unsettling.

"I am originally from Birnhack," the rabbi said. "How may I help you?"

52

E MSBACH DREW IN A LONG, SLOW BREATH, UNCOMFORT-
able with the idea of exposing his personal story to an audience
of strangers. If it wasn't so critical to resolve the doubts that had
been torturing him ever since Uncle Heinrich's attempt to kill him,
he would simply have turned and left. But how could he miss this
opportunity? If he didn't take a chance now, he might never be a
whole person again.

The rabbi with the gray beard scrutinized him, obviously wary
of deceit. The tension in the room thickened. Finally, Emsbach could
bear it no longer. He began to speak, endeavoring to be as clear and
succinct as possible.

"I am a German doctor — a surgeon. I live in Ravensdorf. My
uncle was a Nazi brigadier general."

The faces of the camp residents paled. The oldest rabbi appeared
more affected than the others, struggling to remain calm.

"Go on," he said.

"My parents were killed in an accident when I was a young boy.
My uncle assumed responsibility for my education." He hesitated.
His story was so absurd, how could he repeat it to these strangers?

Their eyes were so skeptical that he almost gave up.

"Please carry on," the older rabbi insisted, his dark-blue eyes burning into the German standing before them.

Emsbach cleared his throat, and continued. "My uncle visited me on the final day of the war. He took me into my private study and pulled out a revolver. He told me that he wanted to go down in history as the murderer of the last living Jew in the world."

Now he spoke faster, the words tumbling off his tongue in a race to be expressed. "I thought my uncle had lost his mind. We were never close. He was always unpredictable, but I never thought that he would harm me. I tried using reason. I reminded him of my mother, his sister, but he just laughed. Then he said something incredible. The brigadier general told me that he had stolen me as a small boy from a Jewish village across the border from Gerlitz, and brought me to his sister's house. He said that they raised me as their own son."

"Do you expect us to believe this ridiculous story?" a clean-shaven rabbi asked angrily. "Who are you? Why are you wasting our time?"

Emsbach felt tears spring to his eyes. He bit his lip and turned his head away, utterly humiliated. Why had he put himself in this position?

One of the other rabbis was more compassionate. "You have to understand," he said softly. "Many of the same Nazis who tortured us and murdered our families are desperate to escape justice. There are reports of Gestapo officers posing as Jews in DP camps in the hope that the authorities will pity them and allow them to leave Germany. How do we know that you are not one of them?"

The room was deathly still. News travels fast. Jewish residents of the camp began gathering around the building, curious about the newcomer. Leizer Levine, standing beside Emsbach, was as surprised as the others. In all the days they'd spent together in the archives, the German had never explained the reasons behind his stubborn search for the Stern family, yet their short acquaintance had given Levine the impression that he was trustworthy.

"This man is not a Nazi fugitive," he declared confidently in Yiddish. "I am sure of it. The doctor is sincere."

"Do you have anything else to add?" the rabbi wearing an American Army uniform asked. The older rabbi was sitting now, his face hidden as he listened to the exchange between the others.

"I understand why you doubt my words. I could not believe it, either. I was sure that the shameful end of his military career had made my uncle delusional. But when he raised his revolver and aimed it at my chest, it was clear that the brigadier general fully intended to pull the trigger. I am only here today because at exactly the last moment, he collapsed. My uncle had a sudden stroke, and minutes later he was dead.

"Since that experience, I've had no peace of mind. The first thing I did was visit an old family servant who had known my parents long before I was born. She confirmed that the story was true. She told me that the servants were all aware of what had happened, and after my parents' death they conspired to keep it a secret."

Emsbach looked around at the faces of the men in the room. "I traveled to the village of Birnhack. I wanted to see it for myself. I went to the synagogue where the brigadier general boasted that he'd snatched me. I have no memories of the place. An elderly gentile told me that there had been a family named Stern living there over 20 years ago, and that they had a child who was stolen by a German officer and never heard from again. I may be that child. I am trying to locate any survivors of the Stern family. When I heard that someone here is looking for survivors from Birnhack, I came to ask for assistance in finding my real family."

The room was silent. The elderly rabbi lifted his head and looked at Emsbach, his features contorted with pain. "Tell me your uncle's name," he ordered, in a voice crackling with emotion. A moment later, the room was electrified by the infamous name, "Brigadier General Heinrich Mauer." At these words, the old rabbi cried out and fell down in a swoon.

Chairs were pushed back as concerned men rushed to help. Emsbach stood transfixed while Levine bent over the prostrate man, gently reviving him from his faint. "Get back! Please, give him air," Leizer requested. People backed away reluctantly, their eyes following the drama.

The rabbi's eyelids fluttered before opening completely. Assisted by Leizer Levine, he struggled unsteadily to his feet and tried to focus on the tall blond German.

"Please sit," Leizer requested, tenderly lowering the frail figure onto a chair. He studied the spectators for a few seconds. "Could someone bring water?" he asked, more to release the tension than because there was a need for it.

The old rabbi lifted his hand weakly, gesturing for Emsbach to approach. Someone thrust a glass of water into his hand and he sipped it before handing it back. Color was returning to his face. The man's voice grew stronger as he began to speak.

"Twenty-seven years ago," he began — and stopped. Recovering, he repeated, "Twenty-seven years ago, my little son was kidnapped from the shul courtyard in Birnhack. It was a few days before his 3rd birthday. Witnesses related that the men on horseback were drunken German soldiers."

The rabbi stopped speaking and momentarily lowered his head to his hands, shoulders shaking with a grief that had never healed. "I tried to pursue them. I called out my son's name again and again, but the men rode their horses into the river and disappeared over the German side of the border

"For years we searched for our child, following any lead. My wife's health was destroyed; our family was broken. For a bribe, one German officer revealed that a certain Captain Heinrich Mauer knew where the boy could be found. It was impossible to leave my wife in her precarious state of health, but I sent faithful messengers. I instructed them to pay any ransom. No price was too high.

"The heartless man cursed them and sent them away, threatening to have me imprisoned. Not long afterward, I received a summons by the Polish police to appear for interrogation regarding the disappearance of a Christian child that Mauer claimed I had kidnapped. Realizing that our lives were in danger, we fled Poland before it was too late. My wife and I moved to America together with our unmarried children.

"Young man, you come here with a tale that breaks my heart." The rabbi choked back a sob, and Leizer Levine put a supportive arm around the man's shoulders. "Perhaps you are my son? But you could also be someone who heard of our tragic story and are playing on our sympathies. My son was very intelligent. If you are indeed my child, surely you must have some memories from before you were kidnapped. Tell me something you remember from when you were very small."

Karl Emsbach hid his face in his palms, closing his eyes and trying with all his might to remember anything from his distant past — but there was nothing. "My first memories are of the house in Ravensdorf," he murmured. "I can remember nothing before that."

Rabbi Stern shook his head in disappointment. "Perhaps you remember your mother lighting Shabbos candles?" he encouraged, but Emsbach could only remember Mutter's parties.

To the men in the room the German appeared sincere, but the general conclusion was that, if his story was true, then he really should remember something.

53

LEIZER LEVINE LOOKED BACK AND FORTH FROM RABBI
Stern to Dr. Emsbach. The doctor's far-fetched story actually
seemed credible to him, but to establish a genuine relationship after
so many years of separation required incontrovertible proof. He
frowned in thought, and then suggested, "Perhaps your son had
a birthmark or some other physical sign that would identify him
undeniably?"

Rabbi Stern shook his head. There had been no physical flaws in
the child who'd been stolen from him. The little boy's beauty and
bravery were the things that had caught the eyes of the drunken
Germans. The rabbi gazed at Emsbach intensely, desperate for a
sign that would allow him to believe that the nightmare was over.

"I am circumcised," Emsbach offered hesitantly. "As a doctor, I
know that some babies are born that way, but it is unusual among
German boys."

The clean-shaven rabbi rejected the idea. "That doesn't prove
anything. As a surgeon, you surely know that such an operation
can be performed at any age, either for reasons of health or to conceal that a man was not circumcised in infancy."

Tense seconds passed until Emsbach said, "I have an unusual scar on my knee. I can't remember *not* having it...and it must have been a deep cut to leave such a scar."

Rabbi Stern's face paled. "Show me!" he said with great urgency. "On which leg is it? Let me see!"

Emsbach pulled his left trouser leg up to reveal a thin, jagged scar twisting down the center of his knee in the shape of the last letter in the Hebrew alphabet. "Yes!" shouted the Rabbi, leaping up from his chair. "Yes! No one could have known about it. Your brothers were going to collect wood for their *Lag B'Omer* bonfire, and they insisted that you were too small to come. You ran after them, but you fell and cut your knee on a sharp stone. I remember as if it were yesterday!" He looked around the room, an expression of ecstasy lighting up his face. "Tanchum, my son!" Rabbi Stern opened his arms to embrace the stunned young man.

No one was able to speak for several minutes and there was not a dry eye in the room. While Emsbach and his father hugged each other, a bottle of *schnapps* appeared from nowhere and shot glasses were passed around. "*L'Chaim! L'Chaim!*" the men shouted. Rabbi Stern clung to his newfound son's arm with one hand and raised his glass with the other. After reciting the *Shehakol* blessing and drinking some of the fiery liquid, the rabbi took both of Emsbach's hands in his own. "I am sorry that I did not have the presence of mind to be like Yaakov Avinu," he told his newfound son. "When he was reunited with his son Yosef, he proclaimed *Shema Yisrael* before anything else. Please, my precious son, say the words with me now, even if you do not understand their meaning."

Emsbach had listened to Chaim *daven* Maariv during the war, and the words were not unfamiliar, though Rabbi Stern's *Litvish* pronunciation was noticeably different from the young boy's.

Unable to take his eyes off the man his lost child had grown into, Rabbi Stern noticed that Emsbach was becoming increasingly pale. Leizer Levine met the older man's eyes, and nodded. "It is wonderful — *gevaldig!* But it is also overwhelming for both of you," he said, urging the two to sit down.

Someone started to hum a *niggun,* and the Jews in the room linked arms, spontaneously dancing around the father and his son. Karl Emsbach, who, in actuality, was Tanchum Stern, felt himself surrounded by a comradeship he had never dreamed of experiencing. His mind did not understand the Hebrew words the men were singing, but on a deeper level his heart understood. He smiled as warmth spread through his body, and he felt a joy beyond imagination.

Word spread through the camp like wildfire. More and more people crowded into the barracks, until it could hold no more. Others stood outside the windows and all around the building. Someone brought a violin and began to accompany the singing men.

Watching the violinist draw his bow, Leizer Levine was caught up in the incredible joy of the reunion between a father and his lost son. With a mind of their own, his long fingers danced in the air until he finally turned to the fiddler and whispered, "I used to play, long ago, before the war. It's been so many years. Would you mind letting me try for a few minutes?"

The man looked at Leizer, but didn't recognize him. "All right, but be careful," he warned. "It's a delicate instrument."

The violinist needn't have worried. Since the day it was carved, his violin had never made such music as it did in Leizer Levine's scarred hands. The eloquence of the music was a reflection of Leizer's deep *Yiddishe neshamah,* and as his bow slid back and forth his lined, tired face was transformed by his own inner light. No Jew could resist participating; even Tanchum and Rabbi Stern joined the circles of dancers, their hearts soaring as one with the others.

The non-Jewish army officers stood restlessly on the sides, disturbed and touched by the mysterious sensations that the music awakened in their hearts. None would admit it, but they envied the suffering Jews who were able to put aside their troubles and dance and sing with such elation.

All too soon, Leizer returned the violin to its owner with a shrug, thanking him and apologizing for being out of practice. The dancers protested, begging for more, but Levine's eyes were moist and he shook his head.

"What happened? Why did he stop playing?"

"I haven't danced like that since before the war!"

Karl Emsbach rested his hands on Levine's shoulders, intending to ask him to stay, but Leizer shook his head in mute refusal. The violinist could not explain to his recently acquired friend how the music had transported him back to his Rebbe's court and the joy he had experienced there before the war. The realization that that world was gone forever had plunged his soul into deep sorrow. He simply could not continue.

Murmuring a few words of appreciation, Emsbach shook Leizer's hand in farewell. Leizer parted from father and son with heartfelt blessings for a wonderful future together, and then he was gone.

"Who was that man?" Rabbi Stern asked his son.

"I wish I knew," Emsbach replied. "I met him in the archives and he helped me for days, translating documents in my search for my family. I was so buried in my own affairs that I never tried to get to know him. I regret that now."

"*A feiner, eidel mann,*" Rabbi Stern said softly, looking through the door where Leizer had disappeared. "I hope we meet him again."

"Gentlemen, shall we consider our meeting adjourned?" It was dark already, and the camp commander was anxious to get home to his wife in the hotel reserved for American Army personnel.

"Captain, have we agreed?" asked the rabbi with the thick glasses. "You will allow our agency to set up a kosher kitchen for the camp residents?"

Captain Prout could no longer remember why he had previously refused this reasonable request. "Yes, yes. Send your men to clean out the smaller kitchen in the last barracks, and make up a list of the supplies you will need. Bring it to my office by 8 o'clock tomorrow morning."

With difficulty, the delegation hid their surprise. Rabbi Stern did not forget his mission. "Captain Prout, sir," he said, "Which room will be available for study and prayer services?"

Prout hemmed and hawed for a moment, but Leizer's music had diminished his resistance. "All right. . . . There is a storage room that could be cleaned out if your men have enough energy. I'll instruct my lieutenant to give you the key tomorrow."

"Thank you, captain. My report to our agency will detail your extensive cooperation," the first rabbi assured him. "But perhaps it is possible to get the key tonight. We would like to hold evening prayers together now, before the delegation leaves."

"You can have the use of this room for tonight," the captain consented, more than mollified by the knowledge that his career would advance by cooperating with these civilians. "But I have to warn you: the storeroom must be cleaned before it will be habitable."

The rabbis in the delegation shook his hand, and the impatient captain left. Word spread that Maariv would be *davened* in the meeting room. For the first time in his life, Tanchum Stern was counted as one of the 10 for a *minyan*.

54

WHERE DO THEY THINK THEY'RE GOING?" RAYA SNIFFED, warming her hands around her glass and allowing the rising steam to tickle her red cheeks. Confined indoors by the winter weather, the usual group of women huddled together at their accustomed table in the cafeteria.

"There's no air in here," Katya grumbled. "Why don't they open a window or something?"

Raya raised her eyes and frowned at Katya, not deigning to comment on the illogic of opening a window in a warm room when it was snowing outside.

Ever practical, Masha simply turned to Mordche, who was bringing up the rear of the procession leaving the dining hall. "Where are you going?" she asked.

The youngster paused impatiently. "Why are you still sitting here? Haven't you heard the news?"

"What news?" Raya yawned, finding it hard to believe that someone could actually know something that she didn't know already.

"There's going to be an announcement in the main office

especially for the Jewish internees. Something important has happened." Mordche hurried after the other men.

"Well, I guess we'd better get moving if we don't want to miss the excitement," Raya declared. The rest of her words were drowned out by the scraping of their chairs as everyone rose at once.

Fraydl stood among the women, waiting for the director to take the microphone and address the camp residents. Promptly on the hour, the man appeared, and after a rather long and unremarkable speech reiterating his accomplishments as director, a new speaker wearing an American Army uniform was introduced.

"As of this moment," the officer informed his audience, "internees may leave and return to camp at their own discretion." The welcome news was met with scattered applause. "Mail privileges are hereby restored, and you may write and receive letters," he continued. "Camp operations are being transferred to the newly established United Nations Refugee Relief and Rehabilitation Administration and the American Jewish Joint. This is the decision of General Dwight Eisenhower, at the behest of President Harry Truman, for your benefit. We wish you success in rebuilding your lives and putting the trauma of war behind you."

There were a few more clarifications, but Fraydl hardly heard. After months of imprisonment, for Jewish refugees the war was over at last! That same afternoon, she wrote a letter to Dr. Emsbach, detailing her experiences since leaving the shelter of his home, and requesting information about Chaim and Yanky.

In the dining hall that night, Solly called for attention. "We need to organize!" he announced in a tone of authority. "The new director told us to elect committees to take over responsibility for administering the camp. Everyone who wants to participate is invited to stay after supper and vote."

This pronouncement was followed by mayhem as everyone began to speak at once.

"I don't know how he thinks we'll ever agree," Raya muttered. "You know what they say: two Jews, three opinions."

Fraydl acknowledged the quip with a smile. Having no interest in politics, she excused herself and went to the dorm. She needed a bit of solitude to consider her plans. Now that communication was possible, she expected to be making crucial decisions in the near future.

Days passed with no response from Dr. Emsbach. Fraydl wrote again, assuming that the first letter had not been delivered. She was so impatient to leave the camp that she hardly noticed the changes taking place. The newly elected committee members organized cultural activities as well as educational and athletic events. Unfortunately, koshering the camp kitchen was not on their list of priorities.

"Did you see the lists on the bulletin board?" Masha asked the other ladies at breakfast. "I think each of you should look into the classes they are offering. I signed up for dressmaking, which is something I can use to make a living. Without family to support us, we must choose a career."

"It's the sensible thing to do," Raya agreed.

"I haven't been in a classroom since I was 13," Fraydl mused.

There was a moment's silence before Raya shook off the melancholy. "The past is over," she declared. "We must prepare for the future."

After some deliberation, Fraydl enrolled in an accounting course to learn bookkeeping skills together with 20 other students from other sections of the camp. She applied herself diligently, though the material was extremely tedious. A few weeks into the course, as she bent over her ledger, Fraydl sensed someone watching her.

Turning to see who it was, Fraydl glimpsed a ghost. It was her brother-in-law Moishe!

"Fraydl?" The man asked in disbelief.

"Moishe?" She could not believe that she had been sitting in the same room with her sister's husband for weeks and hadn't known it!

"Yes!"

"Yes!"

Joy and relief flooded through Fraydl. She wasn't alone after all! The two bombarded each other with questions.

"Where have you been? Do you have any news?"

"Where have *you* been? How did you survive?"

Smiles and tears intermingled, and the accounting class was suspended as everyone joined in the reunion. It would take time to connect the incoherent fragments of stories into an intelligible picture, but meanwhile it was wonderful just to discover someone left from their extended family.

She told Moishe about the family in Vienna following the *Anschluss*. In 1938, Moishe had been deported to Poland together with Fraydl's sister Sarah and their three small children. "We never heard from you after that," Fraydl told him.

"It was a nightmare," he said, his eyes haunted by memories he could never forget. "There were hundreds of us trapped in a no-man's-land between Germany and Poland, young families like mine and elderly people, all exposed to the elements and starving. The local *Yidden* sent us something to eat and warm clothing. Shimon came down with pneumonia. We buried him there." Moishe's voice choked, but he regained control and continued, "They finally moved us to a ghetto across the Polish border. Typhus took away little Ita. Sarah and Esther'ke were shot on the street while I was away on a labor detail."

The two sat in silence. There was nothing more to say. The pain was too deep for words. Fraydl had already heard accounts of the war from other survivors, but this time she relived it through her older sister's eyes, and through her sister's heart. "At least you survived," she whispered. "*Baruch Hashem*, you are still alive."

Hours later, Fraydl and Moishe parted. Fraydl lay on her army cot, listening to the night noises until she fell into a troubled sleep. In the coming weeks, she took comfort in spending time with Moishe. Their common memories and backgrounds drew them together, and she was not surprised when one afternoon Moishe suggested that they marry and begin a new life together.

"Where will we go? How will we make a living?" she asked.

"I have cousins in New York. They will help us get started."

"Are you sure they will sign a certificate for both of us?"

Permission to enter the United States was only granted to immigrants with sponsors willing to take full financial responsibility for them. Since it was extremely difficult to find individuals willing to make such a commitment, few people were able to get visas.

"I will write to them. We should have their answer within a few weeks."

There had already been several weddings in the camp between survivors. Alone and penniless, hope for the future was the only possession they had; it gave them the strength to get through each day. Now Fraydl imagined building her own home. The thought that through bringing Jewish children into the world she would perpetuate the memories of her beloved family comforted her. That night, she went to sleep content for the first time in recent memory.

55

E MSBACH STOOD NEAR THE WALL, TOTALLY DISORIENTED. The other Jews in the newly formed *minyan* were all swaying, facing east with eyes closed, immersed in words that were indecipherable to him. He edged toward the door, fighting the urge to flee and never stop running. What was he doing here?

Gradually, in spite of himself, Emsbach began to feel the words of the unfamiliar chant soothe his stormy heart, pulling him back toward the man who was his father. There was a brief silence after the last *Kaddish* was recited.

"What are your plans now?" Rabbi Stern asked, resting his hand lightly on Emsbach's arm.

"I live in Ravensdorf, an hour from here. My car is outside. I can drive you to your hotel. Would you like to see my home first?"

"Your home is with me, son," Rabbi Stern said firmly. "So many lost years cannot be bridged in only an hour. Come with me to the hotel where our delegation is staying. I cannot bear being separated from you any longer. Even though I feel very tired, I don't want to sleep tonight. All I want is to sit beside you, see you with my eyes, be near enough to reach out and touch you from time to time to know that you are really here. I want to recapture the precious child you were, and I want to meet the man you have become. Let us dream together of the life we will build."

Emsbach hesitated. He felt powerless to refuse the dark-blue eyes, so undeniably like his own, but his mind was gripped by confusion. Since Uncle Heinrich's bizarre revelation had crumbled his old world into dust, Karl Emsbach had searched for his true identity in order to confound the lies he'd been told all his life. Now that search had brought him here, to this point, he found that his courage was deserting him. The reality was too far removed from any of his previous expectations. Overwhelmed, the doctor was unable to either step forward or turn back.

Rabbi Stern's eyes filled with tears of sympathy and pain. "What have they done to my child?" he murmured. "Tanchum, my son, no one is going to force you to do anything you are not ready for. If you feel unable to come with me now, I will not insist. I am so grateful to have found you. Promise me that you will never leave me again?" The tremor in the old man's voice pierced Emsbach with guilt.

"I will come with you." He struggled to recover some of his characteristic determination.

Rabbi Stern smiled encouragingly.

The group of men moved out of the improvised shul in a steady stream. Suddenly self-conscious, they shook hands and parted, the crisp autumn air making them tug their jackets a little tighter against the chill. The night was quiet, and stars glimmered above like scattered diamonds.

Emsbach led Rabbi Stern to his Mercedes and opened the passenger door for him. Taking his place behind the steering wheel, he realized that they were finally alone together. Spontaneously he turned to his father, and they caught each other in a long embrace, as if trying to physically bridge the immense gulf that stood between them.

"*Vater?*" Karl asked uncertainly.

"No, my dear son. 'Tatte' is the name you knew me by. It means 'father' in Yiddish. Call me 'Tatte' and I will call you by your name, 'Tanchum.' "

"Tatte," Emsbach said, and then repeated the word, "Tatte," tasting it thoughtfully. He remembered hearing that word from Fraydl and her nephews, but that seemed long, long ago, in another world, in another lifetime.

They arrived at the hotel. Embach handed his keys to the doorman, who would park his Mercedes. Accompanying his father into the lobby, he wondered what he would do if he encountered a German acquaintance. Fortunately, he was spared that scenario, and the two made their way up the carpeted stairs to Rabbi Stern's room on the second floor.

"May I offer you something to eat?"

Emsbach shook his head. "Please order for yourself," he said. "If I feel hungry, I will call down later."

Rabbi Stern looked puzzled for a moment. "This hotel does not provide kosher food," he explained. Opening a valise to reveal tins of fish and packets of matzah, he added, "I brought plenty of food with me."

Emsbach watched in dismay as his father washed his hands and began his supper. Despite Rabbi Stern's offer to share his meal, Emsbach had no appetite for such fare. An awkward silence rose between them, as each tried to read the other's thoughts. *Does he expect me to observe these ancient laws as well?* Emsbach wondered, while his father admonished himself, *Let it go, Meir! There will be time for everything later. The miracle is that we are together!*

As an afterthought, Rabbi Stern reached into the pocket of his jacket and removed his wallet. Inside was a worn sepia photograph of himself with his wife. "Look, son," he said, handing it to Emsbach. "This is your mother and me, when we first arrived in New York."

Gingerly, Emsbach took the proffered wallet, turning it toward the lamp in order to see it more clearly. The man in the picture was obviously his father, although his beard had dark streaks and was not yet entirely white. A veil of sorrow rested on the woman's face.

"Mamme," he whispered. He turned to his father. "I think I remember something. When she smiles, her eyes almost close. Right?"

Rabbi Stern put down his fork and clasped his son's hands. "Yes!" he exclaimed. "Exactly so!"

A wave of warmth and happiness suffused Emsbach. "I remember," he said, over and over. "I remember."

The rabbi picked up the telephone receiver and called the hotel desk. Emsbach listened as his father spoke: "I wish to make a transatlantic call to the United States. New York area code 212, number Windsor 7-2061. Please inform me when the line is available. Thank you."

"We must speak to your mother as soon as possible," he barely restrained his excitement as he returned the phone to its hook. "You are a doctor, Tanchum. Tell me, what is the best way to break such good news to someone with a very weak heart? We must not shock her."

"Is she at home alone?"

"No. While I am in Europe she is staying with your oldest brother, Dovid, and his wife Hannah."

A shiver sliced through Emsabch. He was not an only child. He had a brother!

"I think it would be best to explain everything to Dovid first, and let him break the news gradually, according to how she responds."

"I agree."

During the time it took for the transatlantic call to go through, Rabbi Stern began describing Tanchum's family for him. Emsbach learned that he was the seventh of nine children, all married and with families except for the youngest, who was engaged. Despite his father's efforts to explain it all clearly, he was soon lost in the details.

"Never mind, never mind!" the rabbi soothed. "I see that it is too confusing all at once. Let's take things one step at a time. Tell me about yourself, from your earliest memories until today!"

Feeling strangely detached, Karl Emsbach spoke of his childhood, his youth in the military academy and his medical studies at the university. When he mentioned Adolph Hitler and Germany, his father's face grew pale, reminding him to whom he was speaking.

"No, no, Tanchum. Don't stop," Rabbi Stern protested. "Of course such things are hard for me to hear, but these are your experiences and I want to know what your life was like. Please continue. I am listening."

Emsbach glanced at the clock on the mantel and saw that it would soon be dawn. "You must be exhausted," he told his father. "Perhaps you want to go to sleep and we will continue in the morning?"

The old man smiled. "I told you already, I will not sleep tonight. There is nothing I want more than to hear your voice. Besides, our call has still not come through and I am anxious to share the news with your mother."

56

THE RING OF THE TELEPHONE INTERRUPTED THEIR discussion. Rabbi Stern's hands trembled slightly as he lifted the receiver and confirmed his desire to accept the transatlantic call. "We have to go downstairs," he told Emsbach. "International calls cannot be put through to regular telephones."

Moments later they were in a booth near the main desk, and Emsbach's father lifted the phone receiver. "Hello, Shaindel?" he began. "Yes, everything's fine. How are you? The children? The delegation has seen success; we can really feel the *siyata d'Shmaya*. Are you taking your medicine? What does the doctor say?"

Emsbach waited anxiously, straining to hear the soft voice speaking beneath the static. "When am I coming home?" Rabbi Stern repeated his wife's question for his son's benefit. "We still have a lot to do, but it won't be much longer. My visa runs out in less than a month, you know. *Ach*," he sighed, involuntarily covering his eyes for a moment, "there is so much work to do, and so few workers. Tell me, Shaindel, do I hear Dovid in the background? I actually called to speak with him. Can you put him on for a few moments, please? Yes, I know this is an expensive call. I have to ask him something important. Thank you, dear. Take care, and *b'ezras Hashem* I'll write to you soon. Good-bye for now."

Rabbi Stern covered the receiver with his hand and motioned to his son, "Do you want to speak to your brother?"

Startled by the idea, Emsbach shook his head. "Not yet, Tatte. I'm not ready yet." The 'Tatte' stuck in his throat. He paused to take a deep breath and regain control. His father was speaking again.

"Dovid? How are you? Sit down, Dovid, I have something *geval-dig* to tell you. Find an excuse to send Mommy out of the room so she won't notice. Any excuse… Ask her to bring you something. Good. Dovid, are you listening? I have found Tanchum! I have found your brother Tanchum! He is alive. He is healthy. It's a miracle!

"Baruch Hashem! He is right here beside me now, but don't tell Mommy just yet. I am afraid for her health. It might be too much of a shock for her to hear it suddenly. She's coming back already? O.K., so we'll talk later. I have so much to tell you. Meanwhile, let the others know and start breaking the subject to Mommy gently. When you think she can handle it, call me back at the hotel. I'll be waiting for your call! Good-bye, son! Good-bye."

Rabbi Stern thanked the concierge and told him that he was expecting another call in a while. "Please call me to the telephone at any hour, no matter the time. I am waiting for a most important call. Thank you."

They returned to their room and waited. Emsbach found himself dozing off in his chair, dreams mixing strangely with reality. Rabbi Stern took out his Gemara and began learning, surreptitiously glancing at his son from time to time in the hope that the ancient tune might awaken some lost memory. At the sound of a knock on the door, both men rose.

"A telephone call from New York," the bellboy announced.

"Thank you." Rabbi Stern dropped a coin into the man's hand and led the way down to the hotel desk.

"Hello?" At first the rabbi thought the call had been disconnected, but then he understood that there was someone on the other end. Emsbach watched his father's eyes mist over. Rabbi Stern thrust the receiver into his son's hand. "Speak to your mother, Tanchum," he said, overcome with emotion.

Rebbetzin Stern had never given up hope, but the years had taken a toll on her health. At this moment her voice was choked with tears, and she could only repeat her son's name."Tanchum! Tanchum!"

Outside of the booth, the concierge turned to the desk clerk. "How strange," he remarked. "The *rabbiner t*old me he was expecting an important call, but neither he nor the German with him are saying a word."

"They are both weeping," the clerk shook his head. "It must be terrible news."

It took a third phone call a few hours later before the members of the Stern family could conduct a conversation that was intelligible. By then it was evening in New York, and all of Tanchum's living siblings had gathered at their brother's house to share in the excitement. Emsbach was visibly shaken by the warmth that poured over the transatlantic line. He promised to come home to his family as soon as his affairs in Germany could be arranged.

Rabbi Stern realized that it was time to *daven*. Karl accompanied his father to the room where eight men were impatiently awaiting their arrival. Once again he stood on the side, but this time someone provided him with a prayer book that had a German translation opposite the Hebrew and he was able to follow the words. *This is beautiful*, he realized, less troubled than he'd felt the previous day. A curious feeling teased his consciousness, until he grasped that it was a sensation of completion. Of belonging.

Over the ensuing days, Emsbach stayed with his father. Rabbi Stern was obliged to accompany the delegation to various Displaced Person camps, offering comfort to survivors and working to influence the authorities to consider the Jewish residents' religious needs. Before he left in the morning, it was his great pleasure to lovingly wrap *tefillin* on his son's arm, correctly position the *tefillin shel rosh* and help him recite the *Shema* in Hebrew.

While his father was occupied during the day, Emsbach began the lengthy process of legally changing his name to the one his parents had given him at his *bris*, and organizing his assets in preparation for leaving Germany permanently. When his father returned to the hotel in the evening, the two spent long hours discussing the past and the future.

"What is in that?" Rabbi Stern questioned, noticing the chest that his son had brought up to their hotel room. A moment later he gave a gasp of admiration, when Emsbach showed him the beautiful pieces of Fraydl's silver. "How did this come to be in your possession?" he exclaimed.

After listening to his son's description of the frightened Jewish children who had tried to hide behind his car in the hospital parking lot, the rabbi shook his head in wonder. "That was extraordinarily brave of you, my son. If the Nazi regime had discovered what you did, you would have been executed!"

"There was no time for me to think about it. I just knew that I could not leave them there."

"Your Jewish heart would not let you abandon them to their fate. I am proud of you! I shudder to think of that wicked Heinrich Mauer, who wanted to transform my kind and gentle child into a monster like himself. I am so grateful that he did not succeed. It is obvious to me that G-d was watching over you all the time."

"I know," Emsbach responded. "Fraydl told me that Jews have a promise that G-d will never forsake them, no matter what."

Rabbi Stern smiled at his son and stroked his cheek tenderly. If Tanchum had a beard, he would look exactly like his brothers. Soon the remnants of their family would be reunited, and the parents would do their best to make up to their youngest son for all the lost years.

57

HIS LIFE HAD CHANGED SO DRAMATICALLY THAT THERE were times when Emsbach did not recognize himself. During the day he was still the son of Mikhail Emsbach, the wealthy industrialist from Ravensdorf. This was how he signed contracts and financial transactions, sold assets and made bank transfers. From early evening until morning, he was Tanchum Stern, son of Rabbi Meir and Shaindel Stern of Williamsburg, New York. He shared kosher meals with his father, attended prayer services with the Orthodox delegations staying at the hotel, and steadily increased his knowledge of Judaism. Afterward, he assumed his former identity again in order to conduct his business.

Emsbach was amazed at how smoothly it was possible to slip from one role to the other, despite a slight sensation of unease that often troubled him. *This is a transition,* he reasoned. *When I leave Germany, Karl Emsbach will stay behind forever. After that I will become Tanchum Stern completely.*

Intending to travel with his father's delegation, he verified the address of the nearest American consulate. He arrived shortly before the end of reception hours, and proceeded to make a formal application for permission to enter the United States. The hall was packed with applicants. Long lines snaked before each desk, amid a constant hum of murmuring voices. Harried clerks glanced periodically at the large clock positioned over the exit, their expressions impatient as if disappointed with the slow, steady sweep of the second hand.

Emsbach filled out the necessary forms in his small, precise script and handed them to the receptionist. Looking about for a place to sit while awaiting his turn, he was surprised when a uniformed guard approached him.

"You are Major Karl Emsbach?" the military attaché asked, holding Karl's application in his hand.

"*Ja*, I am."

"Follow me, please, sir."

He led Emsbach through the crowded hall into a private interview room. "How may I help you, sir?" he asked.

"I am requesting a visa," Emsbach replied.

He waited while the attaché looked over the document in his hands. "Everything seems to be in order," he said in a tone of approval. "How long do you expect to be visiting the United States?"

"I would like to immigrate permanently," Emsbach explained.

"I understand." The official studied the documents again. "You were a soldier in the *Wehrmacht?*" he asked.

"I was a conscript."

"And you are a member of the Nazi party?"

"Every citizen in Germany who did not want to find himself in a concentration camp was a member of the Nazi party."

The officer nodded, perusing the forms yet again. "Do you repudiate the ideology of the National Socialist Party?"

"Of course."

"You are the adopted son of Brigadier General Heinrich Mauer, are you not?"

This information did not appear on the forms Emsbach had filled out, and he was taken aback at the consulate's familiarity with such a minor details of the Nazi hierarchy. "My mother's brother took responsibility for me when my parents were killed in an airplane accident."

The soldier smiled. "We make it our business to know this kind of thing," he explained. "You were not a combatant, am I correct?"

"I am a surgeon. I was drafted into the medical corps immediately after graduating medical school. I spent most of the war working in the Army hospital near my home in Ravensdorf."

"Yes. . ."

Emsbach studied the man's identity tag. "Officer Smalley," he said, "Is there a problem with my application?"

"No, not at all. You are exactly the type of person we want as a citizen in the United States. May I have your passport, please?"

Emsbach handed over his passport and watched as Gaylord Smalley stamped and signed his visa. The two men stood up and shook hands. "May I ask you a question?" Emsbach asked.

"Certainly."

"Out of all the people waiting in line, why did you pick me?"

The attaché smiled mirthlessly. "It's obvious, isn't it? The main purpose of the clerks out there is to disqualify the applicants. We don't need more of *them*." He said the last word with a sneer.

A wave of nausea passed over Emsbach. How many times had he heard anti-Semitic innuendos in the past without even registering them? He turned and left the room, pausing briefly to examine the poor, hopeful souls waiting for their applications to be refused by antagonistic clerks. Yes, most of them appeared to be Jews. He hung his head, not knowing whether to feel ashamed or angry.

Outside he inhaled the crisp, cold air. His boots crunched in the snow, and he decided to walk a little before returning to the hotel. Two blocks from the consulate, he heard the sounds of children playing. *That's just what I need*, he thought, *to redeem my faith in humankind.* He stood outside the fenced yard, watching the youngsters run and slip and slide. Listening to their innocent shrieks and squeals was medicine for his tortured heart.

One little boy drew his attention. The child was huddled near the wall of the building with his face turned away. Emsbach wondered why he wasn't playing with the others. The sign on the gate proclaimed that this institution was the St. Bartholomew's Home for Orphans and Poor Children. He rang the bell, and waited several minutes until approached by a stout figure wrapped in so many scarves that only a pair of narrowed eyes indicated there was a person inside the coat.

"I have come to speak to the director." He spoke in an official tone that demanded compliance. The gate was unlocked and he followed the mysterious figure into the entrance hall of the orphanage.

Like an onion, the person before him unwrapped layer after layer until eventually a wimple and nun's habit emerged. "Follow me," she said, after depositing her many scarves on a chair. "Father James is in here."

Emsbach's first impression was of a squirrel. Short and rotund, the priest seemed to bounce out of his chair. Father James crossed the room and extended his hand in greeting. The questioning expression on his face was heightened by a furrowed brow and raised eyebrows, topped by a widow's peak.

The doctor shook the priest's hand. "My name is Emsbach," he introduced himself. "Major Doctor Emsbach of Ravensdorf. I was wondering if you could help me locate two brothers who have been missing since the end of the war."

"Sit down, sit down," the priest invited. "What are the names of your missing boys?"

Emsbach hesitated. The boys had surely been given German aliases, but he had no idea what they were. His heart sank in near-despair. How would he ever find Chaim and Yanky?

58

MOISHE WANTED TO MAKE THEIR ENGAGEMENT KNOWN immediately, but Fraydl procrastinated. Despite the disappointment in his dark eyes, she asked him to delay the formal announcement for a little while. When Moishe didn't understand, they had their first argument.

"Why not, Fraydl? What possible reason can you have to wait?"

"I don't know, but that's how I feel."

"It doesn't make sense."

"Let's keep it between us for another day or two. Please, Moishe?"

Moishe gave her a piercing look. "Fraydl, you just agreed to become my wife. Have you changed your mind?"

"No. I just want a little time to adjust to the idea… To think it through."

"What on earth is there to think about? Your father chose me for your sister Sarah, may G-d avenge her blood, so obviously your parents approved of me. We have spent hours together over the last month and there is nothing we have not discussed. We share common values and are familiar with each other from the past. Now is the time to go into the future."

"I hear you and I know you're right, Moishe. But something I can't explain is holding me back. I need time to reflect on things first, before facing everyone else's reactions."

"You will never be 100-percent certain. It's normal to have a few doubts. Put them aside, Fraydl. You know that we will share the news with our friends eventually, so why not do it now?"

Fraydl wrung her hands. "I wish I knew how to explain it, Moishe. You are mistaken if you think that I'm worried about your good character or your values. I am not afraid of a future with you. I look forward to building a new life together. Still, something in my heart is not whole. It's as if there is an important task that I must do first, but I don't know what it is."

"You're not making sense. Your fears are groundless. Trust me, and ignore these feelings, Fraydl. They are definitely not in your best interest."

There was something threatening in Moishe's tone that she had never encountered before. It caused her to withdraw instinctively. He wanted her to embrace his point of view, but his impatience with her feelings had the opposite effect. The more Moishe insisted on announcing the news immediately, the greater her insecurity and resistance grew.

His displeasure apparent, Moishe finally accepted her decision with bad grace. He changed the subject. "It's time for lunch. Let's go eat."

She accompanied him in silence, unhappy with the conflict between her mind and her heart. At the door she hung back. "I'm not hungry. I think I'll go rest for a while.

"Do you want me to bring a sandwich to your dorm?"

"No. I have some crackers if I get hungry."

They parted rather stiffly, neither of them understanding exactly how the situation had become so complicated.

It was a balmy winter day. Fraydl did not go straight back to her barracks, but allowed her feet to lead her aimlessly along the paths of the DP camp, lost in her thoughts.

Why aren't I happy? she reproached herself. *Isn't this exactly what I want? Moishe Katz is a fine man from a good family. My parents investigated his background thoroughly before agreeing to let Sarah marry him, which is something I could never do by myself. Before the war, Moishe was a responsible husband and father. Who can promise that I will ever meet anyone else as good as he is?*

Suddenly weary, Fraydl leaned against the gate and stared out at the street, where life moved ahead regardless of her troubled inner world. *Is it possible that the reason I don't feel happy is that I can never be happy again? Perhaps the war has robbed me of the ability to enjoy life, and I should just do what I know is proper, without heeding these strange, contradictory feelings...*

The snow was melting and her shoes were wet. A passing tram sent a spray of slush at the gate, and she quickly turned away.

I will marry Moishe, she decided at length. *It is clearly Providential that we found each other after the war. My sister was happy as his wife, and their children were as sweet as honey. I don't feel connected to him yet, but I will learn over time. It is better to make a life with someone who understands where I come from than with a total stranger.*

Fraydl returned to the dining hall. She wanted to find Moishe and apologize for not seeing things his way in the first place. He was older and more experienced than she. He had her best interests at heart and she was behaving foolishly.

Without warning, a different memory came to mind. *My father's menorah and the rest of the silver are still at Dr. Embach's house. After we marry, we must visit Ravensdorf and reclaim my parents' property. I will show Moishe the attic where Chaim, Yanky and I hid during the war, and introduce him to Dr. Emsbach, the only Nazi in Germany with a human heart. We will find Chaim and Yanky, and see that they are in good hands before we leave Europe.*

Feeling better, Fraydl entered the dining hall. Moishe was not there. Vaguely disappointed that he had not waited, she reminded herself that there was no way he could have guessed that her misgivings would fade away so quickly. She detoured to the men's barracks and asked someone to go in and call Moishe out.

"He's not inside," the man informed her when he came back out. "His bed's empty. His bunkmate doesn't know where he went."

Fraydl thanked him politely and returned to the women's barracks. It was so bright outside that it took a minute for her eyes to adjust to the dim light indoors. "Where is everyone?" she asked, squinting as she tried to focus.

"They decided to go out on the town!" Katya answered. The words were muffled because, at the moment, she was bent over a basin of water and shampooing her long hair.

"And why did *you* stay here, may I ask?" Masha was sitting against the wall, hemming a skirt by the light from the window. "I would have expected you to be the first one out."

"Bring me my towel, will you, luv?" Katya affected an English accent. "I don't want to drip all the way over to my bed!"

Fraydl obliged. "You shouldn't go out with wet hair," she warned. "You can catch a cold like that!"

Katya toweled her black curls dry, smiling broadly. "Herschel is going to propose to me tonight!" she crowed.

"*Mazel tov!*"

"Shh! Not yet! It's still a secret!"

Fraydl envied her friend's lightheartedness. She envied the happy expression on her face. She considered telling her about her soon-to-be-announced engagement to Moishe, but decided to wait. Let him have the honor of sharing the news that evening at supper.

"Ouch! Now look what you did!" Masha brought a finger to her mouth, sucking it pettishly. "I got so excited, I stuck the needle straight into my finger!"

The others laughed good-naturedly. Fraydl rummaged among her private belongings and found a bit of cotton wool for Masha to apply to her aching finger until the bleeding stopped.

"I wish somebody would propose to *me*," the older woman said mournfully. "Anybody would be fine. I'm sick of this place!"

"That's not a reason!" Fraydl was as surprised as the others at the vehemence in her own voice.

"Why not?" Katya challenged, uncharacteristically serious. "What difference does it make? Find somebody with a visa to get out of here. It's better than a million German marks."

I should be happy, Fraydl thought to herself mournfully, turning her head away from her friends. *I should be dancing with joy.*

"Leave her alone," Masha whispered to Katya. "Can't you see that something's happened to disturb her?"

59

"DID YOU KNOW FATHER MATTHEW HOFMANN?" EMSBACH asked the priest.

Father James nodded vigorously. "Father Matthew was a good man. His death is a great loss to the many who loved him."

"His parish was near the military hospital."

"Yes, I am familiar with it."

"Do you know what happened to the orphans who were under his protection? Do you have any idea where they would be today?"

Father James studied his hands, folded in the lap of his cassock, before speaking. "The children who survived the bombings were moved to other orphanages," he told his visitor. "They were moved east at first, until the Russian forces came over the border, and then Father Matthew's orphans were transferred individually to any institution that would accept them."

"Could brothers have been separated?"

"The priority was to save lives, *Herr Doktor*. No one had the leisure for personal considerations."

"Perhaps a list exists of the children's names or other identifying information?"

"Not that I am aware of."

Something about the priest troubled Emsbach. Intuitively, he felt that the man was withholding information. "Might some of those children be here under your supervision?"

The question elicited an evasive response. Father James pursed his lips and rustled through some papers on the table. "Of course, it's not impossible." He cleared his throat several times before deflecting the point. "Some of our orphans were street urchins. Others had widowed mothers who were unable to support them. We regard it as our holy duty to protect these helpless children and endeavor to raise them as good Christians. It is a tragedy that most were lost when the Soviets sealed off their area of influence. At least a few were saved."

"Thank you, Father. I appreciate your taking time from your busy schedule to receive me." Emsbach realized that he would not get any more information from this man.

Obviously relieved, the priest stood up with an expectant expression. "I wish you success in finding your missing children," he smiled, shaking the doctor's hand and motioning toward the door.

Emsbach found his own way back to the lobby. As he reached the door, ruddy-cheeked boys began straggling in from outdoors, trailing wet tracks as the snow on their boots melted.

"Hang up your coats and scarves!" the nun who had opened the gate for Emsbach instructed the children. "Make sure that you don't drop them on the floor!"

One little boy attracted Emsbach's attention. It was the same child he had noticed earlier, the one who was not playing together with the others. Now the little fellow was struggling to undo the buttons on his jacket. As he pulled at his lapels, his cap slid off his head and fell directly into a puddle. This was instantly rewarded with a stinging slap. "You wicked beast!" the nun hissed, her face contorted with outrage at this affront to her discipline.

The child did not resist. On the contrary, he seemed resigned to such treatment. When the bad-tempered nun moved on to cuff a different child for the crime of being clumsy, the first bent down, retrieved his dripping hat and pulled it over his curly head.

Compassionately Emsbach bent over for a moment to help the boy with the stubborn buttons. The child lifted his face to stare suspiciously and then froze with recognition.

"Yanky?" Emsbach asked in disbelief.

"*Herr Doktor!*" the boy sobbed, throwing his arms around Emsbach's neck.

Emsbach couldn't believe it. "Yanky?" he repeated, pulling the boy back to look at him better. "Is it really you?"

Yanky buried his face in the doctor's shoulder, whispering frantically, "Take me home. I don't like it here. Take me back to Tante Fraydl!"

The nun reappeared like a black cloud on the horizon. She seized the child's arms with unnecessary force and yanked him away from Emsbach. "Don't believe a word he says," she warned. "This is a very wicked boy. He is a known liar!" She shook Yanky's shoulders. "You will be punished," she promised. "You will learn to obey and to speak only the truth."

Emsbach inserted himself between the irate woman and the hapless orphan. "I will speak with Father James about this child," he said, and the authority in his voice transformed her rancor into instant submission.

"Yes, sir. Of course, sir," she responded, backing fearfully away.

"Come with me," Emsbach whispered to Yanky, and led him back into the priest's study. "Father James," he said aloud.

The priest's eyes flitted nervously from Emsbach, to the cowering nun in the doorway, to little Yanky, and then back again.

"This boy is one of the missing children for whom I have been searching," Emsbach stated succinctly, wondering cynically if Father James had suspected it all along.

The priest scampered across the room to close the door. "Let us speak in privacy," he said. "Sister Matilda, the children are waiting for their tea."

"Yes, Father." The disappointed woman made haste to leave.

As Father James turned away from the door, he seemed flustered. "I must report this to my superiors," he told Emsbach. "It is not unusual for a family member to ask for a child, but it is extremely atypical for someone who doesn't even know the child's name."

"I know his real name. I did not know what Christian name he was given by Father Matthew."

Father James wriggled in his seat. He wanted to avoid admitting that he was aware that the boy they'd known as Andrew was Jewish. He looked at his increasingly unwelcome guest and pondered his options. Finally he turned to the boy, "Andrew?"

Yanky met his eyes.

"Do you know this man?"

The child nodded.

"Who is he?"

"*Herr Doktor* Emsbach," the boy replied bravely. "He is my friend. I want to go with him, Father James."

The priest sighed. "He seems to know you," he agreed reluctantly. "I suppose that is sufficient proof that you are speaking the truth… but *I* am not acquainted with you. How do I know that you will treat him well and raise him to be a good Christian?"

Emsabach reached into his pocket and pulled out his wallet. He counted out a number of bills and placed them on the table. "In appreciation for the care that Andrew received," he said, deliberately using the boy's Christian name, "and to show you that I am able to care for him properly."

Father James puffed out his cheeks, looking more than ever like a squirrel. "Ah, I see," he said, his eyes opening wide. "Well, then, Andrew, do you wish to go and live with Dr. Emsbach?"

A look of joy lit Yanky's face. "Yes, Father," he replied, hardly believing that it wasn't all a dream.

"So be a good boy then, and remember to say your prayers."

"Yes, Father."

Emsbach took Yanky's hand and headed for the door before the director of the orphanage had a chance to reconsider his hasty decision. He had no idea what he would do next, but he did know they must leave this place as soon as possible. With a formal bow, he bade the priest farewell and they departed with all possible speed.

60

KATYA FINISHED TOWEL-DRYING HER WET HAIR AND twisted it into a tight bun that complimented her pixie face. "Fraydl?" she nudged her friend's shoulder.

Fraydl turned around to face her. "Mmm?"

"You know, you and I are almost the same size. Would you mind lending me the outfit you wear on Shabbos?"

Few of the residents in the DP camp had more than one dress, but Fraydl had a gray woolen suit in addition to her everyday skirt and blouse. Dr. Emsbach had given it to her shortly after the children moved into his attic, with the explanation that one of the patients at the hospital had left it behind after she was released. When no one came to retrieve the forgotten belongings, he received authorization to take them for a "needy neighbor." Fortunately, the lovely suit fit her as if it had been sewn with her in mind, and Fraydl was happy to have something special to set Shabbos apart from the weekdays.

She had planned to wear the outfit tonight when Moishe announced their engagement, but the sparkle in Katya's usually sad eyes was beyond her ability to resist. "Sure," she told the girl. "May it bring you happy memories."

Wreathed in a glowing smile, Katya quickly exchanged her ordinary clothes for the considerably more elegant suit. "How do I look?" she asked expectantly.

"Like a *kallah*," Fraydl assured her.

Katya preened in her reflection from the window, examining herself as well as she could from every side. "Yes, I do, don't I?" she giggled. "Thanks, Fraydl!"

"*Auf simchahs*," Fraydl responded, and Masha added, "Amen!"

When Katya had gone, the barracks seemed very quiet. Masha set aside her embroidery and stretched. "I think I'll go over to the office and see if there is any mail. Want to come with me?"

Fraydl shook her head. She was grateful to be alone at last. The afternoon sun shining through the window passed over her cot, and she studied the dust motes floating in the air. They looked random, but she knew they were not. *Hashem is running the world,* she repeated to herself. *Everything is for the best.*

Fraydl drifted off to sleep. She was back in her parents' house before the war. Her sister Sarah had just become engaged to Moishe Katz, and seemingly endless streams of friends kept coming, bearing gifts and offering congratulations. The *kallah* chattered with animation, and the room echoed with the young girls' laughter. Her mother was sitting in the old rocking chair beside the front window, contentedly embroidering delicate pink roses against a smooth, silky background for her sister's trousseau. Rebbetzin Mertzbach's fingers flashed skillfully as she plied the needle, occasionally glancing with *nachas* at Sarah or smiling at Fraydl.

When she awakened, Fraydl lay motionless in the darkening room for a long time, savoring the pleasant dream. *How different we are,* she mused as she compared herself to her sister. Sarah had been outgoing, drawing people to her like a bee to honey, while Fraydl was shy and introspective. Her sister had been enthusiastic and down to earth, with no patience for books or intellectual discussions. Frequently approached for advice by other girls, Sarah had never lacked a practical solution for any problem.

With explosive intensity, the realization hit Fraydl: she and Sarah were totally dissimilar. Her parents had chosen Moishe Katz for Sarah, not for her. Her sister and brother-in-law had made a charming couple because they complemented each other so well. Unexpectedly, Fraydl felt lighter, as if a great weight had been removed from her shoulders. *Moishe is not the one destined to be my life's partner,* she thought, wondering why it had taken her so long to understand the reason for her inner disquiet.

That evening, Fraydl informed Moishe that she needed to talk to him in private before they ate dinner. Her brother-in-law's jaw tightened perceptibly but he merely nodded and led the way outside. They sat on opposite ends of the bench across from the dining hall and he waited for her to begin.

Without the sun, the air was bitterly cold. Fraydl shivered. She wrapped her coat more tightly around herself and spoke gently, "It was important that I speak to you before you tell anyone, Moishe." She took a deep breath. "I like you and I admire you, but I cannot be your wife. I am not Sarah'le, and I could never take her place. I pray that Hashem will give you a wife who deserves you and who will make you happy. Please forgive me for not realizing this earlier. I was confused, and I had to think it through before I understood."

Moishe did not speak. His eyes focused on some indefinite point between the icicles hanging from the roof of the dining hall. Waiting for a response, Fraydl struggled to keep her teeth from chattering.

"It's too cold to stay out here," he said at last, standing up and straightening his jacket. "I accept your decision. You know how I feel and there is no point in reviewing it another time. We will not speak of this again."

Moishe's bitter disappointment pierced her heart like a dagger. Misgivings flooded her mind, but the words had already been spoken and could not be recalled.

In the ensuing days, Fraydl stopped attending the accounting course. *Moishe needs the certificate more than I do,* she decided. *He will marry and must have a means of supporting his family.* Raya convinced her to join a high-school equivalency class, which at least gave some structure to the empty days that followed.

"What's the matter with you, Fraydl?" Katya demanded. "You look like death warmed over."

Fraydl winced at the cliché and made a half-hearted attempt to return the blithe girl's smile. "I'm a bit downhearted lately," she apologized. "I'll be all right. This mood will pass."

"Put a smile on your face! You need to get out of this camp and see the world," Katya declared.

Fraydl shrugged. Merely getting out of bed in the morning exhausted her. She wished Katya would just let her be.

"What this girl needs is something meaningful to look forward to, not a night of dancing," Raya spoke up.

Surprised at her friend's uncharacteristic insight, Fraydl nodded her agreement.

"She misses her parents," Masha added tenderly, her own expression reflecting Fraydl's loneliness.

"We all miss our families." Katya made a face. "But that doesn't bring them back. Fraydl, you're making me gloomy. Come on, let's go window shopping. That's a guaranteed cure for whatever ails a woman."

"*I'll* go with you, Katya," Raya said. "Don't worry about Fraydl. She's doing better than we are. Her good nature will restore itself soon, I'm sure."

Fraydl realized that Katya was right. She had to do something. She couldn't keep letting her sad feelings pull her into depression. *I have a choice*, she reminded herself, *and I choose to overcome this* test.

One of the representatives of the Joint had given her a *sefer Tehillim*. Fraydl opened it and recited the words, allowing them to comfort her even though she didn't always understand what she was saying. When she had finished, it was as if a great weight had begun lifting from her shoulders. Though still sorrowful, she felt able to smile again.

I must keep myself busy, she decided. Over the next week, Fraydl threw herself into her studies with renewed determination. One afternoon, she was concentrating so hard on her mathematics notebook that she did not even register the new group of visitors entering the camp hall. Providentially, they noticed *her*.

"What is your name, child?"

"Fraydl Mertzbach," she answered softly, looking at the poised and well-dressed middle-aged woman standing opposite her. She wondered who this stranger was, and what she wanted.

Mrs. Frieda Ganz was touring the refugee camps together with the dynamic Mrs. Recha Sternbuch and representatives of the *Vaad HaHatzalah*. Their purpose was to identify children from religious homes and help transfer them to more appropriate venues.

As they continued to converse, Mrs. Ganz expressed interest in hearing about Fraydl's family and education. Fraydl found herself responding to the motherly woman the way parched earth responds to rain.

"For a girl coming from a *frum* background, it must be very hard to live here in the DP camp," the visitor commented.

"Yes, it really is difficult," Fraydl sighed. "The *kashrus* of the food served is questionable, so I depend on bread and vegetables. There's no Shabbos here, and no Yom Tov. The cultural events are not ones my parents would want me to attend, and most of the other residents are obsessed with getting visas to America and erasing their pasts. I miss having someone to really talk to, to discuss *hashkafah* or ask *she'eilos*."

Mrs. Ganz's listening ear invigorated Fraydl. As she poured out her story to the sympathetic woman, the veil of sadness that had settled on her recently began to lift.

"Perhaps you can help us," Mrs. Ganz said. "I serve as an assistant to Mrs. Recha Sternbuch, who has devoted her life to finding and caring for Jewish children who spent the war years in gentile homes. We are looking for people to assist us in this important work. Many of these children were so young that they don't remember their real parents, and very few have parents who can return to claim them. My organization is desperate to discover these orphans before they are lost to the Jewish nation forever. We have *kinderheims* and we need counselors and teachers, young women like yourself. Would you be willing to consider such employment?"

Fraydl was elated. "Yes, of course!" she agreed without hesitation, thanking Hashem for this opportunity to become involved in something meaningful. "I will be glad to help in any way I can."

Her little nephews never far from her mind, Fraydl poured her heart out to Mrs. Ganz about the boys. Perhaps she knew how to find them?

All the details that Fraydl possessed were duly recorded in Frieda Ganz's pocket notebook. "We can only try," the kindly woman promised. "*Netzach Yisrael lo yeshaker.* With Hashem's help, you will meet them again."

Mrs. Ganz waited in the lobby while Fraydl packed her few belongings, hugged and kissed her friends goodbye and returned to her new mentor. They left the camp together, Fraydl's face glowing with hope for a brighter future.

That night when she went to sleep, Fraydl's heart was filled with plan and purpose. The next day she traveled to the industrial city of Bytom, located in the Silesia district of Poland. Fraydl had been engaged by Recha Sternbuch to teach in the orphanage run under the auspices of the *Vaad HaHatzalah.*

61

THE HOUSEMOTHER OF THE *KINDERHEIM* WAS A WIDOW BY the name of Yonah Lederman. She met Fraydl at the train station and accompanied her to the house that served as a temporary shelter for 20 Jewish war orphans. On the way, she briefed her newest staff member about what to expect.

"The number of children varies," Mrs. Lederman explained. "When the house gets overcrowded, we send some of the orphans further west — trying not to arouse the attention of the Communist authorities who control Poland since it was occupied by the USSR. They are very suspicious about our activities." She winked. It was impossible not to feel comfortable in the company of this warm and caring woman.

"Where are the children from?" Fraydl asked.

"A few were rescued from convents or monasteries. Others were given for safekeeping to Christian families, who adopted them and raised them as their own children. A few of the oldest can remember their Jewish families, but most have no recollection at all. Since many of the children thought that their gentile foster parents were their real parents, not all of them are happy to be with us. These poor *kinderlach* believe that they have been abducted. At first they resist our efforts to bring them back to *Yiddishkeit*, but after a period of adjustment they usually come around."

Fraydl felt overwhelmed at the thought of teaching hostile children. This was not exactly what she'd expected to find in Bytom!

"Don't worry, dear," Mrs. Lederman patted her hand lovingly. "They are only children, and they will respond to our caring. We must give them boundless love, and as much happiness as possible. I'll show you to your room, and then we have a staff meeting at 2 o'clock."

The teachers and counselors of the orphanage met together that afternoon. Fraydl was instinctively drawn to the warmth of the young woman responsible for the older children in the *Kinderheim*. A student of Sarah Schenirer in Cracow before the war, Bassy had been discovered by Recha Sternbuch in a DP camp in Stettin, Poland and arrived in Bytom several months ago.

"I'll be glad to help if you need any assistance," Bassy offered. "I have the previous teacher's notebooks. You can look them over to see which subjects the girls were studying."

"That would be very helpful, thank you. What happened to that teacher? Why did she leave?"

Fraydl's innocent question brought a smile to the other teacher's faces. "She left to get married," Bassy replied.

"Working with these children seems to be a *segulah* for getting engaged," Mrs. Lederman explained with a smile of her own. "We have quite a turnover of teachers."

Fraydl blushed. "I have more important things on my mind at the moment," she said. "I'm definitely not looking for a *shidduch* in the foreseeable future."

"Famous last words," murmured Baila, the cook.

"Don't mind her," Bassy reassured Fraydl. "We can't ever have enough *simchahs* — though it does complicate things when we lose a good teacher."

"Fraydl, you will be taking over the class at the lowest scholastic level." The director brought the teacher's attention back to the business at hand. "Obviously, they were unable to attend school regularly during the war, so very few of the children know how to read or write. I suggest that you review the alphabet and move on from there. Keep your lessons brief until they are able to concentrate for longer periods of time."

Fraydl nodded. Her own education had been cut short, so she knew how the children felt. At least, she thought she did... By the end of her first day of work, all her lesson plans had been turned upside down. Instead of a class eager to learn, she found a group of sullen, uncooperative pupils ranging in age from 6 to 12. Yonah Lederman's advice to simply love the children was a much bigger challenge than she'd imagined.

"What am I going to do?" she moaned to Bassy when the first day was finally over. "Maybe I'm not cut out for this job."

"What happened?"

"Ruthy just sat and sucked her thumb while she stared out of the window. She ignored all my efforts to get her to participate. Sarah and Lily were downright antagonistic. Natalie absolutely refused to cooperate; she crumpled every sheet of paper I gave her, and threw her pencil on the floor with such vehemence that it broke in half. When I tried to teach, I was constantly interrupted by either misbehavior or a torrent of irrelevant questions that disrupted the continuity of my lesson. Only little Victoria sat quietly, so sad and withdrawn that it broke my heart." Fraydl sighed, "I'm afraid it was a mistake for me to take this on."

"No! Of course not," Bassy encouraged her. "You have to remember where these children are coming from and try to understand what they're going through. How would you feel if you were torn from the people you knew and the home where you lived, and suddenly reminded that you are Jewish after years of hiding it or not even knowing about it in the first place?"

"I do identify with them," Fraydl insisted. "I keep thinking of my little nephews, and I am really motivated to help these *kinderlach*. The problem is that they don't respond to my good intentions, and I don't know what else to do."

"Talk to Mrs. Lederman," Bassy advised. "She'll give you the support you need."

Yonah Lederman clucked her tongue sympathetically when she heard Fraydl's report. "Just give them time, dear," she said. "Don't worry about the scholastic content of your lessons. I am much more interested in opening their hearts to *Yiddishkeit* and perhaps arousing memories that will help them identify with a Torah-observant life. Tell them stories. Sing songs. It will be fine in the end. *Daven*, and Hashem will help you."

Fraydl put all her energy into developing a relationship with her young charges. As her pupils gradually allowed her entry into their hearts, their minds opened up as well. The children were starved for love, and Fraydl admitted to herself that she herself was not immune to the need for warmth and caring. Within weeks she began to see a transformation, until the girls were laughing and playing and learning. It gave her a deep satisfaction to be part of the devoted care they received.

Yanky and Chaim were never far from Fraydl's thoughts, and she prayed fervently that they would also return safely to *Yiddishkeit*. From time to time, Mrs. Sternbuch or Rabbi Oshry brought another child to the *Kinderheim*. "How do they know where to find the lost children?" Fraydl asked Mrs. Lederman.

"There are rumors," the director told her. "It is hard to keep something like that secret from neighbors and extended family members. When our spies report such rumors or gossip to the *Vaad HaHatzalah*, someone is sent to scout out the situation and decide how to effect a rescue.

"In the best case, the gentile guardians give up the child in their custody voluntarily. Of course, there are always those who are willing to accept a financial incentive for returning the child. The biggest problems are the devout Christians who converted the child to Christianity, and those who have come to regard the adopted Jewish child as their own. They resist giving them up, and special methods are called for."

"Do you mean the *Vaad* literally abducts the children?" Fraydl asked in alarm.

"They use whatever means are necessary," Yonah stated calmly.

"No wonder it's hard for the children to settle down here…"

Mrs. Lederman nodded. "It is a trauma for them," she agreed. "But we have to think of what their parents really wanted. No Jewish child was placed with gentiles for safekeeping with the intention that the child would be raised as a non-Jew. Every parent hoped to return and collect their child after the war. In better circumstances, the mother or father would have come back, and the child would have had to endure the separation from his gentile family anyway."

"What about the children in orphanages, monasteries and convents?" Fraydl asked, her heart pining for her little nephews.

"They are the hardest to reach," Yonah admitted. "We don't have very many inside people who can gain access to those places. Even when we do manage to get into such an orphanage, it's almost impossible to know which children are Jewish and which are not."

"Wouldn't the boys have the sign of the *bris*?"

"Only the older ones, who were born before the war. Many Jewish babies were not circumcised, either because there was no *mohel* available, or from fear that their identity as Jews would be discovered."

Fraydl's eyes welled with tears. "Is there no way to find my nephews again?"

Mrs. Lederman patted her arm affectionately. "Have you heard of the Ponevezher Rav, Rabbi Yosef Shlomo Kahaneman?" she asked. "He went to a monastery near here and spoke to the director of the orphanage. The priest was very cooperative. 'We have no Jewish children here,' he insisted. Harav Kahaneman would not give up. 'Could I just have a look at the children, please?' he asked. The priest was so confident that he agreed. Rabbi Kahaneman was shown into the dormitory just as the children were going to sleep. He strode up and down the aisle between their cots and called out, *'Shema Yisrael, kinderlach!'* Ten children jumped up and ran to him, crying, 'Mamme! Mamme!'

"Can you believe his ingenuity? The priest was very angry, but he had given his word that the Rabbi he could take any Jewish child that he found.

"Here in Poland, the Russians defeated the German Army, and now they control the national and most local governments as well. As you know, the Communists have no empathy for religion. If they find out what the *Vaad* is doing, it means prison! But Rabbi Oshry and Mrs. Sternbuch and the other *Rabbanim* are not afraid of anything. It is a *gevaldige zechus* to work with them!"

62

KARL EMSBACH WANTED TO GET AWAY FROM THE ORPHA-
nage as quickly as possible. When Yanky's short little legs
just couldn't keep up, he lifted the child and carried him all the way
to the American consulate, where his car was parked. Certain that
he was on his way back to the attic and his Tante Fraydl, the little
boy's face was wreathed in smiles.

"Yanky," Emsbach told him, gently touching the child's cold
cheek, "We are not going home now."

A serious expression replaced the happy one. "Not going home?"
he repeated anxiously.

How am I going to explain all the changes in my life to a 5-year-old?

Emsbach sighed. "Here is the car," he said, opening the back
door and depositing the boy on the seat. "It's a surprise," he promised, hoping to alleviate the child's obvious disappointment.

Yanky stared quietly out the window as they drove. When they
reached the hotel, the boy's expression changed to trepidation.
Clutching Emsbach's coat with his small fist, the child insisted,
"You're not leaving me again, *Herr Doktor*! I don't want to stay here!"
Despite the bravado, a tremor of fear resonated in Yanky's voice.

"I'm not leaving you anywhere, Yanky. "We are always going to stay together, from this day forward. The war is over, little one. Many things have changed now."

The child's grasp did not relax. He held onto the hem of Emsbach's coat with all his strength. Noticing that the boy was still wearing his wet cap, the doctor pulled it off and ran his fingers through the dark, tangled curls. Yanky would not let go of his coat until Emsbach gently lifted him in his arms and hugged him tightly.

The feel of the small wet face against his cheek evoked emotions that he did not recognize. He stroked the child's back, murmuring, "It's all right, Yanky. Don't be afraid. I'm not going to leave you again, ever." His heart seemed to melt under the weight of the boy's arms around his neck. "Come on," he whispered. "Take my handkerchief and blow your nose. That's good. Now I'm taking you upstairs to meet someone special."

When he heard the door open, Rabbi Stern turned to greet his son. He stopped short at the sight of the child in Tanchum's arms.

Steadying the boy on the floor, Emsbach told his father, "This is Yanky, the boy I told you about. Yanky, this is Rabbiner Stern. He is my father."

Yanky stared at the man, and blinked. *"Der Zeide?"* he asked.

Rabbi Stern's eyes met with his son's. He shook his head in incredulity. "How did this miracle come about?"

Emsbach sat down, pulling the unresisting boy onto his lap. "It's a long story. . ."

Over the next hour, he detailed for his father all the events that had taken place since they'd parted that morning.

Rabbi Stern arranged a light meal on the table while he listened to Tanchum's account. "Do you have your visa?"

"Yes, my passport is stamped."

"What about the boy?"

"It complicates things, I suppose."

"They are forming a Jewish *Kinderheim* in France under reliable supervision. He could be placed there for the meantime."

Emsbach shook his head. "I promised him that we would not be separated again," he said, tightening his arms around Yanky's shoulders — a gesture that did not escape the rabbi's notice.

"It's getting late. Let us eat. Are you hungry, *mein kind*?" he addressed Yanky.

"I'm starving!" the child replied, jumping to his feet.

"Do you remember how to make a *brachah*?"

The boy was confused. He looked from one adult to the other, then folded his hands into a steeple as he had been taught to pray at the orphanage.

"No!" Rabbi Stern caught the child's hands and pulled them apart. "Jews don't do that," he told him gently. "You are a Jewish child, Yanky. This is how we do it," and he showed the boy how to wash for bread and make the proper blessing.

"He's very young. He forgot," Emsbach defended his ward.

"It's understandable," his father agreed. "There are many things that he will have to learn again, just like you." Emsbach felt his father's love caress him, and he had to blink away a sudden moisture in his eyes.

"When we were with Father Matthew, Chaim and I were together," Yanky said suddenly while chewing the last crust of his sandwich.

"What happened? Why aren't you together anymore?"

"I don't know. He never came back."

"He never came back from where, Yanky? When did you see Chaim last?"

Yanky fingered his napkin. "One night there was lots of noise, and we all had to go down to the cellar."

"You went down to the cellar. What happened next?" Rabbi Stern urged him to continue.

"There was a terrible, terrible boom."

"And then what happened?"

"The house fell down on top of us."

"You were under the house?"

"I couldn't breathe. Chaim moved the bricks and he pulled me out."

The two men looked at the boy, waiting for him to carry on.

"There was smoke everywhere and I was coughing." He looked at Emsbach and whispered, "I was afraid."

"What happened next?"

"There was a big truck. We all got into the truck, but some men told the big boys to help pick up the bricks. I wanted to stay with Chaim but they wouldn't let me."

"The truck drove away with the children on it?"

"Yes, but not Chaim. I thought he would come later, but he never did."

"You don't know where Chaim is?"

"No. *Herr Doktor*, will you go and find Chaim, too?"

"I'll try, Yanky."

Satiated at last, Yanky snuggled into Emsbach's lap and yawned. His eyes never left Dr. Emsbach's face as he fought to keep his eyelids open. The men resumed their previous discussion.

"You know that the delegation is leaving the day after tomorrow," Rabbi Stern reminded his son. "Realistically, I don't think that papers can be arranged for Yanky in such a short time."

"That means that you will have to go without us and we will join you later."

"Are you sure?"

"What choice is there? It's not possible to leave Yanky." After a moment, he added, "I also feel responsible for Chaim and Fraydl. I cannot leave without trying to find them." Emsbach paused. "Tatte, believe me, I want to leave Germany. I want to see my mother." His voice broke and he turned his face away, unable to bear the conflicting emotions warring in his heart.

Rabbi Stern said nothing. A wall of silence grew until it seemed to fill the room. At last, Tanchum's father cleared his throat and stood. "It is late. Let us go to sleep."

Emsbach looked up at his father, grateful for the things that had not been said. "I will come as soon as I can. I promise," he said fervently.

The rabbi nodded. "Of course. I know you will. We will pray that it should be very soon. May Hashem speed your search."

During the last days the delegation spent in Germany, the three spent as much time as possible together. Rabbi Stern taught Yanky about the *parashah,* and reviewed the laws of *kashrus* and Shabbos with his son.

Tanchum wrote a long letter to his mother, explaining the reason for the delay and assuring her of his overwhelming desire to be reunited with her as soon as possible. He handed it to his father at the last minute, and Rabbi Stern slipped it carefully into his briefcase.

"It has been so many years," he remarked sadly. "She will understand, but she won't understand. Do you know what I mean?"

Emsbach nodded. "I think that's how I feel as well," he said. They embraced, and then the rabbi joined his colleagues waiting in the taxi.

With his father's departure, Emsbach felt a terrible emptiness. Yanky tugged at his hand. "Is Cleopatra still in the attic?" he asked eagerly.

Emsbach looked down at the child's innocent face. "No, Yanky. Cleo's gone."

"Tante Fraydl is gone. Chaim is gone. Cleopatra is gone. Everything is gone," the boy recited sadly.

63

TEACHING CHILDREN WAS THE PERFECT MEDICINE FOR
Fraydl. Turning her focus away from herself and out to
others restored her innate serenity. She proved very successful at
awakening in her pupils a longing for a connection to things Jewish,
and her discipline and intelligence were important assets.

Since she'd been a little girl, Fraydl had always loved to sing.
Now she sang to the children, mostly Yiddish lullabies and children's rhymes. Her soft voice stirred something deep within their
hearts. She kept her lessons brief and paced them dramatically, frequently telling stories of *tzaddikim* that opened her pupil's minds
to new concepts of spiritual challenge. Fraydl's own refined behavior contrasted with the coarseness they had grown up with, effectively drawing them ever closer to their Jewish heritage.

Fraydl found that, through the children, she was reconnecting to
the childhood she'd lost during the war. Their innocent love revital-
ized her soul, allowing her to begin the process of growing despite
the losses she had endured. The *Kinderheim* became a refuge for
her no less than for the orphans who inhabited it.

One night, a messenger from the Jewish Relief Agency turned

up at the Children's Home with a frightened little girl in tow. She had been deposited with them that afternoon by a Polish peasant who demanded to be paid for hiding her during the war. Having no known relatives, she was transferred to the *Kinderheim*.

"Who is she? Where does she come from?" Mrs. Lederman queried.

"It's all very strange. The peasant declared that she is Jewish, and that he hid her in his barn until the end of the war. When no one came to claim her, he didn't know what to do with her until he heard that the JRA is paying gentiles who sheltered Jews. He came to us, but he knows neither her name nor where she lived before."

Yonah Lederman bent down to the child's eye level and asked, "What's your name, dear?"

The little girl didn't answer. Mrs. Lederman tried asking in Polish, Hungarian, German and Yiddish — to no avail.

"It doesn't matter," she said at last. "Poor child, she is tired and afraid. Perhaps later she will tell us something."

After several days of loving care and good food, the child finally spoke. Her first whispered words were, "Where is my Tatty? I want my Tatty!"

Yonah was delighted to know that the girl understood Yiddish. Fraydl wanted to take her to her class, but the newcomer clung to Mrs. Lederman, refusing to be separated. The tolerant housemother allowed the child to accompany her all day as she performed her routine duties. Within a few days the girl began to speak freely, but no matter how she tried, she could not remember her name.

"How could she forget her own name?" Fraydl asked in consternation.

"We have no idea what she went through," Yonah replied. "Some children changed their identities many times. While they were in hiding, they had to pretend to be somebody else. Let us hope that her memory returns as she grows older."

"She comes from an *ehrliche* family," Bassy commented.

"How do you know?"

"She knows how to cover her eyes and say the *Shema* before she goes to sleep, and she does *negelvasser* correctly, without assistance."

"We can't leave her without a name," Mrs. Lederman declared. She thought deeply and then decided, "I will call her Lieba. Liebe'le, *zisskeit*," she stroked the child's golden curls."*Tiyera maydeleh.*"

"I want my Tatty," Lieba said soberly. "When will my Tatty come?"

Yonah Lederman gave her a hug and a gentle pinch on her cheek. *Who knows where her father is?* she thought sadly.

"Even if her father is still alive, how will he find her?" Bassy asked.

"I suppose he will contact the peasant into whose care he gave her, and eventually be referred to the JRA. It will be on record that she is with us, and it will be our greatest joy to see them reunited."

"You don't sound like you believe it will happen."

"We try to be optimistic, but there's no point in harboring illusions."

The next day, a registered letter was delivered to the *Kinderheim*, informing Mrs. Lederman that the staff was to pack up and be ready to move the entire orphanage at a moment's notice.

"Why? What happened?" Fraydl was rattled by the unexpected order and didn't understand the urgency.

"Politics," Yonah Lederman answered. "Or call it postwar reality."

"What do you mean?"

"Eastern Europe is in a dangerous situation. The Russian Army disregarded the will of the Polish people and transferred authority to the Polish Communists when they withdrew. Negotiations have been going on for a long time, with pressure from the United States and Britain. Now it seems that permission has finally been secured to bring several hundred homeless Jewish children to the West, but we must move quickly before the window of opportunity closes. Who knows how long it will be before there is another chance to escape the Communists?"

By the end of the summer, arrangements were made to transfer all the orphans to France. Technically, Fraydl was older than 20, but the *Vaad* designated her as a counselor and included her in the children's transport. With her Austrian passport, she was not as vulnerable as some of the other "older teenagers," each desperate to get free of the hostile Communist regime in Poland.

In hopes of diverting the authorities' attention from the accompanying adults whose documents were not valid for the journey, the children sat on the floor in small, scattered groups. Any time police officers tried to inspect their passports, youngsters jumped up and began running around and shouting. Their counselors made a showy effort of running after them, and in the resulting mayhem it was impossible to either count them accurately or match each one to the documents identifying them. Invariably succumbing to frustration, the authorities stamped and signed the papers that allowed the group to proceed.

Fraydl had her hands full keeping track of the children from both her *Kinderheim* and other orphanages as well. The boys were busy fighting, pushing, shoving each other and teasing the girls. The girls bickered among themselves, complained about the boys' behavior and tended to burst into tears at the slightest provocation. She hardly noticed when the train passed through the towns of Czechoslovakia on its way to France. Eventually, the counselors succeeded in setting up a daily schedule that included meals, lessons, naps and story time. The routine had a calming effect and the children finally settled down.

The train stopped in Prague for Rosh Hashanah. "I don't believe it," Fraydl murmured as she gazed around at the ancient and beautiful city. "How is it possible that the Germans were here and didn't destroy everything?"

Prague was miraculously untouched by the devastation of war. Fraydl was grateful to spend her first Yom Tov since she'd been 13 in an authentic Jewish environment. Still, after years of being involuntarily severed from full observance, her feelings were bittersweet. The ancient liturgy opened up wellsprings of tears in everyone who remembered their world before the war. The haunting sounds of the shofar echoed through all the recesses of Fraydl's soul, long after they had left Czechoslovakia behind and continued their journey.

64

T OO BAD FRAYDL LEFT — THIS SOUNDS PERFECT FOR HER."
Katya chewed bubble gum as she scanned the pages of the
Post.

"What is it? Is there anything for us?" Raya tugged the paper
from the younger woman's hands and spread it on the table so they
could each peruse the want-ad section at the same time. Finding
employment had become a critical need for the residents who still
remained in the DP camp. It felt as though they had been here far
too long, but in order to rebuild their lives it was necessary to have
a source of income.

"Here's an ad for a governess in Ravensdorf," Katya said. "The
salary is attractive, but I am an only child. I've never worked with
young children and I wouldn't have the faintest idea how to be a
governess."

"It's not that hard," Masha informed her. "You just have to get
them up in the morning, send them off to school properly dressed
according to the weather, supervise their meals, put them to bed on
time and get up to see what's wrong if they cry at night."

Raya's eyebrows met in a scowl. "I'd rather take care of a stable full of horses than coddle a German child," she said, her voice low and angry.

Her friends nodded their agreement.

"Why Fraydl, specifically?" Masha asked, absently running her finger down the column of ads for seamstresses.

"They want someone who is knowledgeable in Jewish law."

"What?!" Simultaneously Masha and Raya turned to stare at her.

"See for yourselves. It's here in black and white," Katya insisted, miffed at their incredulity.

"Emsbach," Raya said aloud, reading the advertisement in question. "It's an old German name. Why would they want a governess who is knowledgeable in Jewish law?" Raya frowned.

"How could a Jewish child have survived the war?" Masha flicked the newsprint lightly with fingernail. "Perhaps" — her voice caught emotionally — "a German with a heart hid a Jewish child during the war?"

"That doesn't make sense," Raya shook her head. "If they had a Jewish child, the simplest thing would be to turn it over to one of the organizations helping Jewish survivors. If such a person grew attached enough to keep the child, why would they want to raise it Jewish when they could just convert it to Christianity?"

The young women sat in reflective silence while somewhere in the distance an ambulance siren echoed eerily. A dog howled and a metal gate banged shut.

With a sigh, Katya brought them back to the matter at hand. "Do you see any ads for a seamstress?" she asked Masha.

"Nothing realistic."

"Why not try something else?" Raya suggested. "For instance, you could be a housekeeper."

"That's not a bad idea," Masha agreed. Three bent heads reexamined the want ads from a new perspective.

"How about this one? Experienced housekeeper," Masha read. "Able to work independently and manage domestic staff."

"Look! It's the same name and address as the ad for a governess," Katya pointed out.

"Emsbach," Raya confirmed. "I'll write to them. Hmm, maybe they need a cook as well? You know a thousand recipes by heart, Masha. How about that?"

"They do!" Katya exclaimed. "Here, look!" She indicated an ad for a cook, with the unusual clause that the applicant must be familiar with the Jewish dietary laws. "This is really strange!"

"Could the family be Jewish?" Masha pondered.

"Emsbach?"

"They could have adopted a Teutonic surname. During the war I called myself Heidi Shnarrenberger."

Katya snorted. "Shnarrenberger? You couldn't choose something more elegant than that?"

Masha stood up, hands on her hips, and glared at Katya. "I needed a name that would not invite questions!" Sometimes it was hard to hold onto her composure in the face of Katya's characteristic cynicism.

"The important question is whether or not you know how to keep a kosher kitchen." Raya pulled Masha's arm so she would sit back down. "We must be practical."

Masha shifted uneasily before admitting, "I know how to keep a kosher kitchen."

The other two raised their eyes in astonishment. "You used to be religious?" Katya asked in a tone of disbelief.

The color in Masha's cheeks deepened. "So what if I was?" she shrugged. "Things were different before the war."

Ignoring Masha's discomfiture, Katya complained, "And what about me? We always had servants. I can't cook and I can't clean and I don't know anything about children. What can I do?"

"You're about to get married, Katya," Raya reminded her. "Let Herschel worry about those things!"

"Herschel is also looking for a job," Katya fretted.

"Well, maybe the Emsbachs need a handyman," Masha suggested. "Herschel knows how to fix things. He replaced the tiles on the roof when the rain leaked in last winter."

"You know that we're leaving for New York as soon as the visas come through," Katya grew suddenly dreamy. "Herschel says it won't be much longer now, and in America he will open a store. In a few years, we will be rich."

"Well, I wish you good luck," Raya said. "Meanwhile I think I will write to the address in this ad and inquire about the housekeeper position. I'll mention you too, Masha. It would really be nice if we can get out of this camp and also stay together."

A week later, Raya and Masha stood nervously at the back entrance to Dr. Emsbach's home. When the door was opened by the master of the house himself, both women stepped back in alarm. Emsbach's Aryan appearance and erect military bearing overpowered their ability to speak.

While he waited for an explanation for their appearance at his door, Masha closed her hand around Raya's arm and backed away, mumbling, *"Enshuldig, enshuldig.* We must have come to the wrong address."

Raya shook free from Masha's deathgrip. "We're responding to advertisements in the *Post* for a housekeeper and a cook," she squeaked.

"Of course, I am expecting you. Which one of you is *Fraulein* Kellerman?" Emsbach inquired, looking from one to the other.

Raya pointed to Masha, who was on the verge of swooning. "This is *Fraulein* Kellerman." She cleared her throat. "I am *Fraulein* Gutman."

Emsbach nodded. "Please come in," he invited. "The interview will be conducted in my study."

Knees quaking, Raya followed the German through his kitchen and into a comfortable but obviously masculine room, half-dragging Masha behind her. On the carpet beside the desk a small boy lay on his stomach, playing with an old set of toy soldiers. He lifted his eyes when the women entered, and his sweet Jewish face brought inadvertent smiles to their faces even as a shadow of sorrow passed over their hearts.

"Yanky," Emsbach addressed the boy, "please go play somewhere else while I speak with these women."

"I'm hungry," the child addressed the German with familiarity. "May I have some cake?"

"You may take an apple from the counter if you want. Soon I will be finished here and we will have dinner."

The boy swept his toys into a box and put it on the shelf. He looked at the visitors curiously, reluctant to leave the room. "Can I please stay?" he petitioned. "I won't bother."

Emsbach shook his head. "Yanky," he repeated firmly, gesturing toward the door.

"Yes, *Herr Doktor.*" With a last glance at Masha and Raya, Yanky left the room.

The interview was brief and to the point. Emsbach explained the duties involved in housekeeping, and offered the position to Raya on a trial basis. He questioned Masha about the laws of *kashrus* until he was satisfied that she was at least as knowledgeable as he was, and they agreed that the two women would commence work the following day.

"Your letter was from the Austrian DP camp," Emsbach observed. "Traveling back and forth is not very practical. If you are interested, my carriage house is vacant. It is modestly furnished, and I can deduct the rent from your monthly salary. Of course, if you prefer, you may search for lodgings in town."

"No, we appreciate your generous offer and we will be glad to take advantage of it," Raya answered for them both. The dilemma of securing living arrangements had kept the two up late the previous night. The carriage house offered an ideal solution. "We will return early tomorrow morning with our belongings, ready to begin work."

He nodded, satisfied. "I am going out now. May I offer you a ride to the train station?"

"That would be very kind."

On the way into town, Yanky sat in front while Raya and Masha took the back seat. The women were bursting with curiosity as they witnessed affectionate interactions between their new employer and the obviously Jewish child in his care.

"Can I drive?" Yanky pleaded, oblivious to the consternation of the passengers in the back.

"Only until the end of the driveway," Emsbach agreed, allowing the boy to climb onto his lap and hold the steering wheel while he lightly pressed the acceleration pedal. Yanky whooped with joy, and even the German could not suppress a smile as the car slowly swerved from side to side down the driveway. At the corner, Yanky relinquished the wheel and obediently took his place on the passenger side. His animated comments continued all the way to the train station.

"Tomorrow, then?" Emsbach said, opening the back door.

"Tomorrow," Raya affirmed.

"*B'ezras Hashem*," Masha added softly.

65

THE LAST SOUNDS OF THE SHOFAR WERE STILL reverberating in Fraydl's mind when their group was summoned to continue their journey. The train with the orphans from the *Kinderheim* traveled through Germany and entered France. After small groups of children were dropped off at several stations along the way, the number of Fraydl's charges became more manageable. The final stop, near the border with Switzerland and Italy, was a resort that had been requisitioned for refugee children.

The first objective was to help the children catch up on the lost years when they'd had little or no exposure to *Yiddishkeit*. Late in the night, as the children slept, Bassy and Fraydl posed their questions to Mrs. Lederman. The housemother's support was crucial because the inexperienced teachers often felt inadequate to the challenge.

"This is such a beautiful place to live," Fraydl gestured at their surroundings. "You would expect the children to be happy, but look how miserable they are! It's frustrating for me to work so hard with so few results."

"You have to appreciate how difficult the transition is for them," Yonah Lederman explained.

"What is so difficult? Everything here is much better than where they come from," Bassy insisted.

"Of course. But you have to understand the viewpoint of a child. There is a big gap between a child's logic and that of an adult."

"We show them how to *daven* properly — but as soon as we turn around, they kneel again," Bassy complained.

"How are we supposed to react when a girl's actions reflect how she was taught to pray? I've explained how offensive it is over and over, but they still do it." Fraydl bit her lower lip, feeling like a failure.

Mrs. Lederman took a deep breath. "You must remember that most of these orphans have been torn from a world where they were given approval for this behavior such as kneeling to pray. It is futile to tell them they must no longer do it before they internalize Jewish values.

"First of all, you are doing splendidly in the way you set an excellent personal example. Secondly, in class you are gradually teaching them the foundations of *Yiddishkeit*. I am sure that, in the end, it will trickle into their hearts and influence their behavior."

"Some days I feel I'm getting nowhere with them. If only it were possible to speed up the process," Fraydl said.

Yonah nodded with understanding, and smiled. "Just give them love and pretend you don't notice when they say their Christian prayers. You'll see; when the girls finally feel secure, they will let go of their old habits. Have patience, and you'll have the satisfaction of knowing that your labor was not in vain."

Bassy sighed. "Sometimes I feel like giving up."

"G-d forbid! We are *shelichim* and we must fulfill the role that was denied their parents. Look at the whole picture. It is not only these young girls we are concerned with, but also the generations yet to be born from them. Do not doubt that this is holy work, and that Hashem will repay you many times over."

At a loss for words, the young teachers absorbed this message.

"I think we have to create new associations for them," Fraydl said thoughtfully. "We need to create an environment that will draw them out of their despondency."

"How?" Bassy asked. "Where do we start?"

"Fraydl is right," Mrs. Lederman said. "These children need positive experiences to replace the old memories that are confusing them and making them sad."

"Maybe the answer is less schoolwork," Frayd suggested. "Even though they are very far behind, teaching them facts and rules is no replacement for a lost childhood. Perhaps we can just let them be children, and give them as many normal pastimes as possible. When I was in school, we would put on plays about events in Jewish history, and sing songs that taught Torah concepts. They might be more receptive to *Yiddishkeit* if we include it in childhood activities like games and crafts."

Yonah Lederman beamed. "Excellent, Fraydl!" she responded. "We will put your ideas into action!"

After that, there were fewer hours in the schoolroom and more time outside in the bracing autumn air. When the weather permitted, counselors took the girls on early-morning bike rides, to *daven* Shacharis on a hilltop with a spectacular view. At night, they sang around the campfire. Creative classes in sewing, music and art were added to the curriculum. Language skills improved through writing for a *Kinderheim Zeitung*. The children's lives began to mend before their teachers' grateful eyes.

The teachers in the *Kinderheim* had also suffered during the war; they, too, needed to rebuild shattered lives without family support. During the months they worked together, the young women developed ties that bound them like surrogate sisters. Each one felt the other's pain, and shared their happy moments.

The *Kinderheim* became a dynamic place, alive with an air of anticipation as Mrs. Lederman and the *Vaad* searched for warm Jewish homes for the orphans. Visitors came often, hunting for missing relatives or hoping to adopt a child to fill the emptiness left by loss. One by one, many of Fraydl's pupils moved on.

"How are you feeling these days?" the housemother asked Fraydl one spring evening.

"Truthfully, I can say you were right when you promised that we would see fulfillment in our work," she answered quietly. "There can be no greater satisfaction than seeing lost souls rescued and their Jewish inheritance returned to them."

"So why do I sense sadness in your heart?"

Her feelings brought out into the open by Yonah's infallible intuition, Fraydl gave a forlorn smile. "My nephews, Yanky and Chaim, are always in my thoughts and prayers. I can't help but worry about them, and feel responsible. I am happy that I was able to teach the girls in the *Kinderheim*, but I wish I knew that someone was doing the same thing for my little nephews."

"How can you feel responsible? Did you have a choice?"

"You're right. I tell myself that over and over. But I still feel that I should have done more to find them after the war."

"Doesn't Hashem know where they are? Doesn't He care for them even more than you? Let Him run the world, Fraydl. In the merit of your work in the *Kinderheim*, I'm sure He is protecting them, wherever they are."

"You're right, as usual." Fraydl drew comfort from Mrs. Lederman's caring words.

"We have a new project to take on." The housemother changed the subject.

Fraydl sent her a questioning look.

"Many families have recently arrived in Aix-les-Bains from the Soviet Union," she told her. "We've been asked to allow their children to attend our school."

"It seems we have no lack of challenges!"

Mrs. Lederman laughed. "What are we here for, if not for that?" she asked. "The children from Russia also need remedial Jewish education. They must make up for the years lost in the Siberian wilderness. The first group of pupils is due to arrive tomorrow morning."

66

WHY DON'T YOU SIT DOWN, SHAINDEL? STARING OUT THE window won't bring Tanchum home any faster."

Rebbitzen Stern turned her head to look at her husband of over 40 years. "I am afraid he'll never come," she admitted. "It's almost impossible to believe that you found him."

"Actually, I didn't find him. He found me." Rabbi Stern gestured toward the chair next to his. "Come, sit down. Don't strain yourself so; it's not good for you."

His wife let the curtains fall back and sank into the soft cushions with a sigh. "I don't understand why he stayed in Germany," she murmured. "Why would he want to stay in that blood-soaked land?"

It was Rabbi Stern's turn to sigh. "It won't be much longer. He's a fine man, our son. We can be proud of him."

"I don't care about being proud. I want to reach out and touch him after so many years. I want to see his face and hear his voice. I want to be sure that my lost son has been found. Then I can die in peace."

"Please don't speak of dying, Shaindel!"

"Meir, my health is not a secret. I am prepared to leave this world whenever Hashem calls me...But I do long to see my Tanchum just once before I go. Did you tell him that I am not well?"

Rabbi Stern shook his head. "Perhaps it was a mistake not to tell him how serious your condition is," he murmured.

"That's right. Then he might not have stayed behind."

"I'm sorry, my dear. How can I explain? Tanchum's entire life was overturned when he discovered that he had been kidnapped as a child. After an upbringing intended to force him into the mold of a German military officer, an Aryan and a Nazi, he finds out that in fact he is a *Yid*. All things considered, he is coping with sensitivity and dignity — but Tanchum could not hide the turmoil in his heart from me. He was respectful, but I sensed that the connection between us was precarious. I needed to build his trust, to allow him to make the decision to come back when he is ready.

"Tanchum is a grown man now. There is a lot of unfinished business that he must tend to. Much of it is legal, but a fair amount involves his deepest feelings. If I had played on his sense of honor, if I told him how serious your heart condition is, it is conceivable that he would have come with me... but he wouldn't have been fully with us. Part of him would still be torn, still connected to his past. I believe he will come when he is ready. For now, I ask you to accept that and try to be calm and happy."

Rebbetzin Stern laid her head back against the chair and closed her eyes. "Surely Hashem has not brought our child back to us only to take him away again," she said softly. "Talk to me, Meir. You were gone for so many weeks. Tell me about your experiences with the delegation."

The rabbi took off his glasses and methodically polished the lens with his handkerchief. "It was the most moving experience of my life," he told her. "We alternated between joy and sorrow the whole time — and sometimes both of them together."

"What do you mean?"

"In Weimar, Germany, there was a hotel requisitioned by the United States Army. One of the clerks was a Jewish soldier from Brooklyn. He told us about some concentration-camp survivors they employed in the hotel. Two of them were *shomer* Torah and mitzvos. They preferred to walk the seven miles back and forth on Shabbos from their DP camp to the hotel than to ride in the jeep that was sent to pick them up.

"I was with Chaplain Livazer when those two boys were summoned to appear before him. It broke my heart to see how malnourished they were. The oldest was not more than 15. He told us how their parents were murdered by the Gestapo in front of their eyes, and how they spent the war in ghettos and camps. *Oy*, Shaindel, I could hardly breathe from the pain of seeing *cheder yingelech* like that. Instinctively, we all wanted to help. Rabbi Livazer asked what they needed most. He promised to try and get anything they asked for.

"Do you know what they asked for, Shaindel?

"They asked for *tefillin*! They had never put on *tefillin* in their lives, and that's what they wanted. Not food for their emaciated bodies. *Tefillin*!"

Rebbetzin Stern lifted a hand to her face. "I understand what you mean by joy and sorrow at the same time, Meir," she whispered. "*Mi k'amcha Yisrael!*"

"We started out in France." Rabbi Stern strove to lighten her mood. "One of the first things we did was join a Pesach *seder*, organized by Chaplain Livazer in an army base. It was attended by 5,000 Jewish soldiers! "

The rebbetzin blinked. "I can't begin to imagine preparing a *seder* for so many guests. It must have taken a whole company working day and night for weeks just to get it ready."

Rabbi Stern chuckled appreciatively. "Not really. I think there were about 50 Nazi prisoners working to pluck the hundreds of fowl after Chaplain Livazer *shechted* them. Actually, the whole Jewish *kehillah* in Reims worked all night to prepare everything in time."

"But where did you get enough kosher dishes and silverware? And what did they use for linens?"

"They used hundreds of new white bed sheets for tablecloths. The Americans manufactured food trays for field hospitals from the aluminum left behind by the Germans. They gave Rabbi Livazer as many as he could use. We made do with glass covers from captured mines as soup bowls. My delegation supervised the *toiveling* in a nearby lake. It took us two whole days. It was amazing, Shaindel, truly amazing!"

The rebbetzin settled back in her chair with a smile. "It must have been beautiful," she murmured, drifting into a light doze.

"Zeide?"

Rabbi Stern put a finger to his lips and beckoned his grandchild to enter the room quietly. "What can I do for you, Shmuel?" he whispered.

"I want you to *farher* me," the 12-year-old said proudly.

"Let's go in the kitchen, then, so as not to disturb the Baba."

It didn't take long to see that the boy knew the *masechte* inside out. Rabbi Stern pinched the child's cheek with pleasure. Shmuel glowed.

"Here, child, have some of Baba's *mandelbrot* while I boil water for tea."

"*Zeide,*" he said, watching his grandfather bustle about the small kitchen. "Can I ask you a question?"

"Of course, *yingeleh*. What do you want to know?"

"I heard Tatty and Mommy talking about your trip to Europe. They say you found Fetter Tanchum. Could it really be true?"

"Do you doubt your parents, Shmuelik?" The rabbi frowned.

"No, of course not. But how can you be sure it really is Fetter Tanchum and not an imposter? Maybe he is a Nazi who just wants to escape justice and is pretending to be my father's lost brother?"

Rabbi Stern sat down and looked at his grandson gravely. He did not believe that Shmuel had thought of these questions all by himself. He must have overheard his parents discussing such a possibility.

"I understand your concerns," he said slowly, "and I admit that the evidence is all circumstantial. Do you know what that means?"

The boy nodded cautiously.

"I think that when you see him, you will not have any more doubts. Tanchum looks like a younger version of your father and the other uncles. There probably is no way to really prove it beyond any doubt, but the pieces fit together like a puzzle, and it all makes part of the same picture."

"Why didn't he come home with you, then?"

"He will come, *yingele*. As soon as Tanchum finishes up some important business from his past, he will come. "

67

"F RAYDL! FRAYDL!"

Fraydl turned at the sound of Bassy's excited voice. "Did *Mashiach* come?" she asked with a smile.

"Not yet, but almost!" her friend replied. "Look at this!" Bassy danced in place, waving an envelope in front of Fraydl's face.

"If you'd stop shaking it like a *lulav*, I might be able to read it." There was a tremor in Fraydl voice. She had a premonition that Bassy's good news might not be good news for her.

She took the proffered letter and examined it. "A certificate? You got a certificate! Oh, Bassy, *mazel tov!*" Fraydl hugged her friend, suppressing the envy that threatened to spoil the moment. "Who else received one besides you?"

"Chaya Goldshmidt and Ahuva Galitzky!" Bassy was so absorbed in her good fortune that the tears that sprang to the corners of Fraydl's eyes completely escaped her attention. "We have to pack and leave by Monday. Can you believe it? Eretz Yisrael!"

Every member of the *Kinderheim* staff was waiting for the coveted permit that would allow her to leave Europe and begin building a new life in Palestine. The topic most discussed between the counselors was *aliyah*. Should they wait for the official documents that seemed never to come, or would it be better to join the illegal *aliyah* and take their chances on avoiding the British blockade? Now the dream had suddenly become a reality for three of the tightly knit group.

Fraydl surreptitiously wiped her damp eyes on her sleeve and accompanied Bassy back to the dorm, where the girls sang and danced as if it were an engagement party.

That night they argued until very late about the merits of living in the city or on a kibbutz, and whether it was worth leaving *Poalei Agudas Yisrael* to join one of the other factions that offered a more realistic chance of obtaining a certificate from the Jewish Agency. Their knowledge of the difficulties facing pioneers in Palestine faded beside their anticipation of the upcoming journey, and dawn brought fervent promises to be reunited once again in Eretz Yisrael.

After Bassy left, the *Kinderheim* was no longer the same. *Too many things are changing*, Fraydl thought with a sigh as she sat in the unoccupied classroom after the children had been dismissed. Many of her original charges had moved on to adoptive homes or been claimed by relatives. The new pupils from Russia had arrived in Aix-les-Bains together with their families. Their war experiences were very different from Fraydl's, and their mentality was harder for her to understand.

Momentarily surrendering to the sadness that had shadowed her since parting from her close friend, Fraydl allowed the tears she had been holding back to trickle down her cheeks. *I need a good cry*, she rationalized. *It is so lonely without Bassy.*

As often happened when she was sad, she imagined her mother's gentle voice, admonishing her for giving in to such feelings. *You're right, Mamme.* With an effort, Fraydl regained control of her depressing thoughts. *I am grateful to be alive. I must let go of the past and think of the future.* She dabbed at her face with a handkerchief, stood up and squared her shoulders. She was just about to leave the empty classroom when there was a light knock and the door was pushed open.

"Fraydl, are you still here?" The loud voice of the counselor for the middle grades startled her.

"Yes, Chava, I'm just leaving. Can I help you with something?" Fraydl ducked her head, hoping the signs of her recent weeping were not too obvious.

"You didn't come to lunch today, so you didn't hear Mrs. Lederman announce that there's a letter for you in the office. I thought you'd like to know."

"A letter?" Fraydl felt engulfed with sadness again. The only letters she ever received at the *Kinderheim* were negative responses to her requests for information about Yanky and Chaim. Her little nephews seemed to have disappeared from the face of the earth.

"Are you all right?" Chava asked.

"Yes, I'm fine, *baruch Hashem*." Fraydl tried to smile. "Today's been rather a hard day for me and I'm just tired."

"Would you like me to get your letter from the office and bring it to the dorm?"

"That would be very nice of you. I'd appreciate it."

"Go lie down, then, and if you're asleep when I come back I'll just leave it on the shelf beside your bed."

"Thank you, Chava."

I feel like an old woman, Fraydl struggled with herself. *It's wrong to give up hope, but I must be realistic.*

"Is something the matter?" Yonah Lederman asked Chava, when the teacher asked for Fraydl's letter.

"I don't think so. Fraydl said she was tired, and I offered to save her the time and effort."

Chava stared at the numerous postmarks on the envelope. "It's good that the person who wrote this has a clear handwriting. It looks as if it's been around the world before it got here."

Mrs. Lederman nodded. "I hope it will make Fraydl happy. She hasn't really smiled since the girls left for Palestine."

Chava climbed up three flights of stairs and tiptoed into the dorm room the counselors shared. Fraydl stirred in her sleep but didn't awaken, so she left the letter in a conspicuous place and went back out as quietly as she had entered.

Darkness had fallen by the time Fraydl sat up. Switching on the table lamp, she noticed the envelope. *So many postmarks*, she noted in wonder, searching her memory for a clue as to who the sender might be. A moment later, she smothered a cry of recognition. It was her sister's handwriting! Fraydl was born the same year Rivka became engaged to Avraham Abba Feigelbaum, and since the young couple had made their home in faraway Palestine after their marriage, the only thing Fraydl remembered about them was the weekly letter her mother read aloud to her father before sharing the news with the rest of the family.

Fraydl's hands fumbled as she pulled open the flimsy aerogram. It was dated nearly a year earlier, and addressed to her via the Austrian section of the Displaced Persons Authority.

My dearest sister Fraydl,

I can hardly believe the news that you are among the living. My eyes have wept until there are no more tears for Mamme and Tatte and the others, but since I saw your name on the list of survivors in the Palestine Post *my heart is reinvigorated because at least you were saved.*

I have good news for you. Right after the war, we applied for a certificate for my sister-in-law Sarah, but she did not want to wait. By the time we received it, she had run the blockade with a boat belonging to the ma'apilim. It was hashgachah pratis, because now the certificate is yours!

The last time I saw you, Fraydl, you were only 3 years old. Do you remember when we came to Vienna for Malky's wedding? You played so sweetly with my Perel (she is married with a baby now) and everyone called you Tante'le. Write to me right away, please, and tell me when you are coming. I can hardly bear the wait. I hope that you are well. I pray for you constantly.

Your loving sister,
Rivka

68

T HE YOUNG MONK PUT HIS ARM ACROSS CHAIM'S SHOUL-
ders and gave a gentle squeeze. "I understand how hard it
is for you," he told the boy sympathetically. "The war was such a
terrible experience. Many, many people lost everything. It was a
tragedy no one can understand... But life continues, son. There is
no choice but to go on."

The boy's thin shoulders shuddered as he struggled to stifle his
sobs. When gentle Father Simon had informed him that no one
would be coming to take him out of the monastery, Chaim's world
had plunged into total darkness. The horrible war was finally over,
but his hopes were dashed.

"We sent letters to your former guardian and the orphanage
where you and your brother were previously. They were returned
unopened." The monk handed him two canceled envelopes. Chaim
was weeping too hard to make out the handwritten words scrawled
across the addresses, but he understood the priest's meaning.
Father Simon opened his arms, and the lonely boy buried his face in
his mentor's cowl to weep for a world that was gone. "Even Tante

Fraydl? Even little Yanky?" he begged the priest to revise the finality of his message.

"You are not alone, my child," Simon soothed. "We will be your family forever. From this day, you will begin a different life. You will forget your painful past and you will build a new future. From now on, your name will be Thomas."

"Thomas?" The name felt foreign and unpleasant on Chaim's tongue.

"Thomas was a saint. He is venerated all over the world. It is a good name."

Chaim felt dizzy. He caught onto the priest's sleeve as the room spun out of control. Slipping helplessly into the abyss, his terrified scream was reduced to a whimper as the darkness swallowed him.

Moments later, the boy recovered from his faint, blinking in bewilderment. Fathers Simon and Arthur were on their knees on either side of him. From what seemed a great distance, one of the priests was slapping his cheeks and calling, "Thomas, Thomas!" while the other splashed cold water on his face. His cheeks stung. Chaim summoned all his strength to shake his head and make them stop their unwelcome ministrations.

"It's all right, Thomas," Father Simon said in a tone of relief. "You've had a sudden shock. Come upstairs and lie down until you feel stronger."

Chaim did not resist as the two men helped him to his feet. Supporting the boy on both sides, they led him to the dormitory and helped him into his bed.

"Sleep, Thomas," Father Arthur recommended, pulling up the woolen blanket and tucking it in around the boy's shoulders. "You will feel better afterward."

Chaim nodded, closing his eyes obediently. He wanted to sleep. He wanted to shut out the cruel and empty world. He wanted to dream of Tante Fraydl and Yanky and *Herr Doktor*. He wanted to play chess with Dr. Emsbach and watch his little brother line up the toy soldiers on the soft carpet. When he thought of Cleopatra and her kittens, the corners of his mouth flickered with a tenuous smile.

After ensuring that Thomas was asleep, the two priests left the room, softly closing the door behind them.

"Poor child," Father Simon murmured.

"They are all poor children," Father Arthur commented, referring to the 10 orphans under their supervision. "They are also very fortunate to be here under our care. You have seen the street children in the alleys, starving and stealing to survive. We can take great satisfaction from our role in saving them."

"Their bodies *and* their souls."

"Exactly."

"The archbishop is due to visit next week. It will be propitious to have him conduct the baptismal ceremony, don't you agree?"

"Excellent. I am sure he will be very pleased."

Their combined weight caused the old staircase to creak with each descending step. Father Simon paused to make eye contact with his colleague. "I think it would be a good idea to keep the Jewish boys separate from each other for awhile."

"Do you expect resistance?" Father Arthur asked in alarm.

"In my experience, it is better to be careful than sorry."

The two continued their descent in silence, each man sunk in his own thoughts.

Finally Simon spoke. "We will speak of this tonight after prayers." He caught sight of one of the novices. "Josef," he called, "please take up a tray with supper for Thomas. He's feeling weak and I gave him permission to rest until services tonight."

The young man had taken a vow of silence and was allowed to speak only in prayer. He bobbed his head to indicate acquiescence, and immediately turned to the kitchen. Opening the pantry, Josef loaded a tray with bread and cheese. He liked Chaim, and was secretly aware that they were kindred spirits. Five years ago, when he was about Chaim's age, his own parents were taken away by the Gestapo. Josef had cowered under his mother's bed until he was discovered a few hours later by Gretchen, the teenage daughter of their closest neighbors.

"Shh!" she warned him, pressing a finger to her lips. "Don't come out now. I will return when it is dark." During the time that passed,

Yossele had listened while their former neighbors moved freely about his parents' house, searching for valuables and taking whatever found favor in their eyes. Much later, when the house was silent again, Gretchen brought him her little sister's clothes for a disguise. Then she led him through back alleys to her older brother, who was a novice in this monastery, and he was welcomed on condition that he accept the faith of his rescuers. Josef agreed, no questions asked. He would have done anything to escape the terror on the streets.

The newcomer was generously supplied with food to restore the health of his emaciated body, along with warmth and affection to soothe his troubled mind. Josef had once traded his soul for security. Now Chaim was facing the same situation. The monk in training was eager to offer his support.

He knocked on the wooden door before pushing it open with his elbow. Chaim was sitting up in bed, staring at the ceiling.

"You are very pale," Josef whispered, excruciatingly aware that he was breaking the vow of silence imposed on him.

Chaim stared apathetically at the tray of food. Josef was disappointed at the boy's obvious lack of appreciation.

"Aren't you hungry?" he scolded in a whisper, glancing in the direction of the door to make sure no one was witnessing his transgression.

Chaim's head fell back against the wall and he closed his eyes tightly to hide the tears.

"Thomas?" Josef's whisper conveyed concern. "You have to eat. It won't help to starve yourself."

Chaim opened his eyes, blinked a few times, and regarded the novice. "You're Jewish, aren't you?" he asked hoarsely.

"I was Jewish once," Josef corrected the boy. "Now I am a Christian, just as you will be soon. We are brothers."

Chaim shook his head. "No, I can't," he whispered. "I'd rather be dead."

Josef frowned. "No, Thomas. You're wrong. There is no future for the Jews. The Nazis killed your family. Wouldn't your parents have wanted you to live? You have a chance for a good life. Don't throw it away."

"Do you believe the things they say?"

"Like what?"

"Like, that the Jews killed their messiah and that G-d rejects His Chosen People in favor of the Christians?"

Josef shrugged. "What difference does it make? Isn't it clear that G-d blesses the Christians and rewards them with wealth and bounty, while Jews are pursued and expelled from every place they come? Being part of the Chosen People seems to me to be a punishment, not an honor."

Chaim wrinkled his brow in thought. "Who said the purpose of life is to live comfortably and have lots of money?"

"*Ach*, the purpose of life? You are too young to be a philosopher. When you are my age, you will understand. Now is the time to listen to people who know more than you and who want the best for you."

"You mean I should accept conversion?"

"You will eventually. Why make enemies unnecessarily?"

"Did your family keep Shabbos?" Chaim asked, changing track.

The sudden glint of tears in Josef's eyes confirmed that Chaim's words had struck their mark. He began to hum a tune from the Shabbos *zemiros*.

"Stop it!" Josef quickly set down the tray and covered his ears. The light from the lantern on the wall made the wet streaks on his cheeks shine. "You are a wicked boy. I only wanted to help you, but you return evil for good. Do whatever you want! I don't care what happens to you."

Hastily he rubbed the sleeve of his cowl across his face to dry the tears as he retreated to the stairwell. Before descending, Josef hurled one last sentence at Chaim. "You will regret your stubbornness, I promise you!"

69

E MSBACH REPLACED RABBI STERN'S LETTER IN ITS ENVE-
lope. The pool of light from his lamp accentuated the room's
darkness. He rubbed his aching temples in an effort to alleviate
a persistent headache, caused no doubt by the tension that had
accompanied him for the last month.

It was very late, long after midnight. In the past, he would have
been in the midst of night shift at the hospital. He flexed his long,
tapering fingers, admitting to himself that he missed the opportunity to use his skills as a surgeon and to interact with a professional
team. Since his father left for New York, he was preoccupied with
bureaucratic details, getting his visa in order and legally changing his name from Karl Emsbach to Tanchum Stern, concluding
the adoption procedures that would make him the legal guardian
of Fraydl's small nephew, organizing Yanky's passport and travel
documents, translating his medical diplomas and licenses and
obtaining the necessary stamps to authenticate them.

He turned the letter over in his hand and ran his index finger
lightly over the return address. Why was it so hard for him to

imagine himself there? The detectives he'd engaged to find Chaim and Fraydl had filed their reports, concluding that the children were either no longer among the living or had left Germany. These were turbulent times; hundreds of thousands of refugees had passed through the DP camps on their way to new lives in other countries. At first he had expected the children to return to Ravensdorf or to contact him in some way, but the fact that their family's valuable silver Judaica was still in his possession convinced him that the two were truly gone. It was a miracle that Yanky had survived. The precious inheritance would be his when he was old enough to appreciate it.

Each week, Rabbi Stern sent a long letter detailing the family's life. Emsbach — still trying to think of himself as "Tanchum" — sensed the unwritten words between every line, begging him to leave Germany and be reunited with them at last. Weeks were passing, and he no longer had any credible excuse for staying here. The estate lawyers were unquestionably competent to sell the Emsbach assets without his constant supervision. It was time to go.

He made his way up the back stairs and stepped through the door of Yanky's bedroom. The boy was sleeping soundly, an angelic expression of innocence on his face. Emsbach tugged the quilt higher around the little shoulders, gently tucking it in as Rhea had once done for him. He stood beside the slumbering figure for a long time, musing that this child was the bridge between his past and his future. Rabbi Stern had reservations about his newfound son taking on the serious obligation of raising a Jewish child, but in his heart Emsbach knew that he needed Yanky even more than the orphaned boy needed him. Yanky was his anchor to himself, at a time when he was no longer sure of his own identity.

He left the room and passed through the dark hall to his own bedroom, wondering where the calm and certainty he'd once felt in this old house had disappeared to. He slept fitfully until the first pale light filtering through the curtains woke him, a little more than an hour before the servants were expected to arrive. He rose and washed his hands and face. The cold water was invigorating. Perhaps a brisk walk before the rest of the world was awake might help him unwind? He got dressed quickly and let himself out of the house.

It was still dark outside, and the cold wind stung his cheeks. Still, it felt good to walk down the driveway and hear the familiar crunch of gravel beneath his boots. A stealthy movement near a neighbor's gate arrested his attention. Who could it be at this hour except a thief? Emsbach stood silently in the shadows, focusing on the place where his eyes had sensed motion. Moments later, two men burst through the gate and raced along the alley directly toward him.

Impelled by instinct or training, within seconds he had tripped one and jumped on the other's back before either of the men knew what was happening. The first sprawled on the ground, obviously stunned, but the second fought fiercely. It took all of Tanchum's strength to restrain him until he'd locked the man's arms behind his back so he could get a clear look at the fellow's features in the gray dawn light.

A Jewish face full of hatred returned his look. "Let me go, Nazi!" he hissed. "Or we'll kill you, too!"

The man on the ground was scrabbling for something that had fallen when he did. Emsbach was outnumbered, but the men were gaunt and even together did not pose a serious threat to his strength. It was the Luger automatic pistol in the first man's hand that made him let go of the man's companion and raise his arms in surrender.

"You have to kill him. He's seen our faces," the second spoke in Yiddish.

"I know," the first answered, aiming point-blank at Emsbach's face.

"*Shema Yisrael*," the doctor whispered, the events of his life flashing before his eyes, "*Hashem Elokeinu, Hashem Echad!*"

"A *Yid?*" exclaimed the man with the pistol, his hands noticeably shaking.

"Shoot, Meir, shoot!" the second pleaded. "Don't waste time; we've got to get out of here."

"Shoot a *Yid?* Nachman, what if he's a Jew?" Meir replied with a note of hysteria in his voice.

"Give me the gun. I'll do it!"

"He said *Shema Yisrael*, didn't you hear?"

"It's just a Nazi trick. Look at him — he's a German!"

There was enough light by now to make out Emsbach's features, and his Aryan appearance did not correspond with the words his mouth had spoken.

Sudden shouts rose from one of the yards bordering the alley. As the two intruders glanced at each other in alarm, Emsbach grabbed the barrel of the pistol. He yanked it hard to release it from the first man's hand, but the gun discharged and the one called Nachman crumpled to the ground in slow motion, a surprised expression on his face. Nachman peered down at the blood seeping between his fingers where he clutched his side.

The shouts became louder and sounded closer. Someone was obviously searching for these two men in response to whatever crime they'd committed before Emsbach had come on the scene. The accidental gunshot would bring them here any minute.

"If you are a Jew, help us!" Meir pleaded. "My friend needs medical assistance and we are in mortal danger. Help me get him into one of these sheds to hide until we can escape!"

Emsbach hesitated. Aiding and abetting criminals would endanger his future, and he was too rational to ignore his responsibilities to Yanky and to his elderly parents in America. On the other hand, whatever they had done, these two young men were Jewish and one was seriously injured. Could he hand them over to the authorities and continue on with his life as if nothing had happened?

70

THE NEWS THAT FRAYDL'S CERTIFICATE TO ENTER PALESTINE had arrived sent a wave of excitement coursing through the *Kinderheim*. Well-meaning advice about what to do once she reached her new home was interspersed with hugs of joy at her good fortune, personal requests to contact members of her friends' extended families living in Eretz Yisrael and expressions of sorrow at the impending separation.

The intervening days flew by. And then, one morning, Fraydl found herself on the deck of an ocean liner approaching the bay of Haifa in a daze. *Am I really here?* she wondered, straining to see the outlines of land through the blur of her tears. It was impossible to believe that it was really happening. After all she'd been through, she was finally coming home to the land of her dreams.

Sailors threw down heavy ropes, which were quickly wrestled onto posts by husky stevedores. The ship shuddered and bounced off the wharf, rocked from side to side, and finally came to a stop. Fraydl joined the line of passengers maneuvering their possessions along the gangway down to the dock.

The scene on the dock was chaotic. Several times Fraydl lost her way amid the excited pushing and shoving, confused by all the noise. Small children shrieked in protest at finding themselves jostled away from their parents. Frantic voices sought misplaced luggage. From every side, waiting relatives shouted out the names of passengers, stretching their hands through the bars that separated the waiting area from the new arrivals.

Since the Nazi *Anschluss,* Fraydl had been petrified by military uniforms. Knowing Dr. Emsbach personally had not diminished her fear whenever he wore his uniform, and even after the war she'd avoided the gates where British soldiers were stationed in the DP camp. Now, as her eyes beheld armed British officers staring with hostile expressions at the Jewish immigrants streaming off the ship, she was nearly paralyzed with fear.

I could never have made illegal aliyah, she realized, forcing her trembling legs to continue moving forward, past the guards. Would the shadows of war darken her life forever? No, things were going to be different here! With each step her determination grew. *I will build a new life in spite of them!*

After a bored glance at the young woman's face, the clerk scanned her papers and stamped them. She lifted her cardboard suitcase and travel bag and walked through the open door. Outside, stately palm trees lined the boulevard. Colorful vendors hawked their wares from the nearby souk, adding their cries to the cacophony of vehicles on the busy noontime road in front of the building. What was she supposed to do now?

"Fraydl Mertzbach?"

She noticed a teenage boy in a dark suit and hat coming toward her. His still-childish face was framed by long curled *peyos* and a few wisps of beard were evident on his cheeks.

"I am Aharon Feigelbaum," he introduced himself. "I'm looking for my mother's sister, Fraydl Mertzbach."

"Yes, I am Fraydl Mertzbach," she replied, searching through her memory for a photograph to compare to this boy's face. Unfortunately, with everything that had happened in the interval, she could not even remember how her oldest sister looked.

He grinned. "I thought so. You look almost exactly like my sister Malky! Let me take your case?"

She surrendered her bags and followed him through the crowded street until they came to an Arab taxi stand. Fraydl listened in fascination as her Yiddish-speaking nephew began bargaining in Arabic, then took her place in the back of the vehicle while Aharon sat in front beside the driver. The interior of the ancient black Mercedes was hot and stuffy until the men opened their windows, and then a pleasant breeze swept across her flushed cheeks as the automobile gained speed.

Aharon carefully retrieved a bottle and glass tumbler from his briefcase. Turning to face his aunt, he said "Tante Fraydl, you must be thirsty," and offered the water to her. At the sound of his words her heart contracted. She was suddenly reminded of Yanky and Chaim'ke.

Accepting the proffered glass, Fraydl made a soft *Shehakol* and drank deeply from the cool liquid. She hadn't realized how dry her throat was until she swallowed the water. "Thank you," she said, overcome with emotion.

"You must be hungry, too. My mother will have a feast prepared by the time we get home," he reassured her. "Kfar Ata is about half an hour's drive, if everything goes smoothly."

She looked at him quizzically, but he only nodded meaningfully in the direction of the driver and shrugged without elaborating.

Fraydl sat back in her seat, gazing with little comprehension at the sparkling blue sea and the seemingly endless stretches of sand to the left. Closing her eyes, she was assaulted by memories of a far different place in another time. When the taxi halted she opened her eyes, confused about where she was.

"We're home, Tante Fraydl," Aharon said gently. "Look, my mother is coming out to meet us."

Fraydl turned her head and gasped. "Mamme!" she whispered as her oldest sister wrapped her arms around her and they both wept. It was several minutes before the two stepped back to get a look at each other. Fraydl noticed her two nieces for the first time.

"I'm Perel," the older one said shyly.

"I'm Malky," the other chimed in. Their hair was covered, indicating that both were already married.

"Let's go inside." Their younger brother raised his voice slightly. "It's hot out here."

Rivka Feigelbaum led Fraydl into the house, too choked with tears to speak. Sighing deeply, she stroked Fraydl's hand and gazed into her face, clearly unable to believe her eyes.

Fraydl stared at the festive table, set in her honor, with dismay. "I'm sorry," she said, "I can't eat anything right now. I need some time to get my bearings."

"That's perfectly all right." Rivka found her voice. "Would you like to see your room and rest for a while? Your bed is ready, and Aharon already put your bags there. Shall I help you unpack?"

Fraydl's eyes widened as she regarded her only living sibling. "You look so much like Mamme," she whispered, and the two of them embraced and wept again.

Fraydl's first few days with her sister in Kfar Ata passed in a blur. There were times when both began speaking at once, waves of memories carrying them into the past while simultaneously connecting them in the present. At other times, a wall of silence surrounded Fraydl. Words were simply inadequate to express the powerful emotions welling up from so deep inside. Rivka's married daughters returned for Shabbos, and gradually Fraydl began to integrate into the small family.

Fraydl was 17 years younger than her oldest sister. Rivka had married Avraham Abba Feigelbaum when Fraydl was still a baby, and shortly after the wedding the young couple had followed the Husyatiner Rebbe to Palestine. Returning to Austria two years later for her sister Malky's wedding, they brought their daughter Perel'e to meet her grandparents for the first time. It was the last direct contact Fraydl had with her until her sister's letter caught up with her at the *Kinderheim*.

The religious village of Kfar Ata had been founded two years before Fraydl's birth. The young Feigelbaum family joined the community shortly before the Arab riots of 1929 forced residents to abandon the village, and returned with them to rebuild after order was restored by the British one year later. In 1934, business-man Erich Moller established a textile factory that attracted new workers. Many were not Torah observant, and as the social fabric changed most of the religious families moved away. Avraham Abba and Rivka had made the decision to stay.

Aharon's bar mitzvah had coincided with Rivka's husband's first heart attack, when news reached them of the loss of almost his entire family in Europe during the war. Although he lived to see his two daughters marry, Avraham Abba never fully recovered. Shortly after their younger daughter's wedding, Rivka became a widow. Fifteen-year-old Aharon offered to leave yeshivah and work at the textile factory to support his mother, but she preferred to take in ironing and sewing and let him continue in the *beis medrash*. Fraydl was glad to lend a hand, and the two sisters lived in harmony until Rivka's maternal instincts rose to the fore.

"Fraydl, you are 22 years old," Rivka announced one cool morn-ing in Cheshvan. "It is time for you to get married and build your own home!"

71

SAFELY ENSCONCED IN EMSBACH'S ATTIC, NACHMAN AND Meir successfully evaded the intensive police search. Though the gunshot wound was superficial, the loss of blood would have been fatal had the doctor not come to the rescue. The best medicine of all was Masha Kellerman's nourishing meals. When Nachman was sufficiently recovered, both men accepted Emsbach's offer to take over as groundskeepers until their applications for immigration certificates to Palestine were accepted. Within a short time the lush lawn was mown, the trees pruned and the fences repaired.

"I'm going outside now," Yanky declared one June morning.

"What are you planning to do there?" Fully aware of his charge's inclination to mischief, Emsbach was understandably apprehensive.

"I need to help Nachman and Meir plant flower bulbs."

"How will you help them?" Masha asked, collecting the breakfast dishes from the table and carrying them to the sink.

"I like to dig holes. If I dig a very deep hole, will I reach America?"

"I don't think so," Emsbach smiled. He stretched his arms, thinking that some strenuous physical activity would be good for his own health as well. In a playful mood, he lifted the child onto his back and galloped out to the yard to the accompaniment of the little boy's shrieks.

"Yanky wants to help you today," he informed the bemused men leaning on their shovels. "I will be away until the afternoon, but you can call *Fraulein* Gutman at any time and she will take him back into the house."

"Where are you going?" Yanky asked petulantly. "I want to come with you."

Emsbach pinched his cheek. "Not this time. I have an important meeting."

His state of mind had improved immensely with the arrival of Masha and Raya. Now that the old house was once again filled with the scent of cleanliness and home-cooked food, his confidence was also returning. He wrote to his father in New York to tell him that he was delaying his trip until the manor was renovated. He had made the decision to transfer title to a Jewish organization providing convalescence homes for survivors of the concentration camps. The work would take several months, and he felt it was his responsibility to supervise the contractor and suppliers until the job was done.

With the pressure off to make a final decision, he'd considered his options and decided to apply for a temporary surgical position in a civilian hospital in the city. He arrived promptly for his appointment with the hospital administrator.

"May I help you?" inquired the middle-aged receptionist, frowning critically. *Everyone in postwar Germany seems disapproving these days*, he thought. Actually, he might not have even noticed it in the past. Now he often found himself wondering if people could tell that he was Jewish.

"I am here about the position of surgeon."

The woman sat up straighter when she heard his authoritative German voice, and her smile showed him that he'd found favor in her eyes. "Do we have your curricula vitae?" she asked, shuffling the files on her desk.

"Yes, it was sent a few days ago. I am expected for an appointment with the director at 11 o'clock."

"Herr Doktor Stern?" She looked him over again, as if it was difficult to match the name with the person before her.

"*Ja.*" His new name still sounded strange to his ears.

"That will be fine then. Dr. Schiller already has your file. You may go in. He is expecting you."

He felt her eyes on his back as he knocked lightly on the dark mahogany door leading to the inner office. To his surprise, he recognized the man sitting at the desk as a former crony from medical school. Emsbach and Schiller had occasionally partnered as interns, but they'd lost touch after being assigned to separate posts during their military service. Not having expected to meet anyone he knew at this hospital, he was taken aback.

Max Schiller looked up from the file he was perusing and smiled in recognition. "Emsbach! Is it really you? What a welcome surprise. It's good to see you. What brings you here today?"

"I am applying for the position of surgeon on your staff."

"*Wunderbar*! This is excellent news!"

The two spoke for awhile of past experiences in medical school and touched on their military postings during the war.

"I was sorry to hear about your uncle. He was a great soldier and a gentleman." Max offered his condolences for the death of Heinrich Mauer to his supposed nephew.

Emsbach nodded noncommittally. They talked of their classmates who had been killed in the war, and discussed which others were either specializing or going into private practice. Referring to the difficult postwar economics that German was undergoing, Schiller boasted, "You know, for all the drawbacks, there are unsurpassed opportunities as well. Young people with ambition can make unparalleled progress in their careers. Before the war it would have taken years to advance to a directorship, but due to my management positions in the army, I am now the director of a major hospital at the age of 32!"

Obviously proud of his achievement, the director urged his old colleague to fill out an employment application and leave it with his secretary.

"I've already done so," Emsbach explained.

Schiller looked perplexed. He picked up the telephone on his desk and buzzed the secretary. "Bring in Dr. Emsbach's file now, *bitte*," he ordered.

The receptionist informed him that there was no such application.

Max frowned with irritation. "Karl, I must apologize. My secretary is usually impeccably efficient, but it appears that there is a mix-up and she cannot locate your forms. Would you mind filling it out again, just as a formality?"

Emsbach felt blood rush to his face. Taking a deep breath, he explained, "There is no misunderstanding. The application was filled out under a different name than you remember." He hesitated, unsure how to clarify that he was now legally Tanchum Stern, when Max Schiller knew him as Karl Emsbach.

Schiller looked at him with a puzzled expression. "A different name?"

"Tanchum Stern. My name is Stern now. It involves a personal, somewhat complicated series of events."

Max's face lit up and he looked at his old friend with unconcealed admiration. "Emsbach, you were always brilliant! I understand completely. It's a masterly move! You don't have to say another word. I am astute enough to read between the lines. Unfortunately, many of our war heroes have been forced by the difficult postwar circumstances to take an alias, but to choose a Jewish name — what a superb idea! Who would think to investigate a Jew's wartime activities? Our enemies may search the world for those who escaped the Fatherland, but they'll never dream that you had the courage to stay in Germany and even work right here in a prestigious, high-profile German hospital. Magnificent!

"Of course the position is yours," he continued, "I was reviewing the application of Tanchum Stern when you came in and was already favorably impressed. The references are excellent and your surgical skills are recommended by colleagues I respect. Karl, I am looking forward to working with you."

Max winked conspiratorially. "You can count on me, my friend. I won't breathe a word. Some day, when the political climate is less dangerous, I will relish hearing of your exploits. For now, let us go down to the operating theaters so I can introduce you to your new colleagues. "

72

BOTH BOYS WERE PANTING BY THE TIME THEY REACHED THE top of the belfry tower. After Chaim stumbled up the last of the 139 stairs, he threw himself onto the floor, gasping for breath. His chest heaved painfully and he gasped for breath, as did Brother Josef, who slumped against the stone wall, resting his hands on his thighs and letting his head fall forward in exhaustion.

"This—was—a—crazy—idea," he choked out breathlessly.

"But we did it!" Chaim wheezed.

Minutes later, when they could breathe normally, the two were finally able to speak.

"All right. Now that we're up here, what's this all about?"

Chaim rolled over and sat up to face his new friend. "This is the only place where we don't have to be afraid someone will hear us talking. We have to break out of this place!"

"We've already had this discussion, Thomas. I have a good life here. Why should I forfeit a safe life as a Christian for the danger of being a Jew? Anyway, where would I go? Is that why you nearly killed me dragging me up all those steps?"

"You said that if I agreed to convert, we would be brothers, right?"

Josef nodded earnestly.

"But later, I thought, *'We're already brothers! Aren't we both the children of Avraham, Yitzchak and Yaakov?'*"

"You are hopeless, Thomas."

"My name is Chaim, and you know it. What is your real name? It's not Josef."

"Yes it is."

"No, Josef is a Christian name. What did you mother call you?"

"Yosse'le," he said quietly, his eyes momentarily soft with memory. "She called me Yosse'le."

"So your name is Yosef, not Josef."

"Semantics. What difference does it make?" His irritation returned and he glared at the younger boy defensively.

Chaim rubbed his jaw against the back of his hand. He stared up at the huge bell hanging over their heads and thought of Har Sinai hovering over the *Yidden* in the Wilderness. "Hitler killed so many of us," he said. "He wanted to destroy the bodies of our people, just like Haman tried to do. But the people in this monastery want to destroy our souls, and rob us of our heritage."

"They believe that they are saving us from everlasting purgatory," Josef interrupted, and then paused when he caught himself giggling at the words he had memorized from the catechism. "From my point of view, they saved my life. If the priests hadn't taken me in, the Nazis would have murdered me."

"How can you be so sure that your parents are dead? Maybe one of them, your father or your mother, or an aunt or uncle or cousin, survived the war and is looking for you right now?"

"No one in Germany could have survived."

"I did, and so did my little brother and my aunt. There have to be others who were hiding the way we did."

Josef's face drained of color. Slowly he slid down to the floor to sit beside Chaim, who could sense that the other boy was wavering.

"If your mother could see her Yosse'le now, what would she say?" he demanded. "What would she say? How would she feel?"

Josef shook his head, trying to escape the thoughts that this strange boy was planting in his mind. "No one escaped," he whispered. "I was under the bed hiding and I saw the soldiers take them away."

"They could be alive. They could be!"

"No-o-o-o!"Josef's body shook and torrents of tears poured down his pale face.

"Well, you'll never know." Chaim threatened. "If you stay here in the monastery, you will never find out. Perhaps one day you'll be a monk, and they will give you a pulpit and they will tell you to incite the people against the Jews. Maybe you'll do it, and there will be a pogrom. What if the mob attacks any Jew they find — and it turns out to be your own father?"

"Stop it, Chaim! I won't listen to you anymore!" Josef covered his ears with his hands, drew his knees up to his chin and hid his face between them in the skirt of his cassock. The two sat without speaking until the novice calmed down. Finally, Josef said almost inaudibly, "If I help you escape, will you try to look for my parents?"

"Why can't we both run away together?" Chaim asked, resting his hand on Josef's arm. "Two heads are better than one. We'll help each other."

"There's not enough time to come up with a plan."

"What do you mean?"

"The archbishop is expected tomorrow at noon." The thought made him straighten up in alarm.

"Well?"

Josef wrung his hands helplessly. "The plan is for him to baptize all the new boys."

"Did they all consent?"

"You're the only one holding out, Thomas — er, Chaim."

"We have to talk to them. Last night, that little one with the curly hair confided in me that his real name is Simcha Bunim, and the boys they call Mark and Luke understood when I spoke to them in Yiddish, even though they answered in German."

"You're right about Wilhelm. Father Arthur told me that his family paid money to leave him here when he was 3 years old. The monastery promised to return him after the war, but no one ever came to ask about him. He's 10 now, Thomas. He doesn't remember anything except his name. The priests are the only family he knows.

"The other two could have learned Yiddish from Jewish neighbors. I don't think there are any other Jews among the orphans." Josef's confidence returned. "Accept reality, Thomas. You are hardly more than a child yourself. There are things that you don't understand."

"Don't you realize that I am 12 years old already?" Chaim asked. "Shall I spend my bar mitzvah in a monastery, chanting Latin vespers?"

Josef gave him a sharp look. "When there is no other choice, you do what you have to do." He scrambled to his feet. "We need to go down before someone notices that we're gone."

As the boys left the belfry, they had no idea that they were not alone. Two priests stood deep in conversation in the vestibule at the bottom of the steep steps.

"Stubborn, stiff-necked Jew," Father Arthur growled, referring to Chaim. "That boy even has the impudence to argue about our most holy beliefs."

Father Simon rubbed his palms together nervously. "What will happen when the archbishop arrives tomorrow?" he asked, clearly discouraged.

"You'd better hope that everything goes smoothly. I caught Thomas whispering with the other orphans last night. I warned you that we had to keep them apart!"

"Heaven knows I tried to keep them separate."

"Then how do you explain that I found them together repeatedly?"

"It's the work of the Satan himself!" Father Simon declared defensively.

"Well, I assure you that the archbishop will not be amused by your incompetence." Father Arthur sniffed and looked around to be sure no one was listening. "You know that we must have everything arranged by morning or we can kiss our hopes for advancement good-bye. We'll be stuck in this hole until the pope dies."

"I suppose we have no choice now but to consider applying more pressure," Father Simon admitted reluctantly.

"We should have done that from the beginning!" Father Arthur seemed unreasonably pleased at the prospect.

"He appears to be such a gentle child." Father Simon shook his head. "How could I know that such a sweet face hides a will of iron?"

"I recommend that we give him a history lesson."

"History lesson?"

"In the time of the Inquisition, they knew how to deal with Jews." Father Arthur rubbed his hands together.

"He's a clever boy," Father Simon protested. "One hopes it will be sufficient to merely hint, and let Thomas get the idea without our having to actually resort to physical persuasion."

"We can try. But if he proves thick headed, I am prepared to sharpen his mind with a more classical approach."

"Then the boy will have only himself to blame for the consequences of his stubborn nature," Father Simon agreed sadly.

73

THE STREAM OF BANALITIES CONTINUED AS MAX SCHILLER escorted his new surgeon out of the office and down the hall. The lift was manned by a Bavarian with an imposing handlebar mustache and shiny brass buttons bulging over a massive beer belly. Emsbach was disturbed by the disapproving look he received just before the operator pulled the brass elevator doors shut with a jarring clang. *It's only my imagination,* he reproved himself. His newly discovered Jewish identity was making him overly sensitive to nuances he had never noticed before.

The lift operator yanked the pulley to send the lift four floors down to the operating theater, jerking his passengers with each heave. Max frowned at the Bavarian. "It is nearly impossible to find skilled employees these days," he complained sotto voce. "Your coming on board is a great stroke of luck for the hospital."

The elevator descended slowly and noisily down the shaft. Emsbach felt disconnected and bewildered. Max Schiller had concluded that he was a war criminal in hiding. Could he live with that? On the other hand, what were the possible repercussions if he explained the true story behind his change of name?

In the end, he decided to allow fate to make the decision for him.

The antiseptic smell of the operating theaters was invigorating. He'd been away from surgery for several months; now he felt like a fish returning to water.

The director introduced him to the staff. "Dr. Stern will be joining our surgical team," he announced. "He is an old friend of mine, and I know that when you get to know him, you will agree with me that he is a valuable addition to our hospital."

Emsbach accepted the greetings of the doctors, interns and nursing staff. "It is my hope that we will all work well together," he said politely.

Max excused himself. "I wish I could stay longer, but as you know I have a full agenda upstairs. *Auf Wiedersehen!*"

The medical team took a break for coffee and some slightly stale sweet rolls while they worked out a schedule for the coming week. It was mutually agreeable that their new surgeon would assume his duties the following day.

Afterward, department head Professor Dr. Ernst Wagner accompanied Emsbach up to the surgical ward. "I understand you were a military surgeon during the war," he said. "You may find our timetable tedious."

"I have experienced enough trauma," he replied with conviction. "I am looking forward to a less intense schedule."

Wagner nodded. "This is the general surgery ward," he said, holding the door open with one hand and gesturing with the other. There were about 10 beds on each side of the room, all of them occupied. Nurses in starched white uniforms moved quickly among the patients, administering medications and adjusting intravenous bottles. "There are a number of private rooms on the other side of the nursing station for V.I.P.s, or for use as isolation units. Patients after Caesarean sections are housed on the obstetrics ward."

"Sister Lotte," Professor Wagner summoned one of the women in white. "This is the new surgeon, Dr. Stern."

"What are your personal preferences, doctor?" she asked.

"I consider strict preoperative and postoperative care as important as skilled surgery," he replied, slipping easily back into his former role as an empathetic but professional surgeon. "It is my custom to verify that my patients are educated in advance regarding medical procedures, and I wish to be informed of even the slightest suspicion of complications. I have learned to respect the intuition of an experienced nurse above the vital signs recorded on patient charts."

With a nod of approval, Sister Lotte returned to her duties. As Professor Wagner accompanied Emsbach down to the main floor, they discussed various technical arrangements and then parted with a handshake. "I wish to convey my condolences on the loss of your esteemed uncle," Dr. Wagner concluded their conversation. "He was irreplaceable."

"*Danke schön.*"Presumably, Max had filled Wagner in on his former identity.

"We'll see you tomorrow, then."

'Yes, sir."

Emsbach returned home in an ambivalent mood. Had he made the right decision? His innate honesty did not allow him to avoid the truth. His decision to lose himself in his chosen profession was just a tactic, something that would allow him to repress the vacillation that had turned his life inside out. If only there was someone with whom he could discuss it!

Haunting memories of Fraydl teased his mind. What would his life look like now if the young woman had accepted his proposal of marriage? He was sure that they could have built a new life somewhere, raised her nephews and begun their own family. Would he ever meet another person like her, someone to whom he could bare his deepest thoughts? He had felt so connected to the children, and especially to their young aunt. *I never met anyone like her*, he sighed, wishing he could turn back the clock and prevent her from leaving.

"*Herr Doktor!*"

Yanky's voice brought him back to the present. "Yanky?*Ja*, I have returned. What did you do while I was away?"

"I helped Meir and Nachman in the garden," he said, proudly displaying his muddy hands, shirt and trousers as the two young groundsmen watched the interaction between their employer and the child.

"*Sehr gut*. Now go inside and ask *Fraulein* Gutman to wash you and change your clothes."

"I'm big enough to do it by myself," Yanky announced and marched into the house.

"Thank you for your patience.," The doctor turned to Meir and Nachman. "It's not officially part of your contract, but the child has no friends his own age here."

"We don't mind," Meir spoke for them both. "It's been years since we've seen a living Jewish child."

Nachman looked after the boy's retreating figure. "It revives us to see him," he said quietly.

Meir cleared his throat. "Doktor Stern, may I ask you a personal question?

"I don't promise to answer, but I will not be offended if you ask."

"Is Yanky your relative?"

Emsabach felt a shadow pass over him. "His family was killed in the war." After a pause he asked his own question, "Are you brothers?"

"Our fathers were brothers."

For some reason, Emsbach was loath to end the conversation. He remained standing in place, staring at the fresh rows of dirt in the garden. "Perhaps sometime I will tell you Yanky's story." Immediately regretting the implied familiarity in his words, he began detailing the work he wanted done to refurbish the stables.

The men exchanged glances. After the doctor had finished giving his instructions, he left them in the garden.

"Who is that man, really? What is his connection to the little boy?"

"He told us that he's Jewish."

"Do you believe him?"

Meir shrugged.

"I don't. He's a Nazi. It's obvious. He's using the child to hide his past!"

"He cares about Yanky. And the child loves him, too."

Nachman bent to gather up their tools. "That's the only thing that doesn't make sense."

74

I T WAS HARD TO KNOW WHO WAS MORE STARTLED, THE BOYS clattering down the stairs or the monks at the bottom of the staircase.

"Brother Josef!"

"Yes, Father Simon?" Josef felt his knees turn to jelly.

"Whatever were you doing up in the belfry?"

"I saw this young boy sneak into the tower and I followed to see what he was doing, Father."

"And what *was* he doing?" Suspicion laced Father Simon's voice.

"I wanted to look out the window up there," Chaim interrupted, drawing the men's attention from his trembling companion.

Josef's eyes darted from side to side, searching for an escape from the compromising situation.

"And what did you see?" Father Arthur fell for the ploy.

"Just the view. The countryside."

"You were instructed to stay in your room. Have you memorized the catechism?"

Chaim took a deep breath and answered defiantly, "No. And you can't make me!"

Father Arthur smiled. Turning to his comrade he asked, "Then we agree, Father Simon? I do not believe there is any justification for wasting more of our precious time over this issue."

Father Simon sighed. He put his hand on Chaim's shoulder, saying, "I'm so sorry, Thomas. I never wanted it to come to this. It's a great pity that you are such a stubborn child."

Josef inhaled sharply. Waves of alarm rippled over him, even though he did not understand the meaning behind Father Simon's words or Father Arthur's unkind smile.

"You may go, Josef," Father Simon said without looking at him directly. "If we need clarification, we will speak with you later. I believe the boys are awaiting you for vespers."

"Yes, Father Simon," Josef was quick to reply. Gathering his courage, he added, "Come, Thomas. It is time for evening prayers."

"Thomas will not be joining you this time. You are dismissed, Josef."

Head bent in submission and legs heavier than lead, Josef crossed the threshold and followed the stone-paved path leading to the chapel. Though he had no idea what was going to happen, an evil foreboding chilled his blood. As soon as he was out of their sight, Josef prayed for the innocent boy whose words had ignited dormant feelings buried deep within his heart.

The two priests gazed down at the fragile child who was causing them so much aggravation.

"Thomas, you have been informed that the archbishop is coming to our small parish tomorrow?" Father Arthur asked.

Chaim nodded, uncertain what the men expected from him.

"It is a great privilege for the boys that his honor, Archbishop Thiessen, will officiate at their baptism and first Communion."

Chaim waited as Father Simon picked up the thread.

"Of course, you will be one of the boys in the ceremony."

Chaim shook his head from side to side.

"A pity," Father Arthur said, but his voice was cold and hard.

"A pity," Father Simon repeated, clucking his tongue.

"Thomas, no choice is involved. You will be baptized tomorrow, and you will partake of the Communion. Your life was saved by the

Mother Church, and we would be derelict in our duty if we did not save your soul as well."

"I am a Jew." Chaim heard a pounding in his ears. The only thing he could remember was that he had promised Tante Fraydl never to forget that he was a Jew.

Without further speech, the priests each took one of his arms and began to walk. Chaim wanted to resist, but he seemed to have no power in his limbs. Step-by-step they advanced, practically carrying the terrified boy around the back of the monastery's main building and over to a side door. Simon took a large and ancient key from the folds of his robe and inserted it into the lock. He turned it with difficulty until the click of the cylinder told him it was unlocked.

"Let me help you." Father Arthur released his hold on Chaim and grasped a metal ring in the center of the wooden door. He pulled with all his might, beads of sweat standing out on his brow. Suddenly the door gave way, and an unpleasant, musty smell momentarily choked Chaim. He would have run away, but Father Simon was gripping him too tightly.

"It's not too late to change your mind." Father Simon bent down to look in the boy's face, but Chaim turned away and closed his eyes.

"Light the torch!" Father Arthur's voice echoed loudly in the dark chamber. He took the burning torch in his left hand and signaled Father Arthur to close and lock the door. The soft sound of small scurrying feet in the background halted when the great door was secured.

The stairs wound around deeper and deeper. Chaim whispered *Shema Yisrael*. It seemed like hours before the priests stopped, steadying him on a landing.

"It's not too late. . ."

In the flickering torchlight, shadows twisted Father Simon's features until Chaim no longer recognized them. Their footsteps had been muffled, but Father Arthur's harsh voice cut clearly through the heavy silence.

"Do you agree to accept the holy covenant, Thomas?"

Chaim's lungs struggled to breathe the putrid air. The priests' words whirled around him like bats. Instinctively he began to run, but he stumbled and would have fallen if their strong arms had not caught him. The eyes of Father Simon and Father Arthur met above his head before they resumed the downward spiral.

"Let me go!" Chaim screamed. "Let me go!"

"Are you willing to accept Christianity?" Simon asked, halting their descent to wait for an answer.

"Let me go!"

"Not until you answer my question."

"Let me *go*!"

The priests continued down the stairs, ignoring Chaim's pleas. Suddenly they were at the bottom. A long hall stretched into the darkness ahead of them. Chaim resisted, thrashing about in panic as they pulled him relentlessly along the hall. Father Simon fitted the torch into a holder on the wall and slowly took out his ring of keys.

"Let me go," Chaim sobbed.

"Give me the answer I am waiting to hear, Thomas. Then you will be free."

The boy covered his face with his hands. "I cannot, I cannot," he repeated monotonously.

"You must," was Father Simon's terse reply. He unlocked a door and began to shove Chaim into the cell.

"No! Please, no!"

Father Simon pushed the door closed. The two priests began to walk away.

"Come back! I'll do anything! Don't leave me here! Come back. . ."

R IVKA FEIGELBAUM FLICKED OFF THE KITCHEN LIGHT. "Can you come to my room for a few minutes?" she asked her sister. "I want to discuss something with you."

Fraydl's left her seat reluctantly. She had a feeling that Rivka was going to give her another lecture about the importance of getting married — as if she didn't know already.

"Ima, why hasn't Areleh come home yet?" As the two women passed through the living room, Fraydl noticed her niece at the window studying the darkness outside. A year younger than she was, Perel and her husband were staying with them while Perel recuperated after childbirth.

Rikva glanced at the clock on the wall. "He'll be here any minute," she reassured her.

"Aren't you worried?"

"Why should I worry?"

"There are so many disturbances in the Arab villages since the U.N. passed the Partition Plan."

Rivka sighed. "We have to trust Hashem. If I let myself start worrying about everything that could happen, I won't be able to function at all."

"Mrs. Berkowitz said there was an attack on the port in Haifa."

"I heard."

"When the Hagganah tried to retaliate, they were stopped by the authorities."

"Yes, I know. Areleh keeps me up to date. The British offer us no protection from Arab attacks, but they are scrupulous about preventing reprisals."

"Ima…" Perel turned. "I've been here since Yom Tov. I think it's time to go back to Bnei Brak."

"How can you suggest such a thing? You know that it's unsafe to travel on the roads."

Without waiting for an answer, Rivka turned away and motioned for Fraydl to follow her into the bedroom. With the door closed behind them, she showed her sister a letter that had been delivered earlier. "It took a few weeks to get here, but the suggestion looks good," she said. "His name is Yehuda Spitz. Tatte knew his father from the court of the Alexander Rebbe in Vienna, and I learned with his mother in school. He's the oldest of eight children. They live in Jerusalem. All things considered, it seems suitable. What do you think?"

"I suppose it's worth investigating," Fraydl responded in a neutral tone.

Rivka threw up her hands. "I wish there were a way to do that," she complained. After a moment's thought, she added, "We'll just have to put it off until the security situation improves. There really is no choice."

Perel knocked lightly on the open door before entering. "I'm sorry, Mommy, but it's getting late. Areleh is still not back."

Fraydl was relieved at the interruption. Rivka stood up and peered into the darkness from her window. "He should be home by now," she said fretfully.

"Did he say anything this morning about expecting to be late?"

Rivka chewed her lip. "He's probably so immersed in learning that he forgot the time." Her voice sounded unusually shrill.

Rivka's son-in-law appeared in the doorway behind his wife. "I'll go to the yeshivah and remind him of the time," he offered.

"That would take a load off my mind," Rivka thanked him. After a brief pause for reflection, she returned to the subject she'd been discussing with Fraydl previously. "Your sister lives in Yerushalayim," she mused aloud to Perel. "It is possible that Malky's husband is acquainted with the Spitz family. I wonder if he could investigate a suggestion for Fraydl?"

"What's the point in proceeding with a *shidduch* right now, Ima? It's such a dangerous time."

"Life goes on, *sheifeleh*. People get married even in wartime."

Lines of worry creased Fraydl's forehead. She was not sure if she had recovered from the last war, and now she was about to experience another. "Do you think there will be fighting near Kfar Ata?" she asked anxiously.

Rivka shook her head. "Only Hashem knows. When Perel'e was a baby, we had to abandon Kfar Ata during the Arab riots, but we came back the the next year and rebuilt. We were a small village then, but since the textile factory was established many more people have come to live here. That makes it a less likely target for the Arabs."

The door opened, and Shmuel returned alone.

"Where's my brother?" Perel held her sleeping baby tightly in her arms. She hated talk about war.

"He wasn't in the yeshivah," her husband said, avoiding eye contact with his mother-in-law.

"What do you mean, 'He wasn't in the yeshivah'?" Rivka fought a dark sensation of dread that spread through her body like spilled ink. "Where else would he be at this hour? The boy's only 15! He must be learning in a corner and you missed seeing him."

Shmuel shifted his weight from one foot to the other. "I spoke to Rav Binyamin."

"Does the Rosh Yeshivah know where he is?"

"He said he didn't see Areleh in yeshivah today. Not since Shacharis."

"That's impossible! Areleh left the house right after breakfast." Rivka sank into a chair, clasping her hands together to still their shaking. "Of course he was in yeshivah," she insisted. "There's no other explanation."

"I asked some of the other *bachurim*." Shmuel squeezed out the words as if it was painful to utter them.

"Speak up, Shmuel!" his *shvigger* commanded sharply. "Did anyone know where Aharon is?"

"They said. . ." he paused, swallowed, and then continued so quickly that the words merged. "They saw him leave right after Shacharis. With Tzvi Drori."

"Tzvi Drori?" she echoed without comprehension.

"He is the commander of the Hagganah in this region."

Rivka stood up so quickly that her chair turned over, falling back with a crash that woke the sleeping baby. "What does the Hagganah have to do with my son? Areleh is just a child. What connection could he possibly have with a military commander?"

Her questions received no reply, because the answers were obvious. Everyone knew families whose sons had joined the clandestine self-defense organizations of the Hagganah, Etzel and Lechi. They were responding to the blatant British discrimination in favor of the Arab side of the conflict. Many young men were unable to simply stand by and watch. But Areleh? A *frum* boy, only 15 years old?

"They are desperate for soldiers," Shmuel told the women. "I'm sure they won't actually send him out to fight. They'll put him to work peeling potatoes or packing supplies."

"He's just a child." The sorrow in her Rivka's voice brought tears to Fraydl's eyes. Chaim and Yanky were gone. Now Areleh was also in danger.

"You know what Mamme would say." Fraydl touched her sister's arm lightly, before reaching for the worn *Tehillim*.

In the other room, Perel's baby wailed impatiently. "It's time to feed Yosef Chaim," Rivka told her daughter absently, pulling the fallen chair upright. She sat down again and opened her *Tehillim*. "After he eats, you should try to get some sleep, Perel. You are exhausted. Shmuel, please go back to the yeshivah and try to get more information. We need to find Areleh, or at least know where they've taken him. Meanwhile, Fraydl and I will *daven*."

76

ARCHBISHOP THIESSEN ALIGHTED FROM HIS CARRIAGE and surveyed the monastery. A line of dignitaries stretched from the main gate all the way to the front door, and a crowd of common citizens stood reverently behind them. As the archbishop neared the men, they removed their hats in respect, murmuring "Reverend Bishop" while genuflecting piously.

"Your Excellency," the vicar greeted the archbishop, bowing deeply and kissing the man's signet ring.

Monsignor Thiessen graced the assembly of monks and priests with a piercing gaze, responding to their words of welcome with a nod here and a word there. Before disappearing into the dark interior of the monastery, he paused. Addressing the head priest, the archbishop murmured something that the others could not hear.

"Over there, Your Grace," the vicar responded, gesturing toward a group of boys gathered at the edge of the line, closely supervised by the older acolytes.

The archbishop nodded. His severe expression softened as he studied each child for a moment. The younger boys beamed with excitement, but two of the oldest kept their faces down. The monsignor's gaze lingered on them before turning to his host.

"I wish to speak with the religious instructors before the ceremony commences."

"Of course, Your Excellency," the vicar replied. "Please come this way."

The entourage progressed to a large dining room, where a festive meal was set out in anticipation of the honored guest.

"Why do you think he wants to speak to us before the baptism?" Father Simon whispered to Father Arthur.

Father Arthur's dish overflowed with delicacies and his mouth was full. He tore off a chunk of white bread and sopped the gravy from his bowl before answering. "Just something formal," he surmised. "Nothing to worry about. Fill your plate, Father Simon. There are not many opportunities to eat well in this country parish."

After grace was said, the two young priests joined the other teachers in the conference chamber for their audience with the archbishop.

Monsignor Thiessen blessed the assembled men in Latin and then addressed the subject of the future of the Church nationally and internationally after the horrific world war. Several priests were singled out by name and praised for their exemplary sacrifices.

"I had no idea the archbishop was aware of so many details," Father Simon murmured to Father Arthur.

Following the benediction, individual priests came forward to kneel before their holy visitor and offer confession. This was their opportunity to speak of whatever was in their hearts, and to make an impression on the archbishop. Father Simon held back in order to be one of the last. After confessing his sins, he raised his eyes to the fatherly face and asked, "Your Grace, is it true that the Church has assumed final responsibility for all the war orphans?"

"Why do you ask this, my son?"

"I have heard that the Vatican envoy in France is circulating a document directing monasteries and convents not to return Jewish children to their relatives."

Monsignor Thiessen's eyes narrowed and his expression hardened. He requested the vicar to send everyone out of the room so that he could speak privately with Father Simon.

When they were alone, the archbisop interrogated the young priest. "Do you know of any Jewish children among the orphans here?"

Fearing to speak frankly, Simon admitted, "I think it is possible."

"How would you know?"

"It's just a feeling." The young priest's palms were wet with perspiration. He regretted his desire to clear his conscience by asking for the archbishop's endorsement.

"Based on what?" Monsignor Thiessen did not relent.

"Certain boys stand out from the others; they are different in a way. It's hard to explain."

"For example?"

Father Simon swallowed. His Adam's apple bobbed nervously. "They are too obedient," he answered finally, feeling ridiculous. "They are too intelligent, and too polite. They are unfamiliar with the prayers but chant them too loudly. They either kneel at the wrong times or do it too often."

"Do you know where all the children come from?"

"No. There are orphans without families among them, but I assume that most were abandoned by their parents because of mixed or doubtful parentage, or. . ."

"Or?"

"Jewish parents sometimes approached to ask us to provide shelter during the war. When the smaller convents in the city were dispersed during the worst bombings, the older boys were brought here. We have no way of knowing the origins of those children. "

"Did they all have baptismal certificates?"

"Almost all of them had some documentation. The boys scheduled for baptism today are the only ones who did not. Of course, we are honored that they will take their first Communion with the archbishop."

Monsignor Thiessen ignored the flattery. "Have families tried to contact the abandoned children?"

"It's been a year since the end of the war. Father Julius is of the opinion that we may assume there are no surviving relatives."

"I see." Monsignor Thiessen clasped his hands behind his back and raised his face to a nearby window. Father Simon ran the tip of his tongue over his lips nervously, hoping he had not damaged his chances for a transfer to a more prestigious post.

After some introspection, the archbishop spoke quietly. "Although the Fatherland is a Lutheran stronghold, German priests and nuns have always filled important social functions in the areas of education and welfare. During the war we fared better than the monasteries in Poland, which were known as bastions of Polish nationalism. Even so, we were always under suspicion by the Gestapo.

"I, personally, was approached by Jews seeking asylum. During the Nazi period, the Church hierarchy was severely put to the test. Regarding the rescue of Jewish children, each monastic order had to discharge its mission according to the decision of its own leader. There were so many orphans and refugees, and our capacity was limited. I was authorized by the government to allocate funds from the Central Welfare Board, but the support was never enough. Convents were full to capacity and there was barely enough money for food, let alone funds to buy medicine or soap." The archbishop was silent, reliving his memories.

"Admitting Jewish children was never a policy," he continued. "Doing so posed a mortal danger to all the priests and nuns involved. The Gestapo did not hesitate to break into convents or monasteries, and children suspected of being Jewish were taken away. Nazi sympathizers did not hesitate to inform the authorities, and a nun's habit or priest's robe were no protection from the Gestapo."

He peered at the priest. "You are young, Father Simon. Where did you begin your career?"

Father Simon started. He, too, had been reminiscing while the archbishop spoke.

"I was in Berlin," he stammered. "Near my family."

"What was the policy in the monastery there?"

"To the best of my knowledge, no Jewish children were sheltered in our institution."

Monsignor Thiessen nodded. "Do you like it here? It's not too rural for you after Berlin?"

Father Simon perked up. "If the archbishop is asking my opinion, it has been difficult for me to adjust in this place. I would prefer a more urban setting, if that would be possible."

"The point of taking vows is to submit your personal feelings to the absolute authority of the Church, Brother Simon."

"Of course, Your Excellency!" he answered quickly, struggling to hide his disappointment.

"There is a little time remaining before the baptismal ceremony is scheduled. How old are the children taking their first Communion?"

"They range in age from 8 to 12, Your Excellency."

"You may go now, Father Simon. Send the oldest boy into me. I would like to speak a few words with him before the ceremony begins."

"Yes, Your Grace. I will summon Thomas immediately."

77

TANCHUM'S PROCRASTINATION DID NOT BRING HIM THE peace of mind he craved. In fact, he found it excruciating to work with people who assumed that the name "Stern" was a camouflage for past war crimes. Anti-Semitic comments were the rule in his presence, and his continued reticence only seemed to increase his notoriety.

"Come, Stern, join us for a drink!" fellow surgeon Erwin Austerlitz called jovially, giving an exaggerated wink as he pronounced the name "Stern." "We're meeting in *Das Bierhaus* at 5."

"Sorry, can't make it. I have a previous engagement."

His consistent refusals caused a few raised eyebrows and quizzical expressions, but his colleagues' enthusiasm for his company did not diminish.

"Private business," he said as he repeatedly put them off.

"*Jawohl*, we understand!"

Tanchum felt rather than saw their leering expressions as he left the hospital. Notwithstanding his professional behavior, the surgical staff continued to be convinced that Stern was leading a parallel secret life. Even though he declined to satisfy their curiosity, his colleagues managed to supply the lurid details from their own imaginations.

Renovations at the manor were finally completed. On the day that the initial group of survivors moved in, the first winter snow dusted the lawn. Tanchum returned from work to find a short letter from his father.

"Come home, son. Delay no longer. Your mother is progressively weaker and her dearest wish is to see you before it is too late."

Shakily, Tanchum sat down at the desk in his study. Guilt consumed him. He shook his head. What was the matter with him? This endless inner struggle had sapped his strength, turning him into a person he didn't recognize. It was time to face the past and plan a better future. The decision brought him relief, as if a great weight had rolled off his shoulders. Before his identity was challenged, Karl Emsbach had always been a man of action. It was time to make his choice — and to act on it.

"Raya, please call Meir to my office," the doctor requested of the housekeeper.

She stepped into the yard and looked around until she saw the men on the roof of the shed, replacing worn shingles. She shivered in the biting wind. "Meir, Dr. Stern wants a word with you."

"Should I wash up first, or is it urgent?" Meir asked unintelligibly, his mouth full of nails.

"What?"

Meir spit the nails into the palm of his gloved hand. "What happened?" he asked. "What does he want?"

Raya shrugged, pulling her sweater tighter around herself. "He didn't say. He just asked me to call you." She turned around and hurried back into the warm kitchen.

"You'd better be careful," Nachman cautioned. "I warned you about getting too friendly."

Tanchum was pacing the room, hands clasped behind his back, when Meir arrived.

"You called me, *Herr Doktor*?"

"Yes, Meir. Sit down please, I would like to discuss something with you." Tanchum took his place behind the desk. "When you and your cousin came to work for me, it was understood that the positions were to be temporary ones, until you received your certificates to go to Palestine."

Meir nodded, wondering whether Dr. Stern was terminating their employment.

"It's been six months. Your work is commendable, but I do not imagine you see your future as groundskeepers. I would like to know your plans."

"*Herr Doktor* is surely aware of the vote in the United Nations regarding the establishment of a Jewish homeland. When the British Mandate ends, Nachman and I will leave for Palestine."

"You realize that a terrible war is imminent there?"

"We survived the war in Europe. With G-d's help, we will reach our homeland and are prepared to join the fight for Israel's survival."

"I admire you."

Meir met the doctor's eyes. "It is what every Jew wishes to do, sir."

For a moment, Tanchum imagined himself going to Palestine. The thought was revitalizing.

"I have a previous commitment that prevents me from joining you at this time," he said, "but in the future I hope we will meet again in the Jewish homeland."

Meir waited, unsure of where this discussion was headed.

"I am leaving Germany," Tanchum said abruptly. "I don't expect to return."

Meir's eyes widened.

"As you know, my residence is in the process of becoming a convalescent home. The organization managing the institute will take over completely in three months, but I need someone capable to handle the transition period. I am offering you the position.

"A bank account will be at your disposal to cover food and other supplies as well as my workers' salaries. I expect a monthly accounting, but management decisions will be in your hands."

"This is a great responsibility. I need time to consider the ramifications," Meir said slowly. "I must discuss it with my Rabbi."

"You realize that a decision is urgent."

"I understand. I appreciate your confidence in my ability, *Herr Doktor*. With your permission, I will leave to speak with my Rabbi immediately."

"Of course." The two men shook hands.

Once the long-delayed decision was made, Tanchum found that the pieces fell into place far more smoothly than he'd anticipated. He and Meir reviewed the manor records, arranged power of attorney and settled the remaining accounts in Karl Emsbach's name. Max Schiller accepted his letter of resignation, expressing deep sympathy over the unexplained change in plans that was forcing Dr. Stern to leave Europe without prior notice. He wished him success, and asked that he keep in touch.

Yanky was delirious with excitement. "We're going to America!" he sang.

"Get out of the way, *yingele*!" Nachman yelped, after tripping over the boy while lugging a trunk from the storage room.

"When are we leaving? Is it time yet?"

"Yanky, someone's ringing the front doorbell," Nachman told him. "Be a good boy and see who it is."

The staccato tapping of the child's footsteps echoed in the stairwell as he raced down to the lobby and flung open the polished oak door.

"Who's there?" Tanchum called from the living room. No one was expected, but it might be a former patient needing medical attention.

"*Herr Doktor*!" Yanky's high-pitched voice rang out frantically. "Come fast! Don't let him take me! *Herr Doktor*, help! No-o-o-o!"

78

ARELEH TWISTED HIS *PEYOS* UNTIL HE COULD TUCK them up under his cap. It was bad enough being an untried recruit; he didn't want to draw any further attention to himself.

Tzvi Drori noticed, and was pleased. "Come, Ari," he urged. "We have to hurry."

A truck loaded with crates of dates passed near them, slowed and stopped. Tzvi ran ahead, with the Kfar Ata boy trailing behind him. The two climbed into the driver's cabin, crowding together in the cramped space of the dusty van.

"Jordan, meet our new man, Ari Tzipori." Tzvi gestured at the boy on the seat beside him. "Ari, this fellow looks like an ordinary driver, but he is a hero like Bar Kochba. You are looking at the infamous Jordan Shaked, in person!"

Areleh shook the driver's proffered hand as firmly as he could, hoping to make a manly impression. "Pleased to meet you," he said.

"Tzipori?"Jordan asked with a tolerant smile, changing gears and pressing the accelerator.

"Feigelbaum," Areleh explained, blushing.

"Ah! Tzipori it is. Welcome. You've joined us at the best possible time. Oh, the sweetness of scores settled. Tonight the massacre at the Haifa refinery will be avenged!"

Areleh tried to hide his excitement. He leaned back and let the cool wind from the open window bathe his face, concentrating on the banter between the other two in order to avoid thinking about his mother's reaction when she found out he had run away. In any case, it was too late to change his mind now.

The truck continued up winding mountain roads, passing one Arab village after another. They stopped at the British checkpoint. One of the soldiers jumped up into the truck bed to examine the consignment of dates. Tzvi joined him. "I'm in a hurry," he said, slipping a few bills into the man's willing hand. "Maybe you can speed up inspection?"

The sentry jumped down from the truck and waved it through with a laugh.

Jordan lit a cigarette. He offered the pack to his companions. Tzvi Drori lit up, expertly exhaling a stream of smoke while passing a cigarette to Ari with his free hand. Areleh imitated the two older men, only to succumb to a fit of choking at his first puff. Tzvi pounded the boy's back.

Areleh's eyes were tearing and his lungs were on fire, but he refused to give up. Nonchalantly he continued drawing burning breaths of tobacco, struggling to suppress the constant impulse to cough. Finishing at last, he flicked the butt out the window with relief, wondering why men claim they liked smoking so much.

Evening found them backing the truck into a shack on the outskirts of a kibbutz overlooking the Kinneret. On the near side, dark water sparkled in the last rays of sunlight; the far side merged with the horizon in a smear of gray. A small group of teenagers were waiting in the shadows. Under the direction of Jordan Shaked, the boys worked to transfer the top cartons to a second vehicle. Jordan revealed a hidden cavity under the floor of the truck bed.

Tzvi whistled with admiration, but Areleh gasped. Neatly stacked in the hollow space beneath the dates were several crates of ammunition, gunpowder and dismantled handguns. It was a good thing they hadn't told the new recruit about the arms they were smuggling, because his trembling would definitely have given them away to the British soldiers at the roadblock.

"Ari, wake up!" Tzvi Drori playfully shoved Areleh aside and reached for the first box. "We've got work to do!"

Jordan showed the group how to assemble the separate pieces into guns. Areleh forced himself to take part, getting his hands black from the machine grease but earning Tzvi's approval. "You're good with your hands," he praised Ari. "Much better than I expected from a *yeshivah bachur*."

"It's a good night," Jordan said. "There's rain in the air. The Tommies will seek shelter indoors. No one will expect us to be outside."

Areleh stepped out of the shed and squinted, trying to discern something of his surroundings. It was a gloomy night; thick clouds blanketed the moon and stars. A cold wind stung his face. Suddenly, he longed to be in his warm bed at home, with his mother and Tante Fraydl near by.

Back in Kfar Ata, he had felt so guilty for not contributing to the fighting. Every day brought new stories of Arab atrocities and British collaboration with the Arabs. The Rosh Yeshivah had exhorted his students to learn with more fervor in order to protect the Jews in Palestine, but the *bachurim* whispered among themselves with admiration about friends and relatives who had joined the underground. Ever since he'd met Tzvi Drori, Areleh could barely concentrate during *shiur*.

Drori was in charge of Hagganah recruitment in the Galilee. He made it his business to meet potential candidates, persuading them to join the resistance and fight their enemies. Tzvi's words were full of idealism and challenge. He painted a new and better world, free from the chains of the past. A modern world of brotherhood and equality. His words had echoed in Areleh's mind until the boy finally made the fateful decision to follow his dream. That morning he had been brave and confident, but tonight he felt strangely lost and lonely.

Muffled voices from the shed portended an argument. Areleh felt a presence join him outside. "Greetings."He recognized the voice of a boy about his age. "I'm Yossi. Are you hungry?"

"Yes, very," Areleh admitted. He hadn't eaten anything since breakfast, though the nausea from his first cigarette and the excitement of being with Jordan Shaked and Tzvi Drori had almost made him forget that.

"Come with me. I'll take you to the kibbutz dining hall. The Palmach can't expect us to be warriors on an empty stomach."

Areleh smiled. "Are you taking part in the action tonight?" he asked softly as their feet crunched on a gravel path.

"No, they won't let me yet. I was fighting with the partisans when I was 10 years old, but Drori thinks I'm just a kid."

"Were you really with the partisans during the war?"

"Not as a fighter, exactly. I didn't handle weapons. I was a courier between the partisan base camps, and I've seen enough explosives to know how to handle them."

Areleh was impressed. The first drops of rain were falling as they entered the dining hall. It was dark inside, but Yossi knew the way and without hesitation he led him between the tables to the kitchen.

"Where is everyone?" Ari wondered.

Yossi rummaged through the cupboards. "It's late and they've been working in the fields all day, so they're too tired for anything except sleep at this hour. Only the guards are still awake, and they're probably sheltering from the rain under a roof somewhere." Yossi piled some pitas on the counter and pried open a gallon can of green olives. "Help yourself," he offered.

"Where can I wash up?" Areleh asked, feeling self-conscious despite his hunger pangs.

"There's a pump just outside," Yossi replied, narrowing his eyes as he noticed his own filthy hands in the flickering light from the kitchen lantern. "Grab that towel and put it under your shirt to keep it dry. I'll get a bar of soap. No sense eating engine oil when we have perfectly good hummus."

Areleh laughed. He liked this kibbutznik and it made him feel much better to have a friend. After washing away the grime, he dried his hands, took a cup and surreptitiously washed his hands for bread. Yossi noticed but didn't comment, which Areleh appreciated. The boys wolfed down their late supper and drank warm beer that left Areleh light headed.

"We'd better get back," Yossi decided. "Tzvi and Jordan don't like it when we break discipline."

"Will we get into trouble?"

"What can they do? Threaten to tell our parents?" Yossi smirked.

"Why don't we take some food back for the others? They're probably as hungry as we were."

"Good thinking. Then they won't yell at us. You have a good head, Tzipori."

Yossi was right. The rest of the group appreciated the provisions, and within minutes the only thing left of their efforts was an empty olive can. His mood greatly improved by a full stomach, Tzvi Drori cuffed Yossi and Areleh affectionately and told them, "Men, you're coming with us tonight!"

Areleh's heart was bursting with excitement. He could barely believe his good fortune. Yossi punched his arm lightly, and the two stood side by side when Shaked handed out assignments. Moments later, they were huddled with the rest of the team under a tarpaulin. And then the truck was bouncing over ruts on its way to the Arab village of Sassa.

The truck stopped on a hilltop two kilometers from the target. Rain fell in sheets. The men wrapped canvas around their weapons and proceeded single file, slipping on grass made slick by the downpour and stumbling over shin-high rocks that were invisible in the dark. Areleh focused his eyes on Yossi's back, which was slightly less dense than the darkness of the night. He tried to sense when his friend stepped over obstacles so that he would not fall. *We're about as subtle as a herd of elephants*, he thought, wondering why no one seemed concerned with the element of surprise.

"Halt!" The order was whispered from one to the other. After the continuous sound of splashing footsteps, the silence was now broken only by the patter of the rain.

The whispered command came: "Uncover your weapons."

Since Areleh hadn't yet learned how to shoot, he was carrying a backpack of ammunition. *No one even tried the guns after they were assembled,"* he fretted to himself. *"What if they don't shoot?"*

Thunder cracked and the world exploded with zigzags of lightning. Areleh's short life flashed before his eyes. In the brief moment of light, he saw Jordan Shaked's teeth gleam as he grinned. And then the world was plunged into darkness again.

79

"PLEASE COME IN." HIDING HIS SHOCK, TANCHUM TOOK IN the visitor's heavy black cloak and burgundy cassock. He stepped back, inserting himself between Yanky and the priest while gesturing toward the door that led to the living room. Yanky's face was as pale as a ghost and he clung desperately to the doctor's hand. "To what do we owe the honor of this unexpected visit, Reverend?"

"May I introduce myself? I am Monsignor Thiessen of the West Berlin diocese."

"Yes?" Tanchum's mind raced feverishly. Could this be related to the child he had taken from the orphanage? The priest was obviously of high rank. The fact that he was unaccompanied made Tanchum conclude that the visit must be unofficial — perhaps something altogether innocent, such as a request for a donation or an appeal for support for some project.

Archbishop Thiessen glanced at the child cowering behind the German. "I have not come for you," he attempted to reassure the frightened little boy.

Yanky hid his face behind Tanchum. His grip did not relax until the doctor lifted him up into his strong arms. From this more secure position, Yanky regarded the newcomer with obvious distrust.

Monsignor Thiessen stepped closer. "Dr. Karl Emsbach?"

"Yes?"

"I need to speak with you in private," he said quietly. "It is urgent."

Tanchum instructed Raya to take Yanky into another room. "Please bring refreshments for our guest. Yanky may have some scones in the kitchen."

Raya's expression registered disapproval.

"I realize that it is before dinner. Let us hope it won't ruin his appetite."

Once they were alone, the archbishop spoke, "I understand that you knew Father Matthew Hofmann?"

Tanchum met the man's intense gaze. "Yes, I did," he responded. "The orphanage was near the hospital where I was stationed, and we had some contact during the last year of the war. Father Matthew was a good man. His untimely death is a tragedy."

"I received a report that you left two young boys in his care."

Tanchum's heart beat faster. Was this an accusation or a statement of fact? Who, other than Father Matthew and Chaim, could have known? Should he acknowledge the truth of what the priest had said, or take refuge in denials?

He hesitated, and then decided to go with the truth. "Your information is correct," he responded tersely. His neck muscles were tight with tension.

"Please tell me about the children."

"Why?"

The archbishop smiled sadly. "I have taken it upon myself to investigate the background of an orphan in one of the monasteries under my jurisdiction. You were recommended as the person who can authenticate the boy's story, so that he may be reunited with his family."

The festive meal that Masha prepared in honor of Chaim's homecoming was fit for royalty. All those involved with the convalescent home participated in the joyful occasion, as well as Tanchum's employees and Monsignor Thiessen with his entourage. The order to return Thomas to Dr. Emsbach was a controversial one, but the archbishop's absolute authority left no alternative. The monastery complied, and the child was returned to Ravensdorf without delay.

Wedged between the former Nazi who had saved him from enemies intent on destroying his body, and the priest who had rescued him from a life without *Yiddishkeit*, Chaim observed the strangers celebrating his release. He could still hardly believe he was back here, in the refuge that he and Tante Fraydl and Yanky had found so many months before.

Perched on Tanchum's lap, Yanky focused his bright eyes on his older brother, as if Chaim might disappear if he looked away.

"Perhaps the guest of honor could say a few words?" Nachman requested.

Tanchum turned to him. "He only just arrived this morning," he explained politely. "There have been many changes since Chaim was last here. He needs time to adjust."

"I *would* like to say something." Chaim touched Tanchum's sleeve.

Tanchum was surprised. Gazing into Chaim's earnest face, he suddenly realized how much the boy had matured over the past two years. He was no longer the innocent child who had been under his young aunt's guardianship.

"Of course, Chaim," he agreed immediately. He turned to the men assembled at the table and called for their attention. "Chaim has something to say," he announced.

"I want to say thank you," Chaim blushed. He took a deep breath and continued, "Words cannot begin to tell *Herr Doktor* Emsbach and His Grace the archbishop how deeply I appreciate what they have done for me. I can only promise that I will try to be a person who will make them proud. I want to live my life in a way that will give my parents and grandparents, of blessed memory, eternal *nachas*.

"On this day, I remember how my Tante Fraydl taught me the words in *Hallel: Who is like Hashem our G-d. . .He lifts the destitute and seats them with royalty.* That's how I feel right now. Tante Fraydl promised Yanky and me that Hashem watches over us always. She gave me the faith to believe that this day would come. I thank the *Ribbono shel Olam,* and I thank my Tante Fraydl. I *daven* that one day I will be able to tell her so myself."

Chaim sat down abruptly, blinking away tears. The archbishop shook his hand, and Tanchum slid Yanky off his knee so he could embrace Chaim. "We are all so proud of you." Tanchum was so overwhelmed with emotion that he could not say any more than that. Looking at her nephews, he felt Fraydl's absence acutely. Would they ever see her again?

Their ship left Bremen on a stunning winter day. The sky was bluer than Tanchum had ever seen it. White cumulous clouds rose majestically to an unmeasurable height. Chaim and Yanky stood quietly beside him, watching the shores of Germany recede into the distance until there was only a blur on the skyline.

"We're going to America," Yanky repeated for the thousandth time.

Chaim squeezed his shoulder affectionately.

Tanchum Stern stared at the horizon behind them, lost in his thoughts and memories. Germany was so beautiful. A land blessed with mountains and rivers, spacious fields and fertile valleys — but soaked with blood. He led his charges forward to where they could see the ocean's waves breaking on the bow, turning his back on the cursed land that had stolen his childhood and his family. His face to the wind, Tanchum chose to let go of the past and focus on the future.

PART III
NOT TOTALLY, AND NOT FOREVER

80

THE TWO-WEEK VOYAGE PASSED UNEVENTFULLY. THE BOYS spent most of their time in the cabin with Tanchum because they disliked the stinging salt spray that lashed their faces on deck. After the doctor told the children how he'd discovered his true identity, Chaim opened up his heart and shared the events he had experienced after leaving Ravensdorf. They discussed his upcoming bar mitzvah, and talked about becoming part of the family Tanchum had never known.

As the days passed, Chaim's relationship with the doctor deepened. Feeling usurped, Yanky frequently bickered with his brother. He made unreasonable demands for attention whenever he felt that Chaim was monopolizing their guardian. Lacking any experience with raising children, Tanchum found himself nonplussed by his ward's unusual behavior.

"What's the matter, Yanky?" he asked, resting a hand on the boy's forehead to see if he was running a fever.

Matters came to a head when Yanky threw a full-scale temper tantrum in the dining room, kicking and screaming and throwing silverware. As quickly as possible, Tanchum picked up the flailing child and carried him out. Passing near a table of well-dressed European travelers, he heard a woman say, "What that little boy needs is a good spanking!"

"No," someone else responded sadly. "He needs a mother."

Back in the cabin, Tanchum soothed Yanky until his sobs finally stopped and he lay limp in the doctor's arms. Long after the boy's eyelids drooped and closed, Tanchum continued rocking him back and forth.

Chaim came into their compartment. "*Herr Doktor*, please go finish your meal. I will stay with Yanky now."

Tanchum looked at the sleeping child in his arms. "He never did anything like this before," he said. "I don't understand what happened to him."

"Tante Fraydl would have known what to do," Chaim said softly, sitting on the bunk opposite the doctor. "She always understood us."

Tanchum lay Yanky down, removed his shoes and pulled the blanket up to his shoulders. "If he wakes up hungry, bring him back to the dining hall," he told Chaim, and left.

In another two days they would dock in New York. He would see his mother and father, and meet his siblings and their families. Tanchum hoped the reunion would go smoothly. He hoped the family would welcome Yanky and Chaim, and support his decision to raise the two orphans. He hoped the Sterns would be able to accept them all. He also hoped that he and the boys would adjust easily to their new home.

It was a tall order.

"The Statue of Liberty!"

Passengers cheered and hugged each other, laughing as tugboats laboriously pulled the ocean liner into New York harbor. The ship dropped anchor and whistles blew.

"How will we know who they are?" Chaim asked, scanning the crowded pier.

"Our arrival is expected," Tanchum replied, tucking the woolen scarf more snugly around Yanky's neck. "They'll be looking for us."

Followed by porters carrying their luggage, he walked slowly down the gangplank. His posture was erect and his expression calm. No casual observer would envision the turmoil in his heart as he took the final steps marking the division between past and future, moving irrevocably from the familiar into the unknown.

The children were so excited that they didn't know in which direction to look first. Yanky literally danced up and down as they stood in line to present their passports. Beside him, Chaim stood quietly, more than a little overwhelmed by the cacophony surrounding them. The three advanced to the main hall, where throngs of people waited to meet the incoming passengers.

"Tanchum! Tanchum Stern!"

Chaim was the first to hear the voice. "Look, over there!" He tugged at the doctor's sleeve, pointing at a man who was advancing toward them with outstretched arms. The brothers' resemblance was striking. Tanchum extended his hand in greeting, but the man ignored it and caught him up in a rib-cracking embrace instead. Seconds later, the stranger pushed him back, saying, "You are real! I can't believe it! We have waited so long... Let me look at you."

The boys stared. Chaim burst out, "Yanky, *Herr Doktor* is a *Yid*!" Suddenly comprehending the implications of the strange story they'd been told, Chaim burst into tears.

"Who is that man?" Yanky tugged on his brother's sleeve. "What does he want?" His eyes darted back and forth between the bearded stranger and his guardian, and his lower lip quivered.

Chaim hastily dried his wet cheeks on his coat sleeve. "He's a *Yid*, Yanky," he explained. "Like before the war. Like Tatte and Zeidy."

A second man joined them. Like the first, he embraced Tanchum and pronounced the blessing, "Blessed are You, Hashem, our G-d, Master of the Universe, Who revives the dead!"

Finally, Tanchum disentangled himself. He turned to the boys. "*Sie sind mienen bruderen,*" he soothed Yanky, drawing Chaim closer with his other arm.

"*Tiyere kinder,*" Alexander Stern addressed the children warmly, including his own lost brother. "The war is finally over. You're safe now. You're home."

"I am Dovid Stern, the oldest," the first man introduced himself. "This is Alexander, the brother after me."

"Where is my father?" Tanchum asked, searching the crowd behind them for a familiar face.

"The Mamme is very weak," Dovid said soberly. "She couldn't come, so Tatte stayed behind with her. They're waiting for us... We should hurry."

Alexander signaled to the porters, and Dovid guided the group through the exit doors to a taxi limousine. The luggage was loaded. Everyone settled into their seats as Alexander gave the driver directions. Horn blowing with New York fervor, the automobile pulled into traffic.

"How is our parents' health?" Tanchum asked. He felt strange asking this ordinary question. It was hard to feel connected to an unfamiliar family.

"You will see for yourself. Mamme has always been weak, but in the last month she's become almost transparent. It is good that you finally came."

Sensing criticism in his brother's voice, Tanchum felt himself withdraw. "I'm sorry," he said softly. "Now that I am here, I hope it will be beneficial for her."

There was a stiff silence. "You don't remember anything?" Alexander asked, looking at him intently.

"No. Nothing. I have tried and tried, but nothing comes to mind."

"Perhaps it is good that there was a hiatus for all of us to adjust to the idea," Dovid added. "It's so hard to believe."

"I came as soon as I felt I could." Tanchum spoke with a trace of bitterness. "I needed time to accept that I am Jewish, and that for most of my life I lived a lie. I do not want to disappoint anyone, but I am not sure if I will ever be able to find my place in your family. Too much has happened."

"Don't say that, Tanchum!" Dovid interrupted. "Your heritage was stolen, but it is yours to reclaim. Otherwise you are handing victory to the wicked ones who caused us so much pain!"

Tanchum closed his eyes and took a deep breath. It literally took all of his strength to stay calm. He opened them again, and sat staring at the windshield without registering anything he saw.

Dovid touched Tanchum's arm. "It's been hard for you ever since you met our father," he said, "but it's been hard for our parents from the day their youngest son disappeared. And this is not their only sorrow. Two sisters and their families remained behind in Poland when we moved to New York. No one knows their fate. Considering that there has been no contact since the war, we assume the worst."

Tanchum nodded, unable to speak.

"This is Brooklyn," Alexander made an effort to lighten the mood by choosing a neutral subject. "Williamsburg looks a lot like the *alte heim* before the war."

Chaim's eyes were glued to the window, his expression elated. "It's just like I remember," he murmured. "If only Tante Fraydl were with us..."

Yanky moved onto Tanchum's lap. He looked small and frightened.

Thoughts whirled around Tanchum's head like a flock of startled birds. He felt like a prisoner released after nearly 30 years. Now he had to discover what it meant to be part of a family with parents and siblings — and he was also responsible for raising and providing for two traumatized youngsters.

Sensing his distress, Dovid reached out and touched his brother's arm. "Nothing can be accomplished in a single day. We must take it step-by-step. Hashem brought you back to us, Tanchum, and He will help us work things out. Just try to be happy today, and leave the future for tomorrow."

The limousine came to a halt. Tanchum buttoned up Yanky's coat and took his hand. While Dovid paid the driver, Chaim helped Alexander unload the trunks and suitcases onto the sidewalk.

"The driver and I will carry the luggage upstairs," Dovid said. "Sender, take them up already. Don't keep Mamme and Tatte waiting."

A thin layer of ice crackled beneath Tanchum's boots when he crossed the sidewalk. They followed Alexander up the stone stairs leading to the foyer of an old brownstone. The cracked linoleum on the wooden floor had long ago faded into an indeterminate olive color, and the dark wooden stairs creaked and sighed as they climbed to the second floor.

Although it was warm inside the building, the boys huddled close to their guardian, their expressions wary. Tanchum rested a reassuring hand on each of their heads.

"We're almost there," he said. "We're almost home."

81

N O NEWS?" FRAYDL ASKED GENTLY, CAREFULLY POURING
boiling water from the *finjan* onto the tea leaves in the
porcelain cups.

"Nothing encouraging." Rivka sipped her hot tea without really
tasting it. She had just returned from a visit to the Liebman family, whose daughter Peninah was active in the Irgun underground.
Areleh had been gone for over three months.

"He'll come home for the *seder*," Fraydl promised, unable to con-
ceive that her nephew would miss being with his family on Pesach.

Rivka shrugged noncommittally. Lately her brows were perpet-
ually furrowed with worry.

They sat, each wrapped in her thoughts. The silence was so
profound that the sound of the slowly dripping faucet seemed jar-
ringly loud. Fraydl collected their empty cups and carried them to
the sink.

The sound of the front door bursting open shattered the quiet.

"Who is it?" Rivka jumped to her feet.

They ran from the kitchen. A strange figure furtively entered the
house, immediately closing and locking the door behind him.

"Who are you? What do you want?" Fraydl was filled with dread.

"Tante Fraydl, turn out the lights." The intruder's voice was familiar. "There's been an action. The British have declared a curfew. If they find me, I'll go to prison. Hurry, turn out the light and draw the curtains!"

"Areleh!" Rivka gave a piercing cry. "Areleh, my son!" She reached out to touch the apparition, but he pushed her away.

"Mamme, there's no time for that!" His eyes darted about the room. "Soldiers are following right behind me. They'll be here any minute. I have to find a place to hide!"

Fraydl stared in disbelief. This young man with the dirty face and wild mop of hair, dressed in the clothes of a common laborer, was Areleh?

Without hesitation, Rivka grabbed her son's arm and pulled him into the bathroom, pointing at the space between the top of the door and the ceiling, where two small doors concealed a storage place that housed their Pesach utensils during the rest of the year.

Aharon jumped onto a wooden stool and struggled to squeeze himself in, ignoring the sound of breaking glass as he crushed the cartons in his way. Rivka grabbed her son's knees and boosted him higher. When he had wriggled into the narrow space, she climbed on the stool to latch the doors securely.

A violent pounding commenced. "Open up! In the name of His Majesty's officers, open this door immediately!"

The front door shuddered under the soldiers' merciless pounding. Catching her breath, Rivka pushed the stool behind the shower curtain and ran to unlock the door.

Four burly soldiers exploded into the living room. Without explanation, they shoved the frightened women out of their way and fanned out, methodically searching the entire house. The men poked under the beds with their bayonets, threw the down comforters on the floor and emptied every single closet and cupboard.

"Where is the boy?" their leader snarled at the women. "We saw him come in here!"

Rivka's knees could hardly support her. In spite of her trembling, she managed to shake her head emphatically. "I don't know what you're talking about." The woman's voice was hoarse. "There's no one here but me and my sister, and we live alone. Who are you looking for? Why did you break into my house?"

"He's not here, captain."

Her face as pale as chalk, Fraydl sank down on a chair. Rivka stood behind her sister, holding onto the back of the chair, her knuckles white.

"Why are you frightening this poor girl?" she shouted angrily. "Did she survive the Nazi Holocaust, only to have you scare her to death?"

The captain hesitated. He scanned the room again. Where was his missing prey?

"I'm sure he came in here," a private whined in frustration.

The commanding officer turned on him in fury. "Did you *find* him here?" he shouted. "Thanks to your incompetence, the criminal is escaping at this very moment. After him now!"

The soldiers quickly left the house. Rivka shut the door behind them and stood with her back against it, shaking uncontrollably. Fraydl stood up. She walked with unsteady steps toward her sister, whispering, "It's over. They're gone."

"Areleh!" Rivka said. "What are we going to do? They want to arrest my baby." For the first time since her son left she dissolved in tears, her usual mask of competence stripped away.

They heard a rapping from the attic space and Areleh's muffled voice calling for his mother

While Rivka helped the boy out of his hiding place, Fraydl closed the curtains on all the windows and turned off all the lights except the one in the kitchen.

"I'm hungry."

Areleh looked so woebegone that Fraydl nursed the hope that the boy's adventure was over and life might return to normal.

"Wash first," Rivka told him sternly. "Give me your dirty clothes and take clean ones."

After her son had eaten everything edible in the house, he fell asleep on his mother's bed, utterly exhausted. Rivka sat beside him, stroking his long curls and murmuring *Tehillim* from memory. "This is almost how he looked before his *upsheren*," she mused affectionately.

Her sister's unconditional love reminded Fraydl of their mother. It also made her angry. This foolish boy had turned their lives upside down, causing so much unwarranted grief. What were they to do if the soldiers returned? Was it possible to keep Areleh in hiding for the remaining two months until the British mandate expired and the detested occupiers finally left Palestine?

The young man stirred and opened his eyes. For a moment he was their Areleh, the old innocence in his sleepy eyes as he blinked and focused on his mother's face. But that was followed by an abrupt transformation as he jumped out of the bed. "I've got to go now," he announced. "The men are waiting for me."

"No, Areleh!" Rivka protested, catching hold of his pajama sleeve. "It's the middle of the night, and the curfew is still in force. It's too dangerous to go outside now."

"I must." Yanking his arm free, the boy grabbed his clean clothes and closeted himself in the bathroom to get dressed.

Rivka stood outside the bathroom door, trying to reason with her son. "I don't want you to leave, Areleh. I'm afraid. Stay home. We'll discuss it tomorrow."

The door opened and Areleh appeared, fully dressed and ready to go. "*Shalom*, Ima," he said, giving his mother a peck on the cheek. "Don't forget to *daven* for me."

Rivka was speechless at her son's impudence. Was this the same boy she had raised so lovingly?

"*Chutzpah!*" Fraydl responded in defense of her sister's feelings. "How can you talk to your mother like that? First you break her heart and then you just walk out? She doesn't deserve that, and you know it!"

Areleh briefly regarded his aunt. "You spent the war hiding," he told her contemptuously, "but I'm not ready to accept either the Arab's plans to annihilate us or the British collaboration. Together with my comrades, I will resist for as long as I have breath in my body. For centuries Jews have been victims, but no longer! We are building a new land where Jews are strong and not afraid."

Areleh hefted a backpack onto his shoulder and pushed past the women. They heard the click of the door, and then he disappeared into the night.

82

A BOY OF ABOUT 10 OPENED THE DOOR WHEN ALEXANDER pressed the doorbell. "They're here!" Flushed with excitement, he was suddenly overcome with shyness and fled to the interior of the house.

"Come in, come in," Alexander urged Tanchum and the boys.

They were standing stiffly when Rabbi Stern hurried into the front room. "My son! *Oy*, my son!" he exclaimed softly. "What joy it gives me to see you again!" There were tears as they embraced.

Chaim watched them tensely, his lips compressed in a tight line, but Yanky recognized the kind Zeide from the hotel and ran to him eagerly. Rabbi Stern did not disappoint him. He patted the child's head and slipped him a candy bar from his coat pocket.

"Shmuelik," Rabbi Stern called the grandson who had opened the door. "Shmuelik, come meet your new cousins. This is Yanky." Rabbi Stern gave the little one an affectionate pinch on his cheek. "And this young man is Chaim. Chaim, Tanchum wrote me about you, and I am looking forward to getting to know you better now that you are home. Shmuel, take them into the kitchen and serve them some of your mother's delicious yeast cake."

The boys were reluctant to leave the doctor's side, but he nodded for them to follow Shmuel. His father took Tanchum's arm, guiding him gently to the room where his mother reclined. "Don't be nervous," he said softly. "She will understand if you don't recognize her." Remaining in the doorway, he gave his son a gentle push forward.

At first glance, Tanchum saw an elderly woman propped up by many pillows. Her eyes were alert, following his approach as he crossed the room. Tears glistened on her wrinkled cheeks, but she was smiling.

"Mamme?"

Slowly, and with effort, she lifted her arm and reached toward him. Tanchum dropped to one knee at her side. He took her small hands in his own and looked at them, then bent his head and gently kissed the backs of her hands.

"Tanchum," she whispered. Each breath was a struggle. He could see that she was very ill.

Time seemed to stand still. With his support, Rebbetzin Stern lifted her son's hands and held them gently to her lips for a moment. "Now I am not afraid to die," she murmured.

"No!" Tanchum protested, "Mamme, you must live! Please don't talk about death! I have only just come, and I want us to be together."

The rebbetzin held his gaze for a long time before nodding. "You are right, my son. Today I want to live more than I ever did before. May it be the will of Hashem that I stand under the *chuppah* with you at your wedding, and may I one day merit holding your firstborn in my arms." This long speech exhausted her, and the rebbetzin fell back against the pillows. Her eyes closed and her breathing became shallow.

"Tanchum," his father called from the door, "Hannah will stay with Mamme while we go meet the rest of the family. She needs to preserve her strength. Let her sleep now."

A handsome woman in a dark *tichel* slipped into the room and went to her mother-in-law. She rearranged some of the pillows and took the woman's hand in hers. Tanchum looked from his mother to his father. It was hard for him to leave, but he knew the others were waiting and he might as well be done with the formal introductions. "I'll be back soon," he promised, and kissed her cheek before following his father to the dining room where a feast was set out on the table.

Rabbi Stern grasped Tanchum's hand and led him to the crowded table, where he told him the name and his relationship to each person. "You've met Dovid already. He is your oldest brother."Tanchum nodded.

"And you just saw Dovid's wife, Hannah. She is very devoted to your mother. We could never manage without her. . . Your next two sisters, Pessya and Leah, were both already married when the war began.They stayed in Poland when we left for the United States. Also your brother, Mordechai, stayed at his yeshivah in Minsk. It is our prayer that, just as we were privileged to be reunited with you, one day we will hear from them as well…"Rabbi Stern paused. A cloud of grief momentarily passed over his features but he recovered quickly, continuing, "This is Yehuda Leib."

The young man stood and offered his hand to Tanchum, who grasped it, noting his brother's guarded good will.

"Now, this is Shimon, your sister Feige's husband." Rabbi Stern indicated a *yungerman* with a reddish beard.

Shimon followed Yehuda Leib's example and shook hands with his new brother-in-law. "Welcome home. We've been waiting for you," he said.

There were still three men at the table. His father introduced him to Yosef Aaron, but the next one stood and introduced himself, "We've met, of course.I'm Alexander."

Tanchum shook hands with each, trying to keep their names and faces straight in his memory. It was a lot to remember at one time.

"My wife, Devory, is in the kitchen," Alexander said in a hearty voice. "She and Mindy have been cooking and baking all morning just for you."

Tanchum was not sure if that was meant as a compliment or a criticism, but his father was already pointing to the youngest man, who had not yet been introduced. "This is Michoel, your sister

Mindy's husband," Rabbi Stern said with a smile. Mindy poked her head out of the kitchen and waved. "She's our baby," their father said indulgently. "Mindy was born here in America."

Tanchum turned to his little sister. She reminded him of Fraydl. As he'd done a thousand times before, he was distracted by the gnawing mystery: what had become of the girl?

"Tanchum?"

"Yes, Tatte."Tanchum was overwhelmed. He smiled politely and responded appropriately to each person, but it took a great effort for him to do so. He could sense a certain understandable suspicion behind their smiles. Despite his parents' enthusiasm, he would need time to earn his rightful place in this family.

Young Shmuelik was staring at his new uncle. "He looks exactly like Fetter Alexander!" he exclaimed. "Look, Tatte, they have the same face!"

"Of course he does," Rabbi Stern responded. "They are brothers, Shmuel, just like you and your little brother Yitzik."

It was difficult for Tanchum to maintain a flow of superficial conversation while his mind kept returning to his mother's failing health. Her pale skin, labored breathing and the blue tinge around her lips confirmed that her heart was barely functioning. He wanted to consult with her physician, and possibly change her treatment regimen as soon as possible.

Everyone washed for dinner. Gradually a coherent picture emerged from the different pieces of the puzzle. Tanchum pleased his sisters and sisters-in-law by tasting each dish, but his appetite had vanished. Yanky and Chaim made up for his reticence. They ate with relish and asked for more

"This is so good!" Yanky said. "Can I have another serving?"

Tanchum frowned slightly, and Yanky quickly added, "Please, I want more of this."

"You would think that I starved him," the doctor apologized for the child's lack of manners.

"He's just acting like a little boy," Devory said, heaping another helping of meat on Yanky's plate. "Would you like another portion?" she offered Chaim.

"Yes, please," the older boy replied. "I remember that my mother used to prepare kugel like this when I was small. It tastes delicious."

"Please help yourself to another piece. As much as you like."

The thought that the boys would have stomachaches from over-eating flashed through Tanchum's mind, but he decided not to reprove them in front of the others.

After the meal, the women in the family continued to ply Yanky with treats and compliments, which he enthusiastically repaid by sharing his childish recollections of "*Herr Doktor.*" Chaim also contributed an anecdote here and there, painting their benefactor in such heroic colors it made Tanchum blush.

At the end of the meal, Rabbi Stern gave his newly returned son the honor of leading the *bentching.* Tanchum tried to demur, but his brothers all insisted.

"We learned this together in Germany," his father reminded him in a whisper. Tanchum hated to admit that he remembered very little from that time. "I will help you," Rabbi Stern offered.

In the end, Tanchum stumbled through the words, mortified at his failure to do something as elementary as reciting grace after a meal. Young Shmuel's face registered shock at hearing a grown man who could not pronounce these familiar words correctly.

Dovid put an arm around Chaim and spoke loudly, "Everyone understands that you children could not learn properly because of the war. If you are interested, Alexander and I will be glad to help you catch up on some of the learning that you missed."

"I would like that." Chaim gave him a grateful look. "I was worried what the other boys will say when I come to yeshivah and I am not on the level of boys my age."

"There's nothing to worry about!" Alexander assured him with gusto. "We will start reviewing from the very beginning, from *aleph-beis,* and progress from there. With a *kluge kop* like yours, you'll be the best in your class in no time at all!"

Chaim grinned bashfully.

"I already know *aleph-beis,*" Yanky chirped. "My Tante Fraydl made me say it over and over. I can even say it when I'm asleep!"

"That's wonderful!" Dovid smiled. He turned to Tanchum,

"Sender and I will be the *rebbe'im* and you will be the *menahel*. Just tell us what to teach the boys, and we'll do our best."

Tanchum saw through the masquerade, even while he appreciated his brothers' combined attempt to preserve his sense of dignity. Karl Emsbach had been a courageous soldier and an innovative surgeon, but Tachchum Stern was nearly paralyzed by his own incompetence. Over 30 years old, and any 3-year-old in *cheder* knew more than he did!

83

F OR MONTHS, TANCHUM FELT AS IF HE WERE SAILING IN A small boat on a great sea. At times, the waves lifted him higher than he had ever imagined it was possible to go, but at other times he was buried beneath seemingly endless troughs of despair. Under his father's tutelage he learned to fulfill the requirements of a full Jewish life. He mastered the basics, and then progressed step by step until the day came when he completed his first *blatt* Gemara. That was the day that Tanchum discovered himself, and finally understood the purpose of his life.

"*Herr Doktor*?"

Tanchum looked up from his Gemara, and smiled when he realized it was Chaim. "Yes?"

The boy cleared his throat self-consciously. "I would like to discuss something important. Do you have time now, or should I come back later?"

"For you, I always have time." Tanchum closed the Gemara and patted the chair beside him.

Chaim sat. "You know how grateful we are for all you have done for us," he began — and stopped.

"Of course, Chaim."

"*Herr Doktor*, Tante Hannah and Fetter Dovid have suggested that Yanky and I move into their house."

Tanchum's eyebrows rose. "You're not happy here with me and Baba and Zeide?"

"Of course! We are very happy," Chaim quickly reassured him.

"But you want to leave?"

The boy did not meet his eyes.

"Perhaps I have not given you enough attention," Tanchum frowned. "I have been too busy. I'm sorry. Let me rearrange my schedule so that we have more time together. Would you like that?"

Chaim bit his lip. "It's hard here for Yanky," he explained.

"For Yanky?"

"Yes. The Baba is very sick, and we must be very quiet all the time. He's only a little boy, and he's full of energy. I have to occupy him so he doesn't make noise, but there's never any time left for me. My bar mitzvah is only four months away and I still haven't prepared the whole *parashah* because I'm always busy with Yanky."

"I'm sorry, Chaim," Tanchum said, distressed. "I didn't realize."

"It's O.K. I'm usually glad to watch him, but I'm beginning to worry about my bar mitzvah. And when Fetter Dovid suggested that he might be happier in a house full of children, I thought it was a good idea."

"And you want to live there with him?"

"I never want to be separated from my brother again."

Tanchum pressed his forefingers together and rested them on his lower lip, trying to read the meaning between Chaim's words.

"We can still learn together every day!" Chaim tried to sweeten the bitter pill. "After yeshivah, I can come here, or we can meet at shul." He looked at his benefactor with a mixture of trepidation and hope in his hazel eyes.

Tanchum sighed. "I only want the best for you," he said sadly.

"Never mind, then," Chaim shrugged. "We'll manage." He stood up and walked toward the door.

Tanchum raised his voice before Chaim got there. "No, the points you raised are valid. Let me think about it and give you my decision later. . . It's very quiet. Where is Yanky now?"

"I told him he could stay and play with Avreim'l until bath time."

"Tell me when you're ready to bring him home, and I'll come with you. We can walk there and back together."

Chaim smiled. "I usually go to Fetter Dovid's directly after Maariv."

Tanchum looked at his watch. "Good. Now, let me get back to my *sugya*." He reopened the Gemara, but found it difficult to concentrate.

After *davening,* the two walked the few blocks to Dovid's house. The warm spring night made it a pleasant time to be outside and many people were taking advantage of the mild weather.

"I can't believe we've been in New York for half a year already," Chaim said. A narrow sliver of moon peeked at them through the leafy canopy of the trees lining the sidewalk. "It feels like we came only a short while ago."

Tanchum laughed. "For me, it feels like years already," he told the boy.

"For you, it *has* been years," Chaim pointed out sagely. "Your brothers and sisters spent many hours sharing the family's history so that you can feel part of everything. I only had the war years to make up, but you had to rebuild your whole life."

"Are you really only a child?" Tanchum asked in wonder. "When did you become so wise, young man?"

"The war made us old," Chaim answered seriously. "Children of war grow up very fast."

They walked up the steps to his brother's house. Through the open windows came the shrieks and laughter of children playing . Hannah opened the door for them, a baby in her arms and a wide-eyed toddler hanging on to her apron. "Tanchum!" she exclaimed happily. "What a pleasant surprise. Come in, sit down. Dovid just left on an errand, but he'll be right back." She handed the baby to an older daughter and hurried to the kitchen, returning with a platter of fruit for her unexpected guest.

The girls doing homework at the dining table giggled and quickly gathered their papers to make room for him. Chaim pulled out a *sefer* from the bookcase and curled up on the sofa, absently twirling his left *peyah* with his forefinger. Yanky whooped like a wild Indian, tearing through the dining room and circling back to the bedrooms with Avreim'l in hot pursuit. A moment later he emerged from the back of the house yelling, "I don't want to go home, *Herr Doktor*. I want to stay here!" before disappearing once again. Tanchum was unprepared for the intense jealousy that swept through him. He felt bereft.

Dovid hung his hat on the peg and joined Tanchum at the table, while Hannah brought them a plate piled high with small, hot potato knishes.

"It's good to see you, little brother. *Vi machen die elteren?*"

"*Baruch Hashem*, the same," Tanchum replied, enjoying the salty taste of the home-made treat.

"Did you speak with the new cardiologist?"

"Yes. He is not very optimistic, but he did recommend another doctor — someone named John Gibbon, who is researching the development of a pump that could make corrective surgery possible. I was in touch with him, but he thinks it will be years before the machine is perfected enough to use in humans."

"Every day that the Mamme lives is a miracle," Dovid stated emphatically, piercing a knish with his fork and watching the steam rise from it.

"At least she's holding her own for now," Tanchum pointed out.

"Thanks to you," Hannah said with a smile, shifting her baby from one side to the other before his tiny hand grabbed the last knish on the plate. "Your presence gives her strength."

Dovid leaned forward and asked, "Have you given any thought to how hard it is for Chaim and Yanky to live in the same house as an invalid?"

Tanchum wiped his hands on the napkin and studied them. "As a matter of fact, I have."

"They are delightful children," Hannah said. "We would all be happy to have them stay with us."

Tanchum remained silent. He wanted the boys near him. He needed them!

Dovid seemed to read his mind. "Is it fair to the children? Wouldn't they be happier here?"

Tanchum regarded his older brother resentfully. "Do you realize how truly wealthy you are?" he asked. "You have everything: a wife and children, a home of your own. Shall I give away what is the most meaningful to me? Yanky and Chaim are my life. What is left without them?"

"Your whole life is before you," Dovid insisted, resting his hand on his brother's sleeve. "*B'ezras Hashem*, you will marry and have children of your own. But right now, they complicate the situation. You offer Chaim and Yanky your love and accumulated wisdom, but is that enough? They need a mother and siblings. And who will agree to marry a man with your background who also comes with two adopted sons?"

Wounded by the truth in his brother's words, Tanchum turned his face away.

Dovid continued, "You have the means to support them, but no one can give something they don't have. The boys' parents wanted their sons to live in a home where Jewish values are second nature. With all your good intentions, Tanchum, you are still learning what that means. Think about what is best for Yanky and Chaim!"

Tanchum blinked away the dampness that stung his eyes. This was the most difficult decision he'd had to make since he'd discovered his family — and also the most crucial.

84

NACHMAN AND MEIR ARRIVED IN THE FLEDGLING STATE of Israel in April 1948, on the day the British hanged Hagganah fighters Dov Gruner, Yechiel Drezner, Eliezer Kashani and Mordechai El'kachi.

Their first stop was a shul, where they met Dov Weiss, whose sons were active in the underground. "You can stay at my place until you get organized," he offered when he heard that the boys had just arrived. "My house is open, and we usually have youngsters like you for meals."

That night they learned what he meant by "youngsters like you." There was a constant stream of young men, and the only subject discussed was the upcoming war. Everyone seethed with anger at the British duplicity and their open support of the Arabs. Behind the bravado, their fear of annihilation was real.

"I think we should join the Hagganah," Nachman announced.

Meir frowned. "Did we just survive one war in order to dive headfirst into another?"

"What choice is there? The Arabs are intent on destroying us all; they don't care that we are hoping to rebuild our lives after the *Gehinnom* in Europe.

"They just want to throw us into the sea!"

On their fifth day in Haifa, news arrived that Meir Feinstein and Moshe Barazani had blown themselves up with an improvised explosive device shortly before they were scheduled to be hanged by the British. Anger reached fever pitch. There was talk of raiding the citadel in Acre to free the remaining prisoners.

Nachman and Meir approached Dov Weiss. "We want to volunteer," they told him.

"We really need your help, men," he replied. "I'm proud of you. My son will put you in touch with the right people."

The cousins were promptly conscripted into the Hagganah division of the northern region. Their commanding officer was a veteran *kibbutznik* named Jordan Shaked who had famously broken the blockade on Tzefat single-handedly, by maneuvering his truck into a British convoy on the narrow road leading up the mountain.

"How do they expect me to accomplish anything with these poor excuses for soldiers?" Tzvi Drori grumbled.

"Maybe you'd rather serve in the Jerusalem Corridor?" Jordan asked.

Tzvi grimaced. "It can't be worse than this."

"Worse, my friend, much worse. Remember that American reporter we met in Jaffa last month?"

"Kennedy?"

"Right. He traveled to Jerusalem with some of our boys, and couldn't get over what child's play it is to ambush the convoys. The entire surrounding area is under Arab control. They just have to pick us off when the trucks slow down to get through the pass. Kennedy photographed the skeletons of dozens of wrecked trucks strewn along the way. Jerusalem is under siege and it is vital to break through, but the losses are nearly unsustainable."

"What's that got to do with the situation in the north?"

"The best fighters have to be sent to Jerusalem to replace the fallen, which leaves *us* the new immigrants."

"A handful of experienced fighters against seasoned soldiers from Syria, Lebanon, Iraq and Trans-Jordan, rounded out with new recruits who just got off the boat last week and don't even speak Hebrew. How am I supposed to communicate with them?"

"They're good men," Jordan reassured Tzvi. "You've got Yossi and Ari, and they will translate until the new men learn to speak Ivrit. I'm confident they'll pick it up fast. These men are not pampered Mama's boys. They've been through one war already, and they won't run away when you need them."

"I'll do what I can to get them into shape," Tzvi promised, though his expression clearly expressed his doubts.

"Good. I'm off to Haifa for a staff meeting. The Brits may be withdrawing earlier than the original plan calls for, and we have to be prepared. I hope to be back here by morning."

"What's the situation there?"

"The British still control the port area. The Carmeli brigade is consolidating the rest of the city. Fighting is pretty fierce."

"Any Arab civilians left in Haifa?"

"Most of them evacuated, but there are persistent rumors about a substantial number that took refuge in Wadi Nisnas and Wadi Salib."

Jordan climbed into his truck. The men clasped hands through the open window, parting with words of encouragement to disguise the worry in their hearts. The vehicle pulled out with squealing tires, spewing gravel as it fought for traction. Tzvi Drori stepped back and watched until it disappeared, then turned to his ragtag band.

"All right, men. Get into formation!"

Yossi and Ari quickly translated the words into Yiddish, and 50 recruits scrambled to their feet. Tzvi walked up and down the line, shaking his head in disappointment. This was an army?

After hours of rapid push-ups, running and rolling, climbing up cliffs and over walls, the company was near exhaustion. A supper of pita, techina, boiled eggs, tomatoes and cucumbers was followed by elementary military exercises using brooms in place of rifles. "They're marginally better than they were before," Tzvi admitted to Yossi. "Tell them to go to sleep. Tomorrow we fight!"

"Remind me why we agreed to enlist," Nachman groaned. He folded his solitary blanket into thirds, in a vain attempt to cushion some of his aching body from the rocky ground.

Meir lay back against a boulder, wrapping his blanket around himself against the evening chill. "We've been through worse."

"True," Nachman agreed, stifling a yawn. "Better to die in Eretz Yisrael than in cursed Poland."

The next morning, the company was sent to reinforce the out-numbered Hagganah fighters in Tzefat.

"Tzefat!" Meir was ecstatic as they marched. "Do you know where we're going, Nachman? We're on our way to Tzefat!"

The road leading up the mountain was guarded by Arab fighters barricaded in Beit Shalva. Drori's men succeeded in capturing it along with the nearby villages of Ein Zaytim and Biriya. Flushed with victory, the company entered the old city of Tzefat, where they were greeted with cheers from the exhausted defenders.

Nachman and Meir carried a stretcher bearing a wounded fighter. They made their way to the field hospital set up in the ancient Ari Ashkenazi Synagogue. An exhausted doctor pointed to an empty area where they could set their burden down.

Meir bent down beside the man, who was pale and gasping. "We've brought you to the hospital," he told him gently. Addressing the doctor, he added, "He's lost a lot of blood."

"I can see that." As the doctor took out his stethoscope, the young soldier gave a shuddering breath, and expired. The doctor covered him with a blanket and returned to his duties. "The *Chevra Kaddisha* will be here in an hour," he told the boys. "They'll prepare him for burial."

Meir felt tears in his eyes. *"Baruch Dayan Ha'emes.* I don't even know his name. Can we accompany him to the *beis hachayim*?" he asked. "When will the funeral take place?"

The doctor gave him a sympathetic glance. "Not before midnight."

"Why so late?"

"The cemetery is visible to the Arabs. The only way to get there is by crawling on your stomach in the dead of night."

"Can we wait here until the *Chevra Kaddisha* comes? Someone should stand guard over the body and say *Tehillim*."

"You have to get permission from your commander. This is war, boys."

A tremendous explosion rocked the walls of the shul. "What was that?" Meir yelped.

The doctor was impassive. "From time to time, Arabs in the citadel roll barrels of explosives down the mountain into the Jewish Quarter. Sometimes they cause damage, but mostly they just frighten people."

"Where are all the civilians who live in Tzefat? Did they evacuate?"

"Noncombatants are quartered in six stations. This is one of them." The doctor gestured toward the interior of the synagogue. "The men are building trenches and bunkers. A major battle is expected very soon. You boys had better get back to your company."

"Too bad Doctor Stern is not here," Nachman commented as they took their places along the southern wall of the shul, peering through a slit between the stones.

Meir examined his Czech-made rifle. "Better for him that he's not."

"Does he know we left Ravensdorf?"

"I wrote him the day after we arrived in Palestine. He should get the letter next week."

"I wonder how he's doing in America."

"His last letter sounded better than the earlier ones. I think he's beginning to acclimate. He mentioned that his older brother wants to adopt Yanky and Chaim and he thinks it will be better for them to grow up in a family. He said he's making better progress in his learning than anyone expected."

"How long has it been since you and I sat down to a *blatt Gemara*?"

"Too long. Let's make that a priority as soon as we finish this war!"

"Agreed!"

85

C AREFUL, IT'S HEAVY!"

"Are you joking?" Tanchum easily hefted the bundle of *succah* boards onto his shoulder while grabbing the ladder with his other hand.

"Whew!" Alexander gasped, gathering up the hammers and some stray nails. "It usually takes three of us to carry all that down to the basement. Are you sure you can manage by yourself?"

"What? Finished already?" Their youngest sister climbed the ladder after Tanchum had maneuvered his burden downstairs. She was followed by her husband, who was precariously balancing a heavy basket of freshly laundered sheets. "Can you believe it?" she asked, picking up the first sheet. "We never had the whole *succah* down and put away by the day after *Isru Chag*!"

Michoel leaned against the wall and watched his wife with amusement as the wind whipped the wet white fabric around her face and shoulders. "Ooh!" Mindy squealed. "Help me, Michoel!"

Tanchum's brother-in-law grabbed a corner and held it steady while Mindy struggled to pin the sheet to the line. She stood back, watching it flap and snap in the wind.

"Looks like rain," Alexander commented.

Mindy studied the gray sky. "Not yet," she said, despite the clouds blanketing the sky. She picked up another sheet. "The wind will dry them in no time."

"Let me help you." Tanchum returned from the basement.

"No, thank you. Look at your hands! You'll leave black smudges on the sheets and I'll just have to wash them all over again. You and Sender go down to the kitchen. There's still some *kokush* left. Michoel can help me."

"Come on, little brother." Alexander put a hand on his shoulder. "It's getting cold up here and the thought of a cup of hot cocoa is very appealing. "

Tanchum paused. The view of Williamsburg from the roof was dramatically different than the perspective from the street. He didn't mind the cold and he found the wind invigorating.

"Coming?" Sender asked impatiently.

Sensing that the young couple wanted privacy, he followed his brother downstairs. Maybe he would come up again later, just to be by himself for awhile.

Rabbi Stern was puttering around the kitchen. He looked up with a smile. "Need a break?" he asked.

"No, Tatte. We finished already. I have to get home to help Devory. Mindy said something about *kokush*?"

"Here, help yourself. Hannah sent it over and it's very good. Tell Devory that I appreciate her letting you come to help us today."

Alexander polished off a generous slice of cake. "Tanchum did almost everything," he admitted. "I only told him what to do and where to put it all. Next year he'll already know it all, so you won't need me anymore."

"Next year, *im yirtzeh Hashem*, Tanchum will be married and perhaps he will have his own *succah*."

"*Yehi ratzon!* I'll just say good-bye to the Mamme, and then I'll leave. It should be a *gezunte vinter!*"

"Thank you, Sender. A *gezunte vinter* to you, too."

Rabbi Stern refilled Tanchum's mug with hot cocoa and sat down beside his son. "It's been so busy these last few weeks," he said. "Chaim's bar mitzvah and all the Yomim Tovim. We haven't had much time together to really talk. Tell me about the hospital and your work."

Tanchum dabbed chocolate residue from his lips with a napkin. With little fanfare, he had completed the examinations required in order to practice medicine in the State of New York, and recently he had accepted a position as assistant surgeon at Maimonides Hospital. "It's the best thing I could have done," he told his father between bites. "I am very satisfied, and it is rewarding to do something that makes me feel competent."

"I realize the last year has been difficult. We've tried to support you as best we can. We're so proud of the progress you've made, in every way."

Tanchum nodded. "I know that you are always here for me when I need you. I couldn't have come this far without your help, and I hope you will always have *nachas* from me. . ."

"And yet?"

Tanchum shrugged.

"You know that we've had several good suggestions regarding a *shidduch* for you."

"Mamme mentioned it."

"It would give us both such pleasure to see you start building your own family." Rabbi Stern spoke with affection, but there was a tinge of sadness as well. "We really don't understand why you refuse to at least consider any of the suggestions."

"I hear what you're saying," Tanchum responded, without lifting his eyes from the plate still adorned with the last of the *kokush* crumbs. "I realize that it is the next sensible step, and I appreciate your concern — but it's not the right time yet."

"I fear that you are making a mistake, son. As the great Hillel said, 'If not now, when?'"

"If it were logical I could explain, but it's not. Call it intuition, but I am not ready to cope with marriage at this time. I still have so much more to learn."

"Tanchum, I have in mind a certain fine young woman, from an *ehrliche* family. What would happen if you just meet her once? You might discover that your vacillation is unjustified. Won't you give her a chance, for your mother's sake?"

Tanchum did not know how to refuse, but he knew he could not agree. "Tatte," he said, "I have no intention of marrying at this time. It would not be fair."

"But you might change your mind."

"I'm sorry. I really am."

That night, Tanchum had trouble falling asleep. He tossed and turned. The clanking of the radiator grated on his nerves. It was too hot and he threw off the blanket; then it was too cold and he pulled it back on. Finally, he turned on the small lamp beside his bed and tried to read.

A rustling sound outside the door drew his attention. He slipped on slippers and went to investigate. His mother was in the hall outside his room.

"Mamme! What's the matter? Are you feeling unwell?"

"No, my dear, Actually I'm feeling better than usual," she smiled. "I couldn't sleep. I thought I would go to the kitchen and fix myself a glass of milk. I saw the light under your door. You're not sleeping, either."

"Come inside!" he told her, taking his mother's arm and gently leading her to a chair. After tucking a quilt around her, he went to the kitchen and returned with two glasses of warm milk sweetened with honey.

"I rest all day, so it's often hard to sleep through the night," she explained. "But what is keeping my son awake after midnight?"

He sat on the bed facing her, but didn't speak. She shook her head. "Tanchum, tell me what is troubling you. I am your mother. Share your thoughts with me. Perhaps I can help."

She watched him intently, and the devotion in her blue-gray eyes resonated like a chord in his heart. He really wanted to confide, to spill out the contradictions disturbing his peace of mind, but he was afraid. If she knew who he really was, who he had been, would she still love him? The only person he had ever met with whom he felt safe enough to share his deepest thoughts had been Fraydl, during the war.

The memory of the lost girl shook him. Rebbetzin Stern quickly reached out and rested her hand on his arm.

"Trust me, Tanchum," she said softly. "There is nothing you could say that would change the way I feel about you. A mother's love is forever, no matter what. It grieves me to see your distress."

Tanchum shook his head, as if that could make the bad memories go away. "I have begun to realize why I cannot get on with my life," he said.

She waited patiently, her eyes riveted on his.

"Are you sure you're not too tired? It may take a long time to explain everything."

Rebbetzin Stern shook her head. "I have all the time in the world for you," she told him. "Start from the beginning, and the words will come by themselves."

Tanchum began to speak, and the words poured out. He spoke of his earliest memories, about the boy named Karl Emsbach and the woman he called "Mutter." He told her about the servants who were kind, even as they betrayed him by keeping the secret of his real identity. Until now, the rebbetzin only knew what her husband had told her. This was the first time she was hearing the details directly from her son.

By the time Tanchum finished describing boarding school, his military service and the war, the first pale flush of daylight lit the sky. His mother's blue-gray eyes darkened when he spoke of his uncle Heinrich, but she squeezed his hand and whispered, "I am so proud of you," when he described hiding the children from the Nazi mob and then taking them in for the duration of the war.

"I am not proud," he admitted. "I am ashamed. I understand the bitter survivors in the concentration camp who wanted to lynch me. Mamme, I wore the Nazi uniform. I was trained to follow orders. I am tormented by the thought that if I had been commanded to commit atrocities, I would have carried out my orders."

"Hush, my dear. Know that there was not a single day that I did not *daven* for you. I couldn't know what you were going through, but I constantly pleaded with Hashem to protect you from harm, and Hashem hears a mother's prayers. He saved you from the plans of that wicked Heinrich Mauer, may his memory be erased. He brought you home to me."

Her pale cheeks were flushed, but she seemed calm and her breathing was regular. "You are tired now, Mamme," he noticed. "Let me help you back to your room?"

"Yes," she agreed with a rueful sigh. "Having you near gives me strength, but there is a limit. Promise me that we will continue this conversation another time. There is much you have not yet said."

"I promise." Tanchum took her arm and gently guided her back to her bedroom. He kissed her and returned to his own bed, where he fell into a restful sleep. It had been good to unburden his heart. For the first time in years, perhaps in his entire adult life, Tanchum felt at peace. The wounds of estrangement were beginning to heal.

All too soon it was morning. At breakfast, Rabbi Stern handed an envelope to Tanchum. "It's postmarked Israel!" he said with excitement. "Can you believe it, Shaindel?" he turned to his wife. "Israel! Jews have returned to the Holy Land!"

Tanchum studied the return address before opening the envelope. "It's from my former employees," he explained to his parents. "They helped me with all the technical details when my house was made into a convalescent home for survivors."

86

THEIR NEIGHBOR MRS. LIPSCHITZ SETTLED HERSELF INTO the armchair with a sigh. She accepted a glass of tea from Fraydl, chose a lump of sugar to hold between her teeth and sipped thoughtfully.

"Please taste the strudel?" Rivka offered.

"Thank you, I don't mind. Ah, delicious." She gave Fraydl a sharp look that flustered the girl. "You should be married already," she declared in a disapproving tone.

"All in good time," Rivka retorted defensively. "The war is not over yet."

"Who said you have to wait until the armistice is signed?"

"Do you have a good suggestion?"

"As a matter of fact, I do." Their visitor smiled slyly.

Rivka sucked in her breath with surprise. "You do?" she asked. "Who?"

The visitor helped herself to a second slice of strudel. "Two possibilities," she announced blithely. "You can choose either one, whichever you prefer."

Rivka looked at her sister. "Fraydl, I think I should speak privately with Mrs. Lipschitz. Do you mind leaving us alone?"

Fraydl stood up with alacrity. "Good afternoon," she said pleasantly. "It's a beautiful day and I'm happy for a good reason to take a walk." She took her coat from the hook by the door and went outside. The paved street was wet from an early-morning rain and a sharp breeze teased the brown leaves still clinging to the trees, but the sun was shining and the fresh air was invigorating.

She returned an hour later with rosy cheeks, to find her sister still seated at the table. "Is Mrs. Lipschitz here?" she asked, looking about as she closed the door behind her.

"No, she left. Listen to what she had to say and tell me what you think. You know that times are hard and the financial situation is difficult for everyone. Mrs.Lipschitz has a large house and her children are not living at home. She's lonely. After Yom Tov, she decided to take in boarders. Two young men applied. They had recommendations from the Rav, so she accepted them. Of course, she kept her eye on them. According to her, they both have very good characters."

"How does she know?"

"They are tidy, polite and they paid her up front in cash."

"What else does she know about them?"

"They're cousins from a village near Vilna. Not Chassidish, but good *ehrlicher* families. They survived several concentration camps, the only ones left from their family."

"That's not a lot of information."

"They were inducted into the army as soon as they came to Palestine and they were with Aaron when he was wounded. I'll ask him about them tomorrow when I go to the rehabilitation center to visit."

"Are they still serving in the army?"

"Technically, yes. They were given leave for six weeks when the northern border was secured, and that's why they needed a temporary place to stay. That's also why she came here today, because she wants you to meet one of them before they have to return."

"Would the *elteren* have approved?"

"How can we know, Fraydl?" Rivka felt a great responsibility toward her youngest sister. "It was different before the war. These days, such marriages take place often. We can't offer a dowry, so there will have to be compromises. As the mother, you will be the main influence on your children. I think we should consider it, depending on what Areleh recommends."

Fraydl turned her face and blinked away tears. Being a burden was hard. Perhaps one of these cousins was her *bashert* and Mrs. Lipschitz was Hashem's unlikely *shaliach*? Maybe it wasn't even important how she felt. She would *daven* and let things happen as they would.

"Meir, what did our landlady Lipschitz have to say?"

"You won't believe it."

"Try me."

"She has a *shidduch* to suggest."

"A *yenta* is a *yenta* is a *yenta*, in Poland or in Palestine. I thought I saw that look in her eyes."

"So what do you think about it?"

"About her suggesting a *shidduch* for you?"

"For either of us, actually. She sang the praises of a girl who lives here in Kfar Ata. A real *balabusta* , she says. And pretty."

"Money?"

"No."

"Nobody's perfect."

"Neither am I."

Nachman studied his cousin's face. "You're interested, aren't you?"

"I don't know. Maybe. Well, yes. Aren't you?"

"Not yet. I want to finish with this war and get a job. I want to earn enough money to buy a house and a car before I take a wife."

"Would it bother you if I got married before you?"

"I will wish you *mazel tov* with all my heart. You haven't even met her and you're already envisioning the *chuppah*. What if she's ugly or stupid? What do you know about her or her family?"

"She's Ari Tzipori's aunt."

"Ari? He was a good guy. Too bad about what happened. He was in the wrong place at the wrong time."

"It's a miracle the mortar didn't kill him. I wonder if he'll ever be able to walk again. . ."

"The girl is related to him?"

"He's her nephew."

"The Rav knows all the families in Kfar Ata. Ask him about her after Maariv."

"I told Mrs. Lipschitz that I'd give her an answer tomorrow."

"Meir?"

"Yes?"

"You need a haircut."

"We can ask Mrs. Lipschitz for a pair of scissors."

"And Meir. . ."

"*Nu?*"

"You can't meet a girl with those clothes."

Looking down, Meir's face was stricken. "You're right. What am I going to do?"

"We've saved enough between us to buy a second-hand suit. Let's go into Haifa tomorrow and see if we can find something reasonable that fits."

"I set up a *chavrusa* with the Rav tomorrow morning."

"No problem. We're almost the same size. I'll buy a suit for both of us. You'll make a good impression at your *shidduch* meeting, and I'll make a good impression when I go for my job interview at the textile factory."

"You're a genius, Nachman!"

"It runs in the family, cousin."

87

PROFESSOR ZIMMERMAN?"

"Yes, Dr. Stern?"

"I would like to discuss something of a personal nature with you, if you have time."

"Certainly. Let's go to my room."

Tanchum followed the senior researcher and head surgeon through the back passage between the operating rooms and office block. Zimmerman unlocked the door and tossed his scrubs onto an empty chair. "Have a seat," he said, gesturing toward a leather sofa on the far side of his office.

Tanchum waited while the man put on a suit jacket and knotted his tie in front of a small mirror. "I have a meeting to attend in half an hour," Dr. Zimmerman explained. "What can I do for you in the meantime?"

"It's about the cardiac catheterization technique you are developing."

"Ah, yes. I am very satisfied with our progress. Would you like to try performing it on our patient tomorrow morning? You have adequate skill with a scalpel, and a quick mind. In fact, I intended to suggest this to you soon in any case."

"Actually, I have something else in mind. My mother appears to be entering end-stage heart failure, but the exact problem causing the condition is unclear. As one of the foremost experts in this field, I would like to hear whether you would recommend catheterization for the purpose of achieving an accurate diagnosis. She's in her late 60's. Would the procedure endanger her, or does the prospect of improving her condition justify the risk?"

"Have you spoken with John Gibbons? He's leading the research on a heart-lung machine and has successfully repaired lesions using open-heart surgery on animals in his laboratory."

"I have been in touch with him. He is very enthusiastic about his work, but estimates he needs several more years before it will be possible to operate on human patients. Frankly, I fear my mother will not live long enough to benefit from his research."

"I understand." The professor leaned back in his chair and stared at the ceiling with pursed lips, deep in thought. "It's a difficult ethical dilemma," he mused. "On the one hand, with an accurate diagnosis it might be possible to prolong her life, or at least the quality of her life. On the other hand, in her delicate condition she might not survive the experience.

"This is not a decision either of us can make, Dr. Stern. I suggest that your parents seek spiritual counsel. You are a religious man. Address this question to your rabbi."

"I appreciate your time, sir," Tanchum said, rising to leave.

"If she decides to go through with the procedure, I am prepared to accept the case. Bring me your mother's records and make an appointment with my secretary. Obviously time is of the essence, since every day brings further deterioration. In 10 days I am scheduled to address an international conference in Geneva. If you can get back to me by Friday I will work her into my schedule before I leave."

"Thank you, professor. I am grateful for your generous offer."

"It is my pleasure, my friend. I see a future for you and me working together in this field. Once Gibbon's invention is operating effectively, cardiology is going to become a specialty in high demand. With the administrative support of Maimonides Hospital, we can be pioneers in this exciting project and save many lives."

"Thank you for your confidence in me, Professor Zimmerman."

"My best wishes for your mother to have a full recovery."

"Thank you, sir.'

When Tanchum came home, he first spoke to his father about the idea, and then his brothers. A family conference was convened.

After much discussion, Rabbi Stern spoke. "This is a question of *dinei nefashos* and we are not qualified to make a decision. We understand the logic of your argument, Tanchum, but it is natural for us to fear the possible consequences of an experimental procedure. It is not possible to trust our own logic or feelings. We must seek *da'as Torah*."

The others agreed. "Tanchum, you must go to the Rav because you are the only one able to explain all the medical issues involved," his father directed. "Dovid, you are the oldest. You will accompany Tanchum. We will remain here to await the final decision."

A cold rain was falling when the brothers left their father's house. Tanchum drove, keeping a careful distance from the winking taillights of the vehicles ahead. The reflection of the colored traffic lights gleamed against the wet street. "You do the talking," Tanchum told Dovid. "I'll just listen and be prepared to answer any questions."

The venerable Rav himself opened the door to receive them. "Come in, come in." His expression was warm and welcoming. They followed the Rav to his study and described the situation as fully as possible. The Rav asked many questions, clarifying every aspect of Rebbetzin Stern's condition and the chances for improvement. After some thought, he requested their permission to consult with the Chazon Ish in Bnai Brak.

Tanchum and Dovid were shown to an outer room, where a few other men were waiting their turn to speak with the Rav. The monotonous ticking of an old grandfather clock was the only sound other than the murmuring of *Tehillim*.

"How long do you think this will take?" Tanchum whispered to his brother.

"It's not really possible to predict," Dovid said. "I assume it will be a person-to-person call, so it depends on when the operator gets through and whether Rav Karelitz is available." He handed a *Tehillim* to Tanchum and took one himself.

Some time later, the Rav's assistant summoned them back to the study.

"It should be with *hatzlachah*," the Rav said. He appeared tired, but his eyes sparkled with warmth. "A *refuah shelaimah* for Shaindel *bas* Leah!"

It was very late when they returned, and their mother was sleeping. Rabbi Stern received the news from his sons. "While you were gone your mother and I discussed this, and of course we are both prepared to follow the Rav's decision. May your surgeon be a good *shaliach!*" he told Tanchum.

The rebbetzin heard the news the next morning. She nodded her agreement without further discussion. Plans were made to transfer her by ambulance on the same day to the Department of Cardiology. Final tests were performed and surgery scheduled before the end of the week.

Tanchum stayed with his mother until the minute the anesthesiologist administered the drugs to put her to sleep. His heart beat rapidly at the thought that he might have been instrumental in helping to prolong his mother's life or, heaven forbid, the opposite. Quelling his fears, he kissed her cheek and went out to the waiting area to join his siblings in reciting fervent *Tehillim* and praying to Hashem that He guide the surgeon's hands to a successful conclusion.

Outside the operating theater, the family stormed the heavens with prayer for their matriarch's recovery, while inside the catheterization procedure went ahead according to protocol. Professor Zimmerman's newly developed method employed simultaneous catheterization of both sides of the heart. In this operation he was assisted by the most senior surgeons on staff.

"Professor, the left catheter seems to be blocked. I've tried every angle without success."

"I'll take over. Landman, have you injected the contrast medium?"

"Yes, sir."

"Increase the dose of anticoagulant gradually," he instructed the nurse. "Meyers, set up the fluoroscope." There were several moments of tense silence. "Give me another catheter," the professor ordered. "This one could be defective. Give me the smallest size on the tray."

The second catheter entered the intravascular area alongside the first, and halted. Continued manipulation was fruitless. "Let's see the fluoroscope." The surgeons turned their heads to study the green screen.

"It's a massive mitral stenosis," Professor Zimmerman concluded, shaking his head in commiseration. "There's nothing we can do. Remove the catheters."

Before the assistants could carry out his instructions, the figure on the operating table began to convulse. "Immobilize the patient!" Zimmerman screamed, close to panic at this unexpected development.

The paroxysm ceased almost immediately. "Vital signs?" the professor barked, a tremor in his usually confident voice.

"Temperature 98.6. Perfusion 100%. Pulse 80 bpm. Blood pressure 120/90, EKG normal," the nurse read out.

"*What?*" Professor Zimmerman's voice rose in disbelief. "That's impossible! This patient hasn't had vital signs that ideal in years. Double-check the connections."

"Every sign is normal," the nurse confirmed.

"Professor, look at the fluoroscope!"

Zimmerman turned to study the screen. Both catheters had passed through the narrowed valve and blood was flowing freely between the atrium and ventricle of his patient's heart. No one spoke as the catheters were withdrawn and the patient disconnected from the monitors. They all knew that they had just witnessed the impossible.

The professor opened the door from the surgery and was immediately surrounded by members of the Stern family.

"I can't explain it," he began, his breath heaving from a delayed reaction to the shock he'd just endured. "We discovered an irreparable blockage in Mrs. Stern's mitral valve."

The surgeon stopped speaking, unable to continue. Someone handed him a glass of water and he gulped it down. Then he put his arm around Tanchum's shoulder. "I thought we lost her," he confided in an awe-filled voice. "She had a brief seizure at the most critical juncture. It was completely unexpected. It should have killed her, but instead, it unblocked the valve. It doesn't make sense, I know, but the spasm pushed both catheters through at once, and. . ." He didn't know how to continue.

Rabbi Stern blinked. "Doctor, please explain yourself. What is my wife's condition? Will she recover?"

"Rabbi," Dr. Zimmerman said, "your wife is a medical miracle. May you have many years together in good health and prosperity!"

Overcome with emotion, the professor turned and strode quickly away.

88

THERE WAS A HUSHED CLICK AS THE DOOR CLOSED AND Rivka secured the bolt.

"*Nu?*" she turned expectantly. Fraydl appeared frozen, lost in another world.

"*Nu?*" Rivka repeated, raising her voice.

Fraydl lifted her palms in the timeless gesture of helplessness. "What can I say?"

"He seems very nice, Meir Glaser."

"Yes, he is nice. He's quite nice."

"But?"

Fraydl sighed. "I wish I could just tell you, 'He's not the one,' and that would be the end of it."

"Of course you can't." Rivka sat beside Fraydl. She took her hand and stroked it. "You don't necessarily have to know the answer the first time you meet," she reassured her youngest sister. "The main thing is whether or not you felt comfortable with him."

"It's not his fault that I didn't. He tried very hard to make me comfortable."

"Did the conversation flow smoothly?"

"He was talking most of the time."

"That sounds fairly standard."

Avoiding Rivka's penetrating look, Fraydl cast her eyes down.

"So there's no reason to refuse meeting him again?"

Fraydl bit her lip. "I suppose not," she acknowledged reluctantly. "Do you think it will be better the next time?"

"I assume so. It's the first time you ever met a man for *shidduch* purposes, so it's really not surprising that you felt self-conscious and under stress."

"Not exactly." Fraydl hadn't meant to say the words aloud.

"What?"

"Nothing."

"You met someone before you came to Palestine?" Rivka was astounded that such a thing could have taken place without her knowing about it.

Fraydl was thinking of the hours she spent in Dr. Emsbach's study discussing the meaning of life and of *Yiddishkeit* while Yanky and Chaim played with the toy soldiers on the carpet beside them. Those times had been pleasant because she had so fully believed in the ultimate triumph of good over evil. Now her little nephews were gone forever and she was much less naïve. Fraydl closed her eyes tightly to shut out the memories.

Sensing her sister's distress, Rivka insisted, "Fraydl, what happened? I want you to tell me about it."

Fraydl searched desperately for an answer that would satisfy Rivka without revealing the true reason. "Moishe Katz," she recalled with relief. "I met him in the DP Camp shortly after the war ended."

"Moishe Katz, our sister Sarah's husband?"

"Yes. He wanted us to marry and start a new life in America, Rivka. I almost accepted his proposal. But, in the end, I called it off. He left for New York and I have not heard from him again."

Rivka stared into the distance. "Moishe'le Katz," she murmured, reeling from the pain of a reopened wound. It was several minutes before she could collect her thoughts and return to the issue at hand.

"Fraydl, what shall I tell my neighbor?"

"Do you really think there's a point in meeting him again?"

"Do you have any reason *not* to go forward?"

"Not really. I just expected to feel something else… and I don't."

"What *do* you feel?"

"Numb."

"Nothing negative, though?"

"Nothing at all."

"Meet him again. If you still don't feel something positive, then at least you'll know you gave him a fair chance."

Fraydl looked at her sister searchingly. "Rivka, what do you think about it?"

"I did my homework, Fraydl. He's a worthy young man, and would make a good husband."

"I want to get married, I really do. I'm just afraid of making the wrong decision."

"Hashem will help you decide. There's no reason to rush. Take your time. Meanwhile I'll tell Mrs. Lipschitz that she can schedule another meeting."

There was a knock on the door. "That's surely the *shadchan*," Rivka said. "You'd better wait in your room while we talk."

"*Shalom*, Mrs. Lipschitz," Rivka stepped back to let her neighbor enter, taking note of the woman's broad smile.

"*Shalom u'v'rachah!*" her neighbor replied with a wink. "Shall we get right to the point? What does your sister say about *mein* Meir'ke?"

Rivka noticed the possessive pronoun, and smiled. It had been a long time since her friend had looked so full of life. "So far, so good," she replied noncommittally.

"Ahhh," Mrs. Lipschitz nodded with satisfaction. "I thought so. He's such a nice boy, and she's a lovely girl. Anyone with eyes in their head can see it's *bashert*."

Rivka placed a tray with hot tea and sugar cubes before her visitor. "There are still details to work out," she reminded the widow.

Mrs. Lipschitz flicked her fingers in dismissal. "This is a different generation, Rivka. They'll decide what they want to do with their lives by themselves."

"Fraydl and I are old fashioned. I'd like to know what the expectations are."

The other woman took a long sip of tea before getting down to business. "The *shidduch gelt* will be whatever is customary. You know I don't have a lot of experience in the field," she beamed. "I suggest we ask Rav Binyamin. Whatever he decides is fine as far as I'm concerned.

"Meir will ask for an immediate discharge from the army, and considering that an armistice is about to be signed his request is likely to be granted. They can live rent-free by you or rent from me for the first year — we both have enough room, right? Meanwhile Meir will get a job and they'll begin saving money for their own home. Didn't you say Fraydl took an accounting course after the war? I'm sure she can get a position at the textile factory. Now that the war is winding up, they will undoubtedly increase production. The wedding expenses are your responsibility, but of course the wedding will be modest and perhaps they can repay you later. What else remains to discuss?"

"You seem to have thought of everything," Rivka agreed. "I understand that the young man is interested in continuing?"

The woman smiled and raised her hands heavenward. "He's *shikker*," she confided. "Ready to sign on the dotted line."

"Oh." Recalling her sister's obvious lack of enthusiasm, Rivka searched for the right words to respond. "Fraydl is not there yet. She's still unsure."

"What's not to be sure about?" demanded Mrs. Lipschitz, setting her glass down with a clunk.

Rivka sighed. "It's different with girls, I suppose," she tried to soften her answer. "Fraydl wants to think about it. She isn't ready to give a final answer."

"Young people these days!" the widow shook her head. "Where do they get their ideas from? When I was young, we knew to trust our elders with such important decisions."

"Yes, but as you said, things are different today. I suggest that they meet again in another few days."

"*Ach*, the boy's so smitten I thought it would be unnecessary. All right, I'll tell him to come tomorrow evening."

"Tomorrow is a bit too soon for us, Mrs. Lipschitz. I was thinking more about Wednesday, at the earliest."

The visitor clucked her tongue. "That's much too late," she declared. "*Nu*, we'll have to compromise. Tuesday afternoon. If everything goes smoothly, you can hold the vort on Tuesday night." She drained the last drops of tea from her glass. "It should be *b'sha'ah tovah!*"

Rivka peeked out from behind the curtain, watching her ample neighbor plod heavily down the street toward her own home. Life had been so complicated lately. A *simchah* was something they all needed right now.

She thought about Fraydl, and wondered what Tuesday afternoon would bring.

89

I N THE MIDDLE OF THE NIGHT, RIVKA WAS AWAKENED BY bloodcurdling screams. She flew out of her bed and ran to the next room. "Fraydl! Wake up, wake up! It's only a dream, *lubinkeh*." She shook her sister's shoulders until the young woman opened wide, frightened eyes.

"I was running. Someone was after me. There wasn't any place to hide," Fraydl sobbed, covering her eyes with her hands.

"Shhh. It's all over now." Rivka stroked her hair and planted a kiss on her sister's forehead. "Put on your robe and come into the kitchen with me. I'll fix you something hot to drink and then you'll be able to go back to sleep."

Fraydl stared at the cocoa dribbling over the sides of her mug. She dabbed ineffectively at the dark puddle on the blue-checked oilcloth and whispered, "It was so real."

"It was just a nightmare." Rivka wet the dishrag and wiped up the spill. "You're safe now, Fraydl. Look around. Everything is calm and quiet. The danger is gone. It's all over."

Fraydl sipped hot cocoa and closed her eyes. The monotonous ticking of the clock was soothing. Half an hour later she yawned, drowsy enough to return to bed.

Rivka kissed her cheek lightly. She tucked the blanket around her sister's shoulders, the way their Mamme always had when the girls were small. "*Shlufenkeh gehen*," she murmured. Fraydl smiled sleepily. Her bed was soft and warm and she was soon asleep.

It took Rivka longer to calm down. Since Areleh had left, she often woke in the middle of the night and was unable to fall asleep again before dawn. With a sigh she opened her yarn basket and tried to concentrate on the sweater set she was knitting for Malky's youngest.

Fraydl's screams still echoed in her head. Rivka tried to put herself in her sister's place and imagine what she must be feeling. It struck her that she really didn't know very much about Fraydl's experiences. Perhaps it really was too soon to expect her to plunge into marriage?

Rivka had glimpsed the blue number tattooed on Meir Glaser's forearm. She had heard so many stories about the ordeals of concentration-camp prisoners. He must have endured *Gehinnom* there. It was likely that Meir also suffered from nightmares. What implications would this have for his wife? Would these two young people be able to understand and comfort each other? Could the scars ever heal?

Rivka slid her fingers through the nearly finished sleeve and imagined a baby's tiny hand peeking out. *Motherhood will make Fraydl whole again*, she thought hopefully, and exchanged her knitting for a *sefer Tehillim*.

Fraydl met Meir Glaser again the next afternoon. This time they had more to speak about and the meeting lasted a little longer than the first time. Meir asked questions and waited patiently for Fraydl's answers. It was hard for her to open up to him, to describe her parents and brothers and sisters and the lives they had led in Vienna. Despite their common outlook, at the end of his visit the gap between them was still unbridged.

"Are you sure?" Mrs. Lipschitz asked with disappointment, when Rivka informed her that Fraydl was not yet ready to commit. "Is she taking this seriously?"

"Very seriously," Rivka reassured her. "You wouldn't want Fraydl to make such an important decision if she has doubts, would you?"

The neighbor frowned. "Of course she has the right to think things over before giving a final answer," she said, though she was obviously not happy about it. Lifting her arms in a gesture of displeasure, Mrs. Lipschitz shook her head, gave an exaggerated sigh and harrumphed, "I just don't know what is going to happen with this younger generation and their modern ideas. In my day, things were done differently."

Rivka touched her friend's arm affectionately. "I do so appreciate your efforts," she said. "We widows have to look out for each other."

Her neighbor bobbed her head, partially appeased. "They are such nice young men, Meir and Nachman."

"Very nice," Rivka agreed.

"If I had a daughter at home, I wouldn't hesitate a minute. They're so responsible and mature for their age."

Rivka nodded. "It may still work out, you know," she smiled. "You and I have done all we can. Now we must let Hashem take over."

Fraydl was relieved when her sister told her that she had more time. "Thank you for understanding," she said. "I can tell that Meir Glazer is a fine person, and it is flattering that he would want to marry me, but. . ."

"But what, Fraydl?"

"I don't know. There's nothing wrong that I can put my finger on. There are times when I want to agree, but then something holds me back. Does that make sense at all?"

"Partially," Rivka responded. "If you are hesitating because you are shy, then you should take courage and move ahead with the *shidduch*. If you feel uncertain because you don't have the emotional reaction you imagined would come, then perhaps all you need is more time and it will develop.

"On the other hand, if something about him is bothering you, it won't go away. Something like that gets worse over time, not better.

Remember that no one is perfect, Fraydl. You have to decide if you can live with whatever is troubling you or not. No one can make that choice except you. Just be sure the decision is your own and don't let anyone else's opinions or expectations take precedence over your intuition."

"I never had trouble making decisions before," Fraydl fretted. "I used my mind to examine the different sides of a question, I tried to think how Mamme or Tatte would have advised me and then I made my decision. It's totally foreign to find myself vacillating about something that I should actually want so much."

Rivka regarded her thoughtfully. "Maybe you need to get away for awhile," she suggested. "The siege in Yerushalayim is finally over. Why don't we go visit Malky and Lipa?"

Fraydl brightened visibly. "Yerushalayim!" she whispered. "I think I would love that."

"Yes, I also need to get away. It will be good for both of us. I want to see my handiwork on my little *einikel!*" Rivka lifted the nearly finished sweater.

"What about Areleh?" Fraydl frowned.

"It'll only be for a few days. There's nothing I can really do anymore to help him now; at this point it's just a matter of time and prayer. We can *daven* for him in Yerushalayim as well as in Kfar Ata."

The two sisters boarded the bus in Haifa later that week, with Fraydl balancing a pan of sweet *lukshen kugel* on her lap during the bumpy ride while Rivka's knitting needles flashed in an attempt to finish a pair of booties to match the tiny sweater.

The same day, Meir and Nachman parted amicably from their landlady and returned to their platoon. "You boys know that I will be happy to see you again after you are released from the army," she said, fussing over the bag of *eyer kichel* she had packed for them. "I'll think I will be able to hold your room until Purim."

"That's great, Mrs. Lipschitz," Meir told her with a dimpled smile. "We're looking forward to coming back to Kfar Ata."

"And to your *cholent,*" Nachman murmured in a sorrowful tone. There was no comparison between army rations and the food they had been enjoying during their furlough. They would miss both the motherly woman and her culinary talent.

The widow beamed. *"Zie gezunt!"* she called after them, wiping a tear from her cheek when the cousins were finally out of sight. "Such good boys. . ."

90

DESPITE HER WARM COAT, IT WAS STILL VERY COLD ON THE unheated bus. Fraydl felt her innate serenity returning with every kilometer that brought her closer to Yerushalayim. From time to time she used her sleeve to clear the windowpane beside her seat, but a steady rain thrummed monotonously on the glass and obscured the view. Shortly before they reached Tel Aviv, a fierce wind suddenly rocked the bus and an even heavier cloudburst exploded from the sky.

"It seems we're having an exceptionally hard winter this year." Rivka raised her voice to be heard over the deafening roar of the rain on the vehicle's metal roof.

Fraydl thought of the previous winter at the *Kinderheim* in France. "It still hasn't snowed yet," she commented, pulling her coat more tightly around herself.

"That doesn't happen very often in Eretz Yisrael." Rivka chuckled at her younger sister's mistaken assumption about winter weather in the Middle East. "We have a completely different climate from Europe." After a moment, she sighed and added, "I remember how I used to miss the snow. During the first years after Avrumi and I moved to Palestine, I thought the winter rains would never stop. At Kfar Ata we were knee deep in mud and still it poured, day after day." Rivka glanced at Fraydl, who was trying to squint through the rain-streaked window. "I used to long for the profound silence and the blanket of white after a snowfall. Do you miss the winters from back home?"

Fraydl's expression softened with her recollections from the years before the war. "It was the skating I loved the most. Did you like to skate on the ice when you were a girl?" she asked with a broad smile. "I used to be so impatient for the lake to finally freeze over. Sarah'le and I flew over the ice until our teeth chattered from the cold. Then we would thaw out for a few minutes beside the bonfire that our brothers lit, before hurrying back to do it all over again. Oh, I loved racing in and out between the other skaters after her! Until I learned how to skate well, she and her girlfriends used to grab my mittens or scarf and spin me around. It was so much fun... And then to come home to a warm house, and take off our wet wraps and have something hot to drink beside the fireplace. . ." Fraydl's voice tapered off.

Before Rivka could share her own memories, a quick succession of lightning bolts flashed over the churning Mediterranean to their right, almost immediately followed by rolling peals of thunder that drowned out every other sound. Fraydl grabbed hold of Rivka's arm in panic, and the older woman smiled indulgently at the childish reaction.

"It's only a rainstorm, Fraydl," she soothed her sister. "Look, it's already letting up."

Fraydl turned to look out the window at the palm trees lining the highway, their broad green fronds dancing in the wind. "The noise of the thunder," Fraydl whispered. "It reminds me of bombs."

Rivka grimaced in self-reproach. She should have been more sensitive. Giving Fraydl's arm a reassuring squeeze, Rivka reminded her, "It's over now. You're safe. You're free. You're beginning a new and different life."

Fraydl sighed. "I think it will never be over for me," she murmured. "I forget sometimes, for a little while, but then it all comes back."

"It's getting better, though," Rivka reminded her."You're feeling much stronger and happier than you used to."

Fraydl turned to her sister with the hint of a smile."Thanks to you," she said. "I really appreciate how much you do for me. I hope I will be able to repay your kindness some day."

"*Sha*," Rivka admonished. "You mean the world to me, Fraydl. It gives me the greatest pleasure to have you near and to be able to do whatever I can for you." For a moment, her voice broke. She tightened her lips and regained control of her emotions. To lighten the heavy mood that had settled over the sisters, she deliberately changed the subject, "You thought it was cold in Haifa, but it is even colder in Yerushalayim. Some years, it even snows. A person can really feel the winter there."

By the time the bus reached the Ramle main bus depot, the storm was almost played out. Rivka and Fraydl took advantage of the break to leave the bus for a few minutes and stretch their cramped legs; it had been a long, confining ride. Slowly the two picked their way around puddles, breathing in the clean, fresh air.

"Malky knows that we're coming?" Fraydl asked, blinking rapidly against the sharp breeze.

"Her downstairs neighbor has a telephone. I called from the post office and left a message. Don't worry. I know she'll be delighted. She won't want us to leave!"

"Does she have a large apartment? Her husband won't mind?"

Rivka laughed. "Where there's room in the heart there will be a place in the hearth," she quoted. "Yerushalayim apartments are so tiny you can barely turn around in them, but Yerushalmis are the most caring and welcoming people in the world. You'll see."

The bus driver honked his horn and the scattered passengers returned to their seats. The landscape was blurred behind a drizzling rain as the trip resumed. Rivka closed her eyes and dozed. Fraydl wiped the fog off her window and stared out at the breathtaking scenery as the bus chugged up twisting mountain roads. Deep valleys fell away from the road in stony tiers planted with vineyards and olive groves. *This is Eretz Yisrael!* she repeated to herself, hardly able to believe the wonder of it. *This is what the*

olei regel saw when they went up to Yerushalayim for the festivals.
As the engine strained and whined and the bus lurched over the
mountains surrounding Jerusalem, a sense of peace settled over her.

"*Tachanah Merkazit,*" the driver announced. He pulled his vehicle into line at Jerusalem's Central Bus Station. Fraydl and Rivka
gathered their bundles and alighted.

"We'll take a taxi," Rivka decided. "It's still raining and we have
so much to carry."

The narrow streets were no obstacle for the veteran taxi driver,
who took them straight to Meah Shearim. Malky appeared at the
courtyard gate before Rivka had even paid the driver. "*Beruchos
haba'os!*" she greeted them with a big welcoming smile. Baby
Simcha Bunim was in her arms, and 2-year-old Sruly peeked from
behind the folds of his mother's skirt. Fraydl felt her shyness melt
away.

Delicious smells wafted from her open door as they shlepped
their bags up to to Malky's top-floor apartment. She settled them in
the kitchen with bowls of steaming soup to counter the cold outside.

"When is Lipa coming home?" Rivka asked, savoring the hot
soup.

"Any minute," Malky replied. "I'll serve him in the main room
so our chatter won't disturb him. Tante Fraydl, I'm so glad to see
you! How was your trip from Haifa? It's not a very good day for
sightseeing, but tomorrow will be better."

"The sun is coming out already." Rivka reached over to part the
curtains, pointing to an expanding patch of blue shining between
heavy black clouds. "After the storm, it's going to be a beautiful
day."

Fraydl cleared the table and carried the empty dishes to the
kitchen sink, where she quickly washed and dried them. "Tante
Fraydl! You are my guest. Please let me do the dishes," Malky protested, feigning affront.

"You told me to make myself at home," Fraydl responded, tick-
ling little Simcha Bunim's chin, which made him laugh out loud.
"Why don't you let me watch the children while you try to rest a
little?"

Malky laughed. "I warn you: if you become indispensable, I won't let you leave!"

Their visit stretched into a week. Lipa hung a sheet around folding beds in the main room to give the guests a bit of privacy in the small apartment, and Rivka took Fraydl sightseeing to places of interest in Yerushalayim. On the last day before returning to Kfar Ata, the two sisters climbed the stairs to the top of the YMCA across from the King David Hotel in order to get a glimpse of the Wailing Wall in the Old City.

"I visited the Kosel before the War of Independence," Rivka said, pointing out the right direction for Fraydl to look, "when the British were still in charge. It's so sad that the Jordanians won't let us go near it anymore. But at least our eyes can still see it from here."

"You'd better go down now," a soldier warned the women. "When people stay in one spot too long, the Jordanian snipers use them for target practice — and they are sharpshooters."

91

THE PARTING BETWEEN MOTHER AND DAUGHTER WAS NOT easy. "Ima," Malky begged, "I want you to stay here with me. Don't go so soon!" The young woman's eyes filled with tears, and she dabbed at them with her sleeve. "You've only been here a few days, not nearly long enough. Kfar Ata is so far from Yerushalayim and we see each other so rarely. Please stay until after Pesach."

Rivka shook her head firmly. "*Tochter'el*," she said, "My responsibilities are waiting for me. I only intended to be here for a day or two, and now it's already been a whole week. I cannot leave your brother alone in that convalescent hospital with all those other horrifically wounded soldiers. It's such a depressing place and he is only a young boy." Rivka's lower lip trembled for a second. "So young," she sighed, thinking of Areleh.

"He didn't realize what he was doing. It's such a pity that he must suffer so. Hashem should help us." Rivka straightened her posture and took a deep breath. "*B'ezras Hashem*, by the summer Aharon will recover from his injuries and then you will come to Kfar Ata to visit us — or we will make the trip to Yerushalayim again."

Malky dried her eyes. "I understand," she said, though her woe-begone expression clearly contradicted her words.

Rivka's sharp eyes and loving maternal heart immediately perceived the exhaustion in the slump of Malky's shoulders. She regretted the situation that kept them apart for so much of the year. Picturing herself at the same age, so far away from her own mother, Rivka wavered. Didn't Malky also need a mother's encouragement and advice? At the beginning of her own married life in Palestine, hadn't she also longed for her mother to nurture and support her when she was tired or unsure of herself?

Torn between the conflicting needs of her beloved children, Rivka asked, "Would you like Fraydl to stay here and help you for another few days?"

As soon as the words were out of her mouth, Rivka regretted the idea, but Malky's face was transformed by the unexpected offer. She turned quickly to her young aunt. "Say you will stay, please, Tante Fraydl? We've only just begun to get to know each other, and the children love you so!"

Fraydl tried to stifle the relief that flooded her. Returning to Kfar Ata meant giving her unequivocal answer to the proposed *shidduch* with Meir Glaser, a decision she found herself reluctant to finalize. "Yes, of course!" she responded. "I will be delighted to stay and help Malky for a few more days."

Rivka frowned, but the words had been said and it was too late to take them back. Her eyes briefly met Fraydl's. She understood all too well her younger sister's enthusiasm for the delay. "Do you imagine that it is possible to escape from life's difficulties?" she asked under her breath, shaking her head. Fraydl blushed and turned away.

Her curiosity piqued, Malky looked back and forth between the two women, but their expressions were unreadable and she could not determine the source of the sudden strain. Before she could ask for an explanation, the baby began to cry for his feeding, and by the time Malky returned with the satiated infant in her arms all traces of tension had dissolved and her mother and aunt were busy repacking their bundles so that Rivka could take her leave.

To her surprise, Fraydl felt much more relaxed with her older sister gone. Nearly the same age, she and Malky had similar interests and shared many ideas. Over the following days, conversation flowed freely between them. Laughter came easily as they shopped in the open-air *shuk*, worked together in the kitchen and cared for the little boys.

Fraydl was a natural storyteller, and Malky was fascinated by her aunt's memories of life in Vienna before the war. For her part, Fraydl was drawn to her niece's simple life. When she watched the interactions between Malky and Lipa, or between Malky and her sons, she could begin to envision herself married to Meir and building her own family.

Fraydl had almost forgotten what it was like to have a real friend. Her developing relationship with Malky represented the first time since the war that she felt comfortable enough to confide in and really share her feelings with another person. It made her feel young and whole again. The days passed too quickly. Soon it was time for her to pack and return to Kfar Ata — and, possibly, to become a *kallah* at last.

"Can I help?" Malky asked, watching her aunt's struggle to close the bulging valise.

"Something's wrong with the buckle," Fraydl panted. She pulled with all her strength, until suddenly the leather strap tore in half and she found herself tumbling backward.

"I think you should just stay here then," Malky giggled, moving Simcha Bunim to her other hip so she would have a hand free to help her aunt.

Fraydl examined the torn strap from her landing place on the floor. "Can you give me your sewing box?" she asked. "I think I can mend it, at least well enough so that it won't open on the way."

Lipa and Malky's apartment was tiny and rather dark. There was just one bedroom, a tiny kitchen and a main room with a narrow balcony overlooking the street. With little Sruly at her heels, Fraydl stepped out onto the porch to find enough light to thread the needle. Later she would remember the moment with stunning clarity. Simcha Bunim was gurgling in his crib. Malky was standing half- in and half-out of the house, holding out a sweater for Sruly because it was cold outdoors in spite of the sunshine. And then their ears were assaulted by a terrible screeching of brakes and the sound of a crash.

Time seemed to move in slow motion after that. Both Fraydl and Malky simultaneously leaned over the porch railing to see what had happened. Fraydl heard Malky's whispered *"Gevalt!"* and felt rather than saw her run from the house. Without thinking, Fraydl picked up Sruly and held him tightly, still looking down at the street and trying to understand what was taking place. A speeding city bus had hit a pedestrian. People were shouting for help. From the balcony she watched Malky desperately push her way through the crowd, clawing at people to let her pass.

It was Lipa.

Realizing that the figure lying crumpled on the street was her niece's husband, Fraydl bit her hand to stifle a scream. What should she do now? She looked around in helpless panic. The mournful wail of an ambulance split the air. Sruly cried and struggled mightily to get out of her arms. From his crib in the other room, Simcha Bunim screamed.

Something inside Fraydl switched gears. She didn't know where the strength to act came from, but she knew she had to take charge of the situation. "Come, *sheifelah*," she soothed the hysterical toddler, and led him back into the house. She secured the balcony door and picked up the baby with her other hand, rocking the children until calm returned.

It was hours before Malky came home again, her face pale and drawn. Wordlessly she collapsed onto a chair, blinking back tears. Fraydl quickly made her a cup of tea and sat beside her, stroking her niece's arm. "Tell me about it," she asked softly. "Where is Lipa now? How is he?"

Malky rested her head against Fraydl's shoulder, and sobbed. "He's hurt, Tante Fraydl. The doctors say his life is in danger. They say his skull is fractured!"

Sruly wandered into the kitchen. He hesitated a moment and then rushed to his mother. Hugging her little boy seemed to help

Malky recover her composure. "Are you hungry?" she asked, pressing her lips against his soft cheek and then automatically tucking his shirttail into his trousers.

"No, the Tante fed me already," Sruly answered, pushing her away and sliding to the floor. He was too young to understand the seriousness of the situation. Now that his mother was home, all was right in his world and he only wanted to play. "Look, Mommy, I can stand on one leg!" Sruly gave a comical demonstration of his new skill, clutching Fraydl's skirt for balance with one hand and the table leg with the other.

"Very nice," Malky said distractedly. She turned to Fraydl. "Where is Simcha Bunim? He must be starving by now."

"He cried for a long time," Fraydl admitted, "but he finally fell asleep. Wait here. I'll wake him and change his diaper first. "

"Thanks." Malky felt almost too weak to move. While she nursed the baby she told Fraydl as much as she knew. "Lipa is unconscious. The doctors won't know how bad the concussion is until he wakes up. His leg is broken, too. The ambulance took us to Shaarei Tzedek Hospital. The neighbors informed my *shvigger* and she came to the hospital. She told me to go home and take care of the children and that she will stay with him."

"You need to eat," Fraydl told her niece. "You must be strong. The whole street is saying *Tehillim* for his recovery. G-d willing, there will be good news soon."

"Can you stay, Tante Fraydl?"

"For as long as necessary, Malky. I'll be here for as long as you need me."

"Do you mind if I go back to the hospital?" Malky asked, patting Simcha Bunim's little back to burp him after the feeding. "I can't stay away, not knowing. I will go out of my mind!"

"Of course. Don't worry about anything. You know that I love your precious children and will take care of them the best I can."

Fraydl packed some sandwiches and fruit and a *sefer Tehillim* for her niece. Malky gave some last-minute instructions about caring for the boys and then hurried back to her husband's side.

The children kept her busy until late that night, but after finally tucking them into bed Fraydl sat beside the kerosene lamp and, as long as there was enough light to read the words, prayed for all of her dear ones, including Chaim and Yanky wherever they were, and poor, brave Areleh, as well as Lipa ben Basya. She had fallen asleep over her *Tehillim* when little Simcha Bunim woke her at midnight for his bottle.

92

"LIPA IS OUT OF DANGER!" FRAYDL AND MALKY EMBRACED, their tears mingling at the joyful news. Malky's face shone with happiness. "This morning Lipa opened his eyes and began to speak, Tante Fraydl! The doctors are optimistic that he will have a full recovery."

"When will he be able to come home?"

Malky shook her head. "It will probably be a long time yet," she explained. "He is in traction now. After they take the cast off of his leg he must learn to walk again. I'm just so grateful that he is awake and talking. He even asked if his *chavrusa* can come to the hospital and learn with him. The doctors said it will be a while before he can concentrate for long periods, but his mind is clear. After such a severe concussion, it's simply a miracle! Tante Fraydl, I can't thank you enough for being here."

"Hashem always sends the *refuah* before the *makkah*," Fraydl replied briskly, and then added, "I would not want to be anywhere else anyway." During the weeks when her niece spent most of the daytime hours at the hospital with her injured husband, Fraydl had become deeply attached to her sweet nephews. The thought of delaying her departure from Yerushalayim did not cause her any appreciable anguish.

"Did we get a letter from my mother yet?" Malky asked, riffling through the mail on the table.

"Here," Fraydl took an envelope from her apron pocket and handed it to her niece. "It came today, after you left the house."

Although mail might take a week to travel between the north of Israel and the center of the country, it was the prevalent method of keeping in touch at a time when few people could afford the luxury of a private telephone.

"I'm so glad I'll have good news to tell her tomorrow," Malky commented, frowning as she read her mother's terse words regarding Areleh's medical condition. By prearrangement, Malky spoke with her mother once a week from the telephone at the post office. This was a complicated and expensive endeavor, necessitating a wait in line at both the post offices in Kfar Ata and Yerushalayim, but since the accident Rivka needed the regular connection to keep informed of developments.

"I hope you'll have a better connection this time."

"I hope so, too. Last week there was so much static on the line, and we had to repeat everything so many times, that we could barely understand a thing. If I have to, this time I'll yell so loudly that she will hear me even without a telephone!" Malky grinned.

"Let's put some coins in the *pushka*. That will surely help!" Both of them giggled, slightly inebriated with relief at the wonderful news.

The next evening, Malky returned from the post office with news for Fraydl. "Ima said that someone named Meir Glaser asked for your address. She wants your permission to pass it on to him."

"What? Is he coming to Yerushalayim?" There was a tremor in Fraydl's voice.

"I don't think so." Malky's expression was puzzled. "Mrs. Lipschitz says that he wants to correspond with you. If you agree, of course."

"I don't know." Fraydl fretted. She turned her gaze to the window, as if Meir might be coming down the narrow street right now.

"If you don't want to, just say no," her niece advised.

"Malky, there's something wrong with me," Fraydl told her sadly. "There is no reason to say no. I really should be happy to agree."

"But you're not." Malky's response was matter-of-factly.

"No." Fraydl didn't trust her voice to say more.

"Do you want to talk about it?"

"It won't help, Malky'le. There is something wrong with me. Something broken inside." Unbidden tears were tracing rivulets down Fraydl's cheeks.

Malky sensed her aunt's wretchedness. "No, there isn't!" she protested vehemently.

"Malky, Meir Glaser is a fine person, and he wants to marry me. Why can't I feel any connection to him? Don't you think I want to be like you, with a husband and children of my own? Meir is offering me exactly what I want more than anything in the world, and I can't make myself accept it. Something terrible is wrong with me." Fraydl began weeping in earnest.

"He's just not your *bashert*, Tante Fraydl," Malka insisted. "You like and admire him as a person, but that doesn't mean that he's the right one for you."

"And who says there will ever be a right one?"

"What kind of question is that? You are such a special person. You will make a wonderful wife, and a wonderful mother. When your *bashert* comes, you won't have these doubts."

Fraydl hugged her niece. "Thanks, Malky," she said. "I appreciate your confidence." She went to the sink and splashed cold water on her flushed face. "My father used to tell us that despair is the favorite tool of the *yetzer hara*. Your Zeide wanted us to be *b'simchah* and to always see the benefit in everything that happens. Thank you for reminding me to be grateful for all the good things in my life. I'll think about Meir's request and I'm sure things will look clearer tomorrow. What else did your mother have to say?"

"Of course she was thrilled to know that Lipa is awake and recovering. And she told me that Areleh asked for his *tefillin*."

Fraydl's eyes widened. "His *tefillin*?" she asked. "That's wonderful news. I'm so glad to hear this. *B'ezras Hashem*, your brother will come home whole in mind and body — may it be soon!"

Malky nodded. So many young men had left their yeshivahs to fight the British and later the Arab Armies, and too many had lost their precious observance of mitzvahs along the way. There were few families that did not have to cope with this problem; she knew firsthand the anguish it caused. "Today is *Rosh Chodesh Adar*," she reminded her aunt. "*Mishenichnas Adar, marbim b'simchah!*"

Fraydl laughed. "We should only hear good news! May the *simchah* of Adar continue all year long." She grabbed Malky's hands and began to dance.

A groggy Sruly heard the singing and managed to climb out of his bed and toddle into the main room, where he stood with his thumb in his mouth, watching his mother and great-aunt laughing and twirling around. Seeing the little boy's wondering eyes, they scooped him up and he joined in the merriment, all three of them conveniently forgetting that it was long past his bedtime.

93

AHH!" NACHMAN SANK DOWN IN THE MOST COMFOR-
table chair in the room and kicked off his shoes. Recently
released from army service, he and Meir had returned to Kfar Ata
and were once again lodging in the widow Lipschitz's home.

Meir couldn't help smiling. "You certainly look pleased with
yourself."

"You could say that!" Nachman agreed.

"I take it you got the job?"

"Yes, my good man. You are looking at the new Director of
Acquisitions at the Kfar Ata Textile Factory."

"I'm impressed. I thought the ad was for salesmen."

"Yes, it was. Apparently somebody in management discerned
more potential in your humble cousin than the world was aware
of," Nachman answered in mock modesty. He straightened up and
cleared his throat. "By the way, I will no longer need to take a loan
to buy an automobile," he announced. "Since my new position
requires extensive traveling, a company vehicle will be made available for my personal use."

"Well, that's another cause for celebration! Congratulations, cousin. I wish you much success and continued prosperity!"

"Now that I am gainfully employed, I am prepared to put in a good word for you, Meir. How about coming to the employment office tomorrow morning?"

Meir's face clouded slightly. He sighed. "Do I have a choice?" he murmured under his breath. Meir's dream was to sit and learn Torah, but he didn't want to starve. Suddenly, the outside door opened.

"Mrs. Lipschitz!" they chorused as she nudged her way backward into the room with a smile as wide as a rainbow. She was carrying a dishtowel-draped tray laden with fragrant delicacies. Nachman inhaled the intoxicating scent of fresh hot pastry and leaped to his feet to relieve the landlady of her burden.

"You shouldn't have," Meir protested weakly, lifting the corner of a towel to peek before turning to straighten the tablecloth so his cousin could set the tray down.

"It's just my way of saying *mazel tov*," the widow declared. "It's not every day that a young man is offered such a responsible position in the Kfar Ata textile factory. I'm so proud for you, Mr. Glaser! You are looking at a great future!"

The men exchanged glances. *How did she know already?* While Mrs. Lipschitz was busy peeling away the towel from the steaming tray, Nachman found a bottle of *Kiddush* wine in the cupboard and poured three small glasses in celebration. "*L'Chaim*," he pronounced loudly, "May we share many more happy occasions!"

"*L'Chaim! L'Chaim!*" Meir and the landlady responded.

"Mrs. Lipschitz," Nachman said, "I really appreciate this beautiful gesture. Can I ask who told you the good news?"

Mrs. Lipschitz smiled craftily. "I have many sources of information. Kfar Ata is just a small village, and everyone knows everything that happens."

Meir savored a bite of strudel. "*A mechayah*," he murmured. "This reminds me of our Bubby's pastry before the war."

"That is a rare compliment," Nachman informed her sotto voce, his mouth full.

The landlady swelled with pride. "*Ach!*" she said, glowing with satisfaction, "*Ess, ess, kinderlach.*"

A moment later, she recalled another reason for her visit. "I have a letter for you," she told her lodgers. Holding out the envelope, she added, "It arrived a few days after you left Kfar Ata to return to your company, and I've been saving it for you all this time. It's from America!"

Both men reached for the letter at the same moment, and then laughed. Meir turned it over and looked at the date. The letter had been sent before Chanukah. The widow was waiting expectantly, but he didn't want to read it in her presence. He merely held in up so Nachman could see that the return address was Williamsburg, New York.

"Dr. Stern!" Nachman exclaimed. He turned to their landlady and explained, "Someone we worked for after the war, to earn enough money to leave Europe."

"Ah." She looked disappointed. "Your former employer?"

"Yes." Meir put the unopened letter on a shelf and helped himself to another pastry. "These are heavenly," he flattered her. "It was so kind of you to think of us."

"My pleasure…" Mrs. Lipschitz waited a little longer, but when neither Nachman nor Meir seemed inclined to elaborate, she finally shuffled to the door with the empty tray in hand. "I'm glad you enjoyed them. I'm looking forward to having you young men back in Kfar Ata."

"Thank you again, and good evening," Nachman said, politely opening the door wider so she could exit and then closing it gently after her.

"I hope she's not offended, but from now on I'm locking that door," Nachman said, turning the key with a click.

"It's unsettling to have someone come in without knocking," Meir agreed. "I wouldn't offend her for the world, but. . ." His voice trailed off.

"She really bakes delicious pastries," Nachman said, licking the last crumbs off his fingers.

"That she does. And she really means well, too."

"Where's Tanchum's letter?" Nachman reached up to the shelf for the envelope.

"Look," Meir pointed out, "There's no street address. It just says *'Nachman and Meir Glaser, Kfar Ata, Israel.'*"

"Like our landlady says, 'It's just a small village and everyone knows everything that goes on.'"

They held the letter between them, reading it at the same time. *"Baruch Hashem,"* Meir said fervently. "Tanchum's mother is making a good recovery after her surgery."

"The last time we heard from him, he did not expect her to finish out the year — and now they're planning a trip to Israel! This is a real miracle."

"He deserves it. After all they've been through, I'd say their family is worthy of a miracle."

"It was a miracle that they ever found each other in the first place."

"Emes, cousin, *emes."*

Nachman poured wine into his and Meir's glasses. "Another toast," he said. *"Chodesh Adar* is the month of miracles. Just as *Am Yisrael* was saved in the time of Esther and Mordechai, may the Jewish people always be miraculously sustained, no matter how impossible the circumstances."

"Amein! L'Chaim!"

94

AFTER DAYS OF RAIN, THE NIGHT SKY WAS FINALLY CLEAR. Fraydl stood alone on the dark balcony, breathing in the crisp Yerushalayim winter air. Hugging her coat around her for warmth, she watched with amusement how each small puffy cloud vanished after every breath.

She had escaped out to the porch in an effort to distract herself from the melancholy that had hovered over her ever since her niece's husband had come home for good. It meant that her extended stay in Yerushalayim was nearly over. Lipa and Malky were picking up the pieces of their life, and perhaps soon she would also fulfill her own dream and become a bride… So why were tears welling in her eyes? Why, instead of anticipation, was her heart full of sorrow? Would the scars from the war never heal?

Fraydl made an effort to focus on the future, but thoughts of the past always interfered. Tonight she kept remembering the war years, unable to suppress the painful memories. She recalled her childhood home in Austria, her neighbor's basement where she hid after Mamme died, the year of living like a fugitive on the streets and the attic in Ravensdorf with Chaim and Yanky. She might be getting married soon, but her mother's candlesticks were still in Dr. Emsbach's house. Fraydl let the tears fall, feeling sad but safe here in Yerushalayim, far away from blood-soaked Germany.

The enchanting melody of Gemara reached her ears and, for a moment, erased her melancholy. Somewhere nearby a voice was chanting the holy words with a yearning that resonated within her. Fraydl strained to hear better. Tiny teardrops of happiness glistened at the corners of her eyes. There was no more beautiful sound in creation.

Gradually, she became aware of other sounds. In the distance she heard a clarinet playing music that teased and tugged at her heart. Little by little the music came closer, until she was treated to the sight of dozens of schoolboys dancing with lit torches in front of a wedding canopy. In the shadows beneath the *chuppah* a tall man walked with great dignity, embracing a newly written *Sefer Torah*. The *chuppah* was surrounded by men, their voices raised in joyful song. As the procession flowed down the narrow street, a smaller group of young girls and older women unfolded behind the men, holding tightly to the hands of small children who were skipping and prancing with excitement.

The music seemed to enter Fraydl's very soul and lift her up. She floated higher and higher as, unconsciously, she tapped her foot to the rhythm. What a lovely gift Hashem had sent her during her last days in Yerushalayim! The *Hachnassas Sefer Torah* procession moved off into the distance. Impulsively she decided to follow the entourage, unwilling to relinquish the joyful feelings it aroused within her.

Lipa and Malky were conversing quietly in the kitchen. Fraydl waved to her niece and promised to return soon, before slipping out of the house and hurrying down the stairs to the street.

She reached the intersection just in time to see the *chuppah* carried into the courtyard of one of the newer *shtiebels* in the neighborhood. Without resisting, Fraydl allowed herself to be propelled along with the rest of the women to the steep stairs leading up to the *ezras nashim*, which overlooked the men in the sanctuary below.

Packed into the anonymous crowd, she enjoyed the lively, joyous atmosphere. As the music played, Fraydl felt transported back to happier times. When she closed her eyes she could almost see her beloved father carrying a beautiful *Sefer Torah*. Her older brothers danced and sang, while her nephews cavorted with their burning torches until sparks drifted up and over the moving *chuppah* into the blackness of the night.

Fraydl eased out of the *shtiebel* a little later, returning to Malky's tiny apartment with her heart full of light and warmth. That night, there were no nightmares to disturb her sleep.

That Shabbos was her last before returning to Kfar Ata. Something drew her to the little *shtiebel* where she had watched the *Hachnassas Sefer Torah*. Fraydl climbed to the women's section and stood quietly in a back corner, allowing the uplifting prayers to sweep over her. When it came time for the Torah reading, she edged forward to the *mechitzah* and lifted the lace curtain ever so slightly to look down as the *sefer Torah* was brought to the *bimah*.

A very dignified elderly woman was also standing beside the *mechitzah*, watching intently as the crown and mantle were removed. She noticed Fraydl and smiled, gesturing that they could share her *Chumash* and follow the Torah portion together. Fraydl nodded, returning the smile. She bent her head over the words and concentrated as the *ba'al korei* read in a slightly accented but very pleasant and mellifluous voice. There was something familiar about the reader's voice, but Fraydl couldn't quite place it.

"Do you know who the *ba'al korei* is?" she whispered during the *misheberachs*.

"Of course," the rebbetzin replied graciously, her face glowing with *nachas*. "That is my son, Tanchum."

"He has a beautiful voice," Fraydl complimented her. She was puzzled. She knew that voice, but couldn't place from where.

"Yes. Wait until you hear the *ba'al tefillah* for Mussaf! That will be my other son, Alexander."

Fraydl nodded in appreciation. "*Ah sach nachas*," she whispered.

After Mussaf, the elderly woman introduced herself as Rebbetzin Stern from New York. "My husband ordered this *Sefer Torah* to be written over two years ago, when our son returned home after being away for many years," she confided. "I recently recovered from a very serious operation, so we decided to use this occasion to make a *seudas hoda'ah* after the *Kiddush*. I would be honored if you would join us, my dear."

Fraydl could not refuse the delicate and aristocratic woman who had been so kind to her during the prayer service. There was something intangible about her that reminded Fraydl of her own mother. "Of course, I would be delighted," she accepted with a warm smile.

A few moments later, a troupe of *bachurim* spilled into the *ezras nashim*, pushing chairs to the sides and dragging away benches so they could set up tables for the *seudah*. Laughing teenage girls quickly covered the tables with white linen tablecloths and set them with plates, glasses and silverware. Meanwhile, the men improvised a *mechitzah* of white tablecloths draped across a wire that bisected the room. Within minutes, the small shul was redolent with the smell of *cholent* and the guests were settled at their tables on either side of the *mechitzah*.

Yosef Aharon Stern's voice boomed out a beautiful *Kiddush*. After the men returned from washing, it was the women's turn to go to the sink. Rebbetzin Stern took Fraydl's hand and insisted that she sit beside her. She introduced her to the women at the table, including her daughter Feige and her daughters-in-law Hannah and Sarah Leah, who were accompanying her.

The first course of gefilte fish, was followed by *ayir mit griebeness*. "This tastes exactly like my Mamme used to make!" Fraydl exclaimed with delight. The other women smiled with pleasure at the compliment.

Listening to the spirited singing of *zemiros* on the men's side, Fraydl relaxed. She felt content. Once again she was swept away on the tide of her memories, imagining that she was with her own family before the war tore them apart. For a moment it was almost true; then someone asked her to pass something, and she came back to reality. They were all gone now. The gap in her life where her loved ones had been would never be filled. The beautiful memories were gone forever.

Fraydl looked around at the people surrounding her. This family was together, and she was glad for them. Perhaps one day she would be a matriarch to a family like this. Her eyes brightened at the thought, and a smile lingered on her lips. This was the kind of life she wanted to build, a warm family of *erlicher Yidden*.

Just as the *cholent* was being served, the shrieking of a child reached their ears. "Oh, dear," Feige said. "That sounds like my Henny." She stood up and was already moving toward the door when a girl of about 12 entered, carrying a wailing toddler in her arms and accompanied by a boy who looked about 8 years old.

The trio made their way straight to their mother. "It's her elbow again," the older girl told Feige, her voice trembling with apprehension.

To her alarm, Fraydl saw that the little girl's left forearm was dangling at an unnatural angle.

"Her shoulder has a tendency to pop out of its socket if someone pulls her arm," Feige explained, as she examined her daughter and tried to soothe her.

"I lifted her up by the arm to help her jump over a puddle in the courtyard," the older girl admitted. "I didn't mean to hurt her, Mommy!"

"Of course not, I know you didn't. Chaim'ke please call Fetter Tanchum." Feige turned to her mother. "There are advantages to having a doctor in the family," she said with strained amusement.

A tall, bearded blond man entered the women's side behind Chaim'ke and bent over the sobbing child seated on her mother's lap. When he spoke, Fraydl recognized the voice of the *ba'al korei*.

Then, as he worked on the little girl's arm, she realized in terror exactly how she knew him.

95

TANCHUM WAS SO FOCUSED ON HIS YOUNG PATIENT THAT he did not realize the effect his appearance was having on the family's unexpected guest.

"Remember how we did it before?" he gently addressed the little girl.

Henny nodded gravely, and held out her unhurt arm. The normally noisy women's section hushed as the doctor gently took the child's healthy right arm and methodically twisted and tugged each joint, pulling first her elbow, then her wrist and finally each finger of her small hand. Henny's kept her eyes on his face, her expression full of childish trust.

Tanchum reached for the injured arm and calmly repeated the same motions, only this time he gripped her upper arm firmly and gave a quick downward thrust, snapping her forearm out and then expertly popping it back into the elbow joint. Henny didn't have time to cry out before the procedure was complete.

Happy chatter replaced the tense silence, as the women of the family offered profuse appreciation for Tanchum's professional skill and the boisterous youngsters resumed their interrupted games.

Tanchum patted Henny's head affectionately, unobtrusively sliding a candy from his pocket into her hand before turning to speak with his mother. He raised his eyes from the child and noticed the stunned figure standing between his mother and Hannah.

He stared, speechless. When he managed to find his voice, it quivered.

"*Fraulein* Fraydl? Is it you?"

"*Herr Doktor*," Fraydl whispered, realizing without doubt that she was facing the Nazi officer from Ravensdorf.

"Tanchum? What is it?" Rebbetzin Stern looked from her son to the young woman. "Fraydl, my dear, this is my son Tanchum." The elderly woman's smile faded as the color drained from Tanchum's face and Fraydl did not respond to her words.

The gentleman in front of her was dressed in a fine Shabbos suit and hat, but Fraydl's eyes saw his Nazi uniform and was immediately taken back to the war years. Tanchum took a tentative step toward her. In response, Fraydl turned and fled as if pursued by evil incarnate.

Tanchum caught his shoe on the leg of a chair and stumbled. Quickly recovering, he raced after the fleeing figure, his desperate call of "F-r-a-y-d-l !" lingering in the air behind him as he disappeared through the door.

Tanchum paused at the bannister and called out again. "Don't run! *Fraulein*, wait!" She ignored him and continued to race down the narrow stairs. Bracing himself with one hand on the handrail, Tanchum leapt over it and landed on the stairs below, just in front of the panicked girl.

Fraydl was running at full speed, and they nearly collided. At the very last moment she managed to grab hold of the railing with both hands and halt her uncontrolled descent. Trapped, she threw a glance up to the landing where Tanchum's brothers and sisters were gathering, everyone speaking at once.

"*Bitte*, please move away," she begged. "Let me by."

"Listen to me for one minute!" Tanchum panted. "Just hear what I have to say."

Fraydl felt suddenly starved for air. The staircase darkened and began to turn around her. Fighting overpowering weakness, she shrank back against the wall and prayed not to lose consciousness.

"Tanchum, what is going on?" Alexander's booming voice cut through the cacophony. During the fraction of a second when Tanchum turned to answer his older brother, Fraydl flattened herself against the wall and slipped under his arm. She was down the final flight of stairs before he could follow. Seconds later, Fraydl reached the courtyard and vanished through the gate.

"Wait! Don't go! *Fraulein*, wait for me!" he shouted after her, but it was too late. By the time Tanchum reached the courtyard, Fraydl had disappeared.

"Tanchum, she's gone. Come back inside." He felt Alexander's hands on his arm.

"Fraydl." Tears stung Tanchum's eyes as he stared at the place she had stood just minutes earlier. "I searched for her for so many years. I was sure that she must have died. I never harmed her. Why would she run away?"

Alexander put an arm around Tanchum's shoulder. "We'll find her, brother," he promised. "She must be staying near here. We'll ask around. Someone will tell us where to find her."

Partially reassured, Tanchum allowed himself to be led back to the *shtiebel*. Their oldest brother was waiting at the door. "What happened?" Dovid asked. "Who was that?"

"Someone he knew from before," Alexander replied. "I think it might be the girl he hid during the war with Chaim and Yanky."

"Tante Fraydl?" Young Chaim stood immobile for a moment on the stairs behind the men he was following back up to the *ezras nashim* after the excitement died down. "That was Tante Fraydl? Yanky!" He abandoned his post-bar mitzvah dignity and pushed past the adults into the men's section. "Yanky, Yanky! Tante Fraydl is here in Yerushalayim!"

"Did you see her?" Yanky asked incredulously.

"No, but *Fetter Tanchum* did!"

Tanchum resumed his seat at the head table. He tried to eat his portion, but inexplicably the *cholent* was tasteless. After attempting a few bites, he gave up and allowed his feverish mind to wander.

Rationally he understood the impossibility of searching for Fraydl right now, but the intensity of his disappointment interfered with his ability to concentrate on the speeches and *zemiros*. The only thing he wanted to do was walk the streets of Meah Shearim until he found her again. Fraydl was so near, yet still so far away! The thought of losing her again caused him profound pain.

"Pull yourself together!" his brother Alexander's elbow nudged him meaningfully. "The Mamme was so happy. Now she is upset. Do you want to spoil it for her?"

Tanchum glanced at the makeshift *mechitzah*, meeting his mother's worried gaze in the narrow opening between two tablecloths. He forced himself to nod and smile. With a prodigious effort, he channeled his thoughts back to the *seudas mitzvah* and was rewarded by his mother's smile in return.

The youngsters of the family cleared everything away in short order. The boys returned the benches and planks to their places, while the girls organized the used dishes in cartons and gathered up the tablecloths.

The Stern family slowly made their way back to the hotel for their Shabbos rest through the warm and sunny Yerushalayim winter afternoon.

"I never dreamed who she was," the rebbetzin murmured, supported by her daughter Feige and oldest daughter-in-law on either side.

"No one could have known," Hannah reassured her.

"Why didn't I ask her more about herself? I might have guessed, from her answers. Her name should have made me realize. How many young women her age named Fraydl are there? I'm so sorry I didn't realize. I could have explained the story of our family and things would have turned out differently."

"It's not your fault, Mamme. G-d willing, we will be able to locate her after Shabbos and clarify everything. She seemed nice," Feige commented. "Quite *eidel*."

"She is exactly as Tanchum described her to me," her mother agreed. "I was drawn to her the minute I saw her. It is so amazing;

he saved her life, and in a way she was the *shaliach* to draw him back toward his *Yiddishkeit*."

Hannah and Feige looked at each other in surprise. They did not know the whole story, but after Mamme went to sleep they intended to go to Tanchum and pry out every detail.

96

MALKY WAS CLEARING OFF THE TABLE AFTER THEIR *seudah* when Fraydl burst through the door, wide eyed and out of breath.

"*G-tt in Himmel*, Fraydl! What happened?" The plate in Malky's hand crashed to the floor. She had never seen her aunt in such a state, and immediately feared the worst. "Are you hurt? Where have you been? Here, sit down. I'll bring you a drink. Calm down and tell us what happened!"

Fraydl gulped the water from the glass Malky put in her hand, then leaned her elbows on the table and hid her face in her palms.

Lipa hauled himself up onto his crutches and hobbled to the balcony. He looked around, scanning the road in every direction. The sun was shining and people were strolling along the street. Nothing appeared amiss. With no obvious explanation for the young woman's distress, he returned to the house in time to hear Fraydl gasp, "...a Nazi in shul! I recognized him from Germany during the war. A Nazi officer."

Malky's face went white. "A Nazi? In Meah Shearim? Tante Fraydl, that's impossible!" she whispered.

Lipa frowned. "It is not unheard of," he told his wife. "There have been reports of war criminals trying to escape justice by posing as Jews."

"In New York maybe, or Argentina. But Meah Shearim? I can't believe it!" Malky looked at Fraydl's face and knew she was telling the truth. "*Oy*, Tante Fraydl you must have been so terrified... Lipa, what are we going to do? Where is he now?"

"We have to warn people," Lipa spoke decisively. "It's possible that we should do so immediately, even though it is Shabbos. I will have to ask a *she'eilah*. Tante Fraydl, did the Nazi see you? Did the officer recognize you?"

Her head jerked in a nod, tears spilling down her cheeks.

"Thank G-d you made it home!" Malky cried out. "If the Nazi realized that his disguise has been exposed, he could be very dangerous!" She ran to the door and locked it for good measure.

The tension in the air was so tangible that both infants began to wail at full volume. While Lipa and Malky were distracted in an effort to calm their little ones, Fraydl finally got her breath back. She remained sitting stiffly in the chair, hugging herself tightly, reliving memories she had worked so hard to forget. The flashback was so intense that Fraydl literally lost awareness of where she was. Instead of the familiar room, she imagined Heinrich Mauer's contorted visage and heard his wicked laughter ringing in her ears.

"Tante Fraydl! Tante Fraydl!" Malky shook her aunt by the shoulders. "Lipa what are we going to do? *Gevalt!*"

"I'll go ask the Rav," he answered, adjusting his crutches and heading for the door. "Lock the door after I leave, and don't open it again for anyone except me. Stay with the tante; don't leave her alone for a minute!" Moving as quickly as he could, Lipa left the house.

Malky massaged her aunt's shoulders and rubbed her arms. "Talk to me, Tante Fraydl! It's all over now. You're safe here with us in Eretz Yisrael. Don't worry, we'll take care of you. Tante Fraydl, look at me, please! Come back to us!"

Fraydl blinked. She looked up at Malky in confusion, feeling as if she had just woken from one of her nightmares. Relieved, Malky poured boiling water from the urn on the *blech* into a cup and then poured it into another glass. She put tea essence and sugar into a third glass and added the water, then handed the tea to her aunt. Fraydl held the glass with both hands, letting the heat burn her fingers and bring her back to reality. "I'm sorry for alarming you," she whispered. "I don't know what happened to me. *Baruch Hashem*, I feel better now."

Malky sagged with relief. She made herself a glass of tea and sat beside her aunt. "Poor Tante Fraydl. What an awful experience!"

The corners of Fraydl's mouth turned up and she tried to smile. "Where did Lipa go?" she asked.

"To ask the Rav what to do."

"I think that I want to leave Yerushalayim after *Havdalah* tonight. I will go back to your mother in Kfar Ata. He won't follow me there."

"Of course, we understand.We left *cholent* on the *blech* for you. Wash now and eat something."

"No," Fraydl said weakly, taking the last sip of tea and setting down the glass. "I'm not hungry. I really can't eat a thing. I ate something at the *Kiddush* in *shul*. Now I feel so tired, I just want to sleep. Do you mind?"

There was a quiet knock on the door. Malky opened it for Lipa, who was accompanied by the Rav. Fraydl was calm enough to relate what had happened in the *shtiebel* and how she had identified Dr. Emsbach.

"Are you absolutely certain?" the Rav inquired softly. "It is vitally important that there be no margin of error. Could it have been a Jew who reminded you of the Nazi officer? Publicizing this information could cause irreparable damage if people began pursuing an innocent man as a German war criminal. Are you absolutely certain of his identity?"

"The man is definitely a German doctor. I cannot say that he is a war criminal, but he was a Nazi officer. I recognized him and he recognized me. He called me by my name."

The Rav and Lipa exchanged glances. "What did he do then?"

"I ran away and he tried to stop me." There was a tremor in her voice, and she blinked her eyes rapidly. Malky put a reassuring arm around her aunt's shoulder. Feeling her niece's supportive presence, Fraydl was able to slow her breathing and calm herself.

"What is the name of this imposter?" the Rav asked.

Fraydl hesitated. She thought back to the morning, to the lovely family and their *seudas hoda'ah*. "His name is Dr. Karl Emsbach," she replied.

"How did you come to be in that place?"

"She was at a *Hachnasses Sefer Torah* earlier in the week and decided to *daven* at the same shul on Shabbos morning," Malky explained.

"I met a rebbetzin at the shul. She told me that her name is Stern and she is from New York. She and her husband commissioned a *Sefer Torah* because their son returned home after being away for many years. She invited me to stay for the *Kiddush*. In the middle, Dr. Emsbach came over to her. She called him Tanchum, and told me he was her son." Fraydl began to cry again.

"The Nazi must have learned about the loss of their son and managed to convince them that he is that lost child!" Lipa exclaimed.

"Those poor people!" Malky declared. "First they lose a precious child, and then they are tricked by a fraudulent Nazi into believing he is their own son! How wicked to take advantage of grieving parents!"

The Rav stood up. "I will contact the *gabbai* of the *shtiebel*," he promised. "I know him well, and I am sure he will know how to locate the family that donated the *Sefer Torah* to his *shul*. In any case, the Stern family must be informed before this information is made public. Meanwhile, let us keep this secret between us in order to limit their heartache as much as possible."

"Isn't there a danger the Nazi will escape, now that he has been identified?" asked Lipa.

"Yes, but we must accept that risk in order to protect the innocent family that has been deceived. I imagine that they have been through enough anguish. Don't you agree?"

"Is Fraydl in danger?" Malky asked fearfully. "What if that Nazi tries to search her out and harm her, since she is the witness who can identify him?"

"I think that Miss Mertzbach should be moved to another location as soon as possible. In the meantime, she should not leave your house."

"I plan to return to my sister in Kfar Ata on *Motza'ei Shabbos*," Fraydl told the Rav. "I don't think anyone would think of looking for me so far from Jerusalem."

"So it is agreed," Lipa summarized. "The Rav will find a discreet way to inform the Stern family, and Tante Fraydl will leave Yerushalayim as early as possible."

As tired as she felt, Fraydl could not fall asleep after the Rav left the house. For a long time she sat and stared out of the window, watching dark clouds gradually spread over the formerly clear sky. By evening, raindrops were spattering on the pane as winter returned to Yerushalayim.

97

F RAYDL TOSSED AND TURNED, UNABLE TO FALL ASLEEP. SHE got up and drew the curtains to darken her corner of the small apartment, but the minute she closed her eyes the German's face seemed to hover above her in the dim light. The first time she had seen those remarkably blue eyes was on the morning after the mob of Hitler *yugend* had chased them.

Fraydl remembered all too well that shouting pack of boys. She had been so weak that she could hardly run while carrying the featherweight Yanky. Chaim had whimpered fearfully, struggling hard to keep up with her as the gang of drunken teenagers closed in. She remembered her frenzied search for shelter, any kind of shelter. But where in Nazi Germany could three starving Jewish children hide?

The Mercedes in the hospital parking lot had seemed to beckon. It was the only object in sight, and the brief window of time before they would be discovered was rapidly closing. Fraydl had flung herself down to the ground, and the children had crouched behind the back wheel of the big black automobile, numbly praying that Hashem would have mercy and save them.

The Nazi officer had materialized out of nowhere. The moment her eyes met those unforgettable dark-blue ones, Fraydl had known instinctively that he grasped their predicament. Even today, a lifetime later, she experienced wonder at the unexpected expression of human warmth in that brief exchange. In a split second the stranger had opened the trunk of his car, gesturing for the children to climb inside. There was no time to weigh the offer; the voices of the mob were right behind and coming closer.

Fraydl pulled the blanket more tightly around herself, her heart contracting painfully at the thought of her sister Yochi's sons. She had tried so hard to save Chaim and Yanky, but in the end she had been powerless. After the war, not a trace remained. She still *davened* for them, as she did for the other members of her family who had been taken away, hoping against hope that some of them had survived.

Ever since her traumatic encounter with the German this morning, those blue eyes continued to haunt her. There was no question in her mind that it was him. She had heard that voice and seen those eyes almost every day for nearly two years, each time she and the boys came down to his study to eat. The doctor had prepared nourishing meals with his own hands, and he had been adamant that the children finish until the last bite.

Fraydl brushed a tear from her cheek. Suddenly she wanted to talk, to let her heart spill out its memories. She pushed away the curtain dividing her corner from the rest of the main room. Everyone was sleeping; the only sound was the soft tattoo of raindrops against the roof. Now that the day was no longer sunny, the light had drained out of the small apartment.

A small sound caught her attention. Something or someone was moving stealthily in the vicinity of the door. Fraydl sat up quickly, not daring to breathe. She heard it again, a little louder and closer. It couldn't be Lipa or Malky, and the door was locked. She strained her ears. Again, a soft, whispering sound... followed by a thud and the wail of her 2-year-old nephew.

Enormously relieved, Fraydl jumped off her bed, ran over and scooped him up. "Did you fall and get a boo-boo?" she asked tenderly, cuddling his warm little body close. "How did you get out of your bed?"

"*Willst trinken*," Sruly answered petulantly. "I'm thirsty!"

"Come with me, I'll fix you a glass of milk," his aunt promised.

After slurping down half a glass, the little boy pushed it away and looked around for something to do. Fraydl's suggestion that he return to his crib was met with vigorous resistance. "Shhh, Sruly!" Fraydl warned. "You'll wake Mommy and Tatty."

To allow his parents to continue their nap, she pulled the toddler into her bed beside her. He snuggled next to her for a minute and then began to wriggle.

"*Sha*, Sruly. Listen quietly, and Tante Fraydl will tell you a story." He opened his eyes wide and listened as she began, "Do you know that you have a cousin named Yanky? When Yanky was just about as big as you are, he used to sleep beside me just like this. . ."

Fraydl didn't expect the small child to understand what she was saying, but it seemed to calm him so she continued in a low voice. "It was very cold in the attic where we lived then. It was so cold that we could see our breath in the air, but we pulled the comforters up to our noses and then it was warm and cozy." She pulled the blanket up around Sruly's face and he yawned.

"We had a cat named Cleopatra. We called her Cleo. One day she had kittens and Yanky loved to play with them." Sruly's breathing was slowing to a steady rhythm, but his eyes popped open in protest whenever she paused.

"Yanky has a big brother named Chaim. He is so smart, Sruly. I don't know where he is today, but Chaim was bar mitzvah last summer so he must be quite big already. A *bachur*."

Sruly slept deeply, but Fraydl did not stop speaking. She spoke of the German who sheltered the children during the war. "Why did he do it, Sruly?" she asked rhetorically. "He was a Nazi officer, and such a thing put his life in grave danger. He was very intelligent. I always assumed that we were his life insurance if Germany lost the war. And Germany did lose the war, Sruly. Hashem will never abandon His people. I told that to the *Doktor* once, but he didn't believe me. I don't know why we had to go through those terrible years, but looking back I can see that Hashem was with us every minute. And He is still with us, always and forever."

Fraydl looked tenderly at the sleeping child, loving him and intensely missing Yanky at the same time. "Why would *Herr Doktor* choose such a disguise?" she mused aloud. "He seemed different, but he was a German. Perhaps even as he hid us in his attic he was taking part in the atrocities? Why else would he be so desperate to hide his real identity that he would pretend to be Jewish after the German defeat?

"At the end, when the Allies were bombing us almost every night, Dr. Emsbach disappeared. He left the house one day, and never returned." She remembered her letter, which came back unopened when she was at the DP camp in Vienna. "How did he get here to Yerushalayim?" she mused. "What does it all mean? I wasn't even supposed to be in that *shtiebel*. Hashem's ways are mysterious. My father taught me that even when it's not possible to understand, we know that everything is part of His plan."

She stopped speaking for several minutes, looking with affection at Sruly's small hands half-open on the blanket. "I ran away from him once," she resumed, because addressing the sleeping child was providing a much-needed emotional release. "*Herr Doktor* frightened me even more than the certain danger that lurked outside."

Dr. Emsbach really expected me to marry him, Fraydl recalled. *He had it all worked out, and he was sure that I would agree.* "Hashem gave me the strength to reject his offer." She nuzzled her cheek against the face of the sleeping child. "You can't imagine how hard it was, Sruly. He promised me a life that would give me things I could only dream of, starting over with a secure future in a different country, with a husband who would support me and Chaim and Yanky too.

"But my heart told me that such a good life would be worse than being murdered, Srulik. The Nazis were killing Jewish bodies, but if I married the doctor and lived a life far away from *Yiddishkeit*, it would be handing them an even greater victory. Almost our whole family was sacrificed. How could I turn my back on their memories and deny my *Yiddishe neshamah*?

"The most horrible thing , Sruly, is that there was part of me that wanted to accept his offer. I am ashamed to admit even to myself, but I was weary of being pursued and persecuted just for being born Jewish. I was relatively safe in the doctor's house, but I was still a prisoner. I was still young and I wanted to be able to stroll along the street like any normal person, to chat with friends and go shopping for pretty things. I was sick of the constant fear, the constant concern about being discovered and the loneliness of being separated from everyone I loved.

"I also knew *Herr Doktor*. He would pressure me until he overcame my resistance. He was certainly a kind benefactor, but as an officer he was accustomed to obedience. When I realized that he represented more danger to me than the Gestapo, I had to escape before it was too late. I *davened* and asked Hashem to help me make the right decision. "

Fraydl's eyes closed, her hand over Sruly's. Suddenly she was teetering on the icy ledge outside the attic window. It was cold and dark, and the layers of clothing she wore hampered her as she tried to step onto the tree branch. She must have screamed or jumped in her sleep, because the little boy beside her began to cry.

Her nephew's voice startled Fraydl awake. She hugged him close and murmured, "*Sha,* sweet Sruly. Don't be afraid, *sheifelah.* It was just a dream. We're safe now. Hashem is watching and we can trust Him to take care of us."

98

"FRAYDL, ARE YOU ASLEEP?" MALKY'S VOICE WAS HEAVY with worry.

"No, Malky. I'm awake."

"I thought I heard Sruly cry a minute ago, but when I looked in his bed he wasn't there!"

"It's all right. He's here beside me."

"Oh, *baruch Hashem*! I hope he didn't bother you?"

"Of course not."

"Do you feel well enough to get up for *Shalosh Seudos*?"

"Yes, I'm feeling much better. Do you want me to wake Sruly or let him sleep?"

"We'd better wake him. If he sleeps too long now he won't be able to fall asleep again for the night."

Sruly whimpered when Fraydl stroked his cheek and called his name, but a second later he was bright eyed as he scrambled over her to get to the floor. She watched him with amusement. "I will miss you," she said, smiling. "I loved being with all of you here in Yerushalayim."

During *Shalosh Seudos*, Fraydl shared some of her memories with her niece and her husband. Malky and Lipa were spellbound.

"And you are certain that this is the man you recognized at the shul this morning?" Lipa asked. "He is still an imposter, whether or not he is a war criminal."

Fraydl nodded solemnly.

"If he was a righteous gentile, perhaps he converted after the war? He might be a *ger tzedek,*" Malky pointed out.

"I didn't think about that possibility," Fraydl said, her eyes cast down at the tablecloth. "Just seeing him frightened me so terribly that I ran away."

"You told the Rav that he recognized you and called you by name," Lipa reminded her.

"Yes."

"Did he try to talk to you? Did he say anything else?"

Fraydl concentrated, trying to remember something beyond the panic that had consumed her. "He called after me to wait," she said. "When I wanted to pass by him on the stairs he begged me to listen to something he wanted to say."

"What do you think he wanted to tell you?" Malky asked.

"The silver. I forgot about the silver. After we settled in the attic in Ravensdorf, *Herr Doktor* went to see our apartment in Vienna and he brought back a chest with the family silver in it." Fraydl shook her head in distress. "He probably wants to return Mamme's *leichter* and Tatte's menorah."

"Tante, this morning you were so shaken that we didn't know what to think. It was easy to imagine the worst. It is possible that we jumped to the wrong conclusions." Lipa reached for his *bentcher.* "After Maariv I will speak with the Rav about this and we will hear his opinion about how we should proceed."

"Lipa," Malky whispered to her husband as he put on his coat to leave the house. "I don't think it's good for Tante Fraydl to have contact with this man again. You saw how badly she was affected by it. If the German wants to return Zeidy's silver, we can arrange for it to be done without their meeting in person."

"I think you're right," he responded, remembering their aunt's stricken face after she returned from the *shtiebel*. "It would be best that way." He put on his *shtreimel* and left for *shul*.

"Do you think he might have converted to Judaism?" Malky asked Fraydl after her husband left.

"He might have done that," Fraydl agreed, remembering the many conversations with the doctor about the meaning of life. "He saw himself as an ethical person and he was interested in Jewish philosophy; but Rebbitzen Stern told me that he is her son. She said that they commissioned the *Sefer Torah* in gratitude for his safe return to their family. As a German who served as an officer in the German Army, how could he be related to them at all, let alone be their missing son?"

Malky shook her head. "No, that's too bizarre. The man surely never expected anyone to expose his Nazi past. The Stern family would not have accepted him if they'd even imagined such a thing. It's a sad story, but I'm sure the Rav will take care of things in the best way. The good part is that you will get your mother's and father's heirlooms back. Ima will be so happy when she hears about that. She'll be very glad to have you back home in Kfar Ata, too."

"She's not expecting me tonight. She'll be surprised when I turn up at the door."

"It's night already. Let's say '*Hamavdil*' and start packing your things. I hope the bus to Haifa won't leave too late. Are you sure you don't want to wait until tomorrow morning?"

Fraydl tousled Srulik's curls and sighed. "The Rav said I should leave as soon as possible," she said. "Let's get the packing out of the way now, and I can decide later."

After *Havdalah*, Lipa spoke with their aunt about her plans for returning to Kfar Ata. "Tante Fraydl, we have enjoyed having you as our guest, but the Rav is adamant that you must leave as soon as possible," he told her. "He even arranged transport for you in a private automobile, right to my *shvigger*'s house."

"How could he do that?" Malka asked in amazement.

"Zelly Goldberg's son was here with his wife and baby for Shabbos. There have been a string of robberies near where they live, so they don't want to leave the house empty for more than one night. They're leaving Yerushalayim in another hour, and they'll stop here to pick up the tante."

"Do they live in Kfar Ata?" Fraydl asked.

"No, they're from Acco, but Kfar Ata is on their way. It'll take you much less time than going by bus, and you'll be more comfortable too."

"Please tell the Rav that I appreciate his assistance," Fraydl told Lipa. "Actually, I was dreading making the trip alone, and I was also worried about catching the connecting bus from Haifa to Kfar Ata in the middle of the night. This arrangement is very kind."

The trip back to Rivka's house passed in a blur. Fraydl was so weary from the day's events that she dozed most of the way. As hard as it was to leave her niece and nephews, she found that she was looking forward to living with her older sister once again in the spacious and orderly house in Kfar Ata. She was feeling stronger and more confident than she had before coming to Yerushalayim. She felt as if she could finally put her past behind and concentrate on the future.

99

I'M WORRIED ABOUT TANCHUM. HE IS NOT LOOKING WELL since the *Kiddush* yesterday," Feige whispered to her sister-in-law as they waited for the vans that would transport the family to Teveria for the last part of their vacation.

"It's strange," Hannah said. "I don't remember him ever mentioning her name before. Who would have thought that running into her would have such an effect?"

"He looked so upset after those men came last night. Mamme and Tatte were still up sitting with him after midnight when Shimon and I left for our room. They were arguing. Tanchum declared that he won't leave Yerushalayim with the rest of the family this morning."

"How did the *elteren* respond?"

"The idea disturbed them very much. Both of them refused to hear of being separated from him."

Hannah nodded. "He was so determined. I was sure that Tanchum would stay behind to look for her. I wonder what made him change his mind and agree to leave."

Feige unbuttoned her woolen sweater. "Yesterday it was cool and today is almost summery," she remarked, looking up at the clear sky. "My brother is basically a realistic person. How is he supposed to find her when those gentlemen made it clear that she doesn't want to be found? Tanchum is hurt, but it will pass."

"It's a good thing we're leaving today," Hannah said. "We can hope that moving to a different environment, a place he's never been before, will draw him out from behind the walls he's put up around himself."

"He told Alexander that he's been looking for her ever since the war. He thought she must have died."

"At least now he knows she's alive and well." Hannah took off her jacket and draped it across her arm. "That should bring him some comfort."

"Meeting her, and then having her run away, is like losing the connection all over again."

"What about Chaim and Yanky?" Hannah reminded her. "Do they know that their aunt has been found? Or that she is gone again?"

"Chaim knows," Feige responded. "Of course it's not just Tanchum's loss, but they are children and naturally more resilient, and they have settled into your family so well."

" At his age Tanchum should be married already," Hannah said. "If he wasn't alone, he probably wouldn't be so distressed."

Feige looked up and down the street. "For what time did we order the vans?" she asked, peering at her watch.

"They're late, but this is Israel so you almost expect it. . . You're right about Tanchum. Your parents need to put more pressure on him to find a wife. It's for his own benefit. I don't understand how they've been so patient about it until now."

"How well do we really know him?" The usually reticent Sarah Leah surprised them with a contribution to the discussion. The two older women turned simultaneously to stare at the youngest Stern daughter-in-law. "I didn't mean to say it out loud," she apologized, which made them laugh and deepened her blush to bright red.

"Tanchum has been part of our family for more than two years now," Hannah said. "Don't you think that's enough time to get to know him?"

Sarah Leah usually kept her opinions to herself. It was rare for her to openly disagree with what the others had said. "Yosef Aharon says he doesn't know Tanchum at all,"

"That could be because you two don't live in Williamsburg," Feige suggested kindly. "You only see him on the *Shabboses* you come to the *eltern*. We see Tanchum almost every day, so naturally we feel closer."

"I don't understand why he has been so remote since *Motza'ei Shabbos*," Sarah Leah summoned the courage to ask. "When someone speaks to him, he doesn't even seem to hear. That seems like an extreme reaction to just meeting someone he used to know."

Feige shrugged. "It wasn't just somebody he used to know. Tanchum saved her life during the war. Yanky and Chaim are her nephews and she doesn't even know they're safe. Tanchum is a sensitive person. I can understand that her rejection hurts deeply. After he put his life in danger for her, she refuses to speak with him. Actually, I am also offended at such a lack of gratitude."

"I don't think anyone should blame her," Sarah Leah insisted. "The *shver* said she didn't know anything about us or that Tanchum is not who she thought he was. For all she knows, he is a former Nazi soldier who may have committed atrocities."

"The Tatte says that we can't judge anyone who went through the war," Hannah agreed. "It's too bad the way it happened. Tanchum is our brother and we feel his pain, but we have to be *dan l'kaf zechus*... Look, here are the cars!"

Three vans pulled up to the curb and the doormen began loading the Sterns' luggage for the trip north. It took several minutes for everyone to find a place and settle in for the long drive. Taking his seat beside the driver, Tanchum remained wrapped in silence. The ache in his heart was so compelling that it required a conscious effort to respond when anyone spoke to him.

Though Tanchum was totally oblivious to the pleasant weather on this beautiful morning, the rest of the family was entranced. Abundant winter rains had garbed the mountains and plains with wildflowers in a riot of colors. Wadi streams sparkled in the bright sunlight. The temperature was unseasonably warm.

"Look at the green buds on the trees!" Rabbi Stern marveled as they left Jerusalem. "In New York they are shoveling snow, and here we are comfortable even without coats."

"Look at that!" Yanky gestured toward a cluster of trees covered by a carpet of pale-violet blossoms.

"Those are almond trees," the rabbi explained. "They are the first trees to bloom after the winter. Remember, it's only a few weeks after Tu B'Shevat!"

The world was bursting with life on every side.

With his brother Chaim deep in a discussion with Shmuel, Yanky was bored. The little boy turned around on his knees and stared out the back of the van, absently twisting one of his *peyos* around his finger. "Chaim?" he asked.

His brother glanced at him. "Yes, Yanky?"

"Is Fetter Tanchum sick?"

"Of course not. Why do you ask if he is sick?"

"Because he doesn't look like every day. His face is white and he's not talking to anyone."

"Maybe he has a headache or something." Chaim turned to resume his conversation with Shmuel, but Yanky wasn't finished.

"If Tante Fraydl was at the *Kiddush*, why didn't she stay to meet us?" he asked with the bluntness of a small child.

Chaim frowned. "Fetter Tanchum thought it was her, but she didn't stay so maybe it was just someone who looked like her."

Yanky turned back around in his seat. "Why is Fetter Tanchum angry?"

"Who said he's angry? What's the matter with you, Yanky? Why are you asking so many questions?"

"What happened to make his eyes so sad?"

"Yanky, enough questions! Be quiet for a while and look out your window. Watch and soon you'll see some camels or a herd of goats."

Yanky heaved a sigh. He pulled his knees up to his chin and sat looking down at the tips of his shoes. Something was wrong, but no one would explain it to him. Ever since Chaim had become a bar mitzvah he had begun to act just like the other grown-ups.

"Look, *kinderlach*. Yanky! Chaim! Shmuel!" Baba Stern called out. "See those big birds that look like they're floating in circles? Those are storks."

"This is the Hula valley," Rabbi Stern told the children. "Once it was a big swamp. Many settlers died because the mosquitoes carried malaria. It took years for the pioneers to drain the wetlands, but now see how green and beautiful the fields are."

"Is it much longer?" Yanky asked. He was tired of sitting still in the car.

"In another hour you will see the Kinneret," Hannah promised the impatient child. "Just wait until you go back to *cheder* and tell your friends about all the places you've been."

Perking up at that thought, Yanky pushed his nose against the windowpane.

"There's an olive grove," Zeide Stern said. "Olive trees live longer than people. Some of them are hundreds of years old!"

"What are those very tall trees called?" Chaim asked. "They seem to be shedding their bark."

"Those are eucalyptus trees. They were brought here from Australia to help drain the swamps."

Tanchum stared through the window, but saw nothing. If anything, the bright colors outside mocked the gray devastation in his inner world.

100

THE AFTERNOON SUN REFLECTED ON THE CALM WATERS OF the Kinneret left even the most casual observers awe struck. Rabbi Stern instructed the driver to pull over to the side of the road so that everyone could bask in the beautiful sight before continuing their descent into Teveria.

Rebbetzin Stern leaned toward her husband. "Look," she whispered, nodding toward Tanchum, whose face registered pure delight.

Rabbi Stern nodded with satisfaction. "I think I noticed the beginning of a difference in Meron," he whispered. "No Jew could remain oblivious to the *kedushah* at the *kever* of Rashbi. Our Tanchum is resilient. He will be fine."

Reassured, the rebbetzin settled back in her seat. "He will be fine," she echoed her husband. "Everything will be fine, *b'ezras Hashem*."

That evening Tanchum actually managed to put Fraydl out of his mind for a number of hours. Instead of being a captive of disappointment, he chose to focus on this once-in-a-lifetime opportunity of being in Eretz Yisrael together with his extended family. After a relaxed dinner together, he played with the little ones until their bedtime and then took his Gemara to join his father and brothers for an exceptionally exhilarating learning session.

"Are you going to sleep now?" Hannah asked her mother-in-law.

"If you are not very tired, perhaps we could enjoy a short stroll along the lakeshore together?"

"It will be my pleasure," Hannah responded. She checked that her son Shmuel was still learning with Chaim, and then draped a shawl around her *shvigger's* shoulders against the evening chill.

"It has been a good trip, has it not?" Rebbetzin Stern asked as they stood near the sea wall looking out over the undulating waves.

"Yes, it has been wonderful," Hannah agreed.

"You have all been so kind, indulging me like this in the middle of the winter. You must have wondered why I insisted on doing it now and not waiting for a more convenient time."

Hannah inclined her head towards the older woman. "You would never inconvenience anyone, *Shvigger*. We all understood that if it was important to you to make the trip now, there must be a good reason."

The two women stood in quiet harmony for some time, half-listening to the whispering slosh of waves breaking on the pebbles and sand below. Suddenly the rebbetzin spoke, "Hannah, we must find that young woman. She is Chaim and Yanky's only family, and...."

Hannah startled; her mind had been far away. She quickly gathered her thoughts. "You mean the young woman at the *Kiddush*?" She was taken aback by the determination in her mother-in-law's voice, which was uncharacteristic of the elderly woman.

"Yes, of course."

"We know she's in Israel, so it seems to me that we will eventually be able to locate her. Yanky may have forgotten her, he was very young and it was such a traumatic time in his life. Chaim did ask Dovid about it once or twice. He seems interested but not badly shaken up. Only Tanchum had an extreme response and I watched him with Dovid and Yosef Aharon before we left the hotel. I think he's recovering from what happened on Shabbos. Are you still so concerned?"

The rebbetzin looked down at her bony hands, resting on the stone wall. "I feel something," she told Hannah. "Tanchum cannot continue making further progress without closure. It's logical that Miss Mertzbach is also feeling tied to something that is holding her back. It is not enough for Tanchum to ship her family heirlooms to an intermediary. Both Tanchum and Miss Mertzbach will remain imprisoned by the past until they meet and speak about it."

She paused before adding, "I am old, Hannah." When her daughter-in-law began to protest, she shook her head and continued, "I am old, and even though, *baruch Hashem*, I am no longer an invalid, I am not well. I want to live to see my last child married and building a *bayis ne'eman*. Until this matter is resolved, I fear Tanchum will continue refusing our suggestions for a *shidduch*. We must find this girl and convince her to meet us again. We owe it to the boys, too."

"How can we do that, *Shvigger*? We know nothing about her beyond her name and that she apparently lives in Yerushalayim."

"Last night, after the Rav and the *gabbai* left, Tanchum was beside himself. Your *shver* decided to engage a detective to find out where she is. When we do, will you agree to speak with her and persuade her to come? If we have to return to New York before the private investigator finds the girl, will you stay in Eretz Yisrael until you have spoken with her and bring her back with you?"

Hannah was speechless. The suggestion that the others would leave her in this small country, which was permanently under siege by hostile neighbors, took her breath away. If she agreed, it meant undertaking a tremendous responsibility. She would have to speak to a stranger she had met briefly, only once, about a brother-in-law she was not sure she understood. And there would be no one else around to help make the decisions!

When she found her voice, she chose the ancient subterfuge of Jewish woman throughout the ages. "I'll have to discuss it with Dovid."

"I know it sounds difficult." The rebbetzin rested her hand lightly on Hannah's arm. "But I'm sure it will only be a few days. You understand that we cannot delay everyone's return until we have an answer, but the *shver* and I have confidence in you to make contact with the young woman without frightening her away."

Hannah looked out over the water, where a rippling path reflected the moon's pale light. The Stern children revered their gentle mother; refusing her request was impossible. "If Dovid agrees, I will do my best," she promised.

"Thank you, dear. I knew you would not disappoint me. You and I will *daven* that Hashem lead us along the way that He intends."

When Tanchum slipped out of the hotel, he noticed his mother and sister-in-law returning from their walk, but they didn't see him. He strode purposefully toward the sea and climbed down rickety wooden steps to the dock where fishermen were preparing to set out for their nightly catch.

For several minutes Tanchum stood, hands in his pockets, watching the busy men bait hooks and examine their nets. Finally, one of the workers turned a sun-weathered face to the stranger and addressed him in broken English. "Can I help you something, Mister?"

"Do you know where I can rent a boat?"

"Tomorrow, in daylight?"

"No, now. Tonight."

"What kind of boat you want?"

"Does anyone have a kayak here?"

The fisherman squinted up at the tall stranger as if he were speaking Chinese. "A what?"

"Any small boat; a kayak, a canoe, or even a rowboat."

At these words, the man stopped frowning and gestured at a hut further along the shore. "Fellow there, his name Yeshurun," the fisherman said. "You see him out front, he rent you boat. But night no good time for sightsee. The Kinneret, she can be dangerous. In winter, storm blow up sudden. Better wait tomorrow and go on big boat with skipper."

Tanchum nodded his thanks and left the dock. Within minutes, he was walking up to an old grizzled man relaxing on the steps of his hut, smoking a pipe.

"I'd like to rent a small boat," Tanchum told him.

"Now?"

Tanchum nodded.

Yeshurun exhaled thoughtfully. "You a good swimmer?" he asked doubtfully.

"Excellent."

Yeshurun shrugged. He pulled himself up and led the stranger to a rowboat positioned upside down on the sand. "Help me get it to the water," he ordered. A few minutes later, the vessel bobbed in the gentle waves.

"Payment up front," the old man demanded.

When Tanchum handed him a $50 bill. the man's demeanor changed. Considering that the sum was enough to purchase a new boat, it was certainly sufficient to buy his good will. Yeshurun even waded into the cold shallows to help launch the tourist into deeper water.

"If you notice the water getting choppy, don't wait. Come back in right away," he warned with a wave. He noted with approval that the stranger was skillful in applying the oars, but shook his head at the foolhardiness of such an outing at night. The Kinneret might be friendly and placid in the sunshine, but a winter storm had a way of bringing out the worst in her.

101

A T FIRST THE HOUSE IN KFAR ATA APPEARED DARK, BUT when Fraydl pushed open the front door she saw that there was light in Areleh's room. *I should have come back before,* she thought with concern. For days after Rivka's son ran away to join the army, her sister had sat alone in his room, wrapped in a depression that nothing Fraydl said or did could penetrate. She hoped that Rivka's troubles had not caused her to retreat once again into that sad period of their lives.

Fraydl left her suitcase in the main room and tiptoed down the hall. Her sister's voice was audible through the half-closed door. Who could she be speaking to in the empty room? Fraydl tapped lightly on the door before slowly pushing it open. The sight that greeted her eyes caused her to gasp, "Areleh you're home!"

Rivka was sitting on a chair beside her son's bed. Both occupants of the room turned to greet her. "Fraydl! Why didn't you write me when you were coming, so I could meet you at the bus station in Haifa?"

Rivka was clearly elated to see her younger sister.

"It wasn't exactly planned," Fraydl replied with a smile, bending down to kiss her sister's cheek. "What a wonderful surprise to see you here, Areleh! Why didn't your mother write to tell us that you were being discharged?"

Rivka stroked her son's sleeve. "It was a last-minute decision," she explained, her gaze simultaneously caressing him and reassuring herself that he was really there.

"*Shalom*, Tante Fraydl." Areleh's voice was strong, and accompanied by a lopsided smile. In a less robust tone, he added, "It's good to be home."

"Does this mean that you've recovered from your wounds?"

"No." Bitterness flashed across her nephew's still-rounded, babyish face. Rivka compressed her lips to conceal her pain at the boy's words. "It means there's nothing left to be done. There were many other soldiers waiting for my place in the convalescent home. . ."

Fraydl's eyes stung, but she knew that the young man would not welcome her pity. "They don't know everything, those doctors," she said confidently. "Hashem is the *Rofei Cholim*, and only He knows the future. Now that you're home, Areleh, I'm sure you'll improve steadily."

He nodded, a hint of appreciation in his eyes. "I hope so, Tante."

"And just because part of your body is affected, that doesn't mean you can't use your mind!" The determination in Rivka's voice reminded Fraydl of her father. She stood up and straightened her skirt. "Tomorrow morning, Rav Mendelsohn is sending one of his students to be Areleh's *chavrusa* here at home until he feels well enough to return to the yeshivah." There was triumph in her expression, but Fraydl did not miss the boy's downcast eyes. She wondered if he was ready for such a step.

"That's wonderful news," she said. "Lipa would envy you."

"Why would anyone envy me?" Areleh's lips turned down in self-pity and his voice was harsh.

"Because the doctors have forbidden Lipa to learn for at least six months," Fraydl explained. "His head injury was so serious they didn't expect him to survive at all. Of course, we know that medical science does not have all the answers. *Baruch Hashem*, the power of prayer is stronger than their predictions. But Lipa still has problems to overcome."

"Like what?"

"His concentration," she said sadly. "Lipa's short-term memory is not good enough to learn with a *chavrusa* even if the doctors would permit it." Fraydl remembered watching him try to learn on his own, and weeping. "Lipa told Malky that by the time he finishes one segment, he has already forgotten the beginning. He cannot *daven* the whole *tefillah*. Even just saying *Kiddush* on Shabbos is hard for him."

"Poor Lipa!"

"We must continue *davening* that he will have a full recovery," Rivka agreed, shaking her head compassionately. She picked up the tray with the dishes from their *Melaveh Malkah* and headed for the kitchen.

"Tante Fraydl, is everything all right except for his concentration?" Areleh's concern for his brother-in-law had pushed his own troubles into the background.

"His taste buds have been affected," she told him. "He says all his food tastes like sawdust. And he cannot smell. When I commented on the delicious aroma from the kitchen on *erev Shabbos*, Malky told me that Lipa has lost his sense of smell."

Areleh's expression was shocked. "Poor Lipa," he repeated in a whisper. "That must be terrible."

"Areleh, you and Lipa are alive. That is the most wonderful thing in the world. You will learn to walk again, and Lipa will slowly be able to learn again. The most important thing is that you are here with us. So many are gone, Areleh. So many will never come home."

The boy sensed the unshed tears in his aunt's eyes. "I'm glad to be alive," he told her, feeling a need to offer comfort. "I will do my best to be strong."

She brushed her tears away and smiled. "You must be strong, Areleh. You are the man in the family and we need you."

The boy lay back on his pillow, exhausted by the exchange but feeling more content than he had since leaving Kfar Ata with Tzvi and Jordan only two years previously.

Fraydl shut the door quietly and left her nephew to sleep. She went into the kitchen and took a towel to dry the dishes that Rivka was washing. "Are you sure Lipa is doing well enough that you can leave Malky with the children?" her sister asked.

"He's able to get around with crutches."

"Is there something you're not telling me?"

Fraydl pursed her lips. "Mamme used to do that."

"Do what?"

"She knew when there was something I hadn't told her, and she used to ask me the same way you just did."

"So what are you not telling me?"

By the time Fraydl finished telling her sister about the accidental meeting with Dr. Emsbach, it was quite late. "You acted correctly," Rivka told her. "This is the last thing you need right now."

Fraydl nodded half-heartedly. "I thought so," she agreed. "Anyway, I'm glad to be back in Kfar Ata. I missed you, and I'm so glad that Areleh is home again. I just wish I didn't have to face Mrs. Lipschitz."

Rivka cleared her throat.

Fraydl stopped what she was doing and stared at her sister. "What is it? Is everything all right with your neighbor? With Meir Glaser?"

"I assume you will be happy," Rivka said, uncharacteristically hesitant.

"What are you trying to tell me?"

"I would have written. I didn't expect you home yet, you understand..."

"Rivka, what is it?"

"After all your work on yourself, I hope you're not disappointed."

"Will you please get to the point?"

"Meir Glaser became engaged this week. His cousin Nachman is working at the textile factory now. He met a young woman he thought was appropriate, and he introduced her to Meir, and. . ."

Fraydl grabbed her sister in a huge hug. "*Mazel Tov!*" she almost shouted. "I am so happy, you can't imagine. I wish them a wonderful life together. *Baruch Hashem!* The greatest happiness is *hataras hasefekos* — the resolution of doubt. Rivka, I am absolutely thrilled at this news!"

Rivka regarded her sister indulgently. "May you be the next one to find your *bashert*," she murmured. And Fraydl added a fervent *"Amein!"*

102

A LTHOUGH THE NIGHT AIR WAS CHILLY, AFTER HALF AN hour of steady rowing in a northerly direction, Tanchum's shirt was soaked with perspiration. It felt so good to be engaged in a physical activity that prevented his mind from continually processing painful thoughts. When the lights of Teveria were reduced to tiny points in the distance, he rested the oars along the inside of the rowboat and dropped anchor, vaguely amused at the way the little boat jerked in protest before settling down to a gentle dip and sway.

Tanchum stripped down to his swimming trunks and dived off the bow. As he'd anticipated, the shock of the cold water was paralyzing initially, but once his body adapted he began to swim. A lifetime ago, as a soldier, he had been expected to swim in icy water to prove his physical prowess. Even now Tanchum found the swim invigorating. He pushed himself forward, stroke after powerful stroke, savoring his ability to prevail over the strong undertow.

Faint light from a pale sliver of moon and the glimmer of distant stars were the only illumination. After a while Tanchum flipped over onto his back and floated in the gently heaving sea, keeping track of his location in the darkness by listening for the soft slapping of the waves against the wooden sides of the tethered rowboat. *I needed this,* he thought with satisfaction. His body gradually released days of accumulated tension until he felt totally relaxed.

In this lonely environment, it was natural for a man's thoughts to turn to the Creator of so much beauty, and to the destiny that had brought him to this point and place in his life. For the first time in memory, Tanchum felt able to let go, and to accept that he was not in control. *Perhaps the purpose of my life was to save the children,* he thought. *When the children are reunited with Fraydl and the silver is returned to her, then I will have successfully completed my mission.*

Wisps of clouds blew over the moon in a game of peekaboo. Tanchum barely noticed the rising wind or the dark, angry clouds moving in from the north. *Chaim and Yanky.* He would have to return the children as well as the family silver! To flee this unwelcome thought, he began to swim again. Now that he was no longer filled with pent-up energy, the current seemed surprisingly stronger. For the first time he noticed the restless sea and realized that a storm was brewing. The whistle of the wind and the rush of the waves concealed the exact location of the rowboat, as rapidly falling raindrops began to sting his neck and shoulders.

Suddenly the waves seemed to be coming from every direction at once, lifting him up and then plunging him back down. The rowboat was just ahead of him — or had he passed it? The sky flickered and went dark. Conditions on the water had become extremely unpredictable. And dangerous.

Tanchum paused to tread water and get his bearings. Were those lights on the horizon from Teveria or from the other side of the Kinneret? Were they as close as they seemed, or far away? He suddenly realized how unwise it had been to come out here alone in the middle of a winter night! Badly shaken, Tanchum realized that the Almighty was showing him how helpless he was. *Shema Yisrael!*

The rain blinded him. The sky exploded with flashes of lightning interspersed with total darkness. Having no idea where he was,

Tanchum let the waves toss him back and forth, silently begging Hashem to save him from a watery death. In his mind's eye he saw his loving parents, and felt their anguish at losing him once again.

A sudden sharp pain shot through his shin as his body was thrown against a floating object. Instinctively Tanchum threw out his arms, making contact with the stern of his rowboat. *Thank You, Hashem. Thank You, Hashem...* He clung to the side until his breathing slowed to a normal rate. Waves passing beneath him tipped the rowboat down in his direction. He took advantage of the opportunity to haul himself up and over the side, dropping onto the heaving floor. He lay there, exhausted, while the little boat bucked wave after wave.

When he had recovered slightly, Tanchum reached down to explore the extent of his injury. His leg throbbed but the skin was not broken. It might be fractured, but it would take an x-ray to know for sure. As far as he could tell, he seemed to be whole. *Thank You, Hashem!* Slowly, painfully, he climbed onto the seat and pulled up the anchor. Grateful that he had not neglected to lock the oars in place, he set them in the water and began to row.

Getting back to shore took much longer than the trip out, but the storm was abating and the incoming tide helped him reach the empty dock at last. Limping painfully, Tanchum dragged the rowboat up to the spot on the beach where it had lain previously. After tying it securely to the post, he dressed in his wet clothes and made his way to the Eden Hotel.

The lobby was vacant. It was so late that the clerk had fallen asleep across his arms at the main desk.When he entered their suite, Tanchum was taken aback to find his father still awake, sitting before an open Gemara.

Rabbi Stern's relief was palpable. "What happened? Where have you been?"

"I went swimming."

"I can see that."

Tanchum shrugged ruefully. "I didn't expect you to wait up for me."

Rabbi Stern's expression was grave. "I am happy to wait up for you," he said. "But it was wrong of you to do something like this without telling us first."

"You're right. I'm sorry. I didn't say anything because I didn't want you to worry and I wasn't sure how long it would take."

"Do you know what time it is?"

"No, Tatte. I didn't take my watch."

"It's after 3 in the morning, son. Whatever made you do such a foolish and dangerous thing?"

"I had a hard day yesterday, as I'm sure you noticed. I was desperate to get away from it all, and my thinking was just to have some solitude while doing something I usually enjoy."

"Did you enjoy it?"

"No, sir. I mean — yes, at first I did. But later I realized that I shouldn't have done it. I am grateful to be back safely, and I hope you will forgive me for worrying you. I don't think it's something I will repeat in the future."

"I'm glad to hear that." Tanchum's father studied him. In spite of the exhaustion and sopping-wet clothes, he sensed a quality that had not been there before: a kind of contentment.

"Tanchum!" Upon hearing voices, the rebbetzin joined her husband and son. "*Baruch Hashem*, you're back! But why are you standing and talking? Go quickly and change into dry clothes so that you don't catch pneumonia, G-d forbid!"

Tanchum said good night to his parents and went to the bathroom to wash up and put on pajamas. It cost him a supreme effort to walk without a limp, but he had concluded that his leg was not broken and did not want to upset them further. After the door had closed behind him, his father turned off the overhead lights and he and his wife went into their own room.

"That was very dangerous." Tanchum's mother sighed, her forehead creased with worry.

"He gave me to understand that he has done such things before and was confident in his ability to do it again. Also, I believe he sincerely regrets his decision to go out in the first place. Tanchum is usually very responsible. He won't do it again."

"I was so worried." Tanchum's mother parted the curtains at the window. A fog had rolled in, concealing the sea from their view.

"He is a grown man, Shaindel. We cannot expect him to tell us everything, and we cannot tell him what to do."

"I wish he were married."

The rabbi responded with characteristic humor. "Yes, a man must listen to his wife."

"Like you listen to me?" she teased.

"I believe I do."

"Well, now I am telling you to go to sleep. We have a busy day ahead of us tomorrow. The children are planning a trip to Tzefat, and my friend Kreindel will be meeting me afterward for lunch. Imagine — I haven't seen her since she left Birnhack 30 years ago! I wonder how we will recognize each other?"

"She probably looks like an older version of the young woman she was then."

"Life has not been easy for either of us, Meir. Do I look like an older version of the young woman I once was?"

"You look exactly the same to me as on the day we married."

The rebbetzin chuckled and shook her head. "May it always be so," she told him. "I am looking forward to meeting Kreindel. After all these years of correspondence, at last we will see each other's faces and hear each other's voices again."

The next morning, Tanchum did not go on the planned trip to Tzefat with his siblings. When he joined his father and brothers for Shacharis, his father took one look at his flushed cheeks and ordered him back to bed.

"Meir, call a doctor," Rebbetzin Stern declared after resting a cool hand on her son's feverish forehead. "Tanchum is sick!"

Tanchum shook his head in disagreement. "I *am* a doctor, Mamme," he croaked. "A thermos of hot tea and a few hours of sleep are all that's necessary. It's nothing serious, I'm sure. There's no reason to worry."

With wishes for a speedy recovery, Alexander, Yosef Aharon and Dovid left the hotel with their families. His mother fluttered around, fluffing his pillow and smoothing the blanket until Tanchum finally slipped into an exhausted sleep. When she was convinced that he did not need her presence, the rebbetzin went out to the main room of the suite to await her old friend Kreindel's imminent arrival.

103

WAIT ONE MINUTE!" MRS. LIPSCHITZ COMMANDED. "I forgot something important. I'll be right back!" She disappeared into her house.

Nachman used the time to rearrange the tower of packages beside him on the front seat of his company car. "It's too bad your sister isn't coming with you today," he told the passenger in the back seat. "It's really a beautiful day for a trip. You can sense that spring is in the air."

Rivka nodded politely. "I wanted her to come, but she just returned home from Yerushalyim on *Motza'ei Shabbos* and more traveling would have been too much for her. She needs to unpack and settle in. Perhaps another time we will both take advantage of your generosity."

"I saw Areleh in the *beis medrash* this morning. It's good to have him back home again."

"Your cousin came to get him for Shacharis, and I agreed that he could stay in yeshivah as long as he feels strong enough. By the way, *mazel tov*! I hear that you were the *shadchan*!"

"Not really. The *kallah* is a secretary where I work. It was just an idea, and then all the pieces fell into place by themselves."

"That's how *shidduchim* are done." Rivka smiled. "Maybe you have an idea for my sister Fraydl?"

"I don't think her *bashert* will be working in a textile factory. He's probably learning in a yeshivah in Bnai Brak or Yerushalayim."

"I wish I knew. . ."

"I've heard that she is very special. I'm sure it won't be long before you find the right one."

The conversation was interrupted by the neighbor's return. She was staggering under the weight of a shoebox. "Nachman, this is the last thing," she promised, dropping onto the back seat beside Rivka Feigelbaum and fanning her perspiring face with an envelope.

Nachman glanced at his watch and stifled a sigh. He walked around to the other side of the car and took the box from his landlady, grunting at the unexpected weight. "Mrs. Lipschitz," he gasped, "what's in here? Bricks?"

She practically giggled. "Of course not. It's just old photographs. I'm sure my friend Shaindel will want to reminisce with me. It's been so long, I thought that I'd show her the pictures. It will be almost like reliving everything together."

"I remember when your husband bought his first camera," Rivka mused, rolling up her window because the breeze on her face was cold.

"Oh, yes. He even built a darkroom in our house and developed the pictures on his own."

"I remember how he used to pose your daughter in different ways and photograph her at every opportunity. He was very talented. Why didn't he ever take it up professionally?"

Mrs. Lipschitz shrugged. "He lacked ambition," she admitted. "My Shepsel was a wonderful person, a real *mentch*, but if I didn't push him to do something, he would never do it on his own."

"Well, you know what they say: 'Behind every great man is a woman.' I'm sure your husband appreciated your support."

Kreindel Lipschitz blinked away a tear. "I hope so. I really tried…" After a pause, she changed the subject. "You know, I haven't seen my friend Shaindel since Shepsel and I left Birnhack after the First World War. Goodness, that was a long time ago! My Devorah was the same age as Shaindel's youngest son, Tanchum. And then he was lost... Oh, my...."

The old woman's face crumpled. Rivka handed her a handkerchief and stroked her hand. Nachman glanced at his landlady in the rearview mirror. "Is everything all right, Mrs. Lipschitz?" he asked with concern as they drove along the highway toward Teveria.

"I don't know if this was a good idea," Mrs. Lipschitz sobbed. "I was so happy when Shaindel wrote that they would be staying for a week in a hotel beside the Kinneret. I didn't realize how many memories it would awaken."

"Of course it was a wonderful idea," Rivka soothed her neighbor. "You will share many happy memories."

"It's all gone now, Rivka," Kreindel wept. "Everyone we knew is gone."

"I know, dear. I know." Rivka felt a knot in her throat.

"What will I tell her? That my only daughter lives in England and I am all alone now that my husband is gone? That Devorah comes to visit once a year and her children hardly know their grandmother?"

"You will tell her about living in Palestine under the Turks and then the British. You are a pioneer, Mrs. Lipschitz. She will be fascinated by all the experiences you've had. Tell her how the Arabs attacked Kfar Ata and we had to escape to Haifa, and how afterward we came back and rebuilt everything from scratch."

The widow nodded. "That's right. I've had a long and interesting life."

"Why do you speak in the past tense?" Nachman spoke up. "You're the most amazing *balebusta* I have ever known!"

"Thank you, Nachman. It's so nice of you to say that. It really is my pleasure to help such fine young men." Kreindel wiped her teary face and whispered to Rivka, "I think it's a situation where the cow wants to feed the calf even more than the calf wants to drink." They both smiled.

"Here is the *kever* of the Rambam. The *kever* of the *Shelah* is right over there." Nachman slowed the car as they entered Teveria.

"Is this where you wanted to stop, Mrs. Feigelbaum?"

"Yes, exactly here. Thank you so much, Mr. Glaser. It was very kind of you to offer me a ride."

"How will you get back to Kfar Ata?" Mrs. Lipschitz asked her neighbor.

"I'll take a taxi from here to the *kever* of Rabbi Meir Baal HaNes and then walk along the shore back to the Central Bus Station. I should be home in time to serve Areleh and Fraydl their dinner. Have a wonderful visit with your friend, and come over later to tell me all about it, all right?" The women embraced briefly before Rivka left the car.

A few minutes later, Nachman pulled up to the entrance of the Eden Hotel. "Let me help you with your packages, Mrs. Lipschitz," he offered. She took her purse in one hand and a plate of pastries in the other, while Nachman staggered after her with two crates and many more packages containing enough culinary supplies for a small army. The clerk directed them to the suite where the Stern family was registered.

Rebbetzin Shaindel Stern and Kreindel Lipschitz fell into each other's arms, weeping. Nachman shifted from one foot to the other, waiting.

"You look exactly the same!"

"You haven't changed a bit!"

Wiping tears from her eyes, Mrs. Lipschitz turned to introduce her boarder to her friend. "Thank you so much for bringing my dear friend to Teveria," the rebbetzin told him graciously. "We would be honored if you would join our family for the evening meal when you return to take Kreindel back to Kfar Ata."

"I appreciate the offer," Nachman responded. "It depends on how long my business takes. I would like to return home before dark if possible."

They exchanged pleasantries, and then Nachman went back for the shoebox of photographs. By the time he returned, the women were so deep in conversation that they didn't notice him. He set the carton on a table, bade them farewell and left to conduct the day's business in Teveria.

104

Tanchum was awakened much later by the voice of his mother's old friend, which sounded somehow magnified by the closed door separating his room from the suite's main room. The two women were alternately laughing and crying as Mrs. Lipschitz carried on a lively narrative punctuated by his mother's exclamations of admiration or sympathy.

He stretched and blinked at the light streaming into the room from the open window. A glance at his watch told him that it was nearly noon. He had slept well and, as he'd predicted, his fever had subsided. Once he became fully awake, the comfortable bed felt confining. He got up, washed, dressed, davened what he still could of the morning prayers and stepped into the main room.

"Tanchum!" The rebbetzin's voice communicated delight. "You look much better now, son. How do you feel?"

"*Baruch Hashem*, almost fully recovered." In spite of this optimistic declaration, Tanchum's voice was noticeably hoarse.

"Meet my good friend, Mrs. Kreindel Lipschitz," his mother introduced her guest. "Kreindy, please make the acquaintance of our miracle child, Tanchum."

Mrs. Lipschitz examined him carefully from tip to toe. "I can't believe it!" she exclaimed, energetically shaking her head to emphasize the point. "It feels like just yesterday that Tanchum and my Devorah'le were playing together in our garden. You were such a sweet and beautiful child," she added, addressing him directly, "but with an amazing affinity for mischief. My little girl followed you around like a puppy. *Oy*, Shaindel, look at him now, all grown up. It's hard to believe that this is that same little boy with blond curls who was my daughter's playmate so many years ago!"

The rebbetzin radiated *nachas*. Tanchum shifted awkwardly, wishing for a good excuse to escape.

"You slept through breakfast. You must be starving." Rebbetzin Stern offered him a plate of tempting pastries. "Mrs. Lipschitz baked these especially for us." She smiled at her friend. "You must give me the recipe before you go back to Kfar Ata! Meanwhile, Tanchum would you mind enjoying them in the lobby so we can continue our conversation? I doubt if you will find the reminiscences of two old ladies as fascinating as we do, and we still have a lot to catch up on before the others return for dinner."

The tilt of her head and her knowing smile told him that she sensed his discomfort and had come to the rescue. Murmuring polite words of gratitude, Tanchum parted from them, snatching a Gemara from the table on his way out of the suite.

He settled onto a chaise lounge in a corner of a quiet wing off the lobby. The delicate pastries dissolved in his mouth and Tanchum licked his fingertips like a small child, briefly prolonging the sweet sensation. He stretched out his long legs and opened the worn volume.

Less than an hour later, he frowned and set the open Gemara down on the coffee table. Where was his concentration? Was it because he wasn't feeling well, or was it because of what had happened at the Kiddush on Shabbos? He opened an inside pocket and pulled out his pipe. After methodically filling it with fragrant tobacco, he struck a wooden match and held it above the bowl, inhaling deeply. Once again Tanchum tried to focus on the tiny print, but his brain refused to cooperate. After reading the same lines 10 times without comprehending them, he closed the Gemara.

Outside the window, sunlight glinted off the water and waves followed one another like heartbeats. Why did Fraydl run away? Why did she send those men to speak with his father? Was it enough just to know that she had survived and was apparently well?

No. It wasn't enough.

Tanchum had often imagined what would happen when he finally found the girl whose life he had saved. He was certain that when she knew the truth about his secret past and real identity, her delight would validate all the difficulties and challenges he'd had to overcome. For nearly two years during the war, Fraydl had been there to listen as he slowly opened up his inner world, sharing his thoughts and his hopes for a better future. Her obstinate observance of mitzvos had ultimately earned his admiration, though neither of them had realized that one day he would leave the world of Karl Emsbach and become Tanchum Stern. The disappointment of losing her again without even an explanation was devastating.

Tanchum's thoughts returned to the hotel in Yerushalayim only two days earlier. It had been excruciating to wait patiently until after *Havdalah* so he could begin his search. His strategy had been to return to the neighborhood of the shul with his sister and sisters-in-law. He'd been prepared to knock on every door in Meah Shearim until they found the girl from his past.

While he was working out the plan with Feige, three men in rabbinical garb had arrived at the hotel and requested a private audience with Rabbi Stern. Tanchum's mind was so focused on finding Fraydl that he barely registered the strangers until they had already left and his father asked to speak with him.

"I'm sorry, son," he had said, "but those gentlemen were from the young lady in shul today. They were sent to warn us to desist from trying to make any further contact with her."

Tanchum stared at his father without comprehending. When he finally grasped the meaning of Rabbi Stern's words, he could only repeat, "Why?"

"I'm sorry," Rabbi Stern said again. "I tried to explain the situation, but they refused to listen. It seems the young woman identified you as a former Nazi officer and informed someone in her family, who then contacted those three *rabbanim*. The purpose of their visit was to make me and your mother aware of your true identity as they understood it. All my arguments to convince them of the truth failed. When they saw that I remained adamant that you are indeed my son, they gave up. But their parting words were a warning not to contact *Fraulein* Fraydl under any circumstances."

Ignoring the warning, Tanchum and his brothers had raced after the strangers. But the streets were dark and empty. The three *rabbanim* had vanished without leaving a trace. A few guests in the lobby had noticed them departing, but none could tell him which way the men had turned.

Tanchum did not sleep at all that night. He spent the hours pacing back and forth, overcome with anguish at the strange turn of events. In the morning his parents commissioned a private investigator. The family's departure for the north was delayed while Tanchum and his mother gave the detective all the details that they could recall about the mysterious girl who had appeared and then disappeared so suddenly from their lives.

Returning to the present, Tanchum realized that his pipe had grown cold. He emptied it into the ashtray, wiped the bowl clean and returned it to the pouch in his pocket. The contentment he'd briefly enjoyed after last night's harrowing adventure had dissipated. Maybe a walk outside in the crisp winter air would help clear his head? He gave his Gemara to the clerk for safekeeping, buttoned his sweater and stepped through the door.

Before he knew it, the wind had grabbed his hat and sent it somersaulting across the lawn. Tanchum raced after it, but a man just coming up the drive caught the fedora in midair and waved to let him know the truant was safely in custody. Tanchum walked briskly down the path, reaching for the hat with his left and hand while offering his right to the quick-witted young man.

105

N ACHMAN GLASER!" TANCHUM SUDDENLY RECOGNIZED
the man in front of him.

"Dr. Stern!" Nachman grinned.

With the greedy wind still tugging at his hat, Tanchum suggested that they go into the lobby where they could speak in greater comfort.

"You certainly showed up at just the right time," the doctor exclaimed.

"I seem to remember you did that once for me," Nachman responded. "I'm glad to return the favor."

"You're looking good."

"I almost didn't recognize you." Nachman stepped back and looked him over.

"Have I changed so much in these few years?"

"You look the same, but different," Nachman replied. "I don't remember you dressed like this back in Ravensdorf. And you were clean shaven then. You wrote us about the changes, but now I see what you meant."

"You, on the other hand, are exactly the same. I daresay that these are even the same clothes you were wearing when we said good-bye."

Nachman pretended to be offended. "Not to exaggerate! Well, maybe it's the same trousers, but definitely a different shirt."

Both men laughed. "What are you doing here? Coming to visit me?"

"I had no idea you were here. Your latest letter said that your family was coming to Yerushalayim, but you didn't know if you would be able to leave the hospital and come with them."

"It is certainly providential that you showed up."

"My friend, you are looking at the Director of Acquisitions for the Kfar Ata Textile Factory. We have several important clients in Teveria, so I come here regularly."

"And the Eden Hotel is one of your clients?"

"As a matter of fact, it is. But the specific reason I am here today is to pick up my dear landlady and bring her back to Kfar Ata."

Tanchum regarded him with a puzzled expression.

"She is a widow and not a young woman. I guess she must be lonely since she is always visiting Meir and me, and she won't rest until she sees both of us settled down and married. Anyway, Mrs. Lipschitz told us she was coming to the Eden Hotel today to meet an old friend, and out of the goodness of my heart I offered her a ride."

"Kreindel Lipschitz is your landlady?"

"You know her?" Nachman was incredulous.

"She was friends with my mother back in the Old Country."

"What a small world!"

Just then, a van pulled up to the entrance, discharging the rest of the Stern family. Yanky ran over to Fetter Tanchum, chattering a mile a minute about the endless steps in the city of Tzefat, and how they had seen an artist with an easel who painted portraits of cats. In the middle of an account of how he had nearly become lost in the maze of alleys, the child suddenly stopped and stared at the man with Tanchum.

Rabbi Stern and Chaim joined them at that point. "You're looking much better, Tanchum," his father said with satisfaction. "The sleep did you good."

Chaim scrutinized Tanchum's companion. Suddenly, he recognized the former groundskeeper. "*Herr Nachman*! Yanky, remember? It's *Herr Nachman* from Ravensdorf!"

Tanchum introduced his friend to his father. "Do you remember, Tatte, that I told you about the men who took over for me in Ravensdorf when I left? This is Nachman Glaser. He and his cousin Meir helped me convert the manor into a convalescent home for survivors of the concentration camps."

The men shook hands and Rabbi Stern invited Nachman to join them for Minchah and then dinner. "I see this is a good day for reunions," he commented.

In the dining room, Kreindel caught sight of her boarder. "Nachman! We don't have to leave already, do we?"

"After dinner, Mrs. Lipschitz," Nachman reassured her.

"He is such a fine young man," the landlady confided in Rebbetzin Stern. "I really hope he marries a local girl and settles down in Kfar Ata."

"You're all grown up!" Nachman looked from Chaim to Yanky and back. "It's really great to see you again." Reminding them of long-ago conversations, he added, "So, when are you coming to live in Eretz Yisrael?"

The children's faces grew serious. "We used to talk about how we were going to live in Palestine when Tante Fraydl came back," Chaim explained to Rabbi Stern. He turned to Nachman. "Where is *Herr Meir*?"

"The two of us live in Kfar Ata, a village about an hour's drive from here. Would you like to come back with me and meet Meir? He will be so excited to see you again."

"Can we, Zeide?" the boys chorused. "Can we go with Reb Nachman to visit Reb Meir?"

Rabbi Stern stroked his beard thoughtfully. "What do you say, Dovid?" he asked his oldest son.

"How will they return here?" Hannah asked. "It's been a busy day and I think Chaim and Yanky need to make it an early night."

Mrs. Lipschitz brightened. "Shaindel, I have a wonderful idea. Why don't you come and visit me at home? It's on the way to Haifa.

On your return trip to Lod you can stop by Kfar Ata. Then Meir will get to see the boys, and I can show you the garden I told you about."

"How do the hospitals in New York compare to those in Germany?" Nachman asked, sliding a second helping of chicken onto his plate.

"They are satisfactory," Tanchum replied. "I've been asked to consider changing my specialization to orthopedic surgery. It's a developing field with a good future."

As they discussed the pros and cons of such a decision, Nachman remembered Areleh Feigelbaum. "Meir and I have a young friend," he told Tanchum. "We fought in the same unit during the War of Independence. Areleh was very seriously wounded. His pelvis was shattered, and the doctors say he'll never walk again. He's just a kid — not even 18 yet. I wonder if you would know of an orthopedic specialist in America who could offer him any hope?"

106

ANCHUM CONSIDERED THE QUESTION. "I HAVE connections with one of the most prominent orthopedic surgeons at Maimonides Hospital, Professor Sidney Weintraub. When I spoke with him the day before we left New York, he offered me a fellowship position after he returns from an international lecture tour in the summer. If anyone in the world can help your friend, I think it would be Dr. Weintraub."

"How can we be in touch with him?"

"I suggest that I examine the boy and then relay the information to the professor. We'll see what can be done."

Excitement was evident in Nachman's voice. "Will you come with me tonight?" he asked. "You have no idea what a *chesed* it would be for his family to hear that there's even a chance that Areleh will walk again. They were told his case is hopeless."

"I'm not promising anything, of course. Success is in Hashem's hands, but I can try to be a good *shaliach.*"

"*Mezumen, mezumen!* Reb Nachman, will you do us the honor?" Rabbi Stern called.

After *bentching*, the men *davened* Maariv and then farewells were exchanged. Chaim and Yanky begged to be allowed to join

Nachman and the fetter. "Please! Please take us with you!" Chaim pleaded. "During the war I wasn't able to learn. After Archbishop Thiessen rescued me from the monastery, Reb Meir used to learn with me every evening after he finished work. I want to see him so much. Please?"

"What do you say?" Tanchum turned to his brother and sister-in-law.

"Dr. Stern just needs to examine Areleh, and then we will head back to Teveria. It won't take long," Nachman said. "It's 5:30 now. I can have them all back at the hotel by 9 at the latest," he promised.

Dovid shook his head. "I'm sorry," he told the boys, "but we haven't had time to learn yet today. A day without learning can never be replaced. You'll see Reb Meir on Sunday when we pass through Kfar Ata on our way to Haifa."

Hannah looked relieved. "We have a busy day planned for tomorrow," she tried to encourage the disappointed children. "You need a good night's sleep. You won't be sorry."

A tearful Kreindel Lipschitz settled herself into the backseat. "Good-bye, Shaindel." She reached through the open window to clasp the rebbetzin's hand. "I can't tell you how wonderful it was to spend this day together. Now I can hardly wait for you to come to Kfar Ata on Sunday. We must see each other once more before you return to America."

Tanchum's mother bent her head into the car to kiss her friend's cheek. "Drive carefully, Mr. Glaser," she requested. "It was a pleasure meeting you, and I can't thank you enough for making this very special day possible. Good-bye, Kreindel. We'll see each again other on Sunday, *b'ezras Hashem*."

Mrs.Lipschitz made sure that Nachman did not doze at the wheel by offering frequent and unsolicited advice about his driving. Tanchum chuckled as Nachman patiently responded to the ongoing comments. Occasionally he noticed his friend roll his eyes and bite his lower lip, but the only words he spoke were "Yes, Mrs. Lipschitz" and "Thank you, Mrs. Lipschitz."

By the time they reached Kfar Ata, Nachman had a blinding headache. He helped his landlady into her house, carried in the remaining packages and then led Tanchum around to the private entrance of their room. Meir was not there, but there was a note informing his cousin that he planned to eat supper with Areleh at the Feigelbaum house, and that Nachman was invited to join them.

Meir jumped to his feet when he saw the man accompanying Nachman. "Dr. Stern!" The two men greeted each other warmly.

"Will you join us?" Rivka asked, after introductions were made.

"Thank you very much, Mrs. Feigelbaum," Nachman replied, "but we already ate in Teveria." He then explained the purpose of their visit.

Rivka responded with a sudden intake of breath. "Do you think. . .?" She looked at the tall, blond stranger; afraid to believe that a cure might exist for her poor handicapped son.

"I will have to examine Aaron first, but according to the report Nachman gave me I am cautiously optimistic," Tanchum told her.

Areleh's expression was frozen. His hands shook as Meir wheeled him into his bedroom so Dr. Stern could perform the examination. The harried doctors at the military hospital had offered no hope. They said the damage was too severe. Months of therapy had brought no improvement. Was it possible that this American doctor could perform a miracle and restore movement to his legs?

Rivka wished that Fraydl was home to hold her hand while they waited for the verdict, but an hour earlier she had gone to the post office to call Malky in Yerushalayim. Rivka knew from past experience that there was often a long wait for the public phone.

She passed the next half-hour whispering *Tehillim* for Areleh and watching the front door to see if her sister had returned. Rivka sighed. She wondered if Malky had brought the children with her to the post office, or left them with Lipa? Fraydl would tell her that Areleh was back home. It was worth waiting in line for such good news. She looked at the door to her son's room, praying that soon she would have even better news to share.

In the bedroom, Tanchum helped Areleh onto his bed and gave him a pillow to support his head. "Please keep your hands at your sides," he instructed, methodically checking the boy's reflexes, looking for swelling or wasted muscles. He palpated the boy's pelvis, hips and legs and observed their alignment in relation to each other.

"This is called Gaenslen's test," Dr. Stern explained, flexing Areleh's hip joint as far as it would go on one side while extending the opposite one.

Areleh bit his lip to keep from crying out. He knew these exercises well from his months in the hospital. Internal rotation, external rotation. The doctor rolled Areleh onto his side to assess contractures.

Tanchum examined the scars left from the boy's injury and the subsequent surgeries. The whole examination took nearly an hour to complete, but Areleh was uncomplaining except when the physician's probing fingers made contact with points that were too sensitive to bear touch.

"I'm sorry for hurting you, but pain is a good sign," Dr. Stern commented. "It means that the nerves have not been severed."

Areleh lay back against the pillows, exhausted.

Tanchum opened the bedroom door. Rivka rose to her feet expectantly. "What do you say, doctor?" she asked.

"It is possible that there are still very small shreds of shrapnel embedded in the bone sheaths, which would explain the severe pain and the leg's inability to bear any weight," Tanchum told her. "The pelvic bone has healed remarkably well considering the degree of injury, probably because he is still young, but there is a grave distortion of the osteoperimeters. I recommend surgery to alleviate the pain, but I must consult with Professor Weintraub about whether it is feasible to resculpt the bone into the correct shape."

From his bed, Areleh shrugged. "I didn't understand a word of that," he admitted.

Tanchum turned back to his patient. "I said that after I speak with the senior doctor it will be possible to recommend a course of action," he said with a gentle smile. "Can anyone tell me where to find a telephone at this hour?"

"You want to call the professor now?"

"It's about noon in New York. I should be able to speak with him before he leaves the hospital."

"The only public phone is at the post office." Nachman studied his watch. "If we run, we might get there before they close."

107

A FEW MINUTES AFTER THE MEN LEFT, FRAYDL RETURNED. She found her sister in the kitchen. "Was there someone here while I was gone?" she asked, surprised at the unusual number of unwashed dishes in the sink.

Rivka smiled enigmatically. "Yes, we had guests. It's too bad you missed them. Sit down and I'll fix you an omelet for supper while I tell you about it."

"Don't you want to know what Malky said?" Fraydl was surprised at her sister's preoccupied manner.

"Of course I do. Here, take these and make a salad while I'm at the stove." Rivka handed her a cucumber, a tomato, a small onion and a sharp knife. Fraydl took the wooden cutting board and a bowl to the table and began to prepare the vegetables.

The oil sizzled when the beaten egg was poured into the skillet. Soon the familiar smell of omelet tickled Fraydl's nose. "I had to wait over an hour," she explained while slicing the cucumber. "The Katzman family has a new *einikel* to discuss with the *mechutanim* and Mr. Fried is negotiating with someone about buying or selling some property, I'm not sure which."

"That's the thing I hate about a public phone." Rivka slid the puffy omelet onto a plate. "You can never have a private conversation."

"Malky was so happy to hear that Areleh is home. I could almost see her dancing when I told her. It is such good news."

"I may have something even better to tell her next week." Rivka set the steaming omelet on the table. She opened the small icebox and took out a container of *smettina*.

"Are we celebrating?" Fraydl asked, contemplating the unexpected luxury of sour cream with a weeknight supper.

"Perhaps. While you were gone, Nachman Glaser came by with an old friend of his, a doctor who is visiting Eretz Yisrael from New York. This doctor, I forgot his name, has connections with some internationally renowned surgeon. He examined Areleh and seems to think that there might be an operation which can bring significant improvement."

Fraydl's eyes widened. "Mmmm," was all she could say after washing her hands for bread. She picked up a slice and made *Hamotzi*, swallowing as quickly as she could. "What wonderful news!" she exclaimed at last.

"He didn't promise, but he said there is room to hope."Tears stood in Rivka's eyes. "If only..." she whispered.

"We will *daven!*" Fraydl declared. "With Hashem's help, anything is possible!"

"They went to try and place an overseas call before the post office closes. You didn't see them?"

"There were still a few people in line after me, but I didn't notice Meir Glaser. I saw some men on the other side of our street, but I didn't pay attention to them. I was in a hurry to get home."

"That was probably them. They just left here a few minutes before you returned."

"I hope they got in before Luba locks the door. Luba is so soft hearted that she never closes the post office until everyone has finished. If they got there before the last one in line was on the phone, then she'll let them make the call."

"I'm going to sit with Areleh for awhile. Finish eating and then join us, Fraydl. It will help us bear the suspense until the doctor returns with news."

When Fraydl was done, she went to see her nephew. He looked pale, but the bitterness in his face was less pronounced than it had been. To distract him, she suggested that she accompany him on the piano while he played his clarinet.

"I haven't played since I left home," the boy responded with a frown.

"Do you think you've forgotten how?"

He laughed. "No! Ima, please bring me my clarinet and I will show Fraydl how music is supposed to sound."

Aharon got his musical talent from his mother, but Rivka had stopped playing after she heard about the loss of her entire family during the war. Fraydl had been a *mizhinekel*, the youngest, indulged even more than her older siblings. She'd been given private tutors to teach her to play the piano, the violin and the flute. She had even begun to learn music theory in school before all the Jewish pupils were expelled. After the war, it was natural for Fraydl to become the music instructor at the *Kinderheim*. When she came to Kfar Ata she was very pleased to see that there was a piano.

Fraydl sat on the piano stool and ran her fingers over the keys. "Ready?"

Areleh blew a few tentative notes, wet the reed a bit more and then challenged his aunt to begin. It was like a game. He would begin playing a tune and she would figure out how to accompany him, and then she would begin a different one and he had to join in.

Rivka listened with pleasure, occasionally stepping out of the room to look out the front window. When she saw that Nachman and Meir were finally returning with the doctor, she hurried to open the door and welcome them inside.

Tanchum did not keep her waiting. "Dr. Weintraub is very interested in your son's case," he said. "Does Aharon have a passport? We must arrange to bring him to New York as soon as possible, because the professor is scheduled to leave the country for another extended tour."

"I'll take care of it tomorrow," Rivka promised, her heart beating so rapidly that she felt dizzy. "We'll have to go to the Ministry of the Interior in Haifa."

"I am scheduled to be in Haifa tomorrow for a business meeting, Mrs. Feigelbaum," Nachman said. "If you and Areleh can be ready by 8 o'clock, I will be happy to give you a ride."

"I'll come at 6 a.m. to take Areleh to Shacharis," Meir offered. "We can catch the early *minyan*."

"That would be perfect." Rivka was grateful that the pieces were falling into place so well. "Please sit down and let me bring you some strudel before you leave." She went to the kitchen to boil water and prepare a tray of refreshments. A short time later, she reappeared with cups and saucers. "Tea or coffee?"

"Tea, please."

The sound of music could be heard from the back room. "Who is playing?" Meir asked, accepting a steaming cup of tea. "Thank you."

"Areleh plays the clarinet and my sister Fraydl is accompanying him on the piano."

Tanchum blanched. His hands shook, spilling tea into his saucer. "Fraydl?" he said her name in a strangled whisper.

"Yes, my younger sister."

"Fraydl," he whispered as an unmistakable look of sorrow passed over his face.

Rivka held out the platter of apple strudel, but the doctor didn't even notice. "May I speak with Areleh again?" he asked in a shaken voice.

"Of course," she replied, puzzled by the change that had come over her visitor. "You know where his room is."

Tanchum rose and walked slowly back to the boy's room. He put a hand on the wall to steady himself. It couldn't be her, of course. Fraydl, *his* Fraydl, was in Yerushalayim. He had seen her there himself on Shabbos.

Through the open door he watched Areleh sitting propped up by many pillows, his eyes half closed with concentration. On the other side of the room, with her back to him, Fraydl Mertzbach played a lively tune on the piano.

It was her! In Kfar Ata, of all the unlikely places — a place he had never intended to visit. What a miracle that he had met Nachman and agreed to come to examine Aharon Feigelbaum tonight! But what if she ran away again when she saw him?

Areleh opened his eyes. Recognizing the doctor, he began to lower the instrument from his lips, but Tanchum signaled him to continue. Fraydl continued playing without realizing that there was someone else in the room with them.

When Areleh paused between melodies, Tanchum reached for the clarinet and Areleh handed it to him with a smile. The doctor put the mouthpiece to his own lips and blew. After so many years, his technique was rusty, but he managed to keep up with the piano for several bars before the instrument squawked. Her hands still arrayed on the piano keys, Fraydl twisted the stool around to see what had happened. Her dark-brown eyes met the blue ones she had never expected to see again.

108

TANCHUM WAS QUICKER THAN FRAYDL. BEFORE SHE COULD take a step he had already closed the door and was standing guard to prevent her escape. Areleh watched the two of them with a bemused expression. "Do you know each other?" he asked.

"Listen to me," Tanchum's voice was deep with repressed emotion. "You can leave, but first hear what I have to say."

Fraydl backed away until she bumped into the wall. Her knees felt terribly weak. She felt herself sliding down the wall.

"Sit down, *Fraulein*," he directed in the calm and authoritative voice that she remembered so well. He pointed at the chair beside Aharon's bed. Fraydl obeyed.

Tanchum's thoughts were racing, but his mouth seemed paralyzed. Areleh looked back and forth from his aunt to the doctor. "Will someone please tell me what is going on?"

There was a tap on the door and Tanchum moved sideways to let Mrs. Feigelbaum enter the room. Seeing the three of them apparently frozen in a tableau she asked, "What is the meaning of this?"

"This is *Herr Doktor* Emsbach," Fraydl told her sister in a shaky voice. "This is the man I told you about."

Rivka moved protectively in front of her sister. "Is it true?" she asked the doctor.

"No," he replied. "Please let me explain, and then you will all understand, but first I have something to tell you that will make you very happy."

The two sisters regarded him suspiciously. Was he referring to a treatment for Areleh?

"Your sister's children are alive and well. Chaim and Yanky are with my family in Teveria."

Rivka and Fraydl gasped, and then impulsively embraced. "Chaim'ke and Yanky," Fraydl sobbed. "They're safe. They're alive!"

Rivka turned back to the stranger who had entered their lives so unexpectedly, tears still streaming down her cheeks. "Such wonderful news. Tell us what happened. How did they come to be with you? The war is over already for five years. Why didn't you contact us until now?"

"It's a long story. Please sit down and I'll try to explain." For the next hour Tanchum Stern told the amazing story of his kidnapping and the discovery of his true identity, and his rescue of the boys after the war.

"This is unbelievable," Rivka said, shaking her head.

"You're right about that. But every word is true," Tanchum affirmed.

"How can you expect us to believe that you are not Dr. Karl Emsbach? What proof do you have?" Rivka struggled to retain her equilibrium, torn between her son's desperate need for a cure, her sister's vulnerability and their excitement at discovering that Yocheved's children had survived the war.

Tanchum sighed. "My parents recognized me. They knew that the kidnapper was Heinrich Mauer, who revealed the story to me just before he died. There is a strong resemblance between my brothers and me. My former servants verified that I am not the biological child of their mistress. The dates fit."

"These details are all circumstantial," Rivka pointed out.

"I agree. It is not incontrovertible proof, and each detail by itself is not conclusive, but the accumulation of details points to the conclusion that I am, in fact, Tanchum Stern and I never was Karl Emsbach."

Fraydl finally found her voice. "It must have been so traumatic for you," she said sympathetically, "to suddenly discover that you're not who you always believed you were. That all the things you were certain about were suddenly in question."

Tanchum felt the tension in his neck and shoulders relax. Fraydl believed him. He had known she would understand.

Areleh stared at the doctor in fascination. "You mean you were a *goy*?" he asked. "You didn't even know you were Jewish?"

Tanchum nodded sadly. "My real parents had lost hope and moved to America before the war, but they always *davened* for me. I believe it is the power of my mother's *tefillah* that brought me back to them in the end." He looked at Fraydl. "And it is the power of my own *tefillah* that brought me to Eretz Yisrael to meet you again," he added softly.

They heard a knock. Tanchum stepped aside and Rivka opened the door. Nachman Glazer was standing there. "Excuse me," he said uncomfortably, sensing that he had interrupted something important. "Dr. Stern, I promised to have you back in Teveria by nine. It's 10 o'clock already."

"I'm coming," Tanchum said. "Areleh, I hope to see you in New York in the near future. Mrs. Feigelbaum, I appreciate what you are going through. May we see your son's full recovery soon! *Fraulein*, is it reasonable to think that I can see you again before we leave Eretz Yisrael?"

Fraydl stood up and moved close to her sister. "It is possible," she answered, her eyes gleaming with unshed tears.

"Tomorrow?"

"Yes, tomorrow."

"I will bring Chaim and Yanky with me," he promised.

After the men left the house, Rivka turned off the light and told Areleh to go to sleep. She pulled Fraydl from the room and led her to the kitchen. "Tell me again, everything you told me before and anything else you remember. Who is this man?"

On the way back to Teveria, Tanchum was silent, sunk deep in his own thoughts. Glaser glanced at his friend from time to time, struggling to curb his curiosity. There had been electricity in the room when he'd interrupted to remind Dr. Stern of the time. Tanchum finally spoke.

"You are an amazing *shaliach*, Nachman."

Nachman smiled and nodded. "I try to be." He feigned modesty.

"Actually, you have no idea."

"So, tell me."

"Areleh Feigelbaum is your friend."

"Yes."

"Chaim and Yanky are war orphans. Their mother was Mrs. Feigelbaum's sister."

For a moment Nachman lost control and the car nearly swerved off the road. He fought the steering wheel until he could pull over to the side. "You mean to tell me that Chaim and Yanky are Areleh's cousins?" he asked excitedly.

"Yes. The Feigelbaums moved to Palestine long before the boys were born. The children were too little to remember their aunt's name, so I never knew about her existence."

"But how did you figure it out tonight?"

"Yanky and Chaim were with another aunt when I first discovered them. We were all separated in the aftermath of the war. Later I found Yanky, and you remember when Archbishop Thiessen brought Chaim to us — but all traces of their young aunt were lost. I assumed she had not survived. Tonight I recognized Mrs. Feigelbaum's sister as the boys' aunt, Fraydl."

"Amazing! And all this happened because I took my landlady to meet her old friend without even knowing she was your mother!"

"A *gevaldige zechus*," Tanchum agreed.

"I never appreciated myself before," Nachman marveled. "I'm a miracle worker!"

109

AT MIDMORNING THE NEXT DAY, A RENTAL CAR PULLED UP
and parked in front of the Feigelbaum home. Yanky and
Chaim spilled out and then abruptly stood still, staring uncertainly
at the house. From her window, Fraydl watched Dr. Emsbach
encourage them. It was not possible to hear the words he spoke,
but Chaim nodded and Yanky took their benefactor's hand. She
hurried to open the front door.

"Chaim! Yanky!" she called out, almost shaking with excitement
to see her nephews alive and well.

"Tante Fraydl!" Expressions of wonder and gladness lit the children's faces, but they pressed themselves even closer to the doctor
as the small group approached the front porch.

"Good morning, *Fraulein*," Tanchum said. The happiness in his
voice made her feel shy.

"Come in, please," she welcomed them.

To overcome the awkwardness of the first moments, Fraydl began
to chatter in a most uncharacteristic way. "My sister, your Tante
Rivka, had to take her son Areleh to the Ministry of the Interior
to get a passport," she said, to explain why she was the only one

home. "Areleh was injured in the war with the Arabs and needs an operation. Please sit down and I'll bring you something to drink."

"We know," Chaim told her, taking a place at the dining table. "Fetter Tanchum told us about him."

"Your mother was 11 years older than me," Fraydl continued. "Rivka is the oldest sister in our family. She came to live in Palestine right after she was married. I was only a baby then."

Chaim looked interested in these details, but Yanky leaned against Dr. Stern and hung over his shoulder, staring out the window. The younger boy's interest perked up briefly when Fraydl served them fruit and cookies. She watched with interest as the doctor peeled and sliced the fruit for Yanky, and reminded him to make a *berachah*.

"You have been like a father to them," she observed.

He shrugged. "If you remember, I intended to take on that role after the war."

Fraydl blushed at the memory.

"I wish I knew how to raise children, but I have no experience. My older brother Dovid convinced me to let him and his wife, Hannah, take Chaim and Yanky. They have become an integral part of his family, just like their own children."

Both boys smiled and nodded. "We see the Fetter every day and we visit Baba and Zeide Stern almost every day, too," Yanky said. "But we live with Ima and Abba."

"I felt that it was the healthiest option for them. Chaim and Yanky need a father and a mother, and it is good for them to have brothers and sisters, too. I could not give them that." She realized that he was apologizing.

"We have a good life with Abba and Ima." Yanky spoke resolutely. "They are our family now." He stared defensively at his aunt.

"I'm glad to hear that you're happy," Fraydl responded. "I worried about you boys constantly. I could not know whether you were in good hands or if something terrible had happened. My worst fear was that the troubles might make you forget about being Jewish. It makes my heart lighter to know that you have been part of a warm and caring *frum* family. I want to know everything that happened after you left Ravensdorf. Dr. Emsbach told me that he arranged for you to be hidden in an orphanage. What was it like there? Did you stay together? How did you meet again after the war?"

Tanchum winced when he heard her use his former name, but Chaim corrected his aunt, "He isn't *Herr Doktor* Emsbach, don't you know? It was all a mistake."

Momentarily confused, Fraydl quickly recovered. "Of course… yes. I know. Please, tell me where you have been all this time and what happened to you?"

Her older nephew described the orphanage and the end of the war, and finally the time he spent in the monastery until Archbishop Thiessen rescued him.

"*Oy,*" Fraydl murmured from time to time, "*Oy vey!*" When the story was finally completed, she murmured, "Chaim, I'm sure that all our family was watching over you from the next world, and they are proud of you. You lived through a nightmare, but it didn't defeat you. It is *mamash* a miracle that you didn't give in!"

Dr. Stern told the children's aunt as much as he knew about Yanky's experiences. Looking tenderly at the fidgety youngster, Fraydl said, "My poor little Yanky. It must have been very hard for you, too."

Yanky interrupted them, "Do you remember how we used to sit together like this at night when we came down from our hiding place in the attic?"

"Yes, Yankele, I remember." Fraydl smiled.

"I used to play with toy soldiers," the child recalled. He turned to their benefactor, "Where are my toys? Do we still have them?"

"I think they are in the chest with the silver at Zeidy's house," Tanchum answered. "Do you want to play with them again?"

"Yes!"

"You're too big to play with dolls," Chaim's voice dripped with an older brother's condescension.

"When you were my age, *you* played with them. I remember how you lined them up on the floor!" Yanky defended his honor.

"Whoa! No arguing! What will the Tante think?" Tanchum drew Yanky close to him again. "I'm afraid that this young man is getting bored from so much adult conversation. Is there something he can play with — a ball or puzzle, perhaps?"

Fraydl sighed and shook her head. "I think my sister gave all the games and toys to her married daughters for her *einiklach*. Would you like to draw something, Yanky? I can give you paper and a pencil."

"No!" Yanky replied petulantly. "I want to go outside. There's nothing to do here. I want to go somewhere else."

Fraydl was upset. "You've only just come, Yanky. You haven't seen me since you were 5 years old, and now you want to leave so soon? What will I tell Tante Rivka and Cousin Areleh?"

Yanky slumped down onto the floor in a pout.

Seeing that the youngster was almost in tears, Tanchum thought quickly. "How would you like to go for a drive, Yanky?" he asked. "Let's get in the car and see what interesting things there are in Kfar Ata. Maybe we'll find some camels or Bedouin tents."

"There are no camels or Bedouin tents in Kfar Ata. . ." Fraydl began, but both of the boys were already on their feet and heading to the door.

"Please, Tante Fraydl," Chaim turned around to face her. "Let's go out for a little while. Tante Rivka and Aharon are not here now anyway. We'll come back later and then we'll meet them before we go back to Teverya."

"I don't know…" She hesitated.

"What time do you expect your sister's return?" Tanchum asked.

"It could be a few more hours," Fraydl admitted. "Nachman Glaser gave them a ride to Haifa, but government offices have notoriously long lines. Even if they don't have to wait to file their applications, they have to come home on public transportation. I suppose the earliest time they can be back is by noon."

"And it might be later?"

"It will probably be later."

"I think I have time to take the boys for a drive. We'll return by 2 o'clock."

"Tante Fraydl, come with us!" Yanky's enthusiasm was contagious.

"Yes, Tante Fraydl," Chaim joined in. "We'll ask Fetter Tanchum to take us to the sea. It is such a beautiful day. How can you stay behind?"

"I haven't seen you in five years," she said, sorrow resonating in her voice. "I don't want to take my eyes off of you! The only thing I want to do is hear your voices and watch you. It is a dream come true to have you here. I cannot bear the thought of you leaving me. I have so many questions and there are so many things I want to tell you. I want to know what's happening in your lives today and about anything you don't have that you need."

"We don't need anything, Tante Fraydl. The only thing that is missing is you. If you will only come with us, then everything will be perfect!"

"You are invited to join us, of course." Tanchum turned his face away, but the tremor in his voice gave away the intensity of his feelings.

Fraydl hesitated. Finally, against her better judgment, she followed them to the car.

110

B ITTE SCHÖN," FRAYDL MURMURED, FORGETTING TO SPEAK in Yiddish as Dr. Stern opened the rear passenger door for her. Yanky climbed in on the other side and Chaim took the front seat.

"It's windy today," Tanchum commented, putting the key in the ignition and starting up the engine.

"It's often windy during the winter months," Fraydl agreed.

They drove west with the sun behind them until the road began to descend. Tanchum rolled down his window and sniffed. "Who can smell the sea yet?" he asked.

"I do! I do!" Yanky yelled.

"We're almost there!" Chaim sat forward, straining to see the blue line on the horizon that meant they had reached the Mediterranean coast.

Alarmed, Fraydl held on tightly to the armrest when Tanchum left the road behind and began driving on sand. Dunes rose before them, but he carefully maneuvered the car over and around them until at last the restless blue sea stretched ahead in all its beauty.

When Tanchum shut the motor, he told the children, "Listen!" Fraydl found the intermittent cries of the wheeling gulls and the steady lap of the waves strangely soothing. Tanchum opened the car door and they all climbed out. The boys followed him to the trunk, which creaked when it opened.

"Here." He handed a bottle of water to Yanky and two bottles to Chaim. "Carry these down, please." He draped a blanket over Chaim's shoulder, adding "This, too."

"Can I help carry something?" Fraydl asked.

"If this is not too heavy for you?" He pointed to a canvas bag containing wooden sticks, a few old newspapers and some torn rags.

"Are you going to make a campfire?" she asked, mystified.

Tanchum smiled. "No. You'll see." He picked up a wicker basket and hefted it onto his shoulder. "Let's go," he called and led the way toward the water.

"Do you know what's in the basket?" Fraydl asked Chaim as they carefully bumped their way down the steep, sandy path.

"Baba told the kitchen staff at the hotel to prepare a picnic lunch for us. They gave us that wicker basket when we left."

Fraydl nodded. "And do you have any idea why we need these?" she questioned, indicating the canvas bag she was carrrying.

Chaim shook his head. "No idea. Maybe Fetter Tanchum is preparing a surprise for us."

At the bottom of the dune, Tanchum set the heavy basket on the sand and took the blanket from Chaim. He spread it and invited Fraydl to sit. She gratefully sank down onto the sun-warmed sand. While the boys were busy examining the contents of the canvas bag, she removed a scarf from the pocket of her jacket and tied it over her head and under her chin to keep the strands of hair from blowing into her face. Dr. Stern began sorting the various sticks.

"What are you doing?" Yanky's curiosity was insatiable.

"Have patience and you will see."

Tanchum knelt on the sand. With great concentration he laid sticks on the ground in a geometric pattern. It took some rearranging until he was finally satisfied. Then he tied them securely with twine.

"Can you give me the papers, please?" he asked Fraydl. She dug the newspaper out of the canvas bag and handed it over.

Tanchum folded and refolded the newspaper until he had formed a diamond shape. "I haven't done this in 20 years," he muttered. "I hope I haven't forgotten how to do it right." He attached the paper to the sticks and began tearing the rags into strips.

The children huddled around the doctor, their cheeks growing pink in the cool breeze. "It's going to be a kite!" Yanky yelled suddenly. "Tante Fraydl, the fetter made a kite!"

Sure enough, a moment later the strange contrivance of sticks and newspaper and rags was definitely recognizable. They all laughed as Tanchum lifted it over his head, proudly displaying his handiwork. The doctor had to struggle to keep his balance as the wind nearly tore the kite out of his grasp.

"Look how it wants to fly!" Chaim exclaimed.

"Ready, everyone?" Tanchum called.

"Let me! I want to fly it!" Yanky jumped as high as he could in an effort to grab the kite, but Tanchum laughed aloud and held it beyond his reach.

Fraydl found herself laughing with them, enjoying the moment even as she could hardly believe it was happening. How free and happy the boys were! She had never seen Dr. Emsbach so relaxed and in such good spirits.

No, not Dr. Emsbach. There was a *yarmulke* on his golden hair and the breeze had teased the *peyos* from behind his ears. *Dr. Tanchum Stern*, she whispered. *Not Herr Doktor Emsbach. Not anymore...*

Winter surf pounded the sand, cresting into froth near the shore before receding into the depths. Buoyant, looping gulls circled overhead. It had been so long since Fraydl had felt so calm and safe.

Shading their eyes from the sun with their hands, Chaim and Yanky stared up as the kite climbed higher and higher. When it was steady in the sky, Dr. Stern handed the roll of twine to Chaim. "Let it out slowly, son," he instructed the boy. The kite jerked and twisted in the wind.

"Look, the kite is laughing!" Yanky declared as it bounced on the end of its string.

"The pull is so powerful!" Chaim exclaimed with surprise. His arms ached with the effort needed to keep the mischievous kite in line.

"Yes, but you are stronger." Tanchum reassured him. "You're doing very well. Let out a little more string... That's right."

"It's so high!" Yanky cried. "Can my mamme and tatte see it from *Shamayim*?"

"I'm sure your mamme and tatte are watching you all the time," Fraydl told him. A pang of sadness touched her heart and her eyes.

"Do you really think so?" Chaim took his eyes off the kite to look at his aunt.

"I believe they know you are happy, and that makes them happy, too."

"It's my turn!" Yanky tugged on his brother's arm. "I want to hold it!"

"It will lift you up to the sky," Chaim said. "You're too little. Look how hard it is for me to hold on, and I'm bigger than you."

Yanky's eyes filled with tears and his lower lip turned down in a pout. "Fetter Tanchum, tell Chaim to let me hold the kite too!" he begged.

"Let's hold it together," Dr. Stern suggested. "Give a little more string, Chaim. That's right. Now Yanky, come over to this side."

Before Tanchum could take the ball of twine from Chaim, Yanky grabbed it.

"Ouch!" The little boy dropped the string and licked the angry red welt that appeared across his palm.

"It's just a little rope burn," Dr. Stern reassured him. "It will be better in a few minutes."

"It hu-u-urts!" Yanky wailed.

"Look what you've done!" Chaim raced after the bouncing wad of string, but he wasn't fast enough. The kite that had risen almost to the clouds flipped over and dived back to earth, smashing into the sand and exploding into pieces.

The children regarded the broken kite with mournful faces.

"It's not my fault," Yanky sobbed. "I didn't know it would happen."

Tanchum put an arm around his shoulders. "Yanky, you need to listen when grown-ups tell you something," he said gently.

The boy buried his face in Tanchum's side and sobbed. Tanchum patted his back. "Crying won't bring it back," he told the child. "If you learn to be more careful and listen to what you're told, then it is worth the loss."

Chaim kicked at the sand angrily.

"Don't be cross," the doctor said quietly. "He's still young. The kite was just a bunch of sticks and paper tied together with string. Caring about your brother's feelings is more important than a broken kite."

Chaim considered the doctor's words and finally nodded. Tears of disappointment still trickled down Yanky's cheeks. "Come with me," Chaim offered. "I'm going to collect some seashells to take back and show my friends at yeshivah. Want to help?"

Yanky quickly wiped his face with his sleeve and ran after his brother. Fraydl watched the man's eyes following her nephews and pondered the change she could sense in him. *He's different. The kindness and the caring are the same, but this is not the same man man I remember from the war.*

Karl Emsbach had been a refined gentleman, but a German. He had been educated to view the world according to values antithetical to *Yiddishkeit*. But somehow, the lost little boy's *pintele Yid* had survived. Like Chaim and Yanky, Hashem guided Tanchum Stern through the destruction until He'd brought him home again.

111

D ON'T GO TOO CLOSE TO THE WATER!" TANCHUM CALLED.
Obediently, Yanky stepped back from the edge of the wet
sand. Chaim waved at the doctor and then bent down to dig out
another shell.

"Sometimes Yanky's enthusiasm overtakes his common sense,"
Tanchum said, examining the contents of the wicker basket.

"Can I help?"

"Please."

Fraydl withdrew the tablecloth from the basket and spread it
across the wicker cover. "Would you please cut each of these in
half?" she asked, handing him a stack of fragrant pitas and a knife.

"Of course."

While Tanchum cut the pitas, Fraydl opened the glass jars containing cream cheese, techina, olives, hummus and condiments.

"These *knaidlach* look strange," he commented, pointing to a jar
filled with quarter-sized brown balls.

"That's falafel, not *knaidlach*." She smiled at his mistake. "It's
a Middle Eastern staple, made from chickpeas." She set their little

table with plates and silverware, and poured hot tea from the thermos into cups.

"Chaim! Yanky!" Tanchum called the boys. They all used water from the bottles to wash their hands. The food disappeared very quickly.

"This tastes so good," Yanky enthused. "It's the best food I ever ate!"

The others laughed. "A sea breeze and fresh air are guaranteed to whip up a healthy appetite," Fraydl observed.

"Aren't you glad you came with us?" Yanky asked her.

"Yes," she replied. "Very glad."

Tanchum looked as if he wanted to say something, but instead he turned and stared out to sea. When they had eaten their full, he took the soiled dishes to the edge of the water and rinsed them off. The boys lay back on the blanket, letting the sun warm their faces while Fraydl packed the leftovers back in the wicker basket. "Sure you don't want any more?" she asked.

"I couldn't eat another bite." Tanchum deposited the tableware back in the basket.

"Nooooo." Yanky rubbed his full tummy.

Chaim yawned and stretched. "I wish this day could go on forever," he said dreamily.

"We can always remember it," Fraydl said.

"Why not come back tomorrow?" Yanky suggested. "We can come every day until we have to go back to New York."

Tanchum tousled the child's hair. "I'm glad you're having a good time," he said, "but it's time to go back to Kfar Ata now. We don't want your Tante Rivka to worry about what happened to us, and we need to find a *minyan* for Minchah."

The drive back to the house seemed to Fraydl to take only a few minutes. Like Chaim, she felt regret that the outing had come to an end.

"Where is the nearest shul?" Tanchum asked her.

She pointed it out to them and then walked up to the porch.

"Where have you been?" was Rivka's greeting. "What on earth have you been doing? Look at you!"

Fraydl hung her jacket on the hook by the door and glanced in the mirror. A red face with bright eyes gazed back. "Oh, no! Sunburn!" she exclaimed.

"Where are the children?"

"Dr. Stern brought them in the morning, shortly after Nachman picked you and Areleh up. They're so beautiful, Rivka. Chaim is a copy of his father Moishy and Yanky looks just like Yochi — exactly her eyes and expression. I knew it would be a few hours before you returned. The children were restless so Dr. Stern suggested we drive to the beach and back. I didn't realize the winter sun could be so strong. . ."

"So where are they?" Rivka was surprised at how distracted her sister was.

"They went to *daven* Minchah. They'll be back in a few minutes."

"I am so keyed up, waiting to see Yochi's sons. It's too bad we had to go to Haifa, but at least we got the passport applications taken care of. Now we just have to wait a few weeks until they're delivered." Rivka sighed. "We still have to buy plane tickets and make arrangements with the hospital, and I'll need a place to stay while we're there. You might want to stay with Perel or Malky while we're gone." Rivka sat down in her rocking chair. "Fraydl, it's all so sudden. I don't really know what to do first."

"First, let's notify Perel and Malky that Yanky and Chaim have been found. Then we must tell them about Areleh and your trip to New York. I'm sure they'll want to come to Kfar Ata and see the children. When Dr. Stern comes, we can ask him how to go about working out the details of the hospitalization."

A knock on the door interrupted their discussion. "Do I look terrible?" Fraydl fretted.

"They're children. What difference does it make what you look like?"

Fraydl was grateful that the sunburn hid her blush.

Rivka opened the door wide. "*Shalom!*" she cried, "Chaim! Yanky! How wonderful to see you! I am your Tante Rivka. Come in, *kinderlach!*"

Tanchum ushered the boys to the sofa, where they sat on the edge of the cushions, uncomfortable under the scrutiny of an aunt they had never met before. After Tanchum excused himself to go visit Nachman and Meir, Fraydl decided to share Chaim's story with her sister. The boy nodded, occasionally adding a detail. Rivka wept as Fraydl related everything that the child had gone through.

Yanky, meanwhile, squirmed restlessly in his seat. He felt as though he couldn't sit still a minute longer. As unobtrusively as possible, he stood up and slowly sidled away from the others.

"Where are you going, Yanky?" Rivka's question startled the boy. He took a few cautious steps back toward the sofa, until his aunts were once again focused on Chaim. He decided to explore the house. He followed the hall, looking first in the door of Fraydl's room and then passing by the master bedroom. He studied the photographs on the wall and checked out the bathroom and water closet. The last door was closed. Yanky eased it open and found himself face-to-face with a boy about his brother's age.

"Hello," the boy said. "I'm Areleh. Are you Chaim or Yanky?"

112

THE LITTLE BOY STEPPED INTO THE ROOM UNCERTAINLY.
"Chaim or Yanky?" Areleh repeated.

"Yanky."

"Nice to meet you. Where's your brother?"

"He's in the living room, talking with the tantes."

The two cousins inspected each other curiously. "Why are you here all by yourself? Why aren't you with everybody in the other room?" Yanky asked.

Areleh grimaced. "I'm supposed to be sleeping."

"In the middle of the day? Are you sick?"

"I haven't recovered from being wounded in the war yet. I'm a soldier," Areleh informed him.

Yanky's mouth fell open in disbelief. He shook his head. "A real soldier? You don't look old enough to be a soldier!"

"The *yishuv* was in danger, so I lied about my age. They needed fighters so they didn't check too carefully. I was injured in battle."

Admiration filled the younger boy's eyes. "You fought against the Nazis?" he whispered.

"No, not the Nazis. The Arabs. Syrians, Iraqis, Jordanians, Lebanese, Egyptians. We were being attacked on all sides."

Yanky sank down on the chair beside Areleh's bed, his eyes sparkling. "Did you kill them?"

"I tried. I probably did, some."

"Tell me about it!" Yanky begged, spellbound.

Half an hour passed before Fraydl came looking for her little nephew and found the two boys deep in discussion. "Dr. Stern is here," she told Yanky.

"Not now!" the child begged. "Please tell the Fetter that I'll come soon, but not yet."

Fraydl gave Areleh a puzzled glance.

"It's all right, Tante Fraydl. He's not bothering me. I like having him here. He's really smart."

"Where's Yanky?" Rivka looked up when Fraydl returned to the living room.

"He and Areleh are discussing the War of Independence," Fraydl told her with an indulgent smile. "He says he'll come in just a few more minutes."

"It's not *derech eretz* to keep Dr. Stern waiting," Rivka frowned.

"I'll go and get him," Chaim offered, standing up.

"Thank you. Areleh's room is the one at the end of the hall."

Tanchum cleared his throat and tried to look anywhere except directly at Fraydl. At the same time, Fraydl concentrated on her hands, folded demurely in her lap. Seemingly unaware of any emotional undercurrent between Dr. Stern and her sister, Rivka continued the conversation she had begun when Tanchum returned from his visit with Nachman and Meir Glazer.

"Last night I was simply overwhelmed and not thinking straight," she said. "This morning, while we were waiting in line at the Ministry of the Interior, I realized how many questions there are still to ask and all the arrangements that have to be made before putting any plan into action. "

"Of course. Feel free to ask whatever you like. I will explain to the best of my ability."

Fraydl followed the conversation as Dr. Stern patiently cited the credentials of the resident orthopedic surgeon he had contacted, and the implications of the surgery he'd recommended. While Tanchum was engaged in conversation with her sister, she surreptitiously studied his expressions and was impressed with both his sensitivity toward the worried mother and his obvious professionalism. It was similar to the Dr. Emsbach she remembered, but much warmer and more refined.

"Fraydl, go and call the boys, please," Rivka interrupted her thoughts. "Dr. Stern has delayed far longer than necessary."

Dragging Chaim and Yanky away from Areleh was harder than anticipated, but they finally agreed to come after Fraydl promised that she would ask Dr. Stern to bring them again tomorrow.

"Tomorrow?" Tanchum's eyes searched her face.

She nodded, but avoided his gaze. "I promised the children to ask you. It was the only way they would agree to part from Areleh."

"I would like to meet your brother and the sister-in-law who have been taking care of the boys," Rivka told him. "Perhaps they could join us tomorrow? We must discuss the children's future."

Dr. Stern took one of Yanky's hand in his and rested the other on Chaim's shoulder. His expression was thoughtful. "I will tell them," he said, "although I suggest that it is premature to make a final decision."

"Is there any question?" Rivka frowned.

"As I explained to your sister this morning, at the moment the boys are thriving where they are. Mrs. Feigelbaum, you and your son are taking the first steps on a journey that is expected to last many months, and it is impossible to know what unforeseen complications may arise and how they will be dealt with. I realize that you are blood relatives, but in my opinion transferring Chaim and Yanky from their familiar environment under these circumstances is not advisable."

"With all due appreciation, Dr. Stern," Rivka responded crisply, "I have no doubt that my murdered sister and her husband would prefer that their children be raised by me and not by strangers."

An almost invisible intake of breath was the only outward sign that Rivka's words had pierced Tanchum's heart. He bowed slightly, promised to speak to his brother about bringing the boys back tomorrow and led the children out of the house.

"Rivka, do you really think it is necessary to take Chaim and Yanky away from the Stern family right now?" Fraydl said, watching the rental car until it disappeared around the corner.

"What kind of question is that?" Rivka bridled. "Do you think for even a minute that Yochi and Moishy would want anything else?"

"You and Areleh will be in America for months. That's what Dr. Stern said. Where will Yanky and Chaim be during that time?"

"With Perel or with Malky, of course."

"Don't you think you should discuss this with them first?"

"Fraydl, I can't believe we're having this conversation! Yocheved's children belong here with us. There's nothing further to discuss."

113

T HE NEXT MORNING, FRAYDL WAS AWAKE AT DAWN. RIVKA found her in the kitchen when she got up to fix coffee for Areleh before Meir came to take him to Shacharis. "What are you doing?"

"I thought I'd bake a cake for our guests. Where do you keep the cocoa?"

Rivka opened a cupboard and took out a packet of cocoa powder. "You're not usually up so early," she commented.

"I couldn't sleep."

"I know what you mean." Rivka added Turkish coffee to the boiling water in the *finjan* and watched the roiling fluid roll up the sides. "Yesterday was such an emotional day, discovering that Yochi's children had survived the war and seeing them here in our house." She poured the coffee carefully into ceramic cups and returned the *finjan* to the counter. "I still haven't fully grasped that Areleh is home, let alone that we will be traveling to New York for surgery. We've been through so much in such a short while."

Fraydl mixed the dry ingredients of her cake together and began folding it into the whipped egg whites. "Do you realize who Dr. Stern is for me and the boys?" she asked her sister.

Rivka spooned sugar into the four cups of coffee and stirred. She looked at her sister thoughtfully. "He's the Nazi that saved your life."

"It isn't just a matter of giving us shelter during the war. He could have left us in the attic and brought enough food to keep us alive, but he did much more than that. He brought toys and books for the children. He bought us warm clothing. He put his life on the line, Rivka. If it wasn't for him, none of us would be alive today. There is no way that the boys or I could have survived that winter. We were starving and cold. There were enemies everywhere and nowhere left to hide."

Rivka added milk to her cup and nudged one of the others toward her sister. "He was a hero," she agreed. "We owe him a debt of gratitude."

Fraydl poured the batter into the wonder pot, tightened the lid on it and centered it over the flame to bake. She sat down and took her cup, toying with the spoon. "Do you like him?" she asked suddenly.

"Like him? He's a doctor and a *mentsh*, but I don't see what liking or not liking has to do with it."

Fraydl made a *brachah* and took a sip of the rich, hot liquid.

Rivka narrowed her eyes and studied her sister. "Are you trying to tell me something?"

There was a knock on the front door. Rivka opened it to let Meir in. "Good morning, Mrs. Feigelbaum," he greeted her, before going down the hall to help Areleh get ready.

Rivka put the other two cups on a tray and carried them to the dining-room table. Upon her return to the kitchen, Fraydl was swaying over her *siddur,* so she finished drinking her own coffee in silence, engrossed in thoughts of all the changes taking place in her life.

When Rivka heard the sound of Areleh's wheelchair in the hall, she went to wish him a good day. "Did you sleep well?" she asked, handing her son a cup of coffee while Meir helped himself to the other one.

"Yes, very well. When are Chaim and Yanky coming?"

"I don't know. Sometime today, they didn't say exactly when." She handed him an umbrella. "It rained last night. It's still cloudy this morning."

"Don't worry, Ima. We won't melt.'

The remainder of the morning was routine: cleaning, cooking, a short walk to the greengrocer, some mending. "What's wrong with you today?" Rivka demanded when her sister kept polishing the same candlestick long after it gleamed like a mirror. "Do the other one already!"

Fraydl's hands went through the motions, but whenever an automobile passed down their street she hurried to the window.

"You really miss them, don't you?" Rivka's voice was gentle.

Fraydl ducked her head to avoid her sister's eyes. Her thoughts had not been on Chaim or Yanky, but she didn't want Rivka to realize that. "I felt like a mother to the boys during the time we were in hiding," she replied. "I tried to think what Yochi would do, and then fill their mother's shoes as much as possible."

"You were just a young girl. You did the best you could."

"Yes." The slamming of a car door made her jump. But it wasn't them.

Finally, late in the afternoon, a taxi pulled up in front of their house and discharged four passengers. Chaim and Yanky led the way. Following them were a woman and a man that Fraydl assumed was Dr. Stern until he came closer and she realized it must be his brother.

"*Shalom, shalom*! I am so glad you could come," Rivka invited them in.

"*Baruch Hashem, baruch Hashem*. I am Dovid Stern, and this is my wife, Hannah."

"The doctor did not come with you?" The disappointment in Fraydl's voice caused Rivka to stare at her for a moment.

"No, he remained in Teverya. The rest of the family had a tour scheduled today but our parents were tired and decided not to participate. Tanchum stayed at the hotel to keep them company," Dovid explained.

Yanky ran through the hall to Areleh's room, but returned immediately. "Where is Areleh? Why isn't he here?"

"I'll take you to him," Fraydl offered, suddenly needing to escape the scrutiny of the adults. "You too, Chaim."

"Where is he?" Hannah asked.

"At the yeshivah," Rivka told her. "He has a young man from Kfar Ata to help him get back and forth. He's only been home from the convalescent hospital for a few days."

After the children left, Dovid Stern turned to Rivka. "I understand that you want Chaim and Yanky to come and live with you, Mrs. Feigelbaum."

"Obviously. They are my sister's children and they belong with me."

"This is very understandable. How do you suggest we go about it?"

Rivka felt a great weight fall off her shoulders. The expectation of a confrontation with the Stern family gave way to relief. "I would prefer that the children stay here already. Today," she said.

"You must understand," Hannah told her, "that we were completely unaware that Chaim and Yanky had any living relatives. We never intended to separate the boys from their family. Our only desire was to give them a warm and caring home, to heal as much as possible the traumas they experienced in the war."

"Of course. I am very grateful for all that you've done for the boys."

"Everything was done wholeheartedly. They are wonderful children and we love them dearly," Dovid said. "Chaim and Yanky have really become a part of our family and we wish that they could stay with us, but we understand your feelings."

Rivka warmed to the couple. "I would feel exactly the same way in your place."

"It looks as if they've gotten off to a good start. Both Chaim and Yanky told us how much they like your son Aharon. Of course they already know your sister as well, so it is possible they could make the transition without too much difficulty." Dovid turned his head to look around the small living room. "I hope it will not be too hard for you."

"What do you mean?"

"I suppose it's been a few years since active young children lived here."

Rivka smiled and lifted her palms outward in a gesture indicating her agreement with this statement.

"Your house is so tidy and quiet. You're not afraid that it may be difficult getting used to the noise and mess of two active young boys?"

"Maybe a little," Rivka admitted. "Was it hard for you?"

"We still have young children at home," Hannah told her. "We're accustomed to it."

The conversation veered to Areleh's upcoming surgery. "It is a miracle that our neighbor Nachman Glaser met your brother. It was so heartbreaking to think that my son would never walk again. Dr. Stern has given us hope that he may yet lead a normal life."

There was a bit of commotion at the front door as Yanky burst in with a flurry of cold air, followed by Chaim huffing and puffing as he pushed Areleh in his wheelchair. "It's starting to rain!" Yanky yelled.

Rivka quickly went to bring rags to clean the mud off their shoes — but not before Yanky had run around the room, leaving dirty tracks wherever he stepped. She bit her lip in consternation at the havoc one young boy could wreak in less than five minutes.

114

FRAYDL LAGGED BEHIND YANKY AND CHAIM, RELUCTANT to return to the house just yet. Too many things had changed in such a short time. She needed to be alone for a little while, to sort out her tangled thoughts and feelings.

How long ago had it been when the biggest dilemma in the world was whether or not to accept Meir's proposal of marriage? That was before the sight of Dr. Emsbach in shul on Shabbos completely shattered her peace of mind, unexpectedly reawakening terrors she had thought long buried. Fraydl pondered the irony of fleeing Yerushalayim for the safety of her sister's home in Kfar Ata, only to find herself cornered in Areleh's room by the very individual she intended to escape!

The discovery that Dr. Emsbach was actually the scion of a refined Jewish family was earthshaking. How could such a thing be? She had barely processed this information when Chaim and Yanky were suddenly part of her life again. For five long years Fraydl had mourned the loss of the children, pouring her heart out in every prayer, begging Hashem to protect and save them from

12

harm. What a joy to see the two boys healthy and happy and growing up so nicely!

Fraydl thought of her other nephew, Areleh. Fountains of tears had flowed after he disappeared during the War of Independence. Then he'd reappeared — only to break their hearts again with his crippling injury. Month after month, she'd provided emotional support to Rivka as they watched the teenager grow bitter beyond his years, seemingly condemned to life as an invalid. And then Dr. Stern had come on the scene, bringing a ray of hope. And all of these things had taken place in less than one week!

Sporadic raindrops spattered softly in the street, and Fraydl felt tiny wet drops prick her cheeks and forehead. Engrossed in thought, she sheltered beneath a tree across from the house and waited, hardly noticing the ticking of the rain on the leaves above her.

Yesterday she'd spent an improbable morning with Chaim and Yanky and Dr. Stern on the beach. She frowned at the unexpected intensity of her disappointment when the doctor did not accompany Yanky and Chaim again this morning. It was an effort to reframe her memories of this man. She needed to go back and view the years of the war through completely different lenses.

An automobile passed, sending up a lazy arc of spray from the wet street. Then, unexpectedly, the car braked and reversed course until it was even with where she stood. The driver opened the window. "Can I offer you a ride, Miss Mertzbach?" It was Nachman Glaser.

Fraydl shook her head. "No, thank you. I'm on my way back home. I only have to cross the street." She smiled self-consciously, feeling foolish for standing in the rain.

Nachman rolled up the window, but he didn't drive away. He pulled the key out of the ignition, opened the driver's door and came to stand beside her under the tree.

"Is everything all right?"

"Of course," she replied. "Wonderful, even."

"That's good." He did not look convinced.

The front door of the Feigelbaum house abruptly flew open. A small figure shot out of the interior, barreling blindly toward them.

Nachman reacted, instinctively, stepping forward to catch the boy's shoulder, which caused him to spin around. "Hey, what's the matter?" Nachman held on to Yanky so he wouldn't fall.

The child lifted a flushed, tear-streaked face and yelled, "You can't make me!"

"Make you do what? What are you talking about?"

"I *won't* stay here!" Yanky shouted. "I won't! I won't! I want to go back home with Abba and Ima."

Nachman looked at Fraydl questioningly. "Do you know what this is all about?"

"My sister wants our nephews to live with us now," she replied. Fraydl turned to the child. "Yankele, *lubinkeh*, don't cry. Come, let's talk about it. Tell me why you don't want to stay with Tante Rivka and me? We missed you so much, and we are so happy to be together again after the years we were apart. Do you want to leave me again?"

Yanky rubbed his eyes with his fists and hiccoughed. "The tante says we must live in Kfar Ata and not go back with Ima and Abba," he told Nachman. "I don't want to live here. I want to go home! I live in New York. I want to go back to my yeshivah. I want to be with my friends." The child's wide, frightened eyes pierced Fraydl's heart.

She turned helplessly to Nachman. "He's so young. He doesn't understand." Fraydl bent down to the boy's eye level. "Yanky, you will be happy here. I know you will. We are your family, your real family."

"Abba and Ima are my family, and Chaim and Fetter Tanchum. I don't *want* any other family!"

Dovid Stern appeared in the open doorway. His eyes searched for the runaway child until he saw the group under the tree. With a quick glance in either direction, he crossed the empty street to join them. Yanky cast an accusing look at his foster-father. His lower lip quivered.

Dovid put his arms around the boy and hugged him close. He didn't say anything at first, and Fraydl thought she saw tears in the older man's eyes. It was startling how much he resembled Dr.

Stern; it was obvious they were brothers. As Yanky's sobs subsided, the man who had become his Abba began to speak softly to the child.

"Hashem gives us many *nisyonos*, Yanky, but he also gives us solutions to the problems. We just have to search for them in the right places. You can run away from something you don't like, but in the end there is nowhere to run. When we left New York, we were not prepared for this to happen. It should actually make us happy that you are not the last of your family and that you have relatives here in Israel who love you and want you."

"No!" Yanky protested fiercely.

"Yanky, when a Jew has a big problem, what should he do?"

"There's no *time* to *daven*!" Yanky cried. "It will be too late to change anything after you leave me here."

"A Jew should always *daven*," Dovid corrected him. "But what I meant was that this is a problem where we must ask *da'as Torah*."

Yanky's forehead furrowed as his expression slowly changed. "What if the Rav says I must stay?" His voice was shaky.

"Then you must stay," Dovid replied firmly. "But we didn't ask yet, so we still don't know what he will say."

"When will we ask the Rav?"

"Come back to the house with me now, and let's discuss it. I think that your Tante Rivka would prefer that we ask Rav Mendelsohn. He is the Rav of Kfar Ata and a great *talmid chacham*."

Yanky nodded his agreement reluctantly. He accepted his foster-father's handkerchief, wiped his tear-stained face and blew his nose. The two returned to the Feigelbaum home hand in hand.

Fraydl nodded farewell to Nachman and followed a few steps behind them.

115

W HEN ARE THEY COMING OUT?" YANKY COMPLAINED,
pacing around the simple but tasteful anteroom outside
Rav Mendelsohn's study.

Chaim looked up from the *sefer* he was trying to learn. "Will you
please sit still and stop jumping around?"

"How can you just sit there and read?"

"I'm not reading, I'm learning."

Yanky peered over his brother's shoulder at the tiny writing
in the margins of the Gemara. A moment later, he was on his feet
again. "I can't just sit in one place," he declared. "What are they
saying in there?"

He examined the closed door of the Rav's study, wondering if
his vision would penetrate the wood if he just concentrated hard
enough.

"Yanky, come away from that door before somebody opens it
and trips over you." Fraydl waited until the boy had taken a few
steps back before continuing her vigil at the window. The rain had
stopped and it took an effort to avoid looking at the brilliant rainbow in the sky.

"How long does it take to ask a question and get an answer?" Yanky fidgeted. "They should have finished by now."

Chaim sighed. "Asking *da'as Torah* is very serious," he explained. "The Rav must consider if there were precedents in the Talmud and how the problem was resolved. Then he has to decide whether those situations are similar to ours, in order to know which decisions are applicable."

Yanky crossed his eyes and looked down his nose. "Will I be like that when I'm his age?" he asked Fraydl.

"*Im yirtzah Hashem*, yes!" she laughed. "The five years between you might seem like a huge gulf right now, but when you are grown men you won't feel any difference at all."

Yanky rolled his eyes. "I don't want to grow up," he muttered.

Fraydl chuckled in spite of herself, shaking her head. "Everyone has to grow up sometime. You wouldn't like staying in childhood forever. There are so many things you cannot do."

Yanky was mulling this over when they heard a click and the door opened.

Three pairs of eyes turned simultaneously to see Dovid Stern and Rav Mendelsohn come out of the study. The men were followed by Rivka, who kept her gaze ahead and did not meet her sister's searching eyes.

The Rav smiled his trademark warm smile to everyone and blessed them that Areleh's surgery would be successful and the young man would return from America on his own two feet. After shaking hands with Dovid and Chaim and patting Yanky on the head, he excused himself and left for the *shiur* he was scheduled to give at the yeshivah.

Dovid looked at each of the expectant faces in the anteroom, nodding to Fraydl, sending Chaim an encouraging smile as the boy returned the Gemara to the bookcase and holding out his arms to Yanky.

Yanky buried his face in Dovid's jacket, afraid to ask but unable to bear the suspense. "Abba, what did the Rav decide?" he whispered.

Rocking slightly, Dovid hugged Yanky. "You're coming home," he whispered back.

Yanky blinked away the tears that were making Abba's face look blurry. Plaintively, he asked, "Which home?"

"With me and with Ima, for as long as you want."

The younger boy gave a cry of delight and leaped in the air. "Chaim!" he shouted. "We're going home with Abba and Ima!"

Chaim remained standing in place, staring at some indefinite speck on the floor.

"You're not pleased, Chaim?" Dovid asked, regarding him intensely.

"Of course I am, Abba," Chaim answered, but something in his voice was hollow.

Dovid walked over to the youngster and lifted his chin so that he could look into his eyes. "Do you want to stay in Kfar Ata with Tante Rivka?" he asked, not concealing his surprise.

"It doesn't matter."

"Of course it matters. Not every flower blooms well in every climate. I want you to be honest with me."

Chaim met his eyes. "I just don't know, Abba. I was happy with you in New York and I felt good in my *shiur* at yeshivah, but…"

"But what, son?"

"There's something different here. I usually like learning, but if something distracted me in New York it wasn't really difficult to put away the *sefer*. Since we came to Yerushalayim, I feel such progress in my grasp of the Gemara. It's as if a light turned on in my mind and suddenly it all flows together so well. Maybe it's just temporary. Maybe I will just find myself struggling again… But right now, I feel like *shtieging* is the greatest pleasure in the world." Chaim paused, embarrassed.

Dovid put an arm around his shoulder and squeezed. "I'm proud of you," he said. "I think I understand what you are saying. It's not a secret that Torah learning in Eretz Yisrael is at a higher level than learning in *galus*. I'm very impressed that someone as young as you are can discern the difference. It is a sign of maturity."

Chaim blushed.

"Rav Mendelsohn has concluded that the determining factor is where you children want to be. That is why he spoke with both of you individually before he even considered your tante's point of view or my own opinion. In view of the difficult experiences you children went through during the war, stability is the main issue to take into consideration.

"Rav Mendelsohn said that both our home in New York and Tante Rivka's here in Kfar Ata are suitable, but he suggested that it would be best if the current arrangement continues because moving would mean uprooting you. You boys have become accustomed to life in America. You're settled there already."

Yanky bounced up and down impatiently, but Chaim remained deep in thought. "Does that mean I can decide for myself where I want to be?"

"Yes, son, it does. And whatever you decide, I will support you."

Chaim smiled at his adoptive father. "Thank you," he said softly. "I appreciate that."

Yanky looked from one to the other. "You mean that you want to stay in Eretz Yisrael?" he demanded of his brother. "You don't care how I feel?"

"Of course I care about how you feel. You can go back to Williamsburg with Abba if you want to. But I want to stay here."

Yanky's eyes widened and his mouth dropped open. "Without me?"

"Unless you want to stay here."

Yanky's eyes filled with tears. He turned his back on the others and kicked at a pebble on the sidewalk.

Halfway back, Yanky announced enthusiastically, "I have the solution! Areleh and Tante Fraydl and Tante Rivka will come and live with us in New York!"

"Oy, Yankele," Chaim rolled his eyes. "When will you be old enough to understand?"

Yanky's lower lip protruded in an exaggerated pout. "It is a good idea," he grumbled. "Why don't grown-ups ever listen to what children say?" A few seconds later, he turned to his young aunt. "You and Tante Rivka want us to live together, right?" he insisted. "If you live with us in Williamsburg, we will all be together and everyone will be happy."

"Except Chaim," Fraydl pointed out. "Chaim wants to continue learning in Eretz Yisrael."

Yanky frowned. As they passed under a tall tree, he jumped up and grabbed the lowest branch, yanked it down and then released it, spraying water on them all. Before anyone could scold the boy, he'd already raced ahead and ran across the street to the Feigelbaum porch.

For a moment Fraydl remembered the pathetic toddler Yanky had been, so thin and silent and frightened. She had pitied her nephews because they would never know a normal childhood. She glanced at Rivka.

"That child is resilient," her sister commented, dabbing at her wet face with her handkerchief. *"Baruch Hashem.* He reminds me of his father."

Fraydl agreed — Yanky *was* resilient. Still, her heart went out to him. In his few years of life, he'd suffered so much. She prayed that his future would be as joyous as his past had been turbulent.

And now Chaim wanted to stay and learn Torah in Eretz Yisrael. Glancing at her older nephew, she wondered how all of this would play out.

116

T ANCHUM, WILL YOU PLEASE STOP PACING?"

"Oh, forgive me, Mamme. I wasn't aware that I was doing it." He sat down again beside his father and reopened the *Mishnah Berurah* on the table.

"Tanchum, do you mind?"

Tanchum looked at his father without understanding the implied rebuke. Rabbi Stern raised his eyebrows, tilted his head to one side and stared pointedly at his son's fingers. Tanchum glanced down and realized he'd been drumming them on the tabletop. With an apology, he turned a page of the *sefer* and made an effort to concentrate.

Rebbetzin Stern looked up from her knitting. "Do you regret not going with your brothers to visit the ancient fortress?" she asked, obviously expecting him to deny it.

"Of course not." He shook his head in protest. "I am more than happy to stay in the hotel with you."

She resumed her knitting, against the backdrop of her husband's Gemara *niggun*.

Minutes later, Tanchum was once again pacing the room.

"Tanchum!" his parents said in unison. Their eyes met, and they laughed.

"What is it?" She stuck the long needles into the ball of yarn and focused her complete attention on him. Rabbi Stern leaned back in his chair and regarded his son with an expression of grave concern.

"Nothing, nothing. Everything's fine."

"It's obvious that he's not going to tell us." Rebbetzin Stern winked at her husband, her blue eyes dancing mischievously.

"But you know even without his saying it, don't you?" Her husband smiled indulgently at their son.

Tanchum looked from one to the other. "Nothing is wrong," he tried to reassure his parents. "Mamme, Tatte, everything is fine."

"You are sorry you didn't accompany Dovid and the boys to Kfar Ata." It was a statement, rather than a question.

He shrugged, making a vain attempt to escape his mother's scrutiny by answering with a question, "Why should I be?"

She smiled and addressed her husband, "I'm right, aren't I?"

"As usual," he responded, pursing his lips and nodding.

Again Tanchum looked back and forth between them. "Is there some detail here that I'm missing?"

His mother's smile widened and her blue eyes twinkled.

"You know," Rabbi Stern said, closing the Gemara, "I'm feeling much better than I was this morning. Shaindel, do you feel like going for a drive?"

"As a matter of fact, I do."

Tanchum regarded them suspiciously, half-wondering if this dialogue had been rehearsed but still not understanding where it was leading.

"Tanchum dear, would you mind arranging a car and taking us for a little ride?" his mother asked innocently.

"Of course!" He almost leaped to his feet. Tanchum Stern had no idea what their ulterior motive might be, but he welcomed the opportunity to channel his barely controlled restlessness into action.

Once they were settled in the rented automobile and Tanchum had adjusted the driver's seat for his long legs, he felt himself relaxing. After a rainy morning, it had turned into a beautiful day. The sun made the Kinneret glitter so intensely that he had to squint. Rabbi Stern handed him a pair of sunglasses from the glove box.

"Thank you." Tanchum looked at his mother's image in the rear-view mirror and asked, "Where shall we drive?"

She smiled at his jovial mood. It reminded her of a bird just released from its cage. "That way," she gestured, and he drove south along the Kinneret.

They were halfway to Kfar Ata when he realized where they were going. Perhaps his parents wanted to meet the children's aunt, Rivka Feigelbaum, or reacquaint themselves with Fraydl Mertzbach? That was fine with him. If he was honest with himself, it was more than fine. He just wondered why they'd been so mysterious about the destination.

Yanky opened the door when Tanchum knocked. "Fetter Tanchum!" he shrieked, grabbing his hand to pull him inside. "Baba! Zeide!"

Rivka approached her guests with a smile and welcomed them to her house. "Please join us," she said, indicating the empty chairs at her dining table.

Fraydl's eyes met Tanchum's and she blushed, though she turned away quickly before anyone but Yanky noticed. "What's the matter, Tante Fraydl?" he asked loudly, causing her already red cheeks to flush a deeper crimson. She fled to the kitchen, feeling the doctor's eyes follow her. She was trailed by her younger nephew.

Fraydl bent over the sink to wash her hot face with cold water. Yanky's mind was busy trying to comprehend her strange behavior, so she forestalled his questions by handing him a stack of dessert plates and some cutlery, gesturing back toward the living room because she didn't trust her voice. He staggered a little under the load but left the kitchen.

How foolish I am! she thought feverishly. Fraydl had never felt this way before and was ill equipped to deal with it. Hearing the hum of conversation in the other room, she supposed that no one except Yanky had paid attention. She waited until she felt in control before returning to the main room with a tray of fruit and a platter of her sister's apple strudel.

Rebbetzin Stern was deep in conversation with Rivka. Both of them paused to look meaningfully at Fraydl when she came to the table before resuming their low-voiced exchange. Hannah took the heavy dish of fruit from her young hostess and set it in the center of the table, and then transferred slices of pastry onto plates and offered them to each of the guests.

Dovid accepted a pastry and set it before his father before taking another for himself. The two men were discussing Rav Mendelsohn's decision and Chaim's request to stay in Israel to learn, while Chaim listened intently.

"What do you think about sending him to learn in Yerushalayim?" Rabbi Stern asked his son, patting the child's hand affectionately. "My friend Chaim Shmulevitz told me that Reb Leizer Yudel is re-establishing his yeshivah in Geulah. He's been in America for the last few months, raising money. I think you met him. He's staying with Shamshon Raphael Weiss. If I'm not mistaken, Tanchum gave Reb Leizer Yudel a generous contribution. I believe that the new Mirrer Yeshivah would be an excellent choice for Chaim. It's small, so he'll get the individual attention he needs."

Chaim was so absorbed in the conversation that he didn't touch his strudel. After making short order of his own serving, Yanky turned his eyes onto his brother's dish. "If you don't want yours, can I have it?" he asked hopefully.

Fraydl returned from the kitchen, her eyes scanned the room as she served strudel to the women. "Tanchum went to speak with Areleh," Hannah answered the girl's unspoken question. Fraydl nodded. She took her place in the empty seat beside her sister.

Rivka turned sideways to study Fraydl. "I would like to speak with you privately," she said, pushing her chair back away from the table. "Can you come into the kitchen with me for a few minutes?"

117

CHAIM KNOCKED ON ARELEH'S BEDROOM DOOR. "EXCUSE me," he told Tanchum. "Baba Stern asked me to call you."

Dr. Stern stood up. "If you have any more questions, just call me," he told the boy lying on the bed. "We're in Eretz Yisrael until Sunday. After we return to New York, I'll send your mother a telegram as soon as we have a date for the surgery."

Areleh smiled uncertainly. "Thank you," he said. "I feel better after talking things through."

Chaim handed Areleh a plate of strudel and answered *"Amein"* to his *brachah*.

"Are you afraid of your surgery?" Chaim asked as Areleh chewed.

"Why should I be afraid? Nothing can be worse than the way I am now." Areleh used his thumb and forefinger to trap the last crumbs remaining on the plate. "Actually, I'm more scared of being a few thousand meters in the air. What's it like to fly in an airplane?"

Yanky wandered into the room. Areleh had many questions, and the brothers filled in the details of everything they'd been through.

"You'll be with us for Pesach," Yanky said happily. "I hope you stay in America a long time. You can have Chaim's room."

"What about Chaim?"

There was an uncomfortable silence before the younger boy clarified, "He won't be there. Chaim wants to return to Eretz Yisrael for the next *zeman*. Abba and Zeide Stern arranged for him to learn in a yeshivah in Yerushalayim."

"Really?" Areleh turned to examine Chaim's face, his own hazel eyes widening. "I thought you were happy in New York."

"I was. Tante Fraydl always told us about Eretz Yisrael and how wonderful it will be to live here after the war, but then she disappeared and Fetter Tanchum brought us to New York. I was just glad to get away from Europe and all the bad memories. I forgot all about coming to Eretz Yisrael until this trip for the *Hachnassas Sefer Torah*. From the minute we landed, I felt something wake up inside.

"I really didn't expect it to be so different from New York, but it is. Now I don't want to leave! Abba suggested that I fly back with the family to pack my things and get organized. *B'ezras Hashem*, after Pesach I am moving to Yerushalayim."

"When you're back in New York, you might change your mind," Areleh commented.

Chaim shook his head. "I don't think so. I hope not."

Yanky grumbled, "I don't understand why he wants to leave home."

"Don't worry, little brother. We'll visit each other all the time. Abba says it's a good time to buy stocks in the airlines!"

Yanky left the older boys and wandered back through the house. He helped himself to a drink of water in the kitchen, and then meandered through the living room. After mentally counting the adults sitting around the table, he spoke aloud, "Tante Fraydl is not here. Where did she go? And where is Fetter Tanchum?"

"They've gone outside for a little walk," Baba Stern replied, as if this was a perfectly normal thing to happen.

Yanky gave her a surprised look, screwing up his face in concentration. "When did they leave? Maybe I can catch up to them." No one responded to his words.

"I'm bored," he declared. "I'm going outside. I'll come back with the Fetter and the Tante."

"I think you should stay here." Rivka said, pointing to an empty chair.

"Would you like another pastry?" Hannah nudged a plate towards the disgruntled child.

Yanky frowned. "No, I want to go outside."

"You are staying right here in the house," Abba said, without raising his eyes from the *sefer* he was perusing.

Though Baba and Zeide Stern smiled at him with affection, Yanky knew that his foster-father was the final authority. He sighed. At least there was another serving of strudel to compensate. And maybe Areleh would tell him new stories about being a soldier during the Israeli-Arab War.

Meanwhile, Tanchum and Fraydl walked side by side a short distance from the house. Both were too self-conscious to speak first, so they just continued until the sidewalk ended at the edge of Kfar Ata. Tanchum noticed a trail leading through a nearby field dotted with colorful wildflowers. The path seemed to disappear into a small copse of trees, and he could just make out what looked like a park bench on the far side.

"Do you know where this leads?" he asked, pointing to the meandering path.

Fraydl shook her head. "I've never been here before."

"Shall we?"

She smiled shyly and they stepped off the asphalt onto the path. Earlier in the day it must have been muddy, but the afternoon sun had dried the earth enough to make walking pleasant. Accompanied by the trilling of songbirds and the scent of sun-drenched grass, words flowed much more easily. To both Fraydl and Tanchum it seemed as if the whole world was singing.

At first, they spoke about her nephews and Chaim's decision to stay in Eretz Yisrael. Tanchum told her some more about the boys' lives after the war. Fraydl asked questions about Areleh's upcoming surgery, which led Tanchum to describe his work at the hospital and life in Williamsburg. In turn, she shared anecdotes about Malky's family in Yerushalayim and her life in Kfar Ata.

They reached the bench that Tanchum had seen from the road. He took out his handkerchief and brushed away a few dry leaves, and they sat down to continue their conversation. Time passed seamlessly as Fraydl described the *Kinderheim* and the boat trip to Palestine. Gradually they worked their way backward through events, until they were back at Ravensdorf.

Tanchum inhaled deeply. "You have no idea how I searched for you after the war."

Fraydl sensed a wellspring of undiminished pain in her companion. "I wrote to you from the DP camp the day after I arrived," she said. "I mailed it to your home address, but the letter came back a month later unopened, marked 'Undeliverable.' I didn't know what had happened, but in the chaos of those days I feared the worst."

"I never saw such a letter."

"Where were you? One day you left, and you never returned. After a while there was nothing left to eat in the house. I was frightened. I didn't know what to do or where to turn."

"The Allied forces detained me, along with a lot of other German soldiers, for several weeks," he explained. "I hurried home as soon as I was released, but the house was empty. I didn't know if you were still alive or where you could have gone." His voice broke. "You should have left a note."

"I thought about it, but I was afraid. What if your uncle Heinrich found it and came after me?"

"Well, what's done is done. In the end, we met again. Do you believe it?"

"No." She shook her head and laughed. "I find it totally unbelievable."

He smiled, and then became serious. "Do you remember my plan for the future, the night before you fell out of the attic?"

"I could never forget…"

"I want to thank you for refusing me."

"What?" Shocked, she sat up straighter.

"I feel terrible that you were forced to take such an extreme action, but I am eternally grateful that you made the right choice."

Her expression was puzzled.

"If my plan had come to fruition, where would we be today? I would likely be a small-town doctor somewhere in the American heartland, and the children would never know what it means to be Jewish. I would never have met my real parents or my brothers and sisters, or known the truth about where I come from. I would still believe that I am related by blood to Heinrich Mauer!

"From my vantage point at that time it was a good and logical plan, but it would have been the worst possible loss for me and for the people I cared about most: you and Chaim and Yanky. I thank you for being wiser than I was, and I ask your forgiveness for causing you pain."

Fraydl was touched. "There is nothing to forgive," she whispered, feeling the man's complete sincerity. "You always only meant well. There was no way you could have known differently."

"I was raised to use logic over emotion, but by the end of the war it was hard to keep them separate. My heart told me that you and I were meant to be together, and my mind found the rationalization for that to happen."

Their eyes met and held. "Do you remember when you declared that Hashem had forsaken the Jewish people?"

"Of course. And I remember your response as clearly as if that discussion was taking place right now."

She closed her eyes and recited softly, "Not totally, and not forever." Opening them again she added, "It's from *Megillas Eichah*, you know. It's a promise from Hashem that He will never totally reject the Jewish people. There may be times of terrible suffering, but we have His promise that in the end His mercy will prevail and we will return to Him."

For several minutes, the only sound came from the leaves whispering in the slight breeze. At last Tanchum turned to her, his face unusually pale and his voice resonating with a depth of feeling. "I have no doubt that you are the person I have waited for, the one with whom I wish to spend the rest of my life. *Fraulein* Fraydl, I ask you to be my wife. Together let us build a *bayis ne'eman b'Yisrael*."

Fraydl was overcome with emotion. She struggled to form words to reply, "With Hashem's help, I will try my best to deserve a husband as wonderful as you."

The late-afternoon sun was sinking low in the sky, slashing crimson through the trees behind them. "It's getting late," Tanchum said, standing tall and straight. "Shall we return to your sister's house?"

Fraydl stood up and shook out her skirt. "Yes, of course," she replied, feeling lighter and happier than she could have imagined possible. They reached the street just as a small group of sea birds passed overhead, flying through the flushed sky to their nesting site for the night. From a distance they saw Dovid and Rabbi Stern leaving Rivka's house with the boys. Tanchum escorted Fraydl as far as the porch before hurrying to join the men for Minchah. Inside the house, the rebbetzin and her daughter-in-law were *davening*.

"*Nu?*" Rivka whispered, trying to read her sister's thoughtful, somewhat dreamy expression.

Fraydl just smiled and remained in the doorway, her eyes following the men as they walked to shul. She stood there until the daylight dissolved, gently edged away by the coming darkness.

Fraydl came into the kitchen where her sister was washing dishes. Rikva looked up expectantly.

"He is the person I want to spend the rest of my life with."

"Are you sure?"

"More sure than I've ever been about anything."

The sisters embraced tightly before returning to the living room. Hannah and her mother-in-law looked from one to the other. The rebbetzin nodded to Hannah and smiled. Rivka rummaged through the cupboard and took out a bottle of wine and they were ready by the time the men returned from Maariv, their faces wreathed in smiles.

Mazel tov! Mazel tov!

Areleh poured the wine, and even Yanky got a glass. *L'Chaim! L'Chaim!*

The men and boys formed a circle, resting their hands on each other's shoulders and raising their voices in song. Tanchum was swept into the joyful dance as his mother and sister-in-law showered the glowing *kallah* with kisses. Rivka's face shone.

Rabbi Stern briefly disengaged from the dancers and stepped close to his wife. "Is it not sweet revenge?" he whispered. "The wicked Germans, *yimach shemam*, burned the parchment, but the letters of Torah flew free.The Nazis believed that it was in their power to destroy us, but Hashem in His mercy has led us to this day. Mazel tov, Shaindel! Mazel tov!"

Tanchum's mother took a deep, satisfied breath. Without taking her eyes off their son, she whispered, "*Mazel tov*, Meir! ***Mazel tov***!"

THE END

ACKNOWLEDGMENTS

This novel was written and re-written over several years and I owe a tremendous debt of gratitude to those who were close to me through the process. First and foremost, of course, I am grateful to *Der Eibishter* for making the story come to life in my mind and for sending me the special individuals without whom it could never have happened. Thank you, my dear friend, Judy Arev, for always being there, your unquestioning support is priceless. Thank you, fellow author, Tamar Ansh, without your encouragement and insightful ideas, this manuscript would never have been completed. Last, but far from least, thank you, Millie Samson, for being the best writing partner in the world. Chapter after chapter, Millie was there for me, patiently (and relentlessly) suggesting that I need to rewrite or rephrase, rethink and try again, until she was satisfied with my clarity of thought or the rhythm of my writing. As the skilled and talented midwife for this book, *Hidden* belongs to Millie too.

Dear readers, allow me also to express my deep gratitude to Shaar Press. It is an honor that my manuscript was accepted by Reb Shmuel Blitz, manager of the Jerusalem ArtScroll office, and their eminent editor, Mrs. Miriam Zakon; working with them has been a real pleasure. In conclusion, I add heartfelt appreciation to my proficient editors Libby Lazewnik and Judi Dick for their unsurpassed talent and skill.

Rochel Istrin

Adar 5775